BULLET HOLES

&

BROKEN HEARTS

BULLET HOLES & BROKEN HEARTS

by

C.L. LOWRY

Creedom Publishing Company
Philadelphia, Pennsylvania

The Cataloging-in-Publication Data is on file at the Library of Congress.

Creedom Publishing Company

Visit the website at:
www.CreedomPublishing.com

ISBN-13: 978-1-946897-07-7

Printed in the United States of America
10 9 8 7 6 5 4 3 2 1

"Living your life with the sole purpose of making someone else happy isn't living at all."

- Reign Bryant

PROLOGUE

The full moon shined in the dark sky like a spotlight. A nice breeze had finally cooled down the temperature on that summer night. The couple stood at the tall windows admiring the beautiful view of Baltimore, both with a glass of champagne in their hands. *Topside* was one of the best rooftop restaurants in the city and also the location of their first date almost a year ago. The smell of seafood filled the air, reminding the young lady of the delicious meal she just enjoyed. The mussels in a white wine garlic butter were her favorite meal and she couldn't find any other establishment in the city that could match the taste. She couldn't have asked for a more perfect night and it showed by the slight grin on her face.

"What the heck are you smiling for?" Darren asked.

Reign was in a daze and didn't hear Darren's question. He knew exactly what was on her mind but didn't want to mention it. Her thick lips made a simple act such as smiling seem seductive. Everything about her was so sexy to him. She didn't have to do much to attract attention because she was a beautiful woman. There was no need to cake on make-up or enhance her physical features in any way because they were almost perfect. Besides, she hated make-up. She mostly wore eyeliner and lip gloss, that was all she needed. Reign wore her curly hair to the side, just the way Darren liked it. He wasn't only in love with her physical appearance, he loved her mental as well. Reign's personality was humbling and pure. She had a heart of gold and the love was reciprocated. She was in love with him. Unlike a fairytale love, the couple had a different connection; an unbreakable one.

"It's so crazy there are people who never see this side of the city," Reign muttered.

"Yea, I know." Darren looked over at her. "It's a shame."

"Do you think I'm like the city?"

"What do you mean?"

"Baltimore is a beautiful city, but to the world it's nothing."

"Hell no, baby. Everyone can see how beautiful you are. You don't ever have to worry about not being seen for what you truly are," Darren said sincerely, reaching over and caressing the side of her face. They locked eyes and it was as if they were the only two in the restaurant. No one else existed at that moment.

"I love you so much."

His words made her smile. She had never felt this safe and secure with a man.

"I love you too."

Darren leaned in and placed a tender kiss on Reign's soft lips. Wrapping her in his arms, Darren positioned himself behind his lady as they both continued staring out the window. He gripped the champagne bottle, ready to top off their glasses but the bottle was empty. Another one was waiting on ice for them. Picking up the champagne bottle, Darren popped the cork, causing the bubbly to overflow out the bottle. Reign laughed because when they first met, he struggled to open similar bottles. Darren had evolved so much, right before her eyes. She had also evolved. They made each other better. Reign truly felt like he was her soul mate.

"Come on, let's get a better view," Darren whispered as he intertwined his fingers with Reign's and led her to their destination. The restaurant manager gave him a head nod as they approached and walked the couple back past the kitchen. Anticipation was getting the best of Reign. She wasn't a fan of surprises, but she trusted Darren. The manager opened a door, which led to a small flight of stairs. The stairs led to the roof of the building where a small table was set up with two chairs, candles, roses, another bottle of champagne, a tray of assorted desserts, and a violinist. Reign's mouth dropped. Her heart seemed like it wanted to jump out her chest and into Darren's arms. It was his to have forever.

Reign just gazed at Darren in admiration, as the soft tune of the violin set the tone of the night. His slim, tailored suit seemed to fit perfectly. A turtleneck and oxford shoes were his choices to accent the suit. He wore a clean fade and had a thin goatee. Darren's dark skin reminded Reign of Hershey's chocolate and she wanted him all to herself. Everything about Darren was fresh but it was also different. He was a good guy, so growing up in Baltimore girls always overlooked him because they were into niggas that ran the streets and made fast money. That was far from Darren's persona. He aspired to start a tech company, expand his outreach program, and to move out of Baltimore. However, there was something he had to do first.

"I know you hear me say it all the time, but I don't think you know how much I love you," Darren said as he pulled Reign in close.

"Bae, I know how much you love me. You literally changed my life."

"I have wanted you since the first moment I saw you. I want to spend the rest of my life with you."

"I want to spend the rest of my li—"

Just before Reign could finish her statement, Darren dropped on one knee. The princess-cut diamond ring he presented to her shined brightly.

"Reign, will you marry me?" Reign became weak and her knees buckled. She felt lightheaded as memories of her past began to make her head spin. "Reign, are you ok?' Darren asked, noticing her changed behavior.

Once again, her Prince Charming's words brought her back to reality. She was back in the moment. Tears of joy poured down her face like someone left a faucet running.

"YES! Yes, I will marry you."

Darren grabbed Reign's left hand and slipped the stunning ring onto her ring finger. She damn near tackled him to the ground with a tight hug and attacked him with soft kisses. Cheers and applause filled the air as the restaurant manager and staff members congratulated the couple on their engagement. For Reign, this moment was like heaven on earth. Coming from the Gilmor Homes, she never envisioned having a "normal" life. As a young girl, she never thought about marriage, having kids, or building a family. All she knew was crime and survival. It surrounded her. Darren grew up in the same environment but due to his parents' divorce, he and his siblings also spent time in Virginia with their father. Those little escapes to Virginia gave Darren a different outlook on life. The ride from Baltimore to Richmond showed Darren life outside the Gilmor Homes. Interacting with the children in Richmond was much different than the interactions in Baltimore. It was actually safe to play outside without being harassed by crackheads, local drug dealers, or the police.

Reign stood up and took a good look at her ring. It was breathtaking. Darren walked up behind her and embraced his new fiancé. She leaned her head back, resting on his chest. The fabric of his suit was gentle against her head. She didn't want to move. She wanted to stay wrapped in his arms forever

"There's no more hiding our love for each other, baby. I want the world to know about us," Darren said, referring to their discreet relationship.

He grabbed the bottle of champagne and took it to the head, gulping down half of the bottle in one take.

"I'm yours 'til the end of time, bae. You don't ever have to question that."

They kissed passionately and hugged each other tightly. Even with her arms wrapped around Darren's neck during the embrace, Reign couldn't help but take another look at her ring. It all still seemed like a dream, and she didn't want to wake up. The joy she felt was unlike anything else she had ever experienced. Tears fell from her eyes in disbelief.

A notification went off on Darren's phone. It was a text message from his sister. *Did she say yes?* Darren smiled and ignored the message when he noticed it was a few minutes before midnight. The restaurant manager did him a favor by allowing him to have the space to himself for the proposal, but they were supposed to close in three minutes and Darren didn't want to hold them up.

"Come on my beautiful fiancé, let's get out of here," Darren said.

Reign grinned and nodded her head in agreement; she knew they had to get up early and drive to Virginia to meet with his father. Reign already knew Darren's mother and siblings from around the neighborhood, but this would be her first time meeting his father. The meeting would be different than the others because of the exciting news they now had to share with their families. Despite their morning plans, a fire was burning inside of Reign and the only thing she could think about as they headed back into the restaurant was going home and making love to her new fiancé.

Darren swooped her off her feet and carried her to the exit door. They smiled all the way down the stairs, still on cloud nine. Darren was known to be a calm and quiet guy, but inside he had a confidence about him that was on full display. While other men focused on being tough guys, Darren's only focus was being a true gentleman and someone that gave back to his community. He spoiled Reign with everything money couldn't buy; loyalty, trust, and respect. However, once he started his tech company, he planned to give her the world.

They finally reached the outside exit. Reign went to get down, but Darren readjusted his grip and continued carrying her. He didn't let her down until they reached his car, which was parked down the street from the restaurant. Darren opened the front passenger door of his white Dodge Charger and guided Reign into her seat. He hopped into the driver's seat and started the car. The growl from the Hemi engine was music to Darren's ear. He placed his hand on the gear shift, ready to go but Reign placed her hands on his. She guided Darren's hand from the gear shift to her thigh. In a matter of seconds, the couple was lip-locking as their hands were exploring each other's bodies. Darren wanted to rip Reign's dress off and she wanted to do the same with his suit. The kisses were passionate, and the windows of the Charger began to steam up. Reign took another peek at the gorgeous ring. Just beyond her ring, she caught glimpse of a shadowy figure approaching the driver's door.

"Bae, look!" she yelled out.

Darren was startled and turned around to see what had Reign so shook and was greeted by muzzle flash from an AK-47 assault rifle. Reign let out a nightmarish scream as the shots shattered the driver's side window and ripped through the door panel. The gunman emptied the entire clip into the vehicle, before pulling at the handle and attempting to open the door. Darren instinctively threw the Charger in gear and slammed on the pedal. The tires screeched and Darren struck the vehicle that was parked in front of him, but he was able to get on the road after driving over some type of bump. He was speeding down Cathedral Street, as more shots rang out and the rear windshield shattered. Excruciating pains shot through Darren's left arm, shoulder, and leg as he swerved. The Charger bounced off several vehicles before Darren turned a sharp corner. He cut the lights off and continued flying down each street he hit until he was sure he wasn't being followed. A warm liquid began seeping through his suit. He looked down and noticed dark red stains on his torso.

"Baby, I think I got hit," Darren said as he continued focusing on the road. "Baby? Reign?"

An eerie silence filled the car. Darren took a deep breath and looked over at Reign, who was leaning against the window. Her eyes were open, but they were staring into the abyss. Blood was splattered on the side of her face, but it was nothing compared to the large stain that was on her stomach. Her hand covered her stomach and blood was running down each finger.

"Reign, wake up," Darren pleaded. Shaking her shoulder did nothing but make her hand fall by her side, exposing the stomach wound. "Don't worry, baby. Everything is gonna be okay," Darren said as his voice began to crack.

Tears ran down his face. His hands began shaking as he did his best to navigate through the darkness. He had to get to the nearest hospital, but it was hard to focus because he began feeling dizzy.

"God, please don't take her from me."

A chill went up Darren's spine and his vision began to blur. The Charger continued down the street at a high rate of speed. Other vehicles honked their horns and flashed their lights at Darren, in an attempt to get him to cut on his lights. Little did they know, the wounded driver was moments away from death. The Charger drifted into the opposite lane and headed straight towards oncoming traffic. The honking horns weren't enough to prevent a collision with a pickup truck that sent the Charger flipping into the air. The vehicle was totaled, and blood decorated the interior.

BULLET HOLES & BROKEN HEARTS

What seemed like a beautiful ending to a love story quickly turned into a violent tragedy. But to understand the ending, you must know the beginning.

This is Reign's story...

CHAPTER 1

Back in the day

Reign, get your ass in here!" Stoney yelled out as she crawled out the bed and threw on a robe. She watched as her teenage daughter slowly entered the room. "Damn lil girl, you need to clean out ya damn ears. I called you like five times." Stoney walked over to Reign, who had an innocent look on her face. She handed the young girl a crumpled-up dollar bill. "Take this and go get ya'self something from the store."

"Come on, mom. It's about to be ten and I have school in the morn—"

SMACK!

Reign fell back into the wall. The back of Stoney's hand felt like leather going across the side of her face.

"I don't think I asked you a mu'fuckin question, you lil' bitch. I said take your lil' raggedy ass to the store!"

Reign stormed out the room and grabbed one of the backpacks on the living room floor before leaving out the tiny, one-bedroom apartment. Stoney was naive to believe her sixteen-year-old daughter didn't know the real reason why she was sent to the store. That was Stoney's way of getting Reign out of the apartment while she turned tricks. Prostitution had become a lifestyle for Stoney after her husband was murdered. Back then, Stoney was one of the most beautiful women in Baltimore. Her caramel skin, slim body, and silky hair made every single man in the city crave her attention. However, her attention went to a local cocaine dealer everyone knew as Big Mike. The two got married and had a beautiful baby girl they named *Reign*. Big Mike was a legend in the streets and made a lot of money. He even taught Stoney the game and had her dealing with him. Little did he know, his lady also started dabbling in the product they were selling.

Ten years later, there was an invasion at their Baltimore home that changed their lives forever. Five masked men demanding money and drugs. The men found exactly what they were looking for, but one of them believed there was more. They had Stoney pinned down and threatened to kill her if Big Mike did not give them more money. Big Mike begged the men to leave with what they had already stolen, but instead, one of the men sent a warning shot through Stoney's leg. Big Mike rushed the shooter and six shots ripped through his chest before the masked men fled with the stolen goods. Reign was hiding in a closet at the time, and didn't see the shootings, but she heard everything. When the police and paramedics arrived, Stoney was taken to the hospital and Big Mike was pronounced dead at the scene. The police never solved the homicide and Big Mike's killer was never caught. Stoney was left as a single mother with no legitimate form of income. The gunshot left her with a horrible limp. She was always in pain, so working a 9 to 5 wasn't an option for her. The pain medications her doctor prescribed were not very effective, so Stoney turned back to her old habit...cocaine. She still had her beauty and dated a few men after the tragedy but once they realized she was only after money, they'd cut her loose. As the years passed, Stoney's addiction worsened and she was left with nowhere to live until she found a one-bedroom apartment available at the Gilmor Homes, which was also one of the go-to places for illegal drugs. She was able to feed her habit, which quickly evolved over the years.

Once Stoney got hooked on crack, there was no turning back. She began scamming and stealing throughout the neighborhood. Whatever way there was to make money, Stoney was all over it. One day she was walking home from a long day of retail theft when a car pulled up alongside her. The driver offered her some cash for "a good time." Stoney didn't even hesitate to take the man up on the offer. She made $100 in about eight minutes, after servicing the man in the backseat of his Mercury Grand Marquis. Seeing how fast she made that cash, Stoney found her new hustle. Building up clientele was not hard because men from all over wanted a piece of the woman that used to be untouchable. Most men were paying just to fulfill an old fantasy. They used to brag about fucking Stoney until almost everyone that wanted a piece of her, got it. She became used and abused. For the right price, you could do whatever you wanted to her, and she did whatever you requested. She was a sex slave, and her master was crack.

Selling pussy barely kept the rent paid but it surely fed her addiction. Stoney used to make Reign turn the living room TV up to the loudest volume while she handled her business in the bedroom. However, Stoney often caught her clients' eyes wandering when they entered the apartment. The sick men would inquire about the "*pretty young thang on the couch*". Stoney became jealous of the attention that once belonged to her. She didn't want Reign's beauty to interfere with her money, so she started making Reign go to the store, telling her not to come back for an hour or two. Stoney didn't care what time of the night she kicked her daughter out of the apartment. The only thing she cared about was making quick cash and scoring rock.

Reign called her best friend, Brandi, as soon as she stepped outside. Brandi also lived in the Gilmor Homes. She lived with her mother, who worked two jobs. Brandi was usually left unsupervised, one of the reasons why she was able to meet Reign during odd times of the night.

"Girl, ya mom is so nasty," Brandi said while laughing. The heavy-set, dark-skinned girl came strolling up to the corner while munching on a large pack of Twizzlers.

"Shut up. I can't wait 'til I'm eighteen, so I can get the hell up outta here."

"You and me both, bitch. We gonna open up a hair salon and get us a big house down south."

"I don't care if we go down south or up north. As long as we get the hell out of this neighborhood, I'll be happy."

"You got that right. Come on let's go see who your mom gon' lay up with this time."

The two girls sat on the trunk of an older model sedan that was parked on the block. The vehicle never moved, and no one ever yelled at them for sitting on it, so it became their front row seat to Stoney's front door. Brandi dug into the pack of candy and handed Reign a hand full of Twizzlers. The two girls looked like they were in the front row of a movie theater. The only thing they were missing was popcorn and slushies. They made a habit of watching the men Stoney would entertain and even timed how long it would take the men to leave. It was amusing to the girls, but it was also Reign's way of making sure her mother was safe. After her father's death, Reign knew she had to be the one to look out for her mother. She didn't trust any of the men that entered the apartment. When the two were not sitting outside on the car, they sat on the stairs directly outside of the apartment. Reign knew her mother didn't want the clients seeing her, so they only sat inside when the weather was bad.

A black pickup truck drove down the street. The driver seemed to be looking around as he cruised down the block.

"Ewww, Reign. I know your mom ain't out here fuckin' that reject ass, Santa Claus," Brandi blurted out when she saw the older Caucasian male drive by. His bushy white beard made him stand out, along with the dents and scratches on the side of his truck. Both Reign and Brandi began laughing hysterically.

"We ain't got no chimney, so I don't know how Santa gonna get his ass inside the apartment," Reign rebutted.

The laughter continued. Brandi even choked on her own saliva while she was laughing and ended up coughing up a lung. He wasn't one of Stoney's clients. Well, at least that day he wasn't. Everyone knew Stoney wouldn't turn away fast cash, so there were all types of characters that went in and out of the apartment. The girls began looking around to see who else would approach. Out of the shadows emerged a tall, middle-aged black man with a gray goatee and bald head. Everyone in the neighborhood called the man *Slim*, because of his wiry frame. Slim didn't live at the Gilmor Homes but frequented due to his crack addiction. He worked at a warehouse, which kept money in his pockets. Money that went towards buying crack and pussy. Specifically, pussy from Stoney.

"Oh great, here comes this creep," Reign said once she spotted the thin man approaching the front door.

"I know that ain't Slim that's 'bout to walk up in your spot, girl."

"Yea that's him."

"I hate that guy."

"Me too. He's always staring at me."

"Ewww, that would freak me out. Do ya momma know that Slim is a crackhead?"

"She don't care. They probably gonna be in there doing crack together."

"How long you think he gonna be in there?"

"I don't know. Last time he was only in there for like five minutes or something like that."

Brandi couldn't help but break out in laughter again. Slim looked over towards the girls but paid them no mind. Just as the girls suspected, Slim headed up the steps and entered Stoney's apartment. The girls stayed outside chatting and making jokes. Seven long minutes went by and out came Slim, looking disheveled. He was moving a mile a minute as he disappeared back into the shadows.

"You going back in now?" Brandi asked after she let out a big yawn.

Her low eyes were a clear sign of how tired she was getting.

"Nope. I don't want to be around her right now. Can I spend the night at your spot?"

"Yea, but my momma is home so you gotta be quiet once we get in there. She don't work until midnight and if we wake her up, she's gonna kill us."

"Thanks."

Reign gave Brandi a tight hug. She couldn't imagine what life would be like without Brandi. She was always by her side and never judged her. Most kids would have made fun of Reign every chance they got because of her situation, but Brandi wasn't like that at all. She had been a big girl all of her life, so she knew how it felt to be bullied. She didn't want Reign to go through that type of pain. Despite the crazy life she lived, Reign was pretty and was the girl every guy in the neighborhood drooled over and every boy in school was scared to talk to.

Reign followed Brandi to her apartment and watched as the plus-sized girl moved stealthily through the front door, living room, and then past her mother's bedroom. Reign felt good once she entered the apartment. Although she had to tiptoe her way through each room, it felt like a home. It reminded her of the house she lived in when her father was alive. The apartment was clean and smelled like fresh linen. Reign was ashamed of her mother's apartment which looked like a tornado went through it and wreaked of the odors of cat piss, sex, and shit.

Reign was jealous that Brandi lived in a two-bedroom apartment. She dreamt of one day having her own bedroom again. It had been six years since she had a room. Brandi's bedroom was messy, but Reign loved it. There were posters on the wall, clothes scattered everywhere, and a touch of pink on everything in the room. Reign threw her backpack on the ground and used it as a pillow. The spare clothes in the backpack

24

served as the perfect amount of cushion to support her neck. It was not long before the girls were both sound asleep.

CHAPTER 2

Things did not change from that day on. Stoney kept up her antics and Reign spent more and more time at Brandi's apartment. Brandi did not mind the company, but Reign hated it. The visits from random men became more frequent and Reign was rarely seeing her mother. What started out as a few men a week was turning into a few men every other day. By the time Reign got home from school, she only had time to do her homework and get ready to "head out to the store." On the days when Stoney wasn't turning tricks, she was high and on another planet. When Friday night came along, Reign was ready. She knew she didn't have to go to school the next morning, so she could stay up all night with Brandi. Brandi's mom worked extra hours on the weekend, so they had the apartment all to themselves for three days.

"Reign, where you at?!" Stoney yelled out from the bedroom.

Reign dropped her fork and pushed the bowl of oodles and noodles to the side.

"Yes, mom," she said as she scurried to the bedroom. Stoney was sprawled across the bed, with the covers barely draping over her naked body. Reign stood in the doorway for a second and just watched Stoney, waiting for her to move or sit up but she never did. "Is everything ok, mom?"

"Yea, I need you to pass mama that small black bag on the dresser."

Reign slowly inched forward in the disgusting room. The combined odor of sweat, ass, and spoiled milk invaded Reign's nostrils as she headed towards her mother's dresser. Trash and dirty clothes covered the top, but a small black bag sat on top of the pile of junk. Reign grabbed the bag which, was partially open. She already knew what the contents inside were because this was not the first time Stony made this same request in the same manner. The black bag was Stoney's crack kit, which contained two glass smoking pipes, aluminum foil, three lighters, and four small rocks of crack cocaine which were packaged in torn plastic baggies. Reign handed Stoney the bag and make a hasty exit. The last thing she needed to do was watch her mother poison herself with the illegal drug.

Stoney didn't care if anyone was watching or not. Her only concern was the first-class flight she was about to take. Her hand dug into the bag as she removed one of the Pyrex pipes. She shoved a small metal screen into the pipe, using her thumb to inch it into the tube. Stoney bit open one of the plastic baggies that contained the off-white substance. She placed the rock on top of the screen and heated it with the lighter. The flame made the substance melt into the metal. Stoney licked her dry lips and was ready for takeoff. She sealed her lips around the pipe and lit the other end, heating the metal. Smoke emerged from the metal and Stoney inhaled every last bit. The drug wasted no time hitting Stoney. She became excited and a euphoric feeling came over her. She felt like she was floating in space.

Reign grabbed her backpack and headed out of the door. She was ready to get the weekend started with Brandi and not be stuck in the apartment fetching drugs for her mother. She also knew there was about to be a ton of foot traffic going in and out of the apartment. The weekend rush was about to get started. Brandi was supposed to meet Reign at their usual spot, at the abandoned car but when Reign walked outside, she was alone. She was going to head over to Brandi's apartment but the last thing she wanted was Brandi's mom to spot her. Brandi was given strict rules not to have company when her mother was not around, and the girls broke that rule every chance they got.

Reign hopped onto the trunk of the abandoned car and waited for Brandi. Minutes were ticking away, and Reign's eyes were locked on the corner, waiting for her friend to turn it at any moment.

"What the hell you lookin' at?" A voice asked from behind Reign, startling her as she quickly turned around.

Reign was speechless when she saw Omari. The light-skinned, hazel eyed, young man with curly hair walked over to the car and began looking at the corner. He wondered what had the girl's attention. Reign was still in shock. She didn't know what to say. Reign had seen Omari around the neighborhood, but always thought he was trouble. He was always on the corner and hung out with the drug dealers that Stoney copped from. A part of Reign wanted to hop off the car and take off. She was embarrassed because she knew Omari had seen her buying crack on several occasions. Little did she know, his father was also hooked on the powerful drug and Omari did several runs for him too. That was his introduction to the drug game. An old head from his block schooled him to the game and before Omari knew it, he was one of the top hustlers in the city. At the tender age of eighteen, he had already built a name for himself and had a crew under him that sold his product. Although they were the same age as him, the members in Omari's crew looked up to him and appreciated the position he put them in. That made him different than the other young hustlers. Omari had a boss mentality and soon he would have the opportunity to obtain the title as well.

"Where ya homegirl at?" He asked trying to break the silence.

"Huh?" Reign was surprised anything came out her mouth. She didn't know what to say to Omari and felt trapped in his nice eyes.

"If you can huh, you can hear. I asked where ya homegirl was at."

"What homegirl?" Reign asked, finally able to form a sentence.

"I don't know that chick name. I'm talkin' bout the fat one you be with all the time."

"Watch ya mouth. Don't call my friend fat," Reign snarled.

The look Reign gave Omari was one of pure anger. She was protective over her friends and family. She didn't care how fine Omari was, she wasn't going to allow him to disrespect anyone she cared about.

"Damn, calm down. Ain't nobody disrespectin' ya lil friend. I'm just speaking facts. Anyway, what's ya name?"

"None."

"None?"

"Yea. None of ya damn business."

Omari chuckled. "That was so fuckin' corny. Anyway, I'm O."

"I know who you are."

"Oh, you do?"

"Yea. Ain't you a drug dealer?"

"Yea, and ain't you one of the chicks that be copping my work?"

Omari's arrogance was such a turn off to Reign. Her mood quickly went from mesmerized to annoyed. She was seconds away from cursing Omari out until their conversation was interrupted.

"What the hell is going on here?"

Omari and Reign both looked as they were approached. The sound of chips being munched on was overpowering. Their eyes were locked onto Brandi as she kept digging her hand into the large bag of hot chips. Brandi didn't expect Reign to have company. She came out late because her mom overslept and was running around the apartment like a headless chicken. There wasn't even enough time for Brandi's mom to make her a quick meal, so Brandi snagged the chips and some candy for dinner. Brandi always kept a stash of snacks in her room for nights like this.

"Damn, girl, you had me waiting out here forever."

"Well, it don't look like you were too worried," Brandi said as she looked Omari up and down. "How you doing, handsome?" Brandi asked Omari.

"I'm good. What's up with you?"

"Girl, don't speak to his rude ass," Reign interrupted. "He was just over here calling you fat."

"Bitch, I am fat," Brandi muttered. "Besides, he can call me whatever he wants. As long as he calls me." Brandi batted her eyes at Omari, as she licked her fingers.

They were covered in the seasoning from the hot chips, but in seconds Brandi had cleaned them off. Reign rolled her eyes.

"Listen, I wasn't calling you fat in a negative way," Omari lied. "Your friend is just being dramatic. All I wanted to know is where you were."

"Where I was? Boy, let me find out that you were checking for me."

"Yeah, I was. You left your friend out here all alone, so I just wanted to make sure both of yall were cool."

"We don't even know you. It's not your job to make sure we cool," Reign said.

"Reign, chill. Stop being mean."

"Reign? Oh, that's your name, huh?" Omari asked.

"Damn, Brandi. Why say my name and shit all loud? He don't need to be knowing my business."

"My bad. I didn't think it was that deep."

"It ain't that deep," Omari replied. "Like I said, I was just making sure that yall were cool."

"Yeah, we're cool. Have a good night," Reign said, as she hopped off the car, grabbed Brandi's hand a headed around the corner.

"What the hell was that about?" Brandi asked, looking back at Omari.

Reign was pulling her around the corner and Brandi didn't know why. She figured they were going to chill on the car and pull off their usual shenanigans."

"I don't have time for that shit. He was a complete asshole."

"He wasn't that bad. Plus, he gets a pass because he is so damn fine."

"Being fine doesn't give you an excuse to be an arrogant asshole."

"Actually, I think it does."

"Maybe in your world it does, but not in mine. He had no right calling you fat," Reign explained.

A part of her wanted to tell Brandi the truth, that she was more upset Omari mentioned her buying drugs from him. However, him calling Brandi fat was just as upsetting. Reign couldn't believe her first impression of Omari was one of disgust. When she bought the drugs for her mother, she gawked over the handsome dealer but now she wished he never approached her. *Some people are better as fantasies in your head because they are assholes in real life*, she thought.

"At the end of the day, I could care less what people say. All of this shit is depressing and it's fucking up my night. Let's just chill right here," Brandi suggested, leaning up against an older model minivan that was parked near the corner. "We can probably catch the guy your mom is waiting for if we stay right here."

"How are we going to do that? We can't even see my apartment from here."

"You don't need to see the apartment. Most people are going to come from this direction to go to your spot. How much money you want to bet that it's going to be Slim again?" Brandi asked while laughing.

"He better not bring his crackhead ass back here."

"Come on, let's bet. Who do you think it's going to be?"

"I don't know who it's going to be, but it definitely won't be Slim."

"How much you want to bet?"

"A dub."

"Bet," Brandi agreed.

She extended her arm, handing Reign the large bag of Swedish fish she planned on snacking on. The two girls patiently waited, with their eyes focused on the street corner. Deep down, Reign was not sure if Slim would come stepping out of the shadows and into her apartment. When she would sit in the living room, she was able to see the men and get an idea of their routine. At that time, Slim would come around twice a week. Since she was no longer allowed to be in the apartment while Stoney was handling business, it was hard to determine what the current schedule for the men were.

Brandi on the other hand was eager. She wanted Slim to pop out and hit the corner. In her mind, she had already spent the $20. She was going to head over to Popeyes and get the 12-piece family meal with Cajun fries and mashed potatoes as her sides. "You want some of these chips?" She asked as she continued to devour the bag.

"Naw, I'm good."

Brandi didn't even acknowledge the response and placed the bag to her lips and began emptying the remaining chips into her mouth. Reign couldn't help but stare at her friend. *She knew damn well she wasn't going to give me none of those chips.* Time began ticking away and the girls still had their eyes locked on the corner. The Gilmor Homes were action packed. People were running around, cars were driving by and the two still watched. There was no sign of Slim or anyone else that fit the criteria of Stoney's customers.

"Maybe your mom isn't having company tonight."

"Yes, she is. If that was the case, she wouldn't have sent me to the store."

Just as Reign spoke those words, a thin man came strolling by the girls. It wasn't Slim, but his characteristics weren't too far off. The man looked frail. A good gust of wind would have knocked him to his feet. His complexion was significantly lighter than Slim's dark skin tone, but the hair and beard were just as filthy. Both the girls looked at each other with similar disgusting looks on their faces. The man headed to the corner with a little pep in his step. However, he didn't turn the corner and head towards Stoney's apartment. Instead, he continued walking straight. More than likely, he was heading towards the group of teens standing on the corner of the 1600 block of Balmar Court...This was Omari's crew.

As the man staggered towards the group, Reign rolled her eyes and dove back into the bag of Swedish fish. She knew that walk all too well, thanks to Stoney. The quick runs for her mother had her feet moving quickly down Balmar Court and right back. The young men wasted no time serving the crackhead and sending him on his way. This was their routine. They did not value life for themselves, so it was impossible to ask them to value the lives of others. They served their neighbors, friends, and family members. Whatever it took to make money, they did it.

CHAPTER 3

It had been a long night for the girls. Neither Reign nor Brandi had become the winner of the $20 bet of what creep was going to show up to see Stoney. Nevertheless, they both stayed outside until about 2 am and enjoyed the nonsense that went on at The Gilmor Homes on a Friday night. Traffic to and from Omari's crew was nonstop. They were literally flooding the streets with drugs, and nobody batted an eye. Reign was surprised the two of them didn't spot her mom coming out to cop from Omari's crew. That was Stoney's usual routine after earning her cash. She would always head over to buy her drugs and then over to the store to grab essential items. With her lifestyle, essential items included condoms, lighters, and gum.

One thing Stoney made sure she did was try to protect herself from catching an STD. There were always times when the men came over claiming to have forgotten to bring a condom, so Stoney was sure always have them on deck. Lighters seemed to be very common items that always lingered around, but Stoney always found a way to lose them. The gum was just to keep her breath fresh for her company. She didn't mind her teeth were stained dark yellow and that they were rotting away in her mouth. The only thing she cared about was making sure she had a minty scent to mask her halitosis.

The rest of the residents of The Gilmor Homes were also lively throughout the night. Although there was no action going on at Stoney's, that didn't stop the girls from being entertained. Couples were arguing so loud in their apartments, you would have thought they were on the street. Music was blasting from wide body cars that were candy-painted and sitting on 22-inch chrome rims. Young men and women crept around, going to or from booty calls as gunshots rang off in the distance, followed up by police and ambulance sirens. This was Baltimore in the 90s and anyone who experienced it knew this was the norm on any night. The girls loved it. Their heads were on a swivel, trying to keep up with all of the action. By this point, plenty of people had walked around the corner and any one of them could have been going to see Stoney.

"What time your momma getting off work?" Reign asked just before she shoved the last of the Swedish fish into her mouth.

"I don't know. Her ass said she was late, so maybe she'll be getting' off late too."

"Here, you want the rest of these?" Reign asked as she extended the bag to Brandi.

Brandi didn't even respond before she grabbed the bag. It was as if she had been waiting for Reign to offer up the candy.

"Bitch!" Brandi blurted out after discovering that the bag was empty. She crumbled it up and threw it at Reign, who was laughing and running off. "I ain't finna chase your lil' skinny ass!" Brandi yelled out.

She was laughing so hard because she always fell for that trick. Her best friend knew she would never turn down any type of food. Brandi loved to eat.

"Come on, let's go get some more candy."

"From where?"

"Your room, stupid. I know you got more."

"I don't feel like walking all the way down there," Brandi complained. "Plus, if we go all the way to my spot, we are going to miss Slim's creepy ass."

"Slim ain't coming around here, girl. It was probably one of those other men we saw earlier. You know my momma ain't got no picks."

"That's not fair. We made a bet and now you are tryin' to interfere with me winning."

"Ain't nobody worried about that dumb ass bet. I'll just give you $20, if it's that deep."

"You don't even have $20," Brandi said.

"How you know what I got?"

"I know cuz we broke and if you had $20, we could have gone over to Keisha's house and got some food. You know her mom be sellin' those chicken wing platters and shit. I heard they're good too."

Reign smiled. Brandi knew her like the back of her hand, and she was absolutely right. If any of the girls had money, they would have been sinking their teeth into fried chicken wings with salt, pepper, and ketchup drizzled on top. Keisha's mom was also known for her cheese fries and fried fish. Brandi's mouth watered just thinking about it all. "Now you got me hungry. What you got in the house?"

"Nothing. My mom sold her food stamps, so I've been in my stash all week. I don't know how I'm going to last the rest of the month." Brandi laughed. "If she keeps this up, I'll starve. Then I'll probably be a twig like you."

"Girl, you better stop lying to yourself. You damn well, it would be impossible to starve your big ass."

"Well, at least I'd survive. You'd be gone in a day. You, your mom and Slim's skinny ass. Just 3 twigs out here wasting way."

"Fuck you," Reign replied while laughing. She picked up a rock and threw it at Brandi. The rock missed Brandi and hit the rear windshield of the minivan that the girls had been leaning on.

"Hey!" A deep male voice yelled from one of the apartment windows.

Brandi and Reign both took off running and headed for the apartment. They didn't know what damage was caused to the minivan and they were not sticking around to find out. Reign took off in a full sprint and reached the apartment in about a minute. Brandi, however, was slugging along in the back. Her sprint looked more like a speed walk. If someone had come out to confront the girls about the rock that was thrown, Brandi would have been caught after the first five steps she took.

"Damn girl, I ain't never see you run before," Reign said, as she chuckled.

Brandi flashed her middle finger at her best friend, before placing both hands back on her knees. She was so breathing hard and couldn't make it past the vestibule. She needed a break, and she was going to take it. Her body slowly rocked as she took in deep breaths. Reign was still laughing at Brandi. All she could think about was Brandi demolishing that big bag of chips, just minutes before taking off running. Reign laughed so hard, she had to lean on the wall to keep herself up.

"Fuck you," Brandi whispered as she was finally able to get words out between the deep inhales and exhales.

"I wish I had a camera because that was hilarious. That's the first time in a long time that I've seen you run."

"And that's the last time. I'm 'bout to die over here."

"Girl, you'll be okay. All you did was shake up the earth a little with your big ass."

The girls couldn't stop laughing. "At least I got away. You ain't know your girl could move that fast did you?"

"Cut it out. That was not fast."

"The fuck if it wasn't. I was like a fat Flo Jo out there. Wasn't nobody catching me."

"Yeah okay."

"Go check to see if somebody followed us."

Reign immediately followed her friend's order. She slowly pushed open the vestibule door, allowing the cool night breeze to push its way inside where they were posted up. She peeked out to the left. The coast was clear. She peeked out to the right and it was also clear. The girls had made a clean getaway. "Ain't nobody out there," Reign said.

"It better not be because I don't feel like whooping ass over a rock. I may not be the fastest, but I got hands."

"Them hands ain't doing nothin' but stuffing your face."

"Shut up. Speaking of stuffing my face, I'm hungry."

"Well, what you got left in the stash?"

"Let's go find out."

The girls headed up to Brandi's apartment. As soon as they entered, there was a pounding noise coming from her mother's bedroom. The thin walls in the apartment made sure any and every noise traveled between the different rooms. They giggled at each other because the pounding noise was all too familiar to the girls. They both ran into Brandi's mother's bedroom and plopped on the bed. The pounding noise continued, followed up by soft moans.

"It sounds like Darryl is at it again," Brandi said.

Darryl Knight was one of three siblings that lived next door to Brandi. Darryl was a 19-year-old ladies' man, and the older brother of Brandi's friend, Dasia. The middle child was Darren, who was a year old than Brandi, Reign and Dasia. Brandi's mom worked with the Knight sibling's mom, so they had just as much freedom as Brandi. They packed their two-bedroom apartment, with Dasia sharing a room with her mom and Darren and Darryl sharing the other room.

Darryl was one of the star players on the basketball team before graduating, so he was very popular in the neighborhood. He had girls in and out of the apartment the way Stoney had men in and out of hers. These girls were all caught up in the hype that Darryl would one day make it to the NBA. Unfortunately, Darryl wasn't the most disciplined student and didn't have the grades to get a scholarship to a top college. Although he was one of the star players on the team at high school, he was not the best on the team. Darryl's talents only landed him a partial scholarship to Morgan State, where he didn't even make it off of the bench during his freshman year. His 6-foot-5 and 225-pound frame was dominating in high school, but it was average in college. After partying his freshman year away and failing the majority of his classes, Darryl was out of Morgan State and enrolled in Baltimore City Community College. He went from seeing no playing time at the former university to being a starting small forward and averaging 21.5 points, 11 rebounds, 7 assists, and 2 blocks a game. He was back in the spotlight.

It seemed like every night Darryl had a different girl in his room, while his mom was at work. Brandi and Reign were virgins but learned about sex through health education, their peers and movies. Once Brandi realized what Darryl was doing, she found it entertaining to sit in her mother's room and listen in on his intimacy sessions. When Reign came over, she found entertainment in it as well. Brandi used to always ask Dasia about Darryl, but his sister found his actions disgusting so she never stayed home when he had company. Darren on the other hand was also curious about his brother's lifestyle. He often peeked in the room to watch the action, mesmerized by seeing the naked bodies of the beautiful girls that his brother had over.

Darren was the total opposite of Darryl. He was quiet and didn't have an athletic bone in his body. His brother often tried to get him to follow in his footsteps, but it seemed like only one of the Knight brothers was blessed with the talent gene when it came to sports. Dasia was the same way. She stayed in the streets and didn't care much about sports. When she wasn't hanging out with Brandi, she would hang around the neighborhood with her other friends. Most of the time, they were down around Omari's territory trying to get attention from him and his friends. Unlike the sports lifestyle, the lifestyle of drug dealers was appealing to the 16-year-old and her friends.

The muffled sounds of gunshots could be heard coming from outside. Next, the thundering pops of more shots seemed like they were right outside the apartment building. Brandi used her fingers to separate two blinds and scanned the exterior of the building. The darkness made it difficult to see anything from her vantage point. The local dealers had shot out all of the streetlights, so the only thing that illuminated the streets were the moon or headlights from cars. With the moon tucked behind clouds and no cars on the road, Brandi wasn't able to figure out what was going on outside. Although hearing gunshots was common for the residents of The Gilmor Homes, it was still scary to the girls. The girls were no longer interested in what was going on in the Knight's apartment. After the murder of her father, Reign always felt triggered when she heard gunshots. While Brandi was in the window being nosey, Reign tucked herself in the corner, the same way she tucked herself in the closet when she was ten years old. Brandi peeped her friend's current situation and went over to comfort her. They had about six hours left until Brandi's mom got off work and Reign needed to get some rest to clear her mind.

CHAPTER 4

Brandi! What the hell you doing in my room?!" Her mom yelled out as she opened the door. Brandi was knocked out on her mom's bed and didn't realize she fell asleep. She knew the one rule her mom had was to say out of her room and now Brandi was caught. The teenager popped up, wiping the crust from her eyes. "Mom. What time is it?" She asked, not realizing how long she had fell asleep.

"It's time for you to get the hell out of my room!" She barked. She sent her purse flying across the room, hitting Brandi in the arm. The commotion woke Reign up and she sat up. "Reign what the hell? Brandi, I know you ain't have company over while I was at work."

"No ma'am. It wasn't like that. They were shooting last night and we didn't want to be alone. I'm sorry."

"So why are you two in my room?" Neither Brandi or Reign could think of a response quick enough. "You two were in here listening to that nasty boy next door, weren't you?"

"No ma'am," Brandi said.

"No, Ms. Davis," Reign followed.

Brandi's mother wasn't the least bit naïve. She knew exactly why the girls were in her room because she often heard what went on beyond the thin walls connecting to the Knight's apartment. She constantly talked to their mother and informed her of what Darryl was up to, but she always received the same response, *"He's a man and I can't tell him what to do."* She wasn't happy that the girls were in her room, but she accepted their excuse because of the scene she just saw while on her way home.

"Reign, what's going on over at your apartment building?" She asked.

"Umm. I don't know," the confused girl responded. "What happened?"

"Something is going on. When I was walking in, I saw a bunch of cops out there. It looked like the entire police force was outside of your building."

Brandi jumped up and headed to the window. She pulled the blinds up and opened the window to get a look at the corner. Sure enough, she spotted several marked police cruisers at the top of the street. She looked back at Reign, remembering the rock they threw at the minivan. *Oh no, my mom is going to kill me if she finds out what we did,* Brandi thought.

"You see all those cops out there?" Her mother asked.

"Yes, I do."

"Maybe they are out there because of the gunshots that you two heard," she suggested. "I'll call Shelia and see if she knows what's going on. In the meantime, go make me something to eat. I brought home some eggs."

"Yes ma'am," Brandi replied as she scurried out the room.

Reign followed behind her. Brandi was thankful that the police presence had occupied her mom's thoughts because otherwise, she would be getting a whooping for having company and being in her mom's room.

"I'm going to go home before we both get in trouble," Reign whispered, as she headed for the front door.

"You not hungry?" Brandi whispered back, hoping her mom didn't hear the conversation.

"I'll eat at home. I'm not trying to get my ass beat with you," she responded while laughing.

Brandi watched as Reign slipped out of the door and then her eyes immediately cut to her mom's bedroom. Reign's statement about her getting her ass beat had her paranoid. Brandi's mom was a no-nonsense parent and Brandi was now anticipating being punished for not following directions. She could hear her mom on the phone and seconds later her mom closed the bedroom door. The coast was clear for Brandi. The last thing she wanted was to give her mom another reason to be mad, so she dove right into the shopping bags that were on the counter to get breakfast started.

Reign skipped down the steps of the vestibule and exited the building. Everyone on the block was outside, trying to get a look at the police action that was going on up the street. There was chatter, but none of it made any sense to the teen. As she walked by the neighbors, her stomach dropped. The same thought that went through Brandi's mind just went through hers. She was scared the police were there to investigate the culprits that threw a rock at the minivan and fled.

Police officers strolled up and down the street, talking with the neighbors. Reign kept her head down and continued past them. As she approached the minivan, she noticed a crack in the rear windshield and just a few feet away was the rock she threw at Brandi. Reign prayed the owner of the vehicle was not among the small crowds of neighbors that were currently outside. Despite her trying to walk as fast as she could, her steps were slow. Everything was moving in slow motion and it was taking her forever to walk by the damaged minivan. All eyes were on the teen and she began to sweat. *I'm going to get locked up for messing up this van,* she thought. *I didn't even do it on purpose.*

The closer Reign got to the corner of the block, the heavier the police presence became. A weight was lifted from her shoulders as she passed the minivan. Just as she turned the corner and went towards her apartment steps, the chatter from the officers became whispers. *Why are they staring at me?* Reign did her best to make herself small and head up towards the apartment.

"Reign, oh my God. Are you okay?" Hattie Mae asked as she wrapped her arms around the young girl.

Hattie Mae was the nosey neighbor that always knew everyone's business. If something went down in the hood, Hattie Mae either saw it happen or heard about it first. The teens often joked and said that Hattie Mae invented Neighborhood Watch before it was actually a thing. But it wasn't just the neighborhood that knew how nosey she was, the police did too. Anytime something went down in the neighborhood, the first stop the cops made was to Hattie's apartment. Her apartment was right across from Reign and Stoney.

"Yes, I'm okay, Ms. Hattie. Why you ask me that?"

Hattie Mae's eyes began to tear up as she looked into the girl's face. It was the innocence she saw when she looked at Reign that got her choked up. "The cops need to talk to you."

She knows, Reign thought. "Ms. Hattie it was an accident. I'll get it fixed. Please don't tell my mom."

"Girl, I'm not worried about that window that you and your friend broke. I just need you to come with me."

I knew it. She is so damn nosey. My mom is going to kill me. "Where are we going?" Reign asked, noticing that Hattie Mae was taking her back outside.

"Officer, here she is. This is Stoney's daughter."

"Thank you. Did you tell her?" An officer asked.

Hattie Mae shook her head and wiped her eyes with the sleeve of her sweater. The officer took a deep breath and looked at the teen, who was trying her best to avoid eye contact. Reign's heart was almost beating out of her chest as she slowly looked up at the young officer. *Ramos*, Reign read the name tag on the officer's uniform. "Did I do something wrong?" Her voice cracked as she asked the question.

"No, you didn't. Our detectives just need to ask you a few questions."

"About what?"

Just as the words escaped her mouth, a stretcher was being rolled out of the apartment building. This was not too odd for the neighborhood, because ambulances were always up and down these blocks. Whether it was a medical emergency with an elderly neighbor, an overdose by one of the junkies, or a shooting by one of the young stick up boys while they were trying to catch a lick. The red lights and loud sirens were always at The Gilmor Homes.

The only difference about this stretcher was the white sheet that was covering the body. Reign hadn't noticed the coroner van that was parked in front of the apartment building. This scene was very familiar to Reign as she flashed back to the night her father was carried out of the home the same way.

"Reign Bryant?"

"Yes," Reign responded, turning around to acknowledge the person calling her name.

In front of her stood a thin, white man with dark hair that was slicked back. A thick, dark mustache covered his top lip. He wore a baggy gray suit, with his badge draped around his neck and his duty weapon secured to his left hip. The detective stood in front of the confused girl with his hand extended. Reign reached out and shook his hand.

"I am Detective Woodland. Umm, I need to take you inside."

"Okay," Reign muttered.

She was definitely confused now. Hattie Mae took her out of the building and now the cops were taking her back in. Reign followed behind Detective Woodland but looked back at the stretcher that was being loaded in the van. It was like her vision was only focused on the stretcher and slowly expanded to a full view of her environment. Every neighbor had to be outside now. The streets were packed. Everyone wanted to know whose body was about to be carried away.

There was already speculation and rumors that had begun spreading. Some believed the police had raided an apartment and shot someone inside and others believed it was another overdose. Hattie Mae did her best to stay away from the crowds because she knew she couldn't hold water. She would have spilled the beans about what was going on, so she just sat on the steps. Like a hawk, she watched everyone and everything. Reign didn't know what to believe at the time. She still thought this situation was about the minivan and was just waiting for a pair of cuffs to be slapped on her wrists.

They headed up the hallway, towards the apartment. "Why is there tape on our door? Is my mom okay?"

Detective Woodland stopped in his tracks and turned to Reign. "There's been an incident." They were only a few feet away from the door, which was open. Reign stepped to the side and looked into the apartment. There was blood on the wall. She didn't even react. She just looked up at the detective. "Your mom got hurt pretty bad."

"How?"

"Someone came in the apartment and hurt her last night."

"Who did? Who hurt my mom?"

"That's what we are trying to find out. Do you know anyone who would have wanted to hurt your mom?"

Reign shook her head. "What hospital did she go to? I need to go there. She'll need me there."

The detective swallowed the knot that was in his throat. "She didn't go to the hospital," he mumbled. He reached out to embrace Reign, but she backed up.

Reign felt like she got hit by a truck. Any other teen in her situation would have been a mess with the news she just received, but Reign was numb. Her heart was broken but surprisingly she did not feel any pain. It was more of a shock. Thoughts were racing through her mind. *I was supposed to be home. Would I have gotten killed too? Who killed my mom? Was it the same person that killed my dad? Ms. Hattie saw me break the window on the van, she had to see the person that killed my mom.*

"Ms. Hattie," Reign whispered, as she took off running.

Hattie Mae popped up when she saw Reign running towards her.

"Did you see it?"

"Did I see what, darling?" Hattie Mae responded.

"Did you see who killed my mom?"

Hattie Mae was stuck. Tears ran down her face. "No, I didn't. The cops already asked me. I'm so sorry."

Hattie Mae wrapped her arms around Reign again, pulling the teen tightly into her body. The emotions were contagious because seeing Hattie Mae breaking down made Reign break down. Hattie Mae wasn't just a neighbor, but she was Stoney's friend. Hattie Mae knew all about Stoney's demons and would often check on her while Reign was in school. She tried her best to get Stoney to stop using, but that was a battle no one could win.

"I would like to take her down to the station," Detective Woodland informed Hattie Mae. The woman nodded before escorting Reign to one of the police vehicles. With the crime scene unit still processing the scene, Hattie Mae didn't have immediate access to her apartment, so she decided to accompany Reign down to the police station. Reign sunk into the back seat and watched as everyone gawked at her. She even spotted Brandi running around the corner as the detectives pulled off.

CHAPTER 5

"It's so cold in here," Hattie Mae muttered as she and Reign sat in one of the interview rooms. She looked around at the plain gray walls and the multiple cracks that decorated the ceiling. The two-way mirror was even dirty, with fingerprints and smudges all of the glass. Hattie Mae and Reign sat and patiently waited for Detective Woodland to come inside the room; it had been almost 40 minutes.

"This is just like *The First 48*," Reign said.

"Unfortunately, it is."

"Why are we in here? Do they think I had something to do with my mom getting hurt?

"No, honey. They don't think that at all. They just wanted to get you away from the crowds of people out there, and probably didn't want everyone in your face. You need your privacy at this time."

Reign felt a pain in her stomach, as they two continued waiting. She was trying to be patient, but curiosity got the best of her. "I want to go see my mom. Do you know what hospital they took her to?"

"Listen, honey. I'm going to be completely honest with you. I don't think your mom went to the hospital."

"What do you mean she didn't go to the hospital?" Reign began thinking back to the scene outside of the apartment. The sea of police officers and the white sheet being brought out by the coroner. Tears began to fill her eyes. She looked up at Hattie Mae, who was also crying. "My mom is dead, isn't she?"

The door opened before Hattie Mae could answer Reign's question. "Sorry for the wait," Detective Woodland stated as he entered the room. A white woman followed him in but didn't say anything. She wore a blue pants suit with a white blouse. Reign noticed the badge clipped on her belt, it was the same badge that was hanging from a chain around Detective Woodland's neck.

"Is my mom dead?" Reign wasted no time getting right to the point.

Detective Woodland looked at his partner and then dropped his head. He couldn't even bring himself to look Reign in her tear-filled eyes. He placed a manilla envelope on the desk and opened it. Inside were various mug shot photos. "Young lady, I'm so sorry to tell you this but your mother did pass away," he said, not even looking her in the face.

Reign jumped out from the table and ran out of the room. Detective Woodland signaled for his partner to follow her. He removed the mugshot photos from the envelope and closed it, but not before Hattie Mae spotted one of the horrific photos from the crime scene.

"Oh no," she muttered under her breath. "Was that her mother in that photograph?"

"Ma'am, I need you to focus right now. We need your help in trying to solve this case. The last thing we want is for the killer to still be on the loose in your neighborhood and harming someone else."

"A killer?" Hattie Mae took a deep breath. "I knew it. I didn't want to believe it, but something inside of me told me something bad happened to Stoney."

"I need to know if you recognize anyone in these photographs," Detective Woodland said, as he slid the mugshots across the table.

Hattie Mae picked up each photograph and examined them. She then looked at Detective Woodland and nodded. "I know 'em."

"Which one?"

"All of 'em."

He scrunched his face up, not expecting that answer. Well, which one of them have you seen at the victim's apartment?"

Hattie Mae took another deep breath and let out a long sigh. "All of 'em."

"Listen, I don't have time for games."

"I'm not playing any games, sir!" Hattie Mae yelled as she pushed the photos back towards the detective. "You asked questions and I answered 'em."

"So, you're telling me that all of these men frequented the victim's apartment?"

"That's exactly what I'm saying. Stoney used those men and they used her. I knew what went down in that apartment. Everyone did. She would send that poor little girl out on the street and a few minutes later, a man would pop up at her door. They wouldn't be there for long. They were in and out unless they were in there getting high too. Then, they could be in there all night. You know how they nod out and stuff or they be all hyped up. It depended on what they were using."

"And where would her daughter be, when these men were there all night?"

"Most of the time, she was around the corner at her lil' friend's spot. The other times, I don't know where she was going."

"How do you know all of this?"

"Because I watch what's going on. I need to know what's happening in my building."

"That's perfect. So, which one of these people was at the apartment last night?"

She reached over the table and tapped on one of the photos. "Him. His name is Slim. He was there with her. I don't know how long he stayed because I nodded off while I was reading, but I know he definitely was there."

"Did you see or hear anything that would have concerned you? Any yelling or arguing?"

"No. I can't say that I did. I usually don't hear any arguing from down that way. Most of the arguing in the building comes from the couple right above me. It sounds like War World 2 when they go at. It's shame too because they have two adorable children, and I can't imagine what those kids go through."

"What about the gunshots? Did year hear them?"

"Nope. I didn't hear any gunshots. But like I said, I was knocked out."

"Well, I appreciate the information. There's one other thing I need to speak to you about."

"What is it, Detective?"

"We were unable to locate any immediate family for the girl. It seems like you two are close. Would you be willing to take her in for a while, until we can find a permanent home for her?"

Hattie Mae did not even think about the request before answering. "Absolutely not. Detective, I would love to help her out, but I can't. That girl's father was shot and killed and now you're telling me her mother has been killed. For all I know, someone could be coming for her next. I don't want to have that type of drama knocking at my door."

"That's understandable. I would ask before we contact child services."

"So, what are yall going to do? Put her up for adoption?"

"Well, first I need to make sure she had no involvement in the murder. After that, she'll get placed in a group home for teenage girls."

"Involvement? Why would you think she was involved in that? That girl has been through too much and I hope you don't plan on bringing her back in here and making her feel like a suspect."

"I plan to solve this murder. To do so, I have to ask her some questions."

C.L. LOWRY

The door opened and in walked Reign and the detective. Reign's eyes were puffy and tears were still running down her face.

"Reign, are you okay?"

"Yes, Ms. Hattie."

"You don't have to be strong right now. This a lot for you to process."

"I want my mom," Reign sorrowfully said. "I just want my mom."

Hattie Mae hugged Reign tight. She locked eyes with Detective Woodland and shook her head in disgust. She couldn't believe they were planning to question Reign while she was in this current state. "Can you call those people now?" She asked Detective Woodland.

"They were already notified. Once we are finished here, they will take Reign over to the home."

"What home?" Reign asked as she pulled away from Hattie Mae. "Where am I going?"

"The detectives weren't able to get in touch with any of your relatives, so they had to find a place for you to stay."

"Can I just stay with you, Ms. Hattie? I promise I won't be a burden."

Hattie Mae looked over at Detective Woodland and then turned back to Reign. "I already asked them if you could, but they said no," she lied. "They said you have to go to a special home."

"What if I don't want to go there?"

"I don't think you have a choice. Apparently, you have to go somewhere for your own safety. It's kind of like witness protection."

"I don't need to be in witness protection. I need to be with my mom," Reign pleaded.

I can't believe this bullshit, Detective Woodland thought. He gathered the mugshots and slid them back into the folder. "We'll give you two a minute to speak. Child Protective Services will be right up to get everything situated. Reign, I'm sorry for your loss."

The two detectives exited the room. Hattie Mae sat Reign down and gave her a few words of encouragement. She knew how hard life was about to get for the teen, but she also knew how strong Reign was. Reign took care of herself and her mother. The detectives entered the next room and watched them through the 2-way mirror. Detective Woodland hoped Hattie Mae would question Reign to see if she had any information about her mother's murder, but Reign did not mention anything about the crime. She questioned Hattie Mae about where she was going to be taken but unfortunately, Hattie Mae did not have many details. She led Reign on to believe she was going to a facility for her own protection, but Children Protective Services were only able to place her in a group home for troubled teenagers.

CHAPTER 6

Reign stared out the window as she rode in the backseat of the Nissan Altima. The driver was an older black woman who identified herself as Marian. Marian was a representative of the TruGate facility for at-risk teenagers, that Reign was headed to. The facility mostly housed juvenile delinquents and runaways. Reign had never heard of TruGate before and never imagined being in her current situation. She still couldn't believe her mother was killed. She didn't actually know how to feel. She was devastated, but a part of her was also angry. Angry her mother chose drugs over the family. If she weren't so wrapped up in drugs, there would not be men in and out of their apartment. Deep down inside, Reign knew one of those men had something to do with her mother's murder, but she didn't know which one. When she was outside with Brandi, they never spotted anyone coming to the apartment. However, she did remember the gunshots that went off in the middle of the night.

The Nissan came to a stop in front of a large home. Headlights from another vehicle glared through the side mirrors. Reign held her hand up in front of her face to block the reflecting light from shining in her eyes.

"Come on, young lady. Let's get you settled inside because the cops want to talk to you," Marian said.

The cops want to talk to me? For what? Reign exited the Nissan and looked back at the vehicle with the bright headlights. It was dark outside, so she could only see the silhouette of someone walking until the figure stepped closer.

"Welcome to your new home," Detective Woodland said.

Reign did not respond. Seeing the detective was nothing more than a reminder of the tragedy that just took place. It seemed like there was no escape from her new reality. A part of Reign wished it was just a nightmare she would wake up from at any moment, but the other part was prepared for this day to come. Her mother was reckless and didn't care who she double-crossed to get what she wanted. The question wasn't *who would kill Stoney Bryant?* The question was, *who wouldn't have killed Stoney Bryant?*

Reign knew there was a laundry list of sketchy men her mother entertained. In her mind, each one of them was a suspect. *Fat Pat could have done it, he always tried shorting mom on her money when he came over. Eddie from down the street could have done it too, I remember when he roughed mom up. I overheard her telling a friend they were physically fighting. I'll never forget that large knot he put on her head. I know he definitely could kill somebody.* Reign's mind was racing. She was going down the list and unfortunately, there wasn't anyone she thought about taking off the list. Every man Stoney was with could have killed her. None of them were law-abiding citizens.

They both had followed Marian to her office, where she allowed the detective to question the young girl. He disregarded Hattie Mae's feelings and decided to wait until Reign was away from her to get the answers he wanted. "Do any of these men look familiar to you?" Detective Woodland asked as he placed the mugshot photos down in front of Reign.

Seeing each photo flashed her back to each night she was outside, watching the men enter her apartment building. She studied their faces and their mannerisms. The nicknames she called them were made up by her and Brandi. Once they saw someone walking in the building, they had to give them a name. It was their running joke. Only a few of them were actually known by their street names. Fat Pat is an example. Brandi gave him that name because one night he came to visit Stoney with a bucket of KFC tucked under his arm and his stomach hung over his belt. His name was Reginald Packard and the streets called him Biggs. Biggs was known in the hood for shorting people, which is why he did the same with Stoney. Whether he was copping drugs or ordering from his favorite fast-food restaurant, Biggs never had enough money to pay what he owed. "They all look familiar. They all came to see my mom."

"All of them?"

"Yes."

"At one time?"

"No. On different nights."

"Only at night?"

"I think so. When I'm in school, I don't know what my mom does all day."

"Do you think any of these men had a reason to hurt your mom?"

"I don't know. Maybe. None of them were good guys. They were all on drugs."

"How do you know that?"

Reign looked down and began tapping her foot on the ground. "Because my mom was on drugs and she only hung around drug addicts."

"Was there anything valuable in the apartment? Anything that someone would want to rob your mom?"

Reign chuckled. "Nope. We didn't have anything." A tear ran down her cheek. "The most valuable thing in there was my mom."

"Where were you at on the night your mom was killed?"

"I was around the corner at my best friend's apartment," she replied, wiping the tears from her face.

"All night?"

"Yes. I go there when my mom has company."

"Can anyone else confirm this?"

"Confirm?"

"Yes."

"What does that mean?"

"It means is there someone that saw you at that apartment with your best friend?"

"Oh. Her mom can tell you I was there. She came home early from work and saw me in the apartment."

"What were you two doing the entire night?"

Reign immediately thought about the minivan they damaged and having to stay in the apartment because they didn't want to get caught. The last thing she wanted to do was lie to the detective, but she also feared getting in trouble. "We were just watching movies. We didn't do anything special."

"One last question. Did you see any of these men go to your apartment on the night your mom got killed?"

Reign didn't even look down at the photographs. "No. I didn't see anyone go into the apartment."

"Okay, thanks. I'll be in touch if I hear anything. I'm going to do everything I can to catch your mother's killer."

"Thank you."

Detective Woodland exited the office and headed out. Mariam took Reign on a quick tour of the building, before taking her to her room. A room that she was going to share with five other teenage girls. While taking the tour, she saw most of the teens had finished dinner and were now unwinding before bed. Reign noticed how rough the other girls were. They were cursing and play fighting in the living room area. A staff member was monitoring them but didn't seem to be able to control the girls.

"Are you hungry?" Marian asked. "I'm sure there's still some food left from dinner."

"No thank you," Reign replied.

"I understand this transition may not be easy for you, but if there is anything you need just let me know."

"Okay, I will."

"You seem like a nice girl. Just try not to get caught up with the wrong crowd," Marian stated as her eyes cut over to the girls in the living room. Reign followed her eyes and saw a girl standing in the living room. The thin light-skinned girl was staring at Reign. She didn't speak or move. She just stared at the new face in the house. "Let's head up to your room."

Reign followed Marian upstairs and entered one of the six bedrooms. "The bed in the corner with the pink sheets is yours. There should be a bag of clothes next to the bed. Let me know if they don't fit. You can put your clothes in any of the open drawers."

Reign looked around the room, which was much bigger than any of the rooms in the apartment building. There wasn't too much to be impressed by but to her, it was much more than she had. Six twin beds were pushed against the wall. There were four slim dressers and two standing mirrors in the room as well. For the most part, the room was clean, except for dirty clothes that were just tossed around on the floor. "There are some rules that I will go over with you in the morning. I don't want to overload you with information tonight.

The one thing I will tell you; everyone gets punished for the actions of one. This allows for you young ladies to learn about responsibility and accountability. If you have any questions just let me know."

"Thank you."

"No problem. Now, get some rest."

Marian left the room and Reign began looking through the bag of clothes that was left for her. There wasn't much to look through, seeing as though there were only undergarments, a few shirts, and a couple pants in the bag. She took the clothing out and placed them on the bed. A tear dropped onto the shirt that Reign placed on the bed. Folding the clothes reminded her of the way she cared for her mom. She would wash and fold her clothing all of the time, while her mom be high as a kite. Everything reminded Reign of her mother, even the faded yellow paint that covered the walls. *Yellow was mom's favorite color.*

With all of the drama and commotion throughout the day, Reign just realized she hadn't spoken to Brandi since she left her apartment that morning. *I need to find a phone. I need to call Brandi. I wonder if she knows that my mom is dead.*

"Well look at what we got here. We got ourselves a new bitch." Reign looked up and saw the light-skinned girl that was staring at her in the living room. She was standing in the doorway with four other girls. "What's ya name, new bitch?"

Reign ignored the question. She was not in any mood to entertain any nonsense. She wanted to get Marian to get the situation resolved.

"I asked you what your fuckin' name was, bitch," the girl said as she approached Reign. "You think you're too good to answer me? Huh? You think you're too pretty to answer me? Huh?" She stood over Reign, as she continued to inventory the clothing that was given to her. She then ran her hand up Reign's curly hair. "I asked you a question, bitch!" The girl barked as she yanked Reign's hair and pulled her off the bed.

Instinctively, Reign began swinging at the girl. She landed a wild punch before receiving a blow to the face. Her adrenaline was pumping, so the hit to the face didn't stop her from defending herself. She was at a great disadvantage with her hair being pulled but she continued to fight back. Reign reached up to grab the girl's hair, but she was unable to get a grasp. Instead, she drug her fingers across the girl's face. "Get the fuck off me!" Reign yelled. She was hit with another blow. This time the punch busted her nose, she felt the warm liquid running down her face. Reign tried her best to loosen the girl's grip on her hair, but every time she went for the girl's hand, she was hit in the face. Reign started throwing punches again, landing a few on her opponent . The other girls in the room began yelling and cheering as they looked on. Unfortunately, Reign was on the losing end of the fight.

"What the hell is going on in here?!" Marian yelled as she entered the room. "What are you girls doing?"

All of the girls scattered and stood next to their beds. "Tiana! Reign! What are you two doing?"

"She attacked me!" Reign yelled. Blood was still running down her nose.

"She's lying!" Tiana blurted out. "Ask them! This chick hit me first. Look at my face! She scratched me."

"Who started this?" Marian asked the other girls in the room. In unison, they all raised a hand and pointed to Reign. "Reign, come with me," she ordered. "Tiana, I'll send the nurse up to look at your face."

CHAPTER 7

After the fight, Reign had to spend the night under supervision. After the nurse treated her injuries, she slept on a cot in Marian's office. Between the tragedy involving her mother and the fight with Tiana, Reign slept for ten hours. Marian allowed her to stay even as she began her workday. She knew Reign needed rest. It was just before noon when the teen finally woke up.

"Rise and shine."

"Good morning, Ms. Marian."

"Are you hungry?"

"Not really."

"It seems like you've made one heck of a first impression with the other girls." Marian chuckled.

"They lied. I swear I didn't start that fight. That girl got mad because I didn't let her call me a bitch. Then she just grabbed my hair and start hitting me."

Marian shook her head. "I figured Tiana was the one that started the fight."

"Then why am I the one that got in trouble?"

"Who said you were in trouble?"

"I had to stay in here."

"The only reason you're in here is because I didn't want you staying in the room with her friends. Those girls have a habit of causing trouble and putting the blame on other people. This isn't the first incident that they've been involved in."

"So, what am I supposed to do about them? I'm not going to back down from that girl."

"I'm not asking you to back down. We will try to change your rooms but that's only a temporary solution. You two need to learn how to coexist, so we can work towards a permanent solution."

"I just want to go home."

"Now, you know that you can't go there. You shouldn't want to be there anyway. Being there would be too traumatic for you. I'm going to recommend a therapist that specifically deals with helping children in your situation."

Reign did not fully understand what Marian was asking her to do. She never heard of anyone going to a therapist before and she wasn't too keen on the idea of going to see one. The only thing on her mind was her mother. She felt like she was in a bad dream that she desperately needed to wake up from. She just wanted to walk into her old apartment and sit on the couch. She wanted to get her clothes out of there and any pictures that she had of her mom and dad. "I just want to get a few things out of the apartment. That's it."

"Okay. The therapist's office isn't too far from your old neighborhood, so what we will do is take you by there after you complete your session."

"I really don't think I need to go see this person. I don't even know what they do."

"Reign, you have to fully understand the traumatic event that you just went through, and you have to find a way to process everything. A therapist is someone that can assist you with all of this."

"Why can't you just assist me."

"I'm not a professional in that area. You need someone with the expertise and experience to walk you through all of it. I can't do that."

"Okay. I'll go, but only if you let me go to my apartment after I go to the therapist."

"Perfect. We will definitely make that happen. Now, go get yourself something to eat and we will take you over there in about an hour."

Reign walked out the office and headed to the kitchen. She snatched a yogurt out of the refrigerator and a banana off the counter. She wasted no time devouring both. Reign went upstairs to the bedroom to grab a change of clothes. Once she entered the room, she halted after seeing her bed. A dead mouse had been left on her pillow and someone wrote *YOU'RE A RAT* on the sheets in black marker. *Assholes*, Reign thought as she flipped the pillow over, knocking the mouse onto the floor. She knew Tiana had something to do with it, but it would be impossible to prove. She brushed it off and headed to the shower to wash up.

Reign still couldn't believe what she went through on her first night at TruGate. As the vehicle pulled off to take her to the therapist, she just stared at the home. The exterior made it seem like a regular building, but Reign knew the evil that lurked inside. She knew this was going to be a long road to travel. She was only sixteen and couldn't imagine spending another two years going to blows with Tiana. "How long have you been working here?" Reign asked the driver.

"Five years," Deborah responded. Deborah was in her early 50s and was a retired correctional officer. She had seen and dealt with a lot in her career and most of her peers called her crazy to take the job at the group home. *You're going from working with one set of criminals to another*, they would all say. Deborah didn't care what other people thought. Working at the home with the girls was more so a personal decision because she grew up in foster care and remembered how hard the journey was for her. She wanted to make a difference in young girls' lives and lead them in the right direction. This is why her current job seemed perfect and for the most part, it was. After working with adult criminals for over 20 years, there was nothing you could get past Deborah. As soon as she started at the home, she put her foot down and earned the respect of the girls. But teens know how to maneuver through the system, so they knew to start their troubles upstairs in the bedroom after Deborah had left for the day.

This was a common theme for the girls. Deborah worked the 11 am to 7 pm shift and most of the problems occurred after her shift. If Deborah was still working, Tiana wouldn't have dared to pick a fight with Reign. The other workers weren't as strict as Deborah, which is why Tiana and her friends didn't face any type of punishment for the fight.

"Has it always been this way?" Reign asked.

"Has what always been what way?"

"The girls. Doing what they want to do in there?"

"Oh, no. Things used to be a lot different there until the other facilities began maxing out. So, once they ran out of room, a lot of those girls got stuck in sheltering programs. Years ago, some of them wouldn't have qualified to be here. Once you grow up, you'll learn that government-funded programs don't really get enough funding to be ran properly."

"So, what happened? How did it get this bad?"

"Are you referring to that little scuffle you had last night?"

Reign nodded.

"Well, we have a new administrator and I think the girls take advantage of her kindness."

Ms. Marian, Reign thought. "How so?"

"Girl, you ask a lot of questions. The administration at TruGate doesn't really have a sense of what's going on at our level. They have the college degrees that qualify them on paper, but once they step into the world of actually dealing with people, they are lost."

"So what about – "

"Okay, that was your last question," Deborah said. She turned on the radio and tuned in to her favorite station.

A little disappointed, Reign was now left with her thoughts. She wanted to find a way to get out of TruGate, but she needed more answers. She was also confused about what Deborah meant when she was talking about the new administration. She thought Marian was a nice woman that had her best interest at heart. *Am I wrong about Ms. Marian? Why did she take me down to the office after I got attacked? I knew that wasn't right.*

"We're here," Deborah announced.

Reign looked at the small commercial building they were pulling up in front of. She had passed this building so many times while going to school and never paid it any attention. Just as she exited the car, she spotted a familiar face. *Detective Woodland.* So many emotions took over Reign. She didn't know why the detective was at the therapist's office, but something didn't seem right. Deborah approached the front door and opened it for Reign. Reign hesitated to enter and as she reached the threshold, she spotted the other detective that was in the interview room at the police station. Reign took off running up the street.

"Hey, where are you going?" Deborah yelled as she chased after Reign. As soon as Reign hit the corner, Deborah lost sight of her. Thinking the young girl continued up the street, Deborah ran back to the therapist's office. "She just ran off," she said when she entered the office.

"What do you mean she ran off?" Detective Woodland asked.

"As soon as she got to the door, she stopped and just ran off."

"Where do you think she's going?"

"I don't know. She didn't say anything. She just started running."

"This is bullshit. You know how hard it is to schedule these forensic interviews? We need to get her back here right now."

"I'll check the area. She couldn't have gotten far."

"Call Marian and let her know what's going on. I'll get some patrol officers in the area to search too."

Detective Woodland radioed in for backup and Deborah took to the streets in search of Reign. Deborah didn't expect the teen to run off and surely didn't want to be responsible for telling her boss what occurred. Despite the order from Detective Woodland, she never called Marian to inform her that Reign was in the wind. Her car crept up each street as she had her head on a swivel, searching for the teen.

Reign waited patiently for time to pass by. After hitting the corner, she ducked into a vacant home. Just like the therapist building she would pass on her way to school, there was a home around the corner that the kids used as a hangout spot. She never hung out there before, but she heard about it. It was easily recognizable by the red front door and the boarded-up windows. This wasn't uncommon in this area for homes to remain vacant and abandoned for years. If drug addicts didn't take them over, then drug dealers would use them as stash houses.

A few hours had passed, and Reign was still posted in the home. It had been a while since she saw Deborah's car riding up the street. School had let out and she could hear other kids' voices coming from outside. Reign slipped out the house and onto the street. She made sure to blend in with the small groups of teens that were walking home. It didn't take long before she was in her old neighborhood. She noticed neighbors were staring at her but no one spoke or asked her anything. It was like she was a ghost.

Reign hit the corner and halted when she spotted police cars outside of the apartment building. She planned to go in to grab some belongings, but she knew they had to be waiting for her to show up. Instead, she headed straight and went into another building.

"Who that?" Brandi asked, hearing the hard knock at her door. She opened it and saw her best friend standing in front of her. "Reign!" She screamed as she gave her friend a bear hug. "Where the hell did you go? I was so worried. The cops wouldn't tell us where they took you."

"They put me in a placement home," she replied, as she entered the apartment and started peeking out of the windows.

"What are you doing?"

"They're looking for me."

"Who looking for you?"

"The people from the place. I just ran away from them."

"Girl, fuck them people. What happened to your mom?"

Brandi's question hit Reign like a ton of bricks. She was so busy ducking and dodging Deborah, that her mind had briefly been off the tragedy. Now, she was around the corner from the crime scene and all of those emotions came rushing back. Reign sat down on the couch. "Somebody killed her."

"People are saying it was Slim."

"Slim?"

"Yeah. Apparently, he is the one that killed your mom. The cops are looking for him and everything."

"Why the hell would Slim kill my mom?"

"I don't know, but that's the word on the street."

"Who said that?"

"Girl, you know who said it. It was nosey ass, Ms. Hattie. She came back telling the whole hood that the cops are looking for Slim."

Reign sighed. "She is such a snake. She went down to the police station with me and that's probably the only reason she went down. Just to get information."

"Girl, people were saying all type of stuff when you got taken away."

"Like what?"

"In school, Keenan and his little friends are spreading rumors that you shot your mom."

"What?"

"Yup. All because he saw you in the back of the police car but don't pay him no mind, he's so dumb. I told him to shut up and mind his business."

"I fuckin' hate him."

"Me too."

"What else are people saying?"

"That your mom might have killed herself. You know, like an overdose. They are saying someone gave her bad drugs."

"I can't believe people are making up all of these stories. Don't they have anything better to do?"

Brandi shrugged her shoulders. She only told Reign a few things that were being said, but plenty more rumors were going around. By the look on Reign's face, Brandi knew it wasn't worth telling her the rest of the rumors. "So, what you gonna do now?"

"I want to stay here with you."

"You know damn well that my mom ain't having that."

"She don't have to know. Please help me out," Reign begged. "I can't go back to that place."

"Why not?"

"I got into a fight last night."

"A fight? With who?"

"Some girl up there. I don't even know her."

"You beat her ass, right?"

"I couldn't. She snuck up on me and pulled my hair. Plus, she had all of her little friends with her."

"Her friends? Oh hell no." Brandi snatched off her earrings and started rolling up the sleeves on her sweatshirt. "Ain't nobody gonna try to jump my best friend. Let's go get these bitches right now. I ain't fuckin' playing."

Reign loved the idea of showing back up to the house with Brandi and getting a rematch with Tiana. She would run the house if Brandi was with her, but she knew there was no way the staff was going to allow that to happen. "Chill, it's cool. I scratched her all up and the only thing she did was bust my nose. Next time, I'm going to be ready for her."

"Ain't gonna be no next time. I'm coming up there and I'm gonna beat her ass."

Reign laughed.

"I'm serious. But first, let me braid your hair up so she cant's grab it no more."

Reign felt comforted while she was with Brandi. She knew Brandi would support her with anything, but it was actually seeing her in action that made Reign feel at ease. Even though she told Brandi there was no way that she could get into the group home, Brandi was still on a mission. There was no way she would let anyone disrespect her friend. After braiding Reign's hair, they left out on a mission to the group home.

CHAPTER 8

I just don't understand how this happened," Marian said. "How does a teenager that is specifically under a supervised visitation to a therapist get away from the person that is supervising them?"

"I told you a hundred times already, she just ran off," Deborah replied. "By the time I hit the corner she was gone. It was like she vanished in thin air."

"Vanished in thin air? Oh, she's a ghost now?"

Deborah wanted to walk out of the office, but she didn't want to lose her job. She couldn't believe that she was getting blamed for Reign running off. "You can even ask the cops that were there. They tried helping me look for her, but she was gone."

"You can explain it a hundred more times, Deb. I still won't understand it. Your job is to keep these kids safe and to watch them but instead, you let this one get away."

"Obviously, this girl is trouble. She got into the fight last night and then she ran away today. How am I getting blamed for the actions of a 16-year-old?"

"Because you're the adult!" Marian yelled. "You know what type of children we work with, and you know the risk of giving them any type of lead way to make bad decisions. Not only am I surprised that this happened, but I'm also disappointed."

"Well, I don't know what to tell you. I did my best to find that girl and I would still be out there looking for her if you didn't order me to come back here."

"Are you trying to blame me for Reign being missing?"

"No, I'm just saying this seems like a waste of time. I need to go find her."

Just as the two were diving deeper into their conversation, they heard a commotion coming from the hallway. Deborah exited the office and was almost knocked over by teens that were running through the hallway. Marian stepped into the hallway and blocked two kids from running by her. "What are you two doing? Why are you running in here?"

"Ms. Marian, they're fighting," one of the teens responded. She was out of breath.

"Who's fighting?"

"I don't know. But everyone's going outside to see it."

Marian and Deborah took off running. Outside there was a huge melee of punch throwing and hair-pulling. Some teens were solely spectators, cheering on the chaotic fight. On the ground was a bloody Tiana, who had two teeth knocked out after being slugged in the face and then stomped out once she dropped. She and her friends has been chillin' outside after school when Reign and Brandi ran up on them. Tiana was the first victim to face Brandi's wrath, but she wasn't the last. After dropping Tiana, Brandi just started swinging on the other girls. Although it wasn't a fair fight, numbers-wise, Brandi and Reign wreaked havoc on the group of six girls.

Once Tiana got dropped, one of the other girls ran inside the home. With the odds at two against four, Reign and Brandi knew they had to strike first. Brandi did damage with her heavy hands, but Reign struggled with the odds being against her. Reign got a good punch on her first target, splitting the girl's lip but her second target immediately threw a flurry of windmill punches. Reign continued swinging catching the girl with a few good strikes, none of which stopped her attack. The fight continued with both girls swinging on Reign as she punched and scratch her way through the attack. With their adrenaline pumping, they never realized how much damage Reign was doing.

Brandy, on the other hand, was throwing nothing but haymakers. Her hair was pulled into a little bun that her opponents tried to grab but were unsuccessful. Brandi sent both girls to the ground with heavy hits and proceeded to kick each of them while they were on the ground. After grabbing Brandi's leg, one of the girls tried pulling her to the ground. Brandi hit her with two punches to the side of the face, which dropped the girl. She then turned her attention on the girls that were jumping Reign. Brandi tackled one of the girls and pounded on her while they were on the ground. This freed Reign up to go one on one and put a beating on the last girl standing.

"Stop it! Stop this right now!" Marian yelled. She and Deborah pushed their way through the crowd and broke up the fights. They pulled Brandi off her most recent victim and the teen reacted by pushing Deborah. Not initially realizing she was an adult, Brandi was seconds away from swinging on her too. Instead, Brandi grabbed Reign's arm and the two took off running. With their focus on the injured girls, Marian and Deborah didn't even bother chasing after Reign and her friend. Marian called 911 and requested that the police and ambulance come out to the home.

"Come on, girl. Keep up," Reign said as she noticed that Brandi was trailing behind.

"I can't," Brandi responded, breathing heavily. "I need a break."

"Let's go right here."

Brandi followed Reign into an alleyway. The two began walking and suddenly burst out in laughter. "Your big ass always needs a break. We didn't even run that far," Reign joked.

"That's because my big ass had to save your little ass back there. If it weren't for me, those girls were gonna stomp you out."

"Now you know that ain't true. They were light work."

"They all were. Did you see that lady that grabbed me? She's lucky that I didn't knock her head off."

"That's the counselor chick that was chasing me earlier."

"I don't care who she is. The next time she puts her hands on me, I'm gonna lay her ass out."

"Yo, I can't believe we just did that."

"I told you that I was gonna fuck that girl up. Don't nobody mess with my best friend."

"I appreciate you so much," Reign said, giving Brandi a tight hug. Tears of joy ran down Reign's face. She could not imagine life without Brandi. She was the only person she had left that she was close to. Without her mother, she needed someone she could count on and that was her best friend. She felt helpless after the first fight with Tiana and Brandi helped her get that power and confidence back.

"So what are you gonna do now? There's no way you're going to be able to go back to that place. Those girls are going to try to get you back. You have to stay with me for now?"

"What about your mom?"

"What she don't know weren't hurt her. We'll just have to be very careful. Besides, she works so much that she'll never know your there."

The girls headed back to the apartment. Brandi entered first and distracted her mom with small talk as Reign slipped in and snuck into Brandi's room. Not long after the girls got in, there was a knock at the door. Brandi's mom answered the door, greeting two officers that were standing in the hallway.

"Good evening, officers. Can I help you?"

"Hello, ma'am. Sorry to bother you at this time, but one of our detectives sent us over here to speak to you."

"Speak to me about what?"

"We are looking for a girl. Reign Bryant. One of the neighbors told us that she is good friends with your daughter and we were wondering if you've seen her."

"No I haven't, but let me check with my daughter," she replied. "Brandi."

"Yes, mom?"

"Come here."

Brandi froze when she reached the door and saw the officers. *They came to lock us up,* she thought as she began backpedaling. She wanted to make a run for it, but there was nowhere to go. She wished Reign knew what was going on, so they could put their heads together and develop a plan. Brandi locked eyes with one of the officers and to her, it felt like he was staring a hole into her soul. *I gotta get out of here.*

"Have you seen Reign?" her mom asked. "These officers are looking for her." Brandi was too caught up in her thoughts to respond. She kept staring at the same officer, wondering when they were going to make their move. She expected to be in handcuffs already but they were still at the door. "Brandi. Where is Reign?"

Her mother's sharp words cut through Brandi's thoughts. "Oh, umm, I don't know."

"Did you see her in school?"

"Umm, no."

Brandi noticed her mother raise an eyebrow before turning to the officers. "I'm sorry, but we haven't seen her."

"Okay. If you happen to run into her, please call 911."

"Is she in trouble or something?"

"I'm sorry ma'am but we need to go. Like I said, if you see her please give us a call."

The officers walked away and Brandi's mother shut the door behind them. She turned and looked at Brandi. The awkward silence was killing Brandi but it was short-lived as her mother headed towards the bedroom. "What are you doing, mom? Where are you going?"

Brandi was ignored and her mother entered her bedroom. Reign popped up off the bed. "I knew it. What are you doing in here?"

"Mom, it's not what you think."

"It's not what I think? What I think is that you just lied to two police officers. I knew something was up because you have such a big mouth but out there you couldn't even get your words together." Brandi's mom exited the bedroom and slammed the door. "You need to tell your little friend that she has to go," she whispered.

"But, mom. She has nowhere to go."

"That's not my problem. That girl's mother was killed and now she has the police knocking at my door. I've never had the police knocking at my door and I don't want it to ever happen again. Tell her that she has to leave!"

"So where is she supposed to go?"

"I don't know and I don't care. I also don't have time to argue with you. I have to go to work. When I get back, she better be gone."

"I can't do that to her, mom. She needs me."

"You don't have a choice. The last time I checked, your name isn't on any of these damn bills, so you don't get to make any decisions about what goes on in this apartment. I'm going to say this one last time. Tell her she has to leave. If I get back from work and she's here, I'm kicking both of you out."

CHAPTER 9

This is good, Reign thought as she devoured the chicken-flavored Ramon noodles. Brandi had prepared the meal for her friend. It had been a few weeks since Brandi's mother kicked Reign out of the apartment. With nowhere to go, Reign was forced to take up shelter on the streets. Never in a million years would Reign ever guess that she would be homeless at 16-years-old. She couldn't even go back to school because the police had been popping up there looking for her too. They were sure that they would catch her there. She didn't even want to imagine what type of trouble she was in because of the brawl at the group home.

When Brandi's mother was at work, Reign chilled at the apartment with Brandi but on nights she had to work, Reign stayed in the abandoned car that was parked across the street from her apartment. The police detail that was in front of the apartments was still in place, but the officers who worked the detail weren't the sharpest tools in the shed. They had no idea the girl they were looking for was right across the street from them, living in the back seat of a junk car.

Brandi always made sure that Reign had something to eat, even if it meant that she had to take half portions at dinner to ensure Reign was taken care of. She would walk right past the police car and deliver the food to her friend. Life wasn't too bad for Reign, despite the circumstances. Even having to manage on her own was better than being in the group home or being harassed by the police. The only time things got rough was during inclement weather. Because the car's windshield and driver's side window here missing, everything got into the car. On nights that it rained, Reign would set up a big blanket on the back of the seats to act as a shield to keep her dry.

Everything was going fairly well until Detective Woodland received a tip from one of the neighbors about Reign living in the car. He was still on the hunt for her mother's killer and he still had questions for her. Detective Woodland requested that patrol officers conduct checks on the abandoned vehicle during the day and throughout the night. He wanted to find her and was determined to solve her mother's case.

Reign left Brandi's apartment early in the morning, just before Brandi's mother returned home from work. She hit the corner and stopped in her tracks. *What are the cops doing at the car? They are all in my stuff.* The officers were pulling out all of the contents in the car, including snacks that Reign had stashed inside. Reign had no choice but to keep it moving. She headed down the street, looking over her shoulder to ensure she wasn't being followed until she bumped into someone.

"Damn. You just gon' run me over?"

"I'm so sorry," Reign responded. Her eyes focused on the person she bumped into. Her heart began beating fast and she got butterflies in her stomach.

"Yo, you okay? Why you just staring at me?"

"Oh, sorry. Yeah, I'm fine."

"Why you looking over yo shoulder like that?" Omari asked.

"The cops are back there."

"They still looking for you, huh?"

Reign was taken aback by Omari's statement. It was just like their first encounter. He would stop her in her tracks but as soon as he spoke she instantly became annoyed. "No, they're not looking for me. They're probably looking for you," she joked.

"Why would they be looking for me?" He nervously asked.

"You know why."

"No, I don't. Enlighten me."

Reign noticed that Omari was serious. "Because you sell drugs," she whispered.

"Is that so?"

"I don't know. That's the word on the street."

"The streets say a lot of stuff but that doesn't mean it's true."

"So what is that supposed to mean?"

"The streets are saying a lot about you too."

Reign rolled her eyes. "Let me guess. You're referring to my mom." Omari didn't respond. "Whatever you heard ain't true."

"I don't listen to gossip. If it don't come from you or your little fat friend, then I'm not taking it serious."

Reign chuckled. "Didn't I tell you to stop calling my friend fat?"

Omari laughed. "Did you? I don't remember."

"Yes I did, so you better cut it out."

"Or else what? You gon' go tell her?"

"Nope. I'm gonna shut you up."

Omari didn't expect that response from Reign. He looked at her as pretty and petite, which wasn't much of a threat to him. However, he could tell she meant what she said. He didn't know a beast had been unleashed in her and she would never be hesitant to throw hands but he liked what he heard and also what he saw. "How the hell you gon' shut me up?"

"With these hands," she joked.

Omari laughed. "Okay, killa."

"Why you out here this early? I know you not in school."

"How you know what I'm doing?"

"I've never seen you with a book."

"So you watching me now?"

"Boy, ain't nobody watching you."

"Yeah okay. So how you know I don't be having no books?"

"Because I know what you be having."

"I don't know what you talkin' bout."

"I bet you don't. But seriously, what you doing out so early?"

"I'm always out here this early. I'm just going for a walk. Do you always ask so many damn questions?"

"Yup."

"Well go take your ask to school with all those questions."

"I'm not in school."

"What you mean you not in school. How old are you?"

"I'm 16."

"So why you say you not in school?"

"Because I dropped out."

"Now why you go and do that?"

"Because I had no other choice."

"There's always a choice."

"Not when you on the run," Reign replied, trying to make herself sound cool.

"On the run?" Omari asked. He smiled at the teen. "You ain't on the run."

Reign chuckled. "Yes, I am."

"What you on the run for?"

"The cops are looking for me because of my mom."

"That don't mean you on the run. They probably just trynna question you."

"Well, I don't have any answers for them."

"I feel you. Ten toes down. I like that."

"Can I ask you something?"

"Yeah, go ahead."

"I need a job. Can I work for you?"

"You want to work for me?"

"Yeah. I need to make some money, so I can get a place to stay."

"What's wrong with the car you been staying in?" Omari joked.

"What?" Reign asked. She was embarrassed that Omari knew she had been living in her car. "What you talkin' about?"

"Nothing," he lied. "Take this walk with me." The two-headed down the street and towards one of the apartment buildings. "Keep it real with me, what's up with that car?"

Reign really didn't want to get into the details of her living conditions with Omari. She didn't want anyone knowing that she had been staying in there. However, she saw the serious look on his face and knew that he was really waiting for an answer. "My mom got killed and the cops won't let me live on my own in the apartment, so I gotta chill in that car."

"Do the cops know who killed yo momma?"

"I don't think so. If they do know, they sure didn't tell me who did it."

"What did they tell you?"

"They didn't tell me anything. They just tried to harass me. They kept asking me questions that I wasn't ready to answer."

"Like what?"

"They were asking me about my mom's drug habit and where she was getting her drugs from," Reign said as the two continued walking. "I told them that she gets her drugs from you, but I don't think that's what killed her."

"What the fuck? Why you tell them that shit?"

Reign laughed so hard her stomach began hurting. Omari was so nervous and he quickly realized the teen was just messing with him. He wasn't too fond of her specific choice of humor, especially with her suggesting that the police had information on him. "Why you play so much?"

"Cuz you askin' all these questions."

"That's cuz I need to know more about you. Especially if you gon' be working for me."

"So, you gonna give me a job?"

"Maybe. As long as you stop playing so much."

"Okay, Mr. Serious," she joked as she held her hand up to salute him.

"Where yo daddy at?"

"He got killed when I was younger."

"Are you serious or are you playing still?"

"I'm serious. Why would I play about that?"

"I don't know. You seem like the type that would."

"Whatever."

"You hungry?"

"Yup."

"Okay. Let's go in here," Omari suggested as the two approached a breakfast shop."

They entered the shop and the aroma of the food grabbed their attention. Reign wished Brandi was with them because she knew how excited her friend would be to eat at this spot. "Good morning. Are you two dining with us today or picking up an order to go?" A waitress greeted.

"We'll be dining in," Omari responded.

The waitress led them to a table and sat them down. "Can I start you off with something to drink?" She asked as she slid two menus on the table.

"I'll take a large orange juice," Omari ordered.

"And what about you, young lady?"

"I'll take an... umm... an orange juice too please."

"Alright. Two orange juices coming right up. I'll be back to take your food order."

"Why you acting all weird," Omari asked, noticing that she was stuttering to put in her drink order. Sweat beads formed on her head and she looked like she saw a ghost. "You okay?"

"I'm sorry. I'm a little nervous."

"Why the hell you nervous?" Omari began looking around at the other customers. "Is there someone in here that you recognize?"

"No, it's not that. This is... this is my... umm... my first date."

"Date?!" Omari burst out laughing. "This ain't no date. You trippin' youngin'." He continued laughing, even after the waitress approached with their drinks. "I can't believe you thought this was a date."

Reign was embarrassed. She didn't have anyone in her life to explain what an actual date was. She just made assumptions based on what she saw at school and home. She figured spending time and getting something to eat with Omari would classify as them being on a date. Apart of her wanted to get up and run out the shop, but she had nowhere to go. Being with Omari was comforting. Even the short period of time they had spent together that morning kept her mind off her current woes. "Can you stop? You're making me lose my appetite."

"How you gonna get mad at me? That was funny."

"It's not funny."

"Yo, you gotta chill. You was joking all day and now you gettin' mad over nothin'."

"You trynna play me."

"Ain't nobody tryna' play you. You just a kid. We would never be going on a date."

"You not even that old."

"I'm 22. I wouldn't date no kid. That's pedophile shit."

"So why you take me to get something to eat?"

"Cuz I'm hungry and I know you hungry too."

"Thanks for making me feel stupid."

"You made yourself feel stupid. If that's how you gon' be out here moving in these streets then that's going to be a problem."

"What that mean?"

"You can't be out here all gullible and shit. You don't owe anyone anything. Especially no nigga. You need to be a boss in these streets. These niggaz out here will take all that pretty shit for granted and try to use you."

"Then how about you show me how to move."

"I can do that, but this ain't no kid shit. Once you in these streets ain't no getting out."

"That's cool with me."

After that conversation, Omari took Reign under his wing. In a way, he could relate to her. He had also dropped out of school for the street life. The only difference was Omari wanted more than that for Reign. He started her out bagging up weight. He didn't want her standing on corners selling drugs and risking getting locked up. She had an easy gig, maintaining one of his stash houses. Not only did it allow for her to make money, but it also put a roof over her head.

It was also the perfect cover-up for Omari. His stash house didn't raise any red flags because anytime someone drove by it, they saw nothing but teenage girls hanging out at the spot. Reign always had Brandi at the house and they both brought friends from school. Inside the three-bedroom room home, no one would suspect that drugs were being cooked and packaged inside. It was clean and decorated for each season. Reign finally had a home and she cared for it. When it was time to re-up, no physical contact was ever made with Reign. The money was dropped off at another spot and then Reign would leave the product out back to be picked up.

Omari had a well-oiled machine that was the backbone of his drug operation. He also had someone that was loyal to him and that he planned on being loyal to in return. Reign was his gem and he protected her. As the years passed, the two became closer. Omari showed Reign a different type of living. After a few months, the police detail that was outside the apartment was gone and Omari sent a few members of his crew to clean out the apartment. They took everything out and brought it to the stash house. Thanks to Omari, Reign had her memories. She took the items from the apartment and filled one of the bedrooms with them. That was her grieving room. Her mother's belongings were hung up in that room and Reign made sure that no one ever disturbed that room.

Reign also didn't have to look over her shoulder any longer. Her mother's murder became a cold case, as detectives had to focus on other homicides that were occurring in their city. She didn't have to worry about Detective Woodland or the employees of the group home looking for her. She had freedom. Reign loved her new life and was grateful to Omari for putting her in a position to live with such freedom. However, there was one thing that she lacked in her life; *love*.

CHAPTER 10

2 YEARS LATER

Happy **birthday!**" The nail salon owner yelled. "Thank you," Reign replied as she exited the salon. It was Reign's 18th birthday and Omari had paid for her hair, makeup and nails to get done. He even let her drive one of his cars, even though she only had a driver's permit. She always had her eye on the white, 7-series BMW and now he was letting her whip it around town.

Reign had planned on surprising Brandi and picking her up from school, but the hair and nail appointments took longer than expected. It was almost six in the evening, and she figured she would just go home and freshen up before heading over to see Brandi. As soon as she pulled up up the home, saw one of Omari's cars parked out front. *What is he doing here? He said he had plans tonight.*

Reign opened the door and was greeted by the sweet smell of roses. Her mouth dropped when she saw dozens of roses and balloons filling the home, Reign couldn't even see the furniture. Soft R&B music played in the background as Omari appeared in the room. He was struggling to carry multiple shopping bags from designer stores, as he placed them down at Reign's feet.

"What is all of this?"

"It's your birthday and these are your gifts."

"No," she said as tears began to fall from her eyes. "This is too much."

"It's not enough."

Reign embraced Omari, wrapping her arms tightly around him. The scent of his cologne intoxicated her. This was her safe space. When she was around Omari, she felt safe and secure. He had given her a life that she couldn't imagine. The same life her father gave her mother. Omari felt the same way. Reign was his paradise in the hood. She was different. She forced him to be better than he was and to think about someone other than himself. When he planned for the future, it wasn't just his he had planned for. He knew Reign would have a permanent place in his life.

Omari tried playing it cool after hugging Reign, he couldn't deny his feelings for her. She was the most beautiful woman he had ever placed his eyes on. The hair and makeup made Reign look like a model and he felt like her number one fan. It was something about the day that changed everything for Omari. Before he looked at Reign solely as a friend but now that she was an adult, he started to actually notice her.

Reign's hair was styled to the side, allowing her curls to fall on her shoulder. Omari marveled at her unique facial features and beauty. He shook off the feelings and just smiled as Reign looked through her gifts. "This is just way too much stuff," she said. "How much did all of this cost?"

"It's your 18th birthday. Don't worry about the cost. You deserve all of it."

Reign was in tears as she went through each bag. Omari went all out for her and that was only the beginning. In one of the bags, there was a dress he had picked out for her.

"Oh my God, this dress is beautiful."

"I want you to wear it tonight."

"Tonight?"

"Yeah. I'm taking you out to dinner. Our reservation is at 8."

"8?" She said, grabbing his wrist and looking at his watch. "I gotta go get ready."

Omari laughed as he watched her run upstairs to get dressed. He then went into the kitchen to make a few phone calls. Although it was a time for celebration, Omari still had to check on his business. He wanted to make sure everything was running smooth and no issues were going on. Reign got to see the good side of the business because Omari never exposed her to the bad. She didn't know one of his other stash houses had gotten hit, leaving one of his men dead and two others in the hospital. This news couldn't have come at a worst time. If Reign knew that one of the stash houses had been hit, she would be terrified. She would surely think her spot would be next on the hit list. Omari didn't want her living in paranoia and he damn sure wasn't going to allow anything bad to happen to her. After making the phone call, he confirmed that a few of his men were positioned outside the home, to watch it while they were gone.

"How do I look?" Reign asked as she stepped into the kitchen.

Omari turned around and was stunned. His eyes examined Reign from her head to her feet and then back up. The red, silk mermaid dress hugged Reign's body. Her curves were on full display and Omari's eyes followed each one. Reign was nervous because she was used to wearing jeans and a hoodie. This was her first time putting on a formal dress. "You look amazing."

"Do I really?"

"Hell yeah." Once again, emotions started to get the best of him. "Come here," Omari whispered as he opened his arms.

Reign stepped forward, into his arms. She inhaled the scent of his cologne again and closed her eyes. This time when Omari hugged her, his hands wrapped around her waist. The silk dress smoothly guided them to the top of her ass. A fire began burning inside them both. Reign had never been touched like that and Omari hadn't planned on making that move. They both slowly pulled away from the hug and paused as they were face to face. Their lips were only inches apart. Reign slowly opened her eyes.

"Thank you for the dress," she muttered.

Omari bit his lip before responding, "No problem." Their lips almost touched. Omari snapped out of it. "Let's go, before we miss our reservation."

Reign was briefly stuck in the moment. The moment confirmed her feelings for Omari. He grabbed her by the hand, and they headed out. Reign felt so beautiful. Every time she walked by a window or mirror, she snuck a peek at her own reflection. Omari snuck peeks too. He had his share of dealings with women, but Reign was different. If it were any other woman, he would have been all over her in that house, but he couldn't do that with Reign. He didn't want to overstep boundaries and ruin the bond that they had.

He pulled up to Charleston, one of the more elegant restaurants in Baltimore. "Good evening, they were greeted by the hostess. "Do you have a reservation?"

"Yes, we do. It should be under Omari Washington."

The hostess scanned her list. "Here you are. Okay, Mr. Washington. You and your guest can follow me."

Reign and Omari followed the hostess through the main dining room. Reign felt like all eyes were on them. She didn't know why everyone was staring but it made her very nervous. The hostess guided them to The Wine Library, which is one of their private dining rooms. Reign took in her surroundings and gushed over the intimate décor and massive wine selection that was organized neatly around them.

"Happy birthday, ma'am," the hostess said to Reign once they reached the table. "Your server will be right with you."

"How the hell did she know it was my birthday?" Reign asked.

Omari laughed. "Do you like this place?"

"I love it."

"Good, cuz I had to pick somewhere nice for our first official date."

The words pierced Reign's heart. She smiled. "Are you serious? This our first date?"

"Yeah. You're an adult now. You get to experience the benefit of being a woman."

"And you think being on a date with you is one of those benefits?" She jokingly asked.

"Yes, I do," Omari responded.

One thing Reign did best was mask her feelings. She could find humor in any situation, no matter how serious it was and no matter how she was feeling at the time. On the outside, she was joking with Omari, but on the inside she was doing cartwheels. This was her introduction to womanhood. Reign was beautiful, so she always got attention from men but she didn't want it. She was happy with what she had and who she had it with. The bond with Omari was special and that's all she needed in her life. He also taught her how to be street smart, so she didn't fall for the cheesy pick-up lines that were thrown at her on the daily. She was sitting across from the only man she needed in her life.

Omari was mesmerized by Reign and tried his best not to show his emotions. He wanted her birthday to be about Reign and nothing else. They had been out to eat plenty of times before but this time was special and he made sure of it. The sound of music being played caught Reign's attention. She turned and saw a woman in the corner of the room, playing the cello. Her eyes lit up. "This is like something out of a movie." It warmed Omari to see her so happy. His plan to make this the best birthday ever was working. Reign turned her chair around and watched the cellist. She was fascinated by the entire experience and couldn't thank Omari enough.

The server approached and poured the glasses of red wine. Omari lifted his glass and took a sip of the dry wine. Reign grabbed the second glass of wine and began drinking it. She immediately spit the wine back into the glass. "Eww, what is this?"

Omari laughed. "It's wine."

"It's nasty. I thought it was juice." She laughed and slid the glass back on the table. Omari took another sip from his glass. "How are you drinking that?"

"It's not that bad."

"Yes, it is."

"I'll tell the waitress to get you some juice. You ain't even supposed to be drinking that shit. You gotta few more years to go before you can touch liquor and wine."

"Well, if it all tastes like that, I'm never gonna touch any of it."

As usual Reign and Omari shared nothing but laughs during her birthday meal. She had never eaten food so good or ever experienced a night like the one Omari planned. She was truly happy. A part of her thought about where should be if she hadn't bumped into Omari. She would have still been on the streets or locked up for the assault at the group home. She never knew that no one ever pressed charges in that case. Tiana and her friends didn't cooperate with the police and decided to take matters into their own hands. They patiently waited for Reign to be brought back to the home, so they could beat her to a pulp. However, they never got that chance. After the beating that Brandi put on them, they didn't even bother looking for her. All in all, Omari was the best thing that ever happened to Reign.

After dinner, they head back to the house. Omari wasn't ready to break the news to Reign yet about moving her out the hood. It was still her birthday, and he didn't want her stressing out about anything. Besides she was still on cloud nine. Reign didn't know how to react to the events that took place. She never celebrated her birthday in this manner. When she was younger, her parents went all out to spoil her. They threw her a party every year, but she was too young to vividly remember those moments. She had suffered so much trauma in her life, it seemed like every good memory she had was suffocated by pain. Anytime she tried to think back about her life before Omari, the only thing that came to mind was death and guilt. It had been two years and she still blamed herself for not being home the night her mother died.

Even when she thought about how she met Omari, there was pain. The night they first exchanged words was the same night that changed her life forever. However, Omari helped water the rose that grew from concrete. He gave Reign a set of new memories she would never forget, including her birthday.

"I'm glad you enjoyed your birthday," he whispered, placing his hand on her arm.

Reign began to feel warm. She then felt fluttering in her stomach. She locked eyes with Omari and fell into a daze. The young woman was experiencing something new and exciting at that moment. Goosebumps covered her skin. "I did," she muttered, barely able to get the words out.

Omari thought Reign was so cute. He knew how nervous she was. What he did not know was how innocent she was. She never had a man touch her before. Between the trauma in her life and the men that would disgust her. When they came to visit her mother, Reign was not interested in having any sort of sexual experience with the opposite sex. Men literally creeped her out but with Omari, things had changed.

Omari moved a few dozen roses off the couch, so the two could sit down. He was stuffed, so he stretched across the couch and relaxed. Reign plopped on top of him and gave him a tight hug. "I can hear your heart beating," she said as she laid her head on his chest. She then lifted her head and the two locked eyes. Omari leaned in and kissed the birthday girl on the cheek. Reign felt like she was melting. Unable to escape her daze, she smiled and allowed for non-verbal communication to take over the situation. Her eyes lowered to his hand which was traveling down her forearm until he softly held onto her hand. Reign looked back up at Omari, who had parted his lips. He had something important to tell Reign but before the words could escape his mouth, she leaned in and kissed him.

To Omari, the peck on his lips was cute and harmless, but to Reign it was everything. This was her first kiss. She didn't know how Omari was going to react, nor did she care. There were no more mysteries between the two of them when it came to their chemistry. Reign just showed Omari how she felt.

He let out a deep breath. "What was that for?" He asked.

Reign smiled. "I wanted to do that all night."

Omari laughed.

"Why you laughing? Did I do it wrong?" She embarrassingly asked.

"Wrong? Let me find out that was the first time you've kissed somebody."

Reign nodded her head and leaned back in the couch then sat up. She was so embarrassed that she put her emotions on the table and made herself look like a fool. This brought her back to her trauma and feeling like she always makes bad decisions. She didn't have a mother that taught her about these moments. She saw people kissing on television and even walked through the stairwells at school and watched as classmates made out with each other. She never imagined her first kiss would end in awkwardness.

Omari sat up too, after noticing Reign's change in emotion. "Why you always do that?"

"Do what?"

"You joke with me, but as soon as I joke with you, you get mad."

"Because I know you're not joking."

"Come here," he whispered as he turned her face towards his.

Their lips met and Omari led the way. He kissed her softly, allowing the passion to guide them. He then slid his tongue in her mouth, allowing it to dance with hers. His hand glided up her arm until he met her shoulders. Reign was in another world. Omari pulled away, leaving Reign in a daze. Her eyes were closed, and her lips were still moving as if she was still kissing her lover. Omari wanted Reign so bad. It was like a beast was caged and it was only a matter of time until it got unleashed. If any other girl was sitting in front of him, Omari would have her bent over the couch and long stroked her until she climaxed. With Reign, he didn't want to rush it. He wanted to take his time with her and allow her to be in charge of the moment.

Omari leaned in and kissed Reign on the neck. She jumped back, trying to figure out what that feeling was that just shot through her body. Omari smiled at her and kissed her neck again, sending a chill down her spine. "Omari," she moaned as he continued kissing on her neck. Hearing Reign moan his name made his dick hard as fuck. Omari glided his hand back down Reign's arm until he reached her hand. He then placed her hand on his dick, allowing her to feel how excited he was.

Reign's eyes popped open. "It's big and so hard," she whispered. Reign caressed his dick. Omari then slid his hand up the slit in her dress. Warmth consumed his hand, followed up by wetness as he reached her panties. "Yes," she said breathily. Omari rubbed his fingers across the soaked panties, feeling the imprint of her juicy pussy. This sent Reign into a frenzy. She began moaning louder and her legs began to shake. Omari wanted to make her feel good and the mission was accomplished.

"Can I touch it?" He asked softly as he pulled her panties to the side.

"Yes," she moaned. Reign's legs continued shaking as Omari's continued exploring her wet pussy. He rubbed his thumb against her clit, causing her body to tremble. "That feels so good."

Omari's dick was throbbing, and he wanted some action. However, he still wanted to take his time. This moment was about Reign, not him. Omari continued massaging her clit as his fingers continued getting soaked. Reign sat back on the couch, allowing Omari to explore her body.

"Can I taste it?" He asked while looking into her eyes.

Reign nodded her head.

She's about to go crazy, he thought as he went down on her. Omari got on his knees and pushed Reign's legs open. With her now spread wide, he was ready to feast. He kept her panties slid to the side as he softly kissed her lower lips. "You wet as shit." Omari's warm tongue slithered up the lips and danced around her clit."

"Omari!" She moaned loudly as she closed her legs, wrapping them around his head. "I can't take it." The pleasure was too intense for Reign. She had never felt anything like that before and it was causing her body to do things it had never done. This experience was too much for Reign and she was now hooked. She looked at Omari totally different now. Although they didn't have sex yet, Omari made her feel so many emotions and feelings that she never knew existed. Reign had fallen in love and didn't even know it.

CHAPTER 11

3 YEARS LATER

For some people, the word love means nothing. It's just a word used to control someone that feels strongly about you. Omari thought he loved Reign, but he didn't know what true love looked like. Growing up in a single-parent household with just his father, the only love Omari saw was a love for drugs. He wouldn't know what real love was if it smacked him in the face, but Reign was ready to show him. She gave Omari her heart and he promised not to break it. He meant the world to her and she made him a better man. Around the neighborhood, they were the couple everyone wanted to be. The biggest boss in the city and the most beautiful woman in the hood. It was like a ghetto fairytale.

In the beginning, their bond was special. Omari had saved Reign's life and Reign brought a sense of normalcy to his. He needed her just as bad as she needed him. The two were inseparable. They stayed up for hours at night planning their lives and wondering what their next moves would be. The conversations were far from normal. They involved moving large amounts of money, efforts to expand Omari's reach in the streets. They also plans on getting married and having children. They were ready to build an empire together. Omari moved Reign in with him, after his stash houses started getting hit. Come to find out, it was an inside job behind the robberies. Omari had the culprit dealt with for the treachery. Reign never imagined being so deep in the street game, but she was built for it.

The smell of breakfast being cooked woke Reign up from a goodnight of sleep. Sun rays peeked in through the bedroom windows, brightening up the room. Reign hopped up and headed towards the kitchen. Once she stepped foot on the cool tile, she saw two women in the kitchen, whipping up a meal fit for a king; or in this case, a queen. The dining room table was decorated with a delicious spread.

"Well, good morning," Omari whispered as he crept up behind Reign, pressing his body against hers.

"What is all of this?" She asked.

"Happy Birthday, baby. Have a seat."

Reign sat down at the table and one of the women from the kitchen walked over and placed a plate in front of her. Reign's mouth watered once she saw the fresh fruit filling the plate. She grabbed one of the slices of mango from the plate and sunk her teeth into it. The juices from the fruit filled her mouth, just before she devoured the slice in just a few bites. Next, she consumed the pineapple slices, watermelon, and papaya. The women in the kitchen were hired chefs from a local restaurant. Omari hired them to make Reign breakfast for her birthday. He planned to have it served to her in bed, but she got up an hour earlier than her usual time. One of the chefs walked over and slid the plate of fruit to the side. The next plate that was placed in front of Reign contained a southwestern omelet, turkey sausage, and toasted English muffins that were lightly buttered. Reign's eyes widened. She was almost full just off the fruit. She knew she wouldn't be able to finish the entire meal, but after the first bite of the omelet, she couldn't stop.

The chefs also placed a plate in front of Omari but instead of sausage and an English muffin, he had crispy bacon and a cinnamon raisin bagel. Omari wasted no time digging in. As they ate, the couple occasionally glanced up at each other. Reign couldn't hide her happiness. She was grinning from ear to ear and Omari was the reason for that feeling. She had never had anyone do anything special for her before, not even her mother. She was so used to being used by people or them just wanting one thing from her. She was grateful for Omari. It seemed like every year he did something amazing for her, trying to outdo the previous year.

Omari cleaned off his entire plate and reached over to steal a few slices of pineapple from Reign's fruit platter.

"Hey, you didn't ask if you could have some of my fruit?" She said jokingly.

"You not even gonna eat it. Look at your plate," Omari stated, noticing she didn't even put a dent in her omelet.

"Oh gosh, I'm so full."

"Well, don't stuff yourself. We got things to do today."

"What things?" Reign asked as curiosity kicked in.

Omari waved over one of the chefs, who approached with another plate. This one was covered with a steel plate cover. It was placed in front of Reign. Reign peeked up at Omari, wondering what could be under the cover. She couldn't bear to eat anything else. One more bite and she would surely be throwing everything back up. Omari watched her intensely. The chef slowly removed the plate cover, revealing the item on the plate. It was a pink envelope. Reign opened the envelope. "Are you serious?!" She blurted out. She hopped up and dove on Omari, knocking him backwards out the chair. The couple was now on the floor and Reign was smothering Omari with kisses. The chefs were laughing at the affectionate moment.

"Are you serious, Omari? Is this real?"

"Yea, baby. It's real?"

"Well, where are we going?" Reign asked as she looked at the two first-class plane tickets. She had never been on a plane or outside the Baltimore area, so she didn't know what all the writing on the tickets meant.

"I'm taking you to Barbados."

"Where is that at?"

"It's an island in the Caribbean."

Reign began jumping for joy. "When are we leaving?"

"Today. The flight leaves in four hours."

"What?" Reign looked at the tickets to confirm Omari's statement. How the heck am I going to be ready for a trip that fast?"

"Just get yourself ready and don't worry about packing."

Reign was so confused but didn't question her man. She had never been on a flight before, so she listened to Omari. Reign headed upstairs to get showered as Omari took care of the chefs. He pulled a knot out of his pocket and peeled off a few hundred dollars for each of them.

"What would you like to do with the remainder of the food, Mr. Washington?" One of the chefs asked.

Omari looked at the counter and dining room table which were both covered in food. There were sliced fruit, fresh pastries, grits, and steak still being cooked, to go along with the rest of the food they had already cooked. He had no need for all the food, but the last thing he wanted to do was have all the food being wasted and sitting in his home when he got back.

"You both can take what you want and whatever is left over you can give it out around here."

This is what separated Omari from other drug bosses. He was selfless when it came to these types of things. He would give the shirt off his back to those in need and now he was about to have meals handed out to families in the hood who barely get home cooked meals. The chefs even admired him for the decision. They finished the meals that were currently cooking and began packing everything up.

Omari headed up to the bedroom to get ready. Reign was still in the shower. Omari walked past the bathroom door, which was open. As he glanced over, he saw the silhouette of Reign's thin frame through the steamy shower glass. He grabbed a pair of black Prada sneakers out of the closet and placed them next to the bed. He walked past the bathroom door again, this time stopping to stare. It was as if he had never seen Reign naked before. He was admiring the beauty from afar, but he definitely wanted to get a closer look.

As Reign rinsed the conditioner out of her hair, she never noticed the shower door opening and Omari slipping in behind her. Reign almost jumped out of her skin once she felt Omari press up against her. He quickly calmed her down with soft kisses on her shoulder. She turned around and kissed him. Water ran down his face and through his thin beard. With each kiss, a little tongue was added until both of their tongues were intertwined. Reign felt Omari as their bodies pressed against each other. There was no question that he wanted her.

"Do you think we have enough time?" Reign asked softly between moans. Omari was kissing on her breasts and introducing his tongue to her nipples.

Omari didn't respond and he didn't need to. He dropped to his knees and looked up at Reign. Time was currently on his mind. He French kissed her pussy, allowing his tongue to spread her wet lips. Reign attempted to grab anything to keep herself balanced, but her hands just slid down the glass door and shower wall. Her moans became louder and her legs began to shake. Omari used his fingers to open her up and allowed his tongue to guide him to the sweet spot. Once he found the clit, he locked onto it. Slowly licking it, allowing his tongue to flick up and down on it.

"Oh, yes. Don't stop," Reign moaned. Her hands still searched for something stable to hold onto, with no luck.

Reign wrapped her hands around Omari's head, pushing his face further into her pussy. Reign quickly pushed Omari back as her knees buckled and fluid began running down her legs. Omari smiled, knowing he hit her spot. As Reign snapped out of the euphoric state, she looked at her man. His cock was rock hard and standing at attention for her. Reign straddled Omari, causing his cock to slide into her wetness. Her moans turned to sensual screams as she bounced on his hard dick. Omari hooked his arms under her legs and began stroking back. This sent Reign over the edge. Omari was strong but tried his best to be gentle with Reign. Reign's eyes rolled into the back of her head and her nails dug into his back as she reached an orgasmic peak.

Reign loved every minute of the encounter. She was so wet. The water flowed out the shower head and ran down both of their bodies. With each stroke, water splashed around both of their bodies. Omari repositioned his hands and squeezed Reign's breasts. She continued riding him. The water from the showerhead was running down their faces. The water made their vision blurry, but that didn't stop them. They allowed their hands to navigate this love session. Omari slowly sat up and sucked on each of Reign's hard nipples. He was sure to give them both an equal amount of attention. His hands now caressed her back and worked their way down to her ass. He gripped both cheeks and continued stroking. Reign was powerless in his strong arms. She couldn't gain control if she wanted to, and it was a good thing that she didn't want to. Omari was more experienced, and it showed. His right hand slid over to the crack of her ass. He slid his middle finger down the wet crack until he reached her asshole, and he used his finger to caress the surface of the tight opening.

"Oh shit," Reign moaned.

That was exactly the response he wanted. He continued caressing her ass and stroking her simultaneously. The moaning and screaming increased as Reign was introduced to this new form of pleasure. Omari got her to another climax, and she turned into Wolverine on his back. If her nails sunk any deeper into his skin, he would have had to get patched up by a doctor. The chefs were still cleaning up the kitchen and could hear the screams coming from upstairs. They both smirked at each other, jealous that they weren't in Reign's position.

"Damn, I'm bout to cum with you," Omari whispered in Reign's ear.

Just as he spoke, she felt his dick begin to throb inside of her. This turned her on, knowing what was coming next. When he released, Reign felt his cum filling her vagina. It was warm and it felt good. It was exactly the kind of sex she deserved on her birthday.

CHAPTER 12

Reign looked out the window of the plane and took in the beautiful sight of the small island. Her experience had been amazing so far. The flight attendants were extremely nice and she even got to meet the pilot. It helped that Omari purchased first-class tickets because the luxury made her first time memorable. The plane descended and they finally landed at Grantley Adams International Airport. Omari and Reign stepped off the plane and the island heat immediately hit them.

"Wow. It's so beautiful," Reign said once they exited the airport.

Barbados was the complete opposite of Baltimore. It was paradise.

"Here yuh guh. Welcome to Barbados," a young lady said, as she approached the couple and handed two drinks.

"What is this?" Reign asked.

"It rum punch, pretty gyal."

Both Omari and Reign took a sip of the sweet drink. Then they took more sips. The cool alcoholic beverage came at a perfect time as they stood in the hot weather.

"That's good," Reign said.

"Hell yea. Let's go get another one," Omari replied.

The two followed the young lady to a bar that was set up right outside the airport and ordered more drinks. It was a celebration. Reign couldn't believe it. It all felt like a dream. They mingled with tourists of many different nationalities and ages at the little bar. It was like a welcome center for the island. Everyone grabbed a drink before boarding the buses and cabs to their resorts and destinations. After about three rounds, Omari grabbed Reign's hand and they walked towards the taxis and private vehicles. It didn't take long for Reign to notice an older man who was standing near an older model Mercedes Benz and holding a sign that read *Reign Bryant*.

"Omari, you didn't have to do all of this."

"Shut up. It's your birthday and you need to enjoy it."

"Weh a yuh luggage?" The man asked.

"Oh, we don't have any," Omari replied.

"Ok. Mi name Neval but yuh cya call mi Val an di gentleman inna di passenga seat a mi bredda, Ramon."

"What's going on, playa? I'm Omari and this is my girl, Reign."

The man hadn't seen such a beauty in a long time. He couldn't help but stare at Reign for a while. Now he understood why he was hired by Omari. Val and

Ramon didn't just work for a transportation company, they worked for a private security company. They were usually hired to protect politicians, athletes and celebrities while they visited the island. For this week, they would be protecting one of the biggest drug dealers in Baltimore who was planning on taking over distribution in the whole DMV. Omari wanted to be a kingpin and he wasn't going to stop until he reached his goal.

The couple entered the Benz and Reign noticed the steering wheel was on the right side of the car, rather than the left. Everything was different. Even watching the men drive on the opposite side of the road was confusing to her. Reign was taking in every scene as they headed towards Bridgetown. Along with the beauty, the island also had a few rough spots. They drove through areas that reminded her of their hood back in Baltimore. It was unbelievable. Children were begging on the street, buses were packed with locals, and little shacks that people called home. Some of the shacks looked like they wouldn't withstand a strong storm. Reign was a little in disbelief. When she thought about the islands and vacation spots, she never imagined the beauty of these places were hiding some ugly truths.

Although she just landed on the island, Reign was grateful. All she kept thinking about was her mother as she looked at the locals. How easy it was for her mother to disregard their safety and choose drugs over everything else. She now wondered if they weren't in

Baltimore, how things would have turned out. *What if my mom saw this part of the world? What if we lived here instead? Things probably would have been different for her.* Every day people with nothing still did what they needed to do to provide for their families. Even when Stoney was on top back in the day, she never explored the world. The most they did was show off in the hood. This was an entirely new experience.

"What's on your mind?" Omari asked, noticing the scowl look on Reign's face.

"Everything. My mom. My dad. You."

Omari grabbed her hand and held it tight. "Well, I don't want you worrying this week. It is all about relaxation and fun."

Reign smiled. Omari knew all the right things to say to her. She leaned in and kissed his full lips. After the ride to Bridgetown, the Benz pulled up to a large shopping center. The couple was let out the Benz and proceeded to the shops. Val and Ramon followed them, ensuring their safety. Although the island was safe, for the most part, there were still opportunistic criminals that preyed on tourists. Especially tourists who were about to spend the type of money Omari had on him.

"I figured we could just buy clothes and shit from here, since we didn't bring any with us."

Once again Reign was smiling from ear to ear. The first spot they walked in was a Rolex store in the Royal Shop. Reign wanted to stop Omari from taking her in the store because she didn't want him spending a bunch of money on her, but she also remembered it was her birthday and he didn't want her worrying. Omari knew exactly what he wanted to get Reign. He spotted this gift online and thought it would be perfect for her. He had a couple of words with the employee at the store before they went in the back and came out with his order. A gold Rolex watch with a pink dial and jubilee band. Reign couldn't believe it. She never envisioned wearing such an expensive piece of jewelry.

"Thank you so much, bae," she said excitedly. Her arms wrapped around his neck as she jumped up into his arms and gave him the tightest hug she could. Tears of joy fell from her eyes. Reign had come a long way from buying crack on one of Omari's corners to being his leading lady. Her position was unimaginable. Val and Ramon stood guard, knowing all eyes would be on the couple after they walked out the store. Both men were heavily armed and were very good at their jobs. Omari and Reign went from store to store, buying new wardrobes, luggage, art, and weed from one of the locals.

After shopping, the couple was taken to their resort. As soon as they pulled up to the Sugar Bay resort, they both were impressed. A large fountain was the focal point of the exterior of the front of the resort. Omari walked into the lobby and spoke to the receptionist. Once he got his room keys, he went to get Reign so they could get her birthday started.

"Can you make sure our belongings get to the room?" Omari asked Val while sliding a few hundred dollars his way.

"Yea sah. Wi will mek sure there no issues an eff yuh need nuhting else, let mi kno."

Omari and Reign walked through the lobby and headed out towards the beach. The white sand, blue ocean, coconut trees, and clear sky wrapped her in. She was speechless. The delicious smell of curry chicken and other foods flowed through the air. It was evening and everyone that walked by was carrying a drink of some kind. There were frozen drinks, straight on the rocks, shots, and other mixed cocktails. Reign wanted to try them all.

"You hungry?"

"Yup."

"What you wanna eat?"

"I want everything," Reign replied and laughed.

She followed Omari as he walked through the resort. He stopped briefly at one of the bars and grabbed two drinks. They both couldn't get enough of the rum punch. It was their new favorite drink. He then walked out towards the ocean. Reign's feet sunk into the warm sand with each step she took as she continued following Omari. *I guess he wants to go to the beach before we eat*, she thought. The couple walked about twenty yards on the beach when rose petals began to pop up on the sand. Reign paid them no mind at the time. They continued walking until something caught Reign's eye.

"Look, Omari."

He turned to see what had her attention. "It's so beautiful," she whispered. The sun was setting perfectly in the distance, and they had the ideal view. Reign had never seen the sun look so stunning before. It was like everything in her world was magnified and much better than she remembered.

"Yuh table ready," one of the employees said.

Reign turned around to see who was speaking. She saw the waiter who had a towel draped over his arm. He held his hand out, guiding them to a specific spot on the beach. The rose petals on the beach weren't random. They were placed in the sand and created a path that led to a candlelight dinner on the beach. Reign expected to be pinched and woken from this dream. Omari had made her birthday amazing. Nothing would ever compare to this day. She sat at the table and smelled the rose that was given to her by the waiter. She still had a view of the sun setting and an even better view of her man. Omari was just as happy as Reign. She never saw him smile as much as he did in the past twenty-four hours. Usually, he was serious and kept a stern look on his face, especially when he was on the block interacting with his dealers.

Reign ordered jerk chicken, macaroni pie, and corn on the cob. After a recommendation from the waiter, Omari ordered the traditional Bajan meal of fried flying fish and cou cou, which is a mixture of cornmeal and okra. The waiter brought out a pitcher of rum punch for the couple. Everything was delicious. After dinner, they both enjoyed warm rum cake and warm vanilla ice cream. It was now late and both Omari and Reign were tipsy. They began working their way back to the resort to check out their room.

"I don't want to leave yet."

"Reign, you are drunk. You need to go lay down."

"You're drunk too. Let's chill out here for a little bit longer. It's so beautiful."

"They got shows and stuff in the resort that we can go check out if you want."

"No. I just want to be around you," Reign said as she plopped down in a daybed that was in one of the beach cabanas.

Omari made himself comfortable right next to her.

"Thank you for the best birthday ever."

"I thought you said the 18th birthday was the best ever."

"It was but that's for other reasons." She winked at him.

Omari laughed. "No problem, Reign. I hope you are enjoying yourself."

"Of course, I am. I just want you to know that I love you so much."

"I love you too, youngin'."

The cool air and sound of the waves crashing were relaxing. Omari finished the cup of rum punch that he was working on and unbuttoned his shirt. He was getting comfortable. Reign looked over at her man and noticed his six-pack was now on display. She couldn't tell if it was the rum punch or the romantic setting but she was extremely turned on. She stood up and closed the fabric around the cabana, giving herself a little privacy. She laid back down next to Omari and began one hell of a make out session. Clothes were being ripped off and Reign was being tossed around. This led to the couple making sweet love on the beach. Reign had never experienced sex with Omari while he was drunk. Liquor took his passion to another level. They found the perfect way to end the night and it was the beginning of what would be an unforgettable week for the couple.

CHAPTER 13

Taking Reign to Barbados didn't only make her birthday special, it also expanded her horizon when it came to life and their future together. Being on the beautiful island for a week made her not want to come back to Baltimore. She wasted no time looking up other apartments and condos, once they got back home. It didn't take long for Reign and Omari to find a place more suitable than their current home in the hood. She wanted to move to Washington DC, but he didn't to be too far from his business. Moving to DC would be too far from him to keep a strong presence in Baltimore. Word traveled fast and if the hood found out he was gone, it wouldn't take long for someone else to come after his spot. Omari contacted a realtor and after an eight-month search, he was able to find a spot he liked in Perry Hills, Maryland. The house was about thirty minutes away from their current spot, which would allow him to be able to check in on his dealers whenever he needed to.

When the time came to move, Omari and Reign wasted no time getting out of the neighborhood. Although they were excited to get out, Omari was very discreet when it came to moving their belongings. The last thing he wanted was a moving truck outside the spot, announcing the big move. He wanted everyone in the hood to still believe he lived there. The couple made their way towards Perry Hills and Reign could see the extreme change in neighborhoods. Perry Hills was quiet and there weren't many black folks around. There were single-family homes which was surprising to someone who is used to having neighbors above them, below them, and on both sides. Omari pulled onto White Trillium Road and parked in the driveway of a large, four-bedroom home. The home was newly constructed, and they would be the first owners.

They walked into the home, and it looked like something out of a movie. It was entirely too much for Reign. She expected something smaller because it was only two of them, but she couldn't deny the attractiveness of the large home. It reminded her of a home out of a magazine ad. Everything was picture perfect. The cream-colored walls, light carpet, dark hardwood floors, and a kitchen that Martha Stewart would be jealous of. The first thing Reign noticed was the number of rooms. The main floor had a living room, dining room, kitchen, family room, mudroom, laundry room, and office. She didn't even know what a family room or mudroom was, before reading a description of each room in a packet left by the realtor. That didn't even compare to the four bedrooms on the second floor and the multiple rooms in the basement.

"So, do you like it?" Omari asked as he handed Reign her keys.

"I love it, but I think it's a bit much. What the hell are we going to put in all of these rooms?"

"Whatever you want. We need guest rooms so our friends can come visit and when we have kids, we can fill all of these rooms."

Reign laughed at Omari's last statement. She dropped the keys into her purse and continued on her tour of the home. She couldn't believe she was finally out of the hood. She wanted to call Brandi and tell her to pack her bags too. They had enough room in the large home that would allow Brandi to stay there and not be noticed. Reign texted Brandi and told her to be dressed in a few hours. She might not have been able to move her friend into the home, but she was surely going to let her hang out there rather than be in the hood.

"I can't stop thinking about Barbados," Reign muttered as she walked through the home.

"What you wanna go back?"

"Of course, I do. Don't you?"

"Yeah, if you want to. It don't matter to me."

"What you mean it don't matter to you? That island was beautiful."

"I know, but I'm just focused on business right now. I don't have time to be worrying about that stuff right now."

Reign did not like Omari's tone. He seemed very short with her, and she didn't know what he meant by the business comment. As far as she knew, business was going good. "Is there something you want to tell me?"

"Naw. I'm good. I'm bout to head out tho."

"Head out? We just bought this house. Where are you going?"

"I gotta go to the old spot."

"For what?"

"I've told you this already. We still gotta look like we live there. So, I'm gon' go down there and chill."

"Can't you go do that tomorrow? This is our first day in this house."

"Naw. I gotta do it now."

Reign didn't even bother arguing with Omari. She could tell something was up with him. He never spoke to her in that tone before. She couldn't believe she was leaving her in the home alone. She looked at her phone to see if Brandi responded to her text. She had three messages from Brandi, asking her what the new address was. Reign sent it and waited for her friend to show up. In the meantime, Omari headed back to the hood to handle any issue that came up while he was in Barbados with Reign.

Omari couldn't front, the ride from the new home back to the hood wasn't bad. It gave him time to clear his mind. With a possible criminal case being dangled over his head, he was on edge. When he was in Barbados with Reign, one of his dealers got snatched up by Baltimore Police while he was making a run from the stash house. Not only did he have a large amount of drugs on him, but he also had a good amount of cash on him. This was cash and product that Omari couldn't afford to lose. He was in the process of expanding his reach to other hoods and with the product seized by the cops, he didn't have much to distribute to the new dealers.

On top of that, the dealer that got booked had been released by the cops. In Omari's eyes, this only meant one thing. The only way some gets released on those type of charges is if they were cooperating with the police. Omari would easily be able to make his money back, but there was no way that he could keep expanding without product. Plus, he'd needed his whole crew to lay low until he figured out what was or wasn't said to the police.

As Omari pulled up to one of the stash houses, he was met by Ant. Ant was his cousin, but he was more like his brother. Ant and Omari grew up together and stepped into the drug game together. While Omari was more so the brains of the operation, Ant was more so the muscle. He always wanted to put in work, even though Omari wanted him to take more of a backseat role like a true boss. Ant wanted to get his hands dirty and as soon as the opportunity arose, he jumped on it.

"What up, cuz?" Omari greeted as he exited his whip.

"Nothin' much," Ant replied. Both men looked around, to see if anyone was watching them.

"You got the package?"

"Is water wet, nigga?" Ant replied while laughing. "Follow me."

Omari and Ant entered the stash house and headed towards the basement. Ant unlocked the door, which had been bolted shut and secured with a Masterlock. He then looked back at Omari and smiled. Music could be heard blaring from the lower level. When they entered the basement, they saw four people lying on the cold concrete floor. Their hands had been zip-tied behind them, their mouths had been taped shut and wool sacks covered their heads.

"Who are these people?" Omari asked as he tried speaking over the loud music.

"Huh?"

"Who are they?"

"What?"

"Turn the fuckin' music down!"

Ant heard that order clearly and immediately turned off the radio. "Who the fuck is this?"

"That's the rat pack."

"Who the fuck is the rat pack?"

"That's the rat, his mother, his father, and his little sister. We snatched all of them up."

Omari didn't specifically request the whole family be snatched up, but he didn't mind the work that Ant put in. "Sit his ass up," Omari ordered. Ant grabbed the man and brought him to his feet. He pulled the woolsack off his head, revealing a bruised and bloody face. The man that stood in front of him was Lil' Reef.

Big Reef was one of the old heads that used to put in work back in the day and somehow managed to stay a free man, while everyone else around was getting locked down. Rumors flooded the streets about Big Reef possibly cooperating with the police but no one ever found proof to support the allegations. This allowed Big Reef to lay low, start a family and dabble in the drug game here and there. Now, Big Reef was face down in the basement because of his son's actions.

His son following in his footsteps was inevitable. Lil' Reef grew up around the drug game and carefully watched how his dad moved. Unfortunately, he wasn't watching a lion stealthily hunting down its prey or a wolf defending its pack. He was watching a snake slither through the streets. It wasn't long before Lil' Reef was selling nickel bags of weed in school. It was only so far selling weed was going to get him, so he eventually linked up with Omari and asked for a job. Lil' Reef was able to step out of his father's shadow and create his own name. He put in work and successfully moved products on one of Omari's corners. His dad even had him pass on some of his old connections to give to the new crew. This allowed Omari to look at Lil' Reef as more than a corner boy. Lil Reef was set and eventually graduated off the corner. He was now entrusted to move the product from the stash houses and get them to the corner boys. He was climbing the ladder of the organization and it subsequently got to his head. Lil' Reef became flashy like his father. The moves he made were similar to the ones his father made back in the day. All that flashiness led to the police stopping Lil' Reef and his snow-white Ford F-150 with chrome accents. He was one of the only young niggas in Baltimore riding around in a pickup truck and he stuck out like a sore thumb. Especially since he threw 30-inch chrome rims on the truck. It was a reckless move. One that he wouldn't have made if Omari was in the hood and not with Reign in Barbados.

"What happened to my shit?"

"Look, boss. This is on me. I'll take responsibility for this shit, but please let my folks go. They don't got nothing to do with this shit."

Omari looked down at the man's family. He felt nothing. "There are rules to the game and there are also consequences that have to be faced if you fuck some shit up. Omari responded. He looked back at Lil' Reef. "I came to this realization when the stash houses were getting hit and the woman I loved was laid up in one of them and if something happened to her, I would have to live with that for the rest of my life. So, if you don't tell me everything I want to know, I guarantee something bad is going to happen to your family. And afterwards, you'll have to live with that pain."

"Please don't do this," Lil' Reef begged.

"It's already done. Now I'm going to ask you again. What the fuck happened to my shit?"

"Cops," he muttered. "I got stopped by the cops and they took everything from me."

"How did you get stopped?"

"I don't know. They just rolled up on me."

"Uniformed?"

"What that mean?"

"Were they uniformed cops or undies?"

"They had on uniforms."

"You mean to tell me you got stopped by uniform pigs and you let them take my shit?!" Omari barked. "Not the narc motherfuckas' that be watching and shit. Nope. You got stopped by some regular ass ticket-giving cops. How the fuck is that even possible?"

"I didn't have a choice. They locked me up and searched the wheel."

"How you get out?"

"What you mean? I made bail."

Omari hit Lil' Reef with a body shot, causing his knees to buckle. The punch felt like it took all the air out of his lungs. Omari bent over and looked Lil' Reef's in his eyes. "I don't like when people lie to me. If you keep it up, I am going to kill your entire family. One by one."

"Come on, O. I'm not lying," Reef pleaded.

Omari wasn't in the mood to entertain Reef's bullshit. Even the crocodile tears that he tried to form weren't convincing to Omari. Omari gripped up his father and forced him to stand. Big Reef had gotten a beating that was more severe than the one that his son received. The men that attacked him took pleasure in beating him down. He was considered the Alpo of their hood and it was only a matter of time until the streets got a hold of him. With the sack still covering his head,

Big Reef had no idea he was standing side by side with his son.

"Let my pops go. He ain't do shit wrong."

"Are you that naïve motherfucka'? Ya pops did a lot of hit wrong, including passing down that rat gene to you."

"I ain't no rat."

"Prove it."

"How the fuck I'mma do that?"

"By telling me something," Omari said as he paced back and forth.

Although Omari was pacing, his eyes continued to be looked on Lil' Reef.

"What you want me to tell you, O?"

"How'd you get out?" Omari asked sternly.

"I told you already. I made bail."

BANG! The single shot to the back of the head dropped Big Reef. "No! What the fuck?!" Lil' Reef yelled. "You ain't have to fuckin' do that!"

Lil' Reef's mother and sister were screaming, but with the tape covering their mouths, only muffled sounds could be heard.

Omari was quick with the trigger. He had pulled the 9mm Glock from his waistband so fast, Lil' Reef didn't have time to blink for his dad got executed. Now, he staring face to face with that smoking weapon. "You know damn well that I ain't gonna stand here and keep repeating myself. I asked you a fuckin' question and I gave you the option, to tell the truth, but instead, you want to keep playing these games."

"I ain't playing no games, I swear."

"How much was your bail?"

"Come on, O. Stop this shit. It ain't even what you think it is," Lil' Reef begged. "I ain't rat on you. I swear to God."

"You swear to God?" Omari asked, pushing the warm barrel of the gun against Lil' Reef's forehead. "Nigga I am your God. I gave your life purpose. I broke bread with your bitch ass, and turned that motherfuckin' water into wine." Omari lowered his gun. "And what did you do? Did you become a good servant and worship your God? Nope. Your bitch ass turned your back and now you're trying to nail me to the cross."

"No, the fuck I'm not."

"Shut the fuck up!" Omari yelled as he pistol-whipped Lil' Reef. "Ain't nobody ask you to speak, nigga. That's your problem now. You always runnin' your fuckin' mouth. The same problem your snitch ass daddy had."

Lil' Reef was leaking. The strike from the gun split his lip. Pain shot through the entire left side of his face. He started panting, attempting to catch his breath but it was difficult. He was panicking. He wanted to continue defending himself, but he didn't want to risk getting hit again. Omari's words hit harder than he did. Lil' Reef knew the accusations made against him were a death sentence. He stared at his father's lifeless body. Blood leaked out of the soaked woolsack.

"And now here we are. I have to stare in the face of betrayal. I have to look the devil in his eyes and knowing at one point I gave you this life. I gave your entire family a second chance," Omari muttered, pointing the gun at Lil' Reef. "And as the Lord giveth, the Lord taketh away," he said, firing shots at Lil' Reef's mother and sister.

The bullets riddled their bodies. Lil' Reef screamed at the top of his lungs. The deafening scream could be heard blocks away. Omari kept firing until the gun clicked and even still, he slapped on the trigger.

Lil' Reef charged at Omari, and shoulder bumped him. With his hands still tied behind his back, it was the only move he had in the arsenal. Omari fell to the floor and Lil' Reef fell on top of him. "Motherfucka," Omari mumbled, as he hit Lil' Reef in the face with the gun. He then pushed him off and continued the assault. Lil' Reef tried maneuvering his head so that he wouldn't be hit but he was unsuccessful. Omari was relentless with the attack. He continued striking his victim until he beat a hole into his head and blood splattered up onto his face. Lil' Reef was motionless, and Omari continued hitting him like he was defending himself. Ant looked away as his cousin continued to brutalize Lil' Reef's lifeless body.

CHAPTER 14

The ride home should have been a time to decompress, but Omari was still on edge. He still didn't get the answers he wanted out of Lil' Reef. The only thing he knew was that Lil' Reef claimed to have gotten arrested while he had the product, but he didn't offer up any more details. Omari knew something was up because Lil' Reef wasn't bailed out. He knew damn well that any nigga with that amount of weight on him would have gotten a crazy bail, but someone Lil' Reed was released the same day he was arrested. *I know this nigga ratted*," Omari thought.

He looked down at his speedometer, which displayed that he was going 32 mph. The speed limit on the road he was on was 35 mph and he couldn't risk getting pulled over. With a car full of money, guns, and drugs, getting stopped by the cops would have sent Omari away for years. However, he had no other choice but to have Ant and some of the crew pack everything up from the stash houses and put it in his whip. Omari didn't tell them he was hiding it all in his new crib because he didn't know if anyone else had been compromised. His intuition told him there were going be police raids at the stash houses and he was already one step ahead of them if that was their plan. The icing on the cake was going to be the bodies of Lil' Reef and his families being dumped in front of the police station. *This is going to be a message for the whole hood and the pigs. You think about crossing me and this is how you're going to end up.*

Omari was finally home and pulled into his garage. He hadn't seen one police car as he traveled through the affluent neighborhood. That was a peace he never felt before, except when he was away with Reign. It was relaxing to know he had a safe space to go to. No cops were watching the home, no niggas plotting to rob him and nosey neighbors knowing their every move. This was a life Omari could get used to and he wanted to keep it sacred for just him and Reign.

Omari popped the trunk, revealing everything Ant had packed into his vehicle. He grabbed about five assault rifles and tucked them under his right arm and picked up a duffle bag full of cash with his left hand. He entered the home to find a place to start hiding everything.

"Oh hey, Omari," Brandi greeted as she took another bite of a chicken wing. She then noticed what he was bringing into the home. Omari quickly escaped back into the garage.

He turned when he heard the door open. "Babe, you okay?" Reigns asked, stepping into the garage.

"What the fuck is she doing here?"

"Why you cursing at me?"

"Cuz, why the fuck is she in our home?"

"Because you left me here all alone and I wanted to show my best friend my new house. What's wrong with that?"

"That bitch done seen some shit she wasn't 'posed to see."

"What are you talking 'bout?" Reign asked. She looked behind Omari and saw the guns and duffle bag he put on the hood of the car. "Are you serious? You bringing that shit in here, Omari? In our home?"

"I ain't have no choice."

"What you mean you ain't have a choice?"

"We have a little issue right now that's being taken care of, and I think the stash houses gon' get hit."

"So, you made the smart decision to bring this shit up here and risk us getting booked with it?"

"You ain't have no problem when I was stashing shit at the last spot."

"That's because it was already a stash house that you let me move into."

"What's the difference?" Omari asked sarcastically.

"I was a homeless kid back then. I'm a grown woman now and I don't want that shit in the home I plan on building a future in."

"I ain't going back out there with this shit."

Reign took a deep breath. She couldn't believe this. It was bad enough that Omari left her in the home on their settlement day but then bringing guns into their home was the icing on the cake. She immediately flashed back to her father's death and how the men were only concerned about the location of the stash. She didn't ever want that happening to them.

"You have to get those guns and whatever else you thought you were bringing in here and ger it out of this house right now."

"No," Omari responded.

He was starting to get furious. He needed to find a stash spot and Reign was holding him up. This was their first argument, and he was not happy about it. Omari always envisioned Reign as his paradise outside of the hood. When it came to yelling, arguing, and constant strategizing, it always took place in the hood. When he used to come home to Reign there was none of that and he loved that. Now, they had reached a new territory within their relationship. One that neither one of them was prepared for.

"Get that shit out of my house."

"Your house? This ain't your house. I paid for this shit, not you."

"That's what we're doing? So, all this is yours and nothing belongs to me? I'm your girl and I hold you the fuck down. I never asked you for shit and this how you talk to me?"

"You don't have to ask me for shit because I make sure you already got it."

"I earned all that shit."

"How?"

"This just shows how ungrateful you are. I've held you down for five years and this is how you treat me? So, since you paid for this and have the money, you run me?"

"Nothing else matters in this world, except money," Omar replied.

"Loyalty. Love. Trust. Respect. All of those things are worth way more than money. You gon' learn that the hard way."

"What you trynna say?" Omari asked, grabbing her arm.

Reign pulled away from him. "I'm trying to say that since this is your house, I'll find somewhere else to stay."

"So you gon' leave because I said that I paid for this house?"

"Naw. I'm leaving because I gave you a choice between your woman and your guns, and you chose your guns," Reign said, as she walked towards the door. She opened the door and Omari ran towards it and shoulder it shut. "What the fuck are you doing? You ain't leaving me."

"Omari I'm out. I need so time to process everything that was just said to me, so get out of my way." Reign tried to push by him, but he continued blocking the door. "If you don't get out of my way, I'll just go through the garage doors and make as much noise as possible. I'm sure all the white neighbors would love to call the cops on the niggas that just moved in."

Omari looked over the guns on the hood of the car and then back to Reign. "You ain't stupid enough to do that." Reign ran over and pressed the large button on the wall, opening the garage doors. Omari hurried to hit the button, closing the doors. He then pushed Reign to the ground. "What the fuck do you think you're doing?"

"Are you fuckin' serious? You put you're fuckin' hands on me?!" She yelled, standing to her feet and brushing herself off.

"I told you to chill the fuck out. Now go back in the house and cut this shit out and tell that bitch to leave too."

"You're fuckin' disrespectful. I don't know what has gotten into you but I'm not staying in this house with you."

"I tired. I'm tired of you ungrateful motherfuckas' taking my kindness for weakness. I'm the only reason you and all these other niggas are even living these fuckin' lives and all I get is problems in return."

"I don't know what problems you talkin' bout, but I ain't one of them. Now get the fuck outta my way," Reign said as she ran towards the button. Omari tackled her to the ground and pinned her to the ground. "Get the fuck off me!" She yelled.

"Shut the fuck up!"

The door to the home burst open. Brandi ran over and pushed Omari off of Reign. "What the fuck you doing?"

Omari pulled out the Glock and aimed at Brandi. "I'm bout to kill you bitch. You got five seconds to get out my fuckin' house."

Brandi threw her hands in the air. She saw a look in Omari's eyes. A look she hadn't seen before. She considered him a good friend, ever since he began taking care of Reign, but now he was an enemy. She thought long and hard about rushing him and trying to take the gun, but Omari was not a small man and there were plenty of times she had seen him beat up other grown men.

"Omari, are you crazy? Put the fuckin' gun down!" Reign ordered.

"5 – 4 – 3 – 2..."

"Ok, nigga. I'm leaving. Reign, come on. Let's go."

"She ain't going nowhere."

Brandi looked down at Reign. She didn't want to leave her friend, but she also didn't want to take a chance pissing Omari off and forcing his hand. She knew enough about him that she knew he wouldn't hesitate to blow her brains all over the garage. As dangerous as Omari was, she never saw him display any of that behavior towards her or Reign. Brandi slowly backed up until she reached the kitchen and then out of Omari's view. The sound of the front door closing and a car starting outside the home calmed Omari's nerves. He tucked the Glock back into his waistband and grabbed the duffle bag and guns. He walked over to Reign and threw the bag next to her.

"Get up and help me take all of this shit upstairs. We ain't got much time."

CHAPTER 15

Omari and Reign stashed everything in the attic above one of the bedrooms. He went as far as to place everything between insulation just in case the police ever followed him home. There was no telling what time of information Lil' Reef gave up, so he had to be precautious. Omari's intuition was right. In the week following Lil' Reef's arrest, the police had raided all of Omari's stash houses. Due to his forward-thinking, the raids left hadn't them empty-handed. Lil' Reef had made a deal with the police, but it wasn't exactly what Omari had suspected. Lil' Reef planned on telling him about the raids, so they could develop a plan, but he never was awarded the opportunity to explain himself.

When the bodies of Lil' Reef and his family popped up in front of the police station it sparked outrage in the community and spearheaded one of the most extensive internal investigations in the history of the Baltimore Police Department. Once the Internal Affairs Division began digging into the case, they were able to find the arrest of Lil' Reef but no processing information. The officers' that stopped him had brought it to the Narcotics Unit at the time of the arrest and they were so eager to move on Omari's properties, they didn't follow protocol. Lil' Reef was never booked and processed. The information he provided was only verbal and the police never obtained a signed statement. This led to the determination the subsequent raids should have not gotten the stamp of approval from the commanding officers. Heads began to roll as Interviews Affairs continued to unpack the entire situation. There were rumors a dirty cop could have been behind the murders of Lil' Reef and his family, out of retaliation for bad information for the raids.

The rumors had spread to the street and were music to Omari's ears. Even with the police under fire for the Lil' Reef situation, he was still paranoid. He decided to get rid of the stash houses, so he had his men find multiple families to take up occupancy in the homes. Omari allowed them to live in his old stash houses and used their leased apartments as his new stash spots. Once those moves were made, they were back in action. So, even if the cops reviewed the raids and started looking into the old stash houses, they wouldn't find anything there except loving families. This would throw the police off and also because there was no paper trail connection to Omari and the new stash spots.

Everything with Omari's business was back to flourishing, but things at home were broken. He and

Reign had not been the same since the incident in the garage. Even after moving everything the guns and drugs to the new stash spots, Reign was not happy. She was locked on to the words that Omari said during the argument. She couldn't help but think he was right about him owning the home. Throughout their entire relationship, he had been a very generous man, which made her finally realize how dependent she was. Something needs to change, she thought as she began researching how to build something of her own. Reign looked at many professions, but none of them stood out as something she wanted to get involved in. The only work experience Reign had was working for Omari when she was a teenager. She became frustrated as she realized just how dependent she was on him. She also noticed the education requirements for each job. Being a high school dropout was only going to get her so far in the business world. At that moment she made her decision.

"I'm going to get my GED."

"What?" Omari asked as he counted the money that he collected from Ant.

"I'm going to apply for a GED program."

"Fuck you need that for?"

"So, I can get a job."

"A job? Are you still on this bullshit?"

"It's not bullshit," she said placing the laptop on the table next to the piles of cash he still had to count. "Look! This place is in South Baltimore."

Omari didn't even turn his head to entertain the idea. "You don't need that shit."

"I do need it. Can you please support me on this?"

"Babe, I know what this is about, and I don't know why you won't let this shit go. I already apologized for the shit I said. I thought we moved past the day." Omari was serious.

He did think they moved past that situation, but the words he said to Reign in the garage haunted her daily. They both were on edge for weeks after the incident. There was very little communication between the couple. Omari also spent several nights out. He stayed in the hood and made sure his presence was felt in the streets. He wanted the Police and the streets to know that he was ten toes down, especially with the entire stash being at his home.

"This has nothing to do with you. I'm doing this for me."

"But you don't have to. These jobs treat you like shit and pay you pennies. You gon' go get a GED to do what? Make forty thousand dollars a year? That ain't shit," Omari barked. He stopped counting the cash that was in front of him and picked grabbed a small designer bag that was on the table. "Here," he said as he reached out the bag to give to her. "It's fifty thousand in this. Fuck all that dumb shit you talking 'bout and just enjoy this life I'm giving you."

Reign rolled her eyes. "This is exactly my point." She grabbed the laptop and headed up to the bedroom.

"You still trynna go to dinner?" Omar yelled as she was walking away.

"Nope!" She yelled back.

Reign was so irritated. She was invisible in Omari's world. He acted like her opinion didn't matter when it came to making decisions. She thought about the money he just offered her. She clicked the tab on the browser she was viewing. She stared at the job description from a Certified Nursing Assistant. Her eyes scrolled the text until Reign found what she was looking for. *Salary: $12/hour. Fuck. He's right.*

Reign clicked back on the tab with the information on obtaining her GED. Slamming her fingers on the keyboard, she filled out the online application for the program and submitted it. Every time she thought about Omari counting that money downstairs, she thought about the life she and her mother lived after her father died. It was no way that Reign was going to allow that to happen to her. She needed a backup plan. Unfortunately, she had to create this plan without the support of the man she loved.

Reign walked downstairs and sat at the table with Omari. He smiled and slid the bag across the table to her. Reign took the bag and slung it across her chest. Then she assisted Omari with counting the money on the table. Reign is that she never stopped playing her role with Omari. Although he completely removed her from his street shit, she still chipped in to help him do little things. Omari's phone rang and he checked it. He looked at Reign and took a deep breath. He answered the phone and put it on speaker. "Yo," he said as he continued counting.

"Yo, cuz." They both could hear the concern in Ant's voice.

"What's wrong?"

"Them niggas was some goofy shit."

"Da fuck you mean they was on some goofy shit? This was already worked out."

"Yeah, I know it was but that nigga Juante was on some goofy shit. He said he want to meet with you on some boss shit."

"On some boss shit?"

"Yeah. It was weird as shit. He was acting a fuckin' groupie. Kept asking me where you was at."

"Did he accept our offer?"

"He ain't do shit. I put the keys on the table and everything. This nigga just kept asking for you."

"Fuck."

"Exactly. I don't know what type of funny shit he got going on but that was a waste of time. Why we even gotta fuck with these niggas? We making enough money on our own."

"Because we gotta expand. We gone fuck with these niggas, because they got Eastern Shore on lock. With them moving our shit out there and them niggas in Cherry Hill moving our shit too, we gon' live like kings. You see how Gilmor dried up. All those fuckin' abandoned homes. Imagine if all our money was tied up in there like back in the day. We'd be broke as shit."

"Shiiiiiit. We are fuckin' hustlers. We would have found a way."

"But now we don't even gotta worry bout that shit. If Cherry Hill dries up, then we still got that shit out Eastern Shore. Plus, we still got our niggas moving on the west side."

"You a fuckin' smarty arty nigga. You always got a plan."

Omari laughed. He knew his cousin didn't understand the importance of the meeting he sent him to. "We gotta always have a plan. Something is always going to go wrong and you gotta be ready when it does."

"You damn right."

"So, when this nigga say he want to meet me?"

"Tomorrow."

"Fuck. I got dinner plans with Reign tomorrow."

"Nigga, I thought yall was going to dinner tonight. That's the reason you said you couldn't make the meeting."

"Yeah, I know. Something came up and we had to cancel tonight's plans."

"Everything cool?"

"Yeah. It's all good."

"Well, I'll call him and see what he says. I'm sure he's gon' which the meeting location too. Just make sure you ready too. I'm gon' have you meet me there."

"Cool."

"Okay cuz. I'll see you tomorrow."

"Gotchu."

Omari put the money down he was counting and headed to the kitchen. Reign continued counting the money but was also trying her best to decipher the conversation between Omari and Ant. He never spoke to her about his expansion plan, and she felt a bit out of the loop. Before their big argument, he told her that he wanted to expand but he hadn't brought it up afterward and now he was scheduling meetings.

"So, we got chicken and spicy beef," Omari said, walking back into the room with two cups of Ramen noodles. He smirked when he saw Reign's disgusted expression. "If you don't want this, I could try to call one of the chefs and see if they are available to come up here."

"No don't do that. It's last minute and I don't want to bother them."

"You not going to bother them. They get paid good money. I'm sure they won't mind."

"It's okay. Just order a pizza or something."

"Okay. Pepperoni?"

"Half."

"Got it."

The last thing Reign wanted to do was eat Ramen noodles. She grew up eating them and didn't want to be reminded of her past in any way. For Omari, it was a quick meal but for her, it was more traumatic. It was a reminder of her mother's flaws and the impoverished life that they lived. That was the only food that her mother purchased when she got a couple dollars.

Eating that would send Reign's mind back to the Gilmor Homes and she didn't want to do that.

"It should be here in a half," Omari said, returning to the table.

"Cool."

"Can you promise me tomorrow's dinner plans won't be canceled?"

"Why would they be canceled?"

"You told Ant that you would make that meeting."

"Don't worry about that. We'll make it to dinner," Omari responded. "Now, let's talk about you not accepting my apology." Omari slid his hand across the table and grabbed Reign's hand.

"You messin' up my count," she joked.

"Fuck that count," he said, pulling her towards him.

Reign dropped the money on the table but most of it fell to the ground.

"I'm hungry," Omari whispered in her ear.

"You said the pizza was on the way."

"I ain't talkin' bout that." Omari stood up and picked Reign up, putting her on the table. The skirt she was wearing rose up and exposed everything underneath. "No panties? You were ready for me."

Omari dropped to his knees, and nothing else mattered at that moment. Reign wasn't worried about the GED program, her mother, or their argument. She was focused on his next move. The anticipation was killing her as she felt Omari's warm breath against her inner thigh. Her heart was beating fast in her chest. She swore he could hear it.

"You still mad at me?" Omari asked, looking up at Reign. She instantly became turned on just by looking at his face as it was only inches away from her pussy. He shook her head, giving him the answer he was looking for. In response, he dove face first into his meal. Reign moaned loudly. She placed one hand on his head and the other gripped the table.

Omari's thick tongue traveled up her slit, parting the lower lips apart. He followed up with sensual kisses, tasting her pretty pussy. "Ohhh shit," Reign moaned, knowing she couldn't handle the ride he was taking her on. Her nails dug into the tabletop and with the other hand, she attempted to push Omari's head away from her throbbing pussy. She was ready to explode. He grabbed both of her wrists and pinned her hands on the table as he continued devouring her.

Reign leaned back on the table, knocking over stacks of cash as Omari feasted on her. It was something about getting her pussy ate on piles of cash that sent her body into a frenzy. Omari continued parting her lips, causing her body to tremble, and then he latched onto her clit.

"Yesss!"

Reign gasped loudly as she tried to scoot back and prevent Omari from continuing to hit her spot. His hands transferred from her wrists to her hips as he pulled her back towards him. It was too late for Reign. He had her right where he wanted her as the strongest orgasm she ever felt took over her body.

"You ain't going nowhere, baby," he uttered.

"Fuck!" She softly moaned knowing that she was his prisoner of passion. After that powerful release, Reign's body went limp. Omari took all the fight out of her. He stood up, smirking. Reign bit her lip. Omari grabbed something from under her and held it up. It was a hundred-dollar bill that was soaked from her love juices. "Oops," she said sensually.

Omari didn't give her any time to recover as he dropped his shorts and boxers and slid his rock-hard dick inside of her wetness. "Tell me you love me," Omari said as he thrusted his hips forward and went deep with every stroke."

"I love you, O," Reign moaned.

"Tell me you want to have my baby."

"I do."

"Tell me. I wanna hear you say it."

"Oh fuck!" She yelled as Omari began pounding harder and deeper.

His grip on her hips got tighter, as he pulled her forward with each stroke. Reign couldn't contain herself. She tried to grab onto the table but instead knocked off the cash. Seeing her this way burned a fire inside Omari. He kept one hand gripping her hip and the other tugged on the strap of the shoulder bag Reign was wearing. She was stuck.

"Say that shit."

"I want to have your baby," she moaned. "Fuuucckk!" She came again.

Her eyes rolled into the back of her head. Reign felt like she was floating. Sex with Omari had always been great, but this was something completely different. This was more passionate and more intense.

Omari slowly pulled and leaned over and kissed Reign. The soft kisses brought her back down from cloud nine. She rubbed her hand up his beard and to the back of his head. Locking him in place. She didn't want him going anywhere.

Omari kissed his way down her body, as her grip loosened. One minute she had him locked in and the next, his soft kisses were felt on her stomach. Reign tried to sit up and gather herself, but Omari had turned her on her left side. She was now facing a large mirror that was in the living room. Looking at the reflection, she watched Omari remove his shirt and run his hands down her body. Staring at the reflection of his chiseled body and long dick caused me to whimper.

"Damn, you look good," Omari muttered. There was a slight growl in his tone that made Reign crave him even more. Omari looked down and admired the beauty in front of him. The two things that mattered most to him in the world, were on the dining room table. Hundred-dollar bills were still stuck to Reign's back, legs and plump ass. "You ready for this?" He asked, introducing her to a new position. Reign nodded her head and he entered her again. Reign's mouth dropped in disbelief as his dick immediately hit a sensitive spot inside of her that sent her through the roof. He felt bigger. He felt thicker. It felt like he was deeper. "Damn!" He groaned, feeling just as good as Reign.

"Oohh, my God!" She cried out as his dick sent me into another world. Omari noticed that Reign never looked up at him. His eyes followed hers and they both met at the mirror. He smiled when he realized that she was watching him. This made him feel the need to put on a show. He put one leg on the table and continued stroking as he stared back at her in the mirror. Reign moaned loudly as the new angle caused her to reach another orgasm.

"This shit is too good," Omari growled as he reached his peak.

Reign stared as his eyes drifted shut. Then she felt it. It was so warm, and it felt intoxicating as he filled her with his love seeds. He finally opened his eyes and panted as he slowly pulled out of her. Cum leaked out of her pussy and onto the money that was under her. Omari didn't care though. He enjoyed the finale of the moment. He then pulled up a chair and sat at the side of the table, in Reign's face. His dick was still hard and covered in cum. Reign stared at it, wanting it to taste it. Just as she reaches out for it, they were interrupted by the doorbell ringing.

"I guess that's your dinner. I already had mine," Omari joked.

They both laughed.

"Go get it."

"Not yet, it seems like you were about to do something."

Reign blushed. "Get the food and I'll show you exactly what I was about to do."

Omari got his shorts from the ground and threw them on really quick. After grabbing the pizza, the two went right back at each other for another round.

CHAPTER 16

Omari pulled up in the Ferrari. It was just his like him to always try to stunt. Reign sat in the passenger seat, wondering what they were doing outside the rundown apartment building. She told him she wanted to go to dinner and based on the current setting, this was not the current destination.

"I'll be right back," Omari said, as he tucked his gun in his waistband and exited the vehicle.

Regin had so many questions for him, but none of them escaped her mouth at the moment. Omari had business to handle and wanted to make sure everything was in order. Reign had never been to the part of town they were in, and she was shocked to see how familiar it was to The Gilmor Homes. Their current lifestyle left her disconnected from the hood, but so many childhood memories began flashing in her head. The only difference between this apartment building and the Gilmor Homes was the number of junkies that were roaming up and down the street. The number was triple the amount that used to be around her old apartment building.

There were men and women of all ages, races and backgrounds staggering up the sidewalk. It honestly looked like they were cast as zombies in The Walking Dead. Reign activated the locks on the door. *He better hurry up*, she thought. As a child, she did not truly understand the effect drugs had on the people around her because the addicts she saw were much older than she was. However, she spotted a few junkies that had to be around the same age as her. Reign's heart skipped a beat as a child ran by the car. The young girl could not have been any older than 8-years old and was carrying a bag from one of the local pharmacies. Reign noticed an item held fell from the bag but the little girl didn't.

"Hey!" Reign yelled out. "Hey!" She shouted again as she exited the Ferrari.

The little girl continued running across the street. Reign picked up the bottle of peroxide that fell from the girl's bag and then chased after her.

The little girl headed into a dark alley, stopping midway just behind an abandoned building. Reign stopped in her tracks when she entered the alley and saw what appeared to be an encampment. There were makeshift tents made of old tarps, cardboard boxes stacked up as shelter and some people wrapped up in dirty sleeping bags. The alley was filled with homeless people, addicts, and broken families. The little girl crawled under one of the tarps.

Reign inched her way towards the tarp. The hairs on the back of her neck stood up as she walked deeper into the alley. It was an eerie feeling being around so many people in need, while she was draped in expensive clothing and jewelry. Most of the residents of the alley were either getting their next fix or already on cloud nine from shooting up. Those who were not being consumed by crack or heroin were focused on the beautiful young woman that had infiltrated their domain. A diamond amongst stones. All eyes were on Reign and her eyes bounced around as she did her best to watch her surroundings.

"You dropped this," Reign said as she pulled the tarp back.

The little girl quickly turned around, to put a face to the unfamiliar voice. There was so much innocence in her deep brown eyes. Reign felt heavy when she saw the girl's cute face. She was reminded of herself when she was a kid, sitting on the couch when her mother had company or when she had to bring her mother drugs to feed the addiction. A single tear fell from Reign's eye. Dirt covered the little girl's face, and her hair was pulled up into a nappy bun that looked like it had not been washed in a long time. "Thank you," the little girl replied, grabbing the peroxide from Reign.

The little girl opened a pack of cotton balls and poured the peroxide on a handful of them. She took two of the soaked cotton balls and placed them between her mother's foot. Her mother, a heroin addict, was passed out on the cold concrete. A syringe was stuck in between her toes. The little girl pressed the cotton balls on the puncture location, as she gently removed the syringe. Reign's mouth dropped to the floor.

"Here, let me help you," Reign whispered as she picked up the cap to the syringe and grabbed the sharp object from the girl.

The girl took another batch of soaked cotton balls and replaced the others, squeezing the peroxide onto the track mark. Reign reached into the shopping bag and opened the pack of bandages. She placed a bandage on the woman's foot. Doing so, took her back to the filthy one-bedroom apartment that she used to call home. Reign felt like a young girl again, caring for her mother when she got high. The awful stench in the alley was not too far off from the odor that lingered in her mother's bedroom.

"Thank you, for helping me," the girl said.

"No problem," Reign replied. "I used to help my mom too. You're so brave."

The girl smiled. "My mommy said I'm her nurse."

"Yes, you are, and you take good care of her."

"Are you a nurse for your mommy too?"

The question hit Reign like a ton of bricks. Finding it difficult to find an answer the girl, answered "Yes." She looked up. "I'll always be a nurse for her."

The girl picked up a trash bag and placed it under her mother. The bag was filled with all their personal belongings and now served as a pillow to support her mother's head. Reign was impressed by the girl but also heartbroken. No matter how bad her life was, at least she had a place to live. This girl was on the street. "Where is your dad?" Reign asked.

"I don't have one. My mom always says that I don't need one because I have her. She said she's my mommy and my daddy."

"Are there any other kids around here that you play with?"

The girl shook her head. "I can't play because I have to be a nurse."

"You can do both. There is always time to play. "

"No. Mommy said that playing is for little kids and I'm a big kid."

"How old are you?"

"Seven and a half."

"Wow. You are a big kid," Reign lied. She could not even imagine living this type of life at that age. When Reign was that age, things weren't as bad as they were when she became a teen. To be on the streets at seven was unbelievable. "What's your name?"

"Aliya."

Well, Aliya it's nice to meet you. My name is Reign."

"I like that name."

"I like your name too. It's pretty, just like you." Reign helped the girl clean up the cotton balls and the used syringe. Reign just had to help Aliya. There was no way she was leaving that alley without offering the young girl some type of assistance. She reached down for her purse to give the girl some cash but realized that she left it in the car. "I'll tell you what, I'm going to come right back and give you something that will help you and your mom out. Would that be okay with you?"

"Yes."

Reign crawled from under the tarp and made her way back out to the alley. The distance from her current location to the street seemed so much further than it did when she entered the alley. She swiftly walked back towards the car. Her heels clicked on the cobblestone ground. Once again, all eyes were on the outsider as she made her way through the dark pathway.

"STONEY!"

Reign whipped her neck around, after hearing her mother's name begin called out.

"It can't be. Stoney is that you?" A male asked as he emerged from the shadows and headed straight for Reign.

The haggard man used a cane to assist him with walking. Reign's face was turned up, but she had not yet responded. She was curious as to who would be calling for her mother. As the man stepped forward under the dim streetlight, she backed up. The voice did not immediately trigger her recollection, but she recognized the face that haunted her for years. "Slim?"

He thought he was seeing a ghost. No one from The Gilmor had seen Slim since the night her mother was murdered. He was a person of interest in the investigation and even the police could not locate him and now he was standing in front of her. "Yeah, Stoney it's me. I thought you were dead," Slim said. "Listen, I found a new drug that will be you harder than crack. It's called smack. You gotta' try it, Stoney."

He dug into his pocket and pulled out a small, clear plastic bag that was holding a blue folded wax paper that contained a tan powder substance.

"You know the cops are looking for you right?"

"The cops? What they looking for me for? I ain't do shit," he mumbled. Although he was using a cane, Slim was still stumbling around and appeared to be nodding off. A syringe was dangling from his arm and heroin was flowing through his veins. "I thought you were dead, Stoney. I thought that bastard killed you."

Reign just stared at Slim. His eyes were beginning to roll to the back of his head. Reign didn't understand why he was calling her by her mother's name but then realized how much she resembled Stoney, especially before the drugs got a hold of her mother. Stoney used to be the beauty queen of the hood. Slim was one of the people that knew Stoney back when she was the treasure that everyone talked about and Reign was a spitting image of her. "What are you talkin' about? You're the one that did it?"

"Me? I ain't do shit," Slim said in a slurred speech. "He did it, not me. He shot both of us and now I gotta walk around with this fuckin' cane."

Reign looked down at the cane. "Who are you talking about? Who shot you?"

"Why you acting dumb, Stoney? You know that triflin' Omari shot us that night we took his drugs. I knew we shouldn't have done that shit. I thought that nigga killed you. I know damn well his bitch ass tried to kill me. Had me hidin' out for all these damn years. Crazy ass nigga."

Reign's heart felt like it was ripped out of her chest and stabbed a million times. Hearing Omari's name being associated with her mother's death broke her. Reign dropped to her knees as the air felt like it was being pulled from her lungs. She gasped.

"Reign." Omari sprinted down the alley. When he came back to the car she was gone, so he began looking around for her. He saw the thin man hovering over her and was in full attack mode. Slim was too high to react and was tackled to the ground by Omari. Strong punches to the face broke Slim's nose as Omari repeatedly stuck him. Slim curled up and did his best to protect himself, but the drugs flowing through his system had left him defenseless. The fight got a lot of attention as the residents of the alley were all focused on the action. "Reign, are you okay?" Omari asked as he stood up.

Reign was in shock and could not respond to his question. Omari tried embracing her, but she pulled away from him and stood to her feet. "What's wrong with you?" Omari asked. She still did not respond. "What the hell did you do to her?" He asked the battered man. "Hold up," he followed up, noticing some familiar features on the man. "Slim?" *This can't be*, he thought.

"Leave me alone," Slim begged as he tried crawling away.

He was petrified. He was looking at the devil in the flesh. After shooting Stoney, Omari chased Slim down the streets. The gunshots that Brandi and Reign heard that night were intended for Slim. All but two of those shots missed the fleeing man. The two hits had ripped through Slim's right leg and would cripple him. It took Slim a week to go to a hospital. He tried patching himself up but leaving the wounds neglected dd more damage than the actual bullets. In the end, he was left with unrepairable nerve damage which made him unable to put weight on his right leg. After that terrifying night, he spent his years on the other side of town, hoping to never see Omari again.

"So, this is where you have been hiding out, huh?"

"I don't want no trouble nigga."

"Too bad because I do," Omari responded. "Did you say something to her?"

"I told her the truth. I told her what you did."

"And what was that?"

"You tried to kill us," Slim said. "Stoney, run!" He yelled at Reign.

"Stoney?" Omari asked, looking back at Reign. He laughed. "You dumb motherfucka'. You think that's Stoney?"

"It is Stoney."

"You're high as shit, Slim. You are talking to a ghost because Stoney ain't here."

"You didn't even have to do that to her. She didn't take your drugs. It was just me. I did it."

"I know it was you," Omari muttered as he pulled out the gun from his waistband. "You should have kept your fuckin' mouth shut." Omari pulled the trigger four times, riddling Slim's chest with bullets. People began screaming and scattering throughout the alley after the gunshots rang off. Reign froze. "Come on let's go," Omari ordered, grabbing her by the arm and pulling her with him.

Reign was still attempting to process what took place. She looked back at Slim's body, which was nothing more than a lifeless object that was getting smaller as the distance between them increased. Reign watched the residents of the alley flee like roaches. With nowhere in particular to go, most of them ran towards the next alley while others hit turns and headed down the street.

"Get the fuck off me!" Reign yelled, pulling her arm back.

"What the fuck are you doing?" Omari barked back. The gun was still in his hand. "We gotta get the fuck out of here."

"I'm not going anywhere!" She snapped. "Did you do it?"

"Did I do what?"

"Slim said you shot my mom. Is it true?" Pools began to form in her eyes.

"You gon' sit here and believe a fuckin' crackhead over me?"

"I'm not believing anyone. I'm asking you."

"Let's go, right now," Omari ordered, raising the gun to Reign's face.

She immediately flinched, trying to deflect any shot that came out of the gun. Omari grabbed her by the arm again and pulled her to the car. Reign tried her best to escape his grip but was unsuccessful. Omari pushed her into the passenger seat of the Ferrari. The sound of sirens traveled through the air. He looked down the street before tucking the gun back in his waistband and hopping in the vehicle. Omari peeled off and began hitting the side streets. The last thing he wanted to do is get caught on the main roads and risk a cop seeing him.

Reign was still in shock. Her eyes widened like a deer in headlights, as she heard the gunshots. The shots she and Brandi heard the night that Stoney was killed. *If I would have just gone home, I could have saved her.* Guilt began weighing heavy on Reign's shoulders. *I saw him walk up. Omari was there. He was the only one there. He talked to me and Brandi that night, knowing he was going to kill my mom.*

"Yo," Omari said.

His words went in one ear and out the other, but not before triggering more memories and thoughts. *He couldn't have done it. He loves me. He was there for me when nobody else was. There's no way he killed my mom. There has to be a reasonable explanation for all of this.*

"Yo. Don't let that fuckin' crackhead ruin our evening. I just closed out the expansion deal with East

Shore niggas, so now we have a reason to celebrate at dinner."

Reign slowly turned to Omari. "Did you do it?"

"Are you still on this shit?"

There was pain in Reign's eyes. Not just the pain of losing her mother but also the pain of being betrayed. She thought about Slim and how bad he looked. The police had spread his name throughout the entire city, and he could have been an innocent man. They put a target on his back. Which was basically a living death sentence. Then there was Omari. Reign thought about how much Omari grew since taking her in. While Slim was rotting away in an alleyway, they were making love on the beautiful beaches of Barbados. Reign felt like she was dying inside. "Stop the car!" She yelled, causing Omari to slam on the brakes. Reign opened the passenger door and vomited on the street. Her head was spinning. The sight of Slim's face was stuck in her head and then suddenly she blacked out.

CHAPTER 17

"Whoever did this made sure this guy was dead," One of the officers said.

Detective Raven Ramos walked over to the bloody body. "Let me see," she said. The coroner pulled the sheet back, revealing the face of the victim. "It's Slim," she muttered.

"You know this guy?" Detective Jonathon Allen asked. Detective Allen was one of the newer detectives assigned to the Homicide Division. He was a middle-aged man that was living the American dream. He had a beautiful wife, three kids, two dogs, and his dream career. He bled blue, being the son of a Baltimore Police Officer and nephew of a Maryland State Trooper. His mother retired from the police department years ago, but her legacy lived on through him. His mother was his hero growing up. He saw the good and bad that she went through. Whenever it wasn't the department working her nerves, it was his father. Before the fatal car crash, his father frequented the bottle. He hid his addiction well as a postal inspector, however, it would ultimately lead to his demise, after driving drunk and hitting a truck head on, while bar hopping.

"I don't know him personally," Raven replied. "He was a person of interest in a homicide a while back, over at the Gilmor Homes. I was looking for this guy for years."

"Looking for him? Since when did the Special Victims Unit start investigating homicides?" he asked, sarcastically.

Raven shot him a look that could kill. "First of all, we weren't investigating the homicide, and second of all, I wasn't even with Special Victims yet. I was still on the beat and was the first on the scene. Someone just left the victim for dead. It was sad."

"Looks like karma finally caught up to him."

"I guess it did." Raven looked up and spotted officers tearing down the makeshift shelters that the residents of the alley had set up. "Hey, what's going on?" she asked an officer that was pulling out someone from under a tarp. A young girl was also screaming at the officer.

"Help me get this junkie out of here. Homicide wants all of these people identified and interviewed," an officer said. He was a thin, pale-skinned young man. His age and his actions automatically let Raven know that he was a rookie.

"Stop pulling on this woman in front of her child," Raven ordered.

"I have orders to follow."

"And I am giving you a direct order," Raven shouted, grabbing the officer's hand and pulling it off of the woman.

"What the hell do you think you're doing?" he said as he jumped up in Raven's face.

"I'm stopping you from assaulting this woman. Listen rook, I suggest you go back to the academy and relearn the chain of command. I outrank you, and you disobeyed a direct order. Now Officer..." Raven looked closely at his badge and name tag. "Tanner, get the hell out of here."

The officer was not happy being told what to do by Raven, but she was right. Per their department policies and procedures, detectives outranked patrol officers. Disobeying her direct order could result in some form of disciplinary action being taken against him. Additionally, being disciplined while on rookie status could have resulted in his immediate termination from the force. Officer Tanner put his pride to the side and took a walk back to his patrol car.

"Are you okay," Raven asked the woman, who still appeared shaken up by the officer's aggressive actions."

"Yes, I'm fine," the woman responded in a slurred speech.

The band-aid and old track marks on the woman's arm immediately captured Raven's attention. Then the adorable face of the little girl that was inside the tarp gathering belongings. "What are your names?" Raven asked.

"My name is Aliya and this is my mommy," the little girl interjected as she stepped out from under the tarp. She placed four packed backpacks on the ground, in front of her.

"And you?"

"I'm Anna," the woman followed up while scratching her arm.

"Anna, I think you need some medical attention," Raven said. She noticed that Anna had scratched the band-aid off her arm and her fresh track mark was now bleeding.

"I'm fine," she replied, as she continued scratching.

"You're not fine. You're bleeding and you need to get that looked at. Sooner than later."

"It's okay, I'll take care of her," Aliya interrupted, opening one of the backpacks and taking out the supplies she got from the pharmacy.

"I need to ask you a couple questions about the shooting that took place. Did you see anything? Do you know the person that got shot?"

Aliya perked up. "I saw the pretty lady that helped ..."

"We ain't see nothing," Anna barked, placing her hand over Aliya's mouth.

Raven looked at Anna and then at Aliya. "Listen, you don't have to lie to me. I'm just here to help."

"No, you're not here to help. You are here to do a job. Yall don't give a fuck about us. Just like I told that other cop, we don't know shit." Just as she spoke her last word, Anna collapsed. Her body began to violently seize.

"Mama," Aliya yelled.

"Get me an ambulance here now," Raven shouted. "It's okay. Your mom is going to be fine. We are going to get her some help."

Aliya was in tears. Unfortunately, this isn't the first time she witnessed her mom experience a seizure. She also witnessed others in the alley experience seizures. Some never came out of them. They went from seizing to still and the next thing Aliya remembered was a sheet getting thrown over their bodies. She was devastated because she did not want the same fate for her mother. Although she could patch up her mother's minor wounds, the young girl did not know what to do for a seizure.

Raven kept Anna in the recovery position. "What happened?" one of the homicide detectives asked when he ran over to them.

"I don't know, one minute she was talking and then the next, she had passed out and started seizing. What's the ETA on the medics?"

"They're around the corner."

The sound of the ambulance sirens bounced off the buildings. The volume seemed to be much louder in the alley. As the ambulance got closer, Anna seemed to be losing consciousness. "What did she take?" Raven asked Aliya. The girl did not respond to the question.

Two paramedics rolled a stretcher through the crime scene and pulled up to Raven's location. They checked Anna's vitals and immediately hoisted her onto the stretcher. Raven helped Aliya grab the bags and the two followed the paramedics.

"I'm going to follow them over to the hospital," Raven said to the homicide detective. "Do you want me to contact you with her information?"

"No, I don't need it. She's just another junkie and won't be much help to me."

Raven shook her head and walked towards her car. She could not believe what that detective just said. In her mind, everyone was essential to a case and if she was in the unit, she would have interviewed every single person that was in the alley. Instead, the Homicide Unit had patrol officers ripping people from their living area and tossing them in patrol wagons. These people were going to be dropped off at shelters or just to another section of the city and tossed out like garbage. In her mind, the unit was getting rid of possible eyewitnesses to Slim's murder.

"Hey, I need you to do me a favor," Raven said, after calling into the office.

"What do you need now Raven?" Sharon asked. Sharon was one of the investigators assigned to the Special Victims Unit. She had been transferred there after putting in a request with just four years on the job. She latched on to these cases and immediately knew that SVU is where she belonged. She was also one of Raven's good friends and knew her like the back of her hand.

"Don't say it like that." Raven laughed.

"Listen, I know you were assigned any new cases, so you have to be poking around in someone's business." Sharon laughed.

"I'm not doing any poking around. I'm just following up on a cold case."

"Which cold case?"

"Not one of ours?"

"Well if it isn't ours, then who does the case belong to?"

"Homicide."

"Girl, if you don't leave them alone. Don't you remember what happened last time you started poking around in their cases?"

"Yes, I remember. But it's not like that this time. I just want to see something."

"What do you want to see?"

"I need you to pull up the name "Slim" in the database."

"Are you serious?"

"Yeah, I'm serious."

"Ray, there are probably a million people with the alias slim in Baltimore. You need to be more specific."

"There should be an unsolved homicide case. The victim was a woman in her late 40s. He is a person of interest in that case."

"When did it happen?"

"About 5 years ago."

"Where?"

"The Gilmor Homes."

Sharon's fingers were moving a mile a minute as she typed in the information. Raven's request was actually minor and Sharon did not mind helping her. Usually, when Raven called she had an outlandish request that could probably result in both of them losing their jobs and maybe even getting arrested. Sharon did not hesitate to help Raven out on those favors as well. "Ok, I got it. The victim was Stoney Brooks. The cause of death re several gunshot wounds to the chest. The suspect is Sean "Slim" Nichols."

"That's it. The victim had a daughter. Is her information in there?"

"Let me see," Sharon muttered as she scrolled through the case. "It looks like they have Reign Brooks listed as the daughter."

"Perfect. Can you run her and send me a recent picture and her current address?"

"Sending it over to you right now."

"Thanks," Raven turned the car on and waited for the paramedics to pull off, so she could follow them. The notification on her phone let her know that Sharon's email had just come through. Raven opened up the attached photograph of Reign. *I saw the pretty lady that helped...* Aliya's brief statement was stuck in Raven's head. *It can't be*, she thought as she stared at Reign's picture.

The ambulance pulled off and headed to the University of Maryland Medical Center. Raven followed, with one hand gripping the steering wheel and the other scrolling through her phone. The paramedics took Anna right in when they pulled up to the hospital. Aliya hopped out of the back of the ambulance, trying to gather the backpacks with their belongings.

"Here, I'll put those in my car," Raven said, as she grabbed the bags.

"Thank you," Aliya responded.

Raven placed the bags in the trunk of her vehicle. "Can I ask you a question?" Aliya stayed silent and looked back towards the entrance of the emergency room. "It's okay, you're not in any trouble. Neither is your mom."

"Mommy said don't talk to the police."

"I know that's probably what your mom said, but I'm not the police right now," Raven replied, removing the badge from her belt and placing it in her pocket. "I'm your friend."

The young girl smiled. "Can I go with my mommy?"

"Yes, you can. Right after you a couple questions. I need your help, Aliya."

"But I want to see my mommy, right now. She needs my help."

"Your mom is in good hands. The doctors are going to take care of her and then they are going to send her to a nice clean room. I'll take you up to the room and you'll be able to take a hot shower and get a hot meal. Does that sound like something you want to do?"

"Yes."

"Okay. I'll help you out if you help me out. Deal?"

"Deal," Aliya proudly replied.

"Earlier you mentioned a pretty girl. Is this her?" Raven asked, pulling out her phone and showing Aliya the screen.

"Yup. That's her."

"Did she shoot that man that was in the alley?"

"No. She helped me and my mommy."

Raven let out a sigh of relief. "Did she?"

"Yup. I like her. She looks like a princess."

"Yes, she does," Raven said, smiling. "Did you see the person that shot the man in the street?"

Aliya paused and then nodded her head.

"Did you ever see him before?"

"No," she said, shaking her head.

"Where did he go?"

"He took her and left."

"He took her?" Raven asked, holding the phone up again.

Aliya nodded again.

"Do you want to help me save the princess? I think she needs our help."

"Yup."

"Do you think you would recognize the guy that took her, if I had a picture of him?"

Aliya shrugged her shoulders. "Okay. Let's go see your mommy. We can finish this later."

CHAPTER 18

Omari watched as Reign danced around the kitchen. When she cooked, she also performed and he was enjoying the show he was currently viewing. Dressed in only a bra and lace panties, she moved her hips from side to side while she enjoyed the sounds of Beyonce. Watching her made him smile because he was experiencing a different type of life. One that was filled with love. He felt grateful to have her as his lady. For the first time, he felt relaxed. He didn't have to worry about the nonsense the hood had to offer. No arguing in the middle of the night from neighboring apartments, no gunshots, no police sirens, and no dope heads meandering about the streets at all types of hours. It all seemed like a dream. That's because it was.

Omari slowly leaned up, waking up from an unexpected nap. The lights were dim in the living room and Sports Center reruns were playing on the tv. He looked over at the kitchen and it was dark. Reign wasn't in there cooking and dancing around in lingerie. She was curled up in a blanket, on the floor. She had been there for days, only getting up to use the bathroom. The day she saw Slim had taken a toll on her. After passing out in the car, Omari brought her home to rest. He didn't even stay with her to make sure she was fine. Instead, he left out and celebrated his new partnership with Juante and the East Shore crew.

Reign was left to sulk. The guilt and stress weighed her down to the floor like sandbags on a banner. She felt paralyzed. She was still in denial about Omari and the role he possibly played in her mother's murder but after being left in the house alone for a few days, she couldn't help but wonder if that was a sign. She hadn't returned anyone's calls or text messages, not even Brandi who had been blowing her up.

"Let me know if you want something to eat," Omari said. "I'm 'bout to go get a platter." He was sitting on the couch, waiting for a response that he never received. Omari was not sure what his next move was going to be. He hadn't planned on running into Slim that day, so killing him was not in his plans. The move was sloppy, especially with all those witnesses in the alley. After going out to celebrate the first night, he realized it wasn't wise to be out. The police would surely be investigating Slim's murder and he didn't want to be caught slipping, especially not out cruising in the Ferrari. He had parked it in the garage and now needed to find a new ride to make moves in.

Omari's phone was blowing up, but he kept declining the call. Finally, he put the phone on *Do Not Disturb* and placed it face down on the table. Omari got up and sat at the dining room table. He began flipping through the thousands of dollars on the table. He needed to grab a new car until the Slim situation died down. He was waiting for Ant to come to the crib, so he could go and get the car for him. But first, he had to get the money straight.

The last thing he wanted to do was park up his brand-new Ferrari, but he had no choice. That was his dream car. Ever since he was a little boy, he promised himself that he would buy that car and that's precisely what he did. Only now, that car is associated with a homicide. Omari wanted to grab another coupe, but he knew he had to switch it up. He sent Ant a link to a used Ford Expedition that was being sold by a dealer near him. After counting out the thirty thousand dollars, Omari slid the cash into a large manila envelope and waited for Ant to come pick it up.

Omari walked over to Reign and stared at her for a minute. A part of him blamed her for the events that took place. If she never exited the car and gone down that alley, she would have never run into Slim. They would have just been on their way to dinner and had a magical night. Now, he had to lay low and hope no one could identify him as Slim's shooter. "Listen, you can't just sit here like this. I'm about to head out with Ant and I'll be back later. I'm going to have to take your car too. Hopefully, you aren't still on this ground when I get back." Omari leaned down to kiss Reign, but she pulled her head back. He looked at her and saw the same expression on her face that she had in the alley. "I already told you that I had nothing to do with your mom getting killed. I don't know why you aren't believing me, but I swear that I didn't. I wasn't even around there when it happened, so stop believing whatever bullshit Slim said."

Omari went upstairs to grab a pair of sneakers. He didn't even wait around long enough to see Reign's reaction to his statement. Her sadness suddenly turned to rage, as she got up from the floor. She didn't have much time before he would come back down for the keys.

Reign stormed out of the house and hopped into her vehicle. She had to get as far away from Omari as possible and did not want to look back. Anger and pain filled her mind and body. She felt betrayed by the one person she thought would never hurt her and he just subtly admitted that he was involved with her mother's murder. With just her purse and cell phone, Reign needed to get away. Her whole world had just fallen apart and there was no way to piece it back together.

Her vehicle swerved in and out of traffic as she made her way out of the elegant Ellicott City neighborhood. Omari's last words played over and over in her mind, *"I wasn't even around there when it happened, so stop believing whatever bullshit Slim said."*

The thing about lies is that you have to build a false world around the story you are telling, and Omari hadn't thought about that before opening his mouth. After all these years, Omari forgot he walked up to

Reign while she was waiting for Brandi, on the night Stoney was murdered. *He just lied. He knows damn well that he was there that night. He was there to kill my mom*, she thought. Tears flowed down her face. They were uncontrollable. She remembered sitting on the corner with Brandi, waiting to see what man was going to enter her apartment. *He was the one my mom was waiting for. That's why we never saw anyone approach the apartment because he was standing next to us the entire time.*

The blaring horn snapped Reign out of the mental abyss she was falling into. Her vehicle had crossed over the double yellow lines, and she was now headed into oncoming traffic. She pulled the wheel to the right, maneuvering back into her travel lane. More horns blared at her reckless driving. Reign headed towards Columbia Pike when red and blue emergency lights flashed in her rearview mirror. The siren was next to grab her attention.

Reign slowly pulled over to the side of the road. Tears were still falling from her face. She quickly tried to wipe them away, but it was no use. They continued like waterfalls from her eyes. She rolled down her window after hearing a hard knock at it.

"Can I see your license, insurance, and registration?"

Reign did her best to gather herself and get the documents for the officer. Her hands shook as she reached into her glove compartment and then to her purse. She wasn't even sure how she was able to focus enough to get the documents. Her hands continued shaking as he handed them over to the officer.

"Do you know why I stopped you, ma'am?"

Reign looked over at the officer and nodded her head.

"Oh my God, what's wrong?" The officer asked, noticing Reign's emotions.

"Nothing," Reign muttered sorrowfully.

"There is definitely something wrong with you. It's okay. You can tell me."

"It's... nothing."

"Is it Slim?"

Hearing that name felt like a stab to the heart. Reign looked up at the officer, wondering why they mentioned that name to her. Raven stood at the side of the car, watching the traffic that was flying by her. "Why did you say that?" Reign asked.

"Say what? Slim? You know why."

"I don't know what you're talking about."

"Let's get off this street. Pull in that lot over there," Raven instructed, before walking back to her vehicle.

Reign did not even have a chance to respond. She wanted to ask why she was being asked to move off the roadway, but Raven had already cut her emergency lights off and pulled into the parking lot of a shopping center. Reign thought about just pulling off and going about her day, but she remembered that she handed over her documentation and never got it back. Instinctively, she wanted to call Omari and let him know what was going on, but she refrained from doing so. He was the last person she wanted to talk to.

"What are you doing?" Reign asked, as she pulled behind Raven and hopped out of her vehicle.

"We need to get out of here. Get in my car."

"What? Are you crazy? I'm not getting in your car. You got five seconds to give me my license and stuff back before I call my lawyer."

"Listen Reign, it's not going to be long until those officers leave your house, and he comes looking for you."

"What are you talking 'bout?"

Raven chuckled. "How many people do you think drive a Ferrari around here? I guess you were too distracted to see the officers sitting at the top of your block when you left the house. They're looking for your boyfriend."

"I still don't know what you're talking about."

"You know what I'm talking about. So, you can either get in this car voluntarily or I can place you under arrest for Slim's murder."

"I don't know what you're talking about. I don't know nobody named Slim and I definitely don't know nothin' about a murder. Just give me my shit back."

"Don't do this to yourself, Reign. I know you were there. I have several witnesses from the alley that say you were there when Slim got shot. Now I come here and see you in tears. That's more than enough to bring you in. If I do that, all bets are off, and I can't help you."

Reign could tell that Raven was not bluffing. A part of her wanted to keep giving the officer the run-around, the other part of her felt like the officer was right and Omari would be pulling up any second looking for her. "What do you want from me?"

"I just want you to be safe."

Reign entered the car and Raven took off. After about a 10-minute silent ride, Raven pulled into Centennial Park. "What are we doing here?" Reign asked.

"You don't remember me, do you?" Raven followed up, ignoring Reign's question.

"I don't know you, so how would I remember you?"

"I was there when your mom was murdered. You were just a teen then, but I was the officer that gave you..."

"The hot chocolate," Reign added. She could not believe that she was looking at the only officer that comforted her on that tragic day. She was never able to get Raven's name that night before Child Protective Services came and scooped her up. It was unbelievable that she was looking at Raven. Reign never forgot her because she always remembered how young Raven looked. Just seven years older than her, Raven was in her early 20s when Stoney was murdered. "How did you find me?"

"I never stopped looking for you or Slim. Your mom's murder always stuck with me because it seemed so odd. But with Slim in the wind, we never got a chance to find out what really happened that night.

That was up until we found Slim over in Cherry Hill last week."

Reign looked out the window, as more tears began to fall. "Do you know that for years, I had nightmares about that man?" She muttered.

"I can imagine you would."

"Once the police posted his picture on the news as a person of interest, I just knew he was the one that killed my mom. I hated him before she was killed, so seeing his face on the news just validated my hatred."

"Who killed him, Reign?"

"I don't know."

"You were there though."

Reign shook her head. "I wasn't."

"You remember the little girl from the alley? Aliya?" Reign snapped a look at Raven. "She said you looked like a princess." Reign smiled at the compliment from her new little friend. "She also said that a man took the princess away after Slim got shot." Reign's smile quickly faded.

"I don't' know what that girl is talking about. I wasn't anywhere"

"Listen Reign, I don't work for homicide and I'm not going to go telling them what I know, but it's only a matter of time before they find out about you. They are already looking to question Omari and you'll be next. I'm sure Aliya wasn't the only one to see the princess in the alley that day. Just being there allows you to be charged as an accessory to the murder. I don't want to see that happen to you. Not after all you've been through."

"It sounds like I need to contact my attorney."

"Don't do this, Reign. It's not worth it. Whoever you're trying to protect isn't worth it."

"I'm not protecting anybody. Can you give me my shit back and take me back to my car now?"

"You can have your stuff back, but I'm not taking you back there. By the way, your phone keeps vibrating, I'm sure he's already at your car or the officers are. Is there anywhere else I can take you?"

"No. I'll just get an Uber," Reign barked, opening the door.

"Wait. Take my card." Raven extended her arm, passing her business card to Reign. "Don't hesitate to call me."

Reign headed towards Centennial Lake. She could not even wrap her brain around the emotional roller coaster she was on. Between Slim's death, Omari's betrayal, and now a blast from the past, she needed a quick escape. She wanted to ask Raven about Aliya and how she was doing, but she did not want to incriminate herself in any way.

Raven watched Reign walk away. Once she was out of her view, she hopped on the phone.

"You know, one day I'm just not going to answer it?" Sharon answered.

"And that would be the day that I quit, because you know I can't do this job without you."

"Sure, you will. What do you need?"

"I need a full work-up on someone."

"You still working that cold case that you're not supposed to be working on?"

"Yup. I just ran into the girl. She isn't giving up the shooter. But I did notice that her car is registered to someone named Omari Washington. I want to know everything about him."

"Copy. I'll send you everything I find."

"Thanks. You're a lifesaver."

"I know I am. Are you coming back to the office?"

"Not yet. I need to make a stop first."

"Don't do it."

"Don't do what?"

"Don't step on their toes."

"Who? Homicide? They'll be fine. Plus, any information that I get will go straight to them. So basically, I'm doing them a favor."

"You know damn well they aren't going to see it that way."

"I can't help what they see. All I can do is help solve these murders and I have a feeling I'm headed in the right direction."

CHAPTER 19

This film is so good, Brandi thought as her eyes were glued to the television. Dasia recommended the short film *Vengeance* which she pulled up on Amazon Prime. She stuffed her face with microwave popcorn. Brandi had a few minutes to kill before she was meeting up with Dasia for lunch. The hard knock at the door grabbed her attention away from the film. Brandi grabbed the remote and paused the film before getting up to answer the door. There was another knock.

"Hold on. Damn. I'm coming," she announced.

Brandi answered the door and was surprised to see the person that was standing in the hallway.

"Where is she?" Omari asked as he barged into the apartment.

Two other men followed him in. Brandi tried blocking the doorway, but they pushed her aside.

"Hold the fuck up. What are yall doing?"

"Where your friend at?"

"I should be asking you that. I haven't heard from her in a week."

"I don't believe you!" Omari barked, getting in Brandi's face.

"You don't gotta believe me, nigga. I said I don't know where she at. Now, get the fuck outta my apartment."

Omari turned to the men that came with him. "Flip this shit and see if she in here."

The men wasted no time following the order. They began tossing things around, looking for Reign.

"What the fuck are yall doing? I said she ain't here."

"Well, if she ain't here then tell me where the fuck she at?"

"Even if I did know, I ain't telling your dumbass shit."

Omari grabbed Brandi by the neck and pushed her up against the wall. "You think I'm fuckin' playin' with you. You got five seconds to tell me where she at." Brandi could barely breathe, let alone speak. She tried her best to escape his grip, but she couldn't match his strength. Omari was hellbent on hurting someone and Brandi was in his grasp. "I wanna know why the fuckin' cops was just at my house? So, when you see your fuckin' friend, tell her I need some answers."

"I found a phone, boss," one of the men said.

"Look through that shit and see if it's any messages or calls from Reign in there."

All Omari wanted to know was if Brandi was lying to him because he was ready to snap her neck. She continued her attempts to break free but was unsuccessful. Omari waited patiently as his henchman scrolled through Brandi's phone.

"Naw it ain't nothin' in here. Looks like she sent a bunch of messages but it ain't no response to them."

"Yo, what the fuck is going on in here?" Everyone in the apartment turned to the doorway. "Get the fuck off her!" Darryl barked.

Omari loosened his grip when he saw the man pointing the Draco at him. Ironically, that was the name the hood gave him because he was so fond of the tool. A red bandana was wrapped around the assault rifle, keeping the clip snug inside the weapon. His brother, Darren, had a shotgun aimed at Omari's head. Dasia stood behind her brothers with a little Ruger .380 tucked in her purse.

Omari freed Brandi and she ran over to Dasia. Her eyes were bloodshot from the pressure that Omari had on her throat. His men were strapped, but they knew if they reached for their pistols, it would be a blood bath in the apartment.

"Just calm down, my man. This is all just a big misunderstanding. I was just having a little discussion with Brandi," Omari exclaimed.

"Fuck all that shit you talkin' bout," Darryl said, as his grip tightened on his weapon. "Give me one reason I shouldn't air yo' asses out right now."

"Cuz you know who I am."

"That shit don't mean nothin' to me, blood."

"It should. I can make you a lot of money." Omari removed a wad of cash from his pocket and dropped it on the floor."

Darryl smirked. "So, your life is only worth a couple racks?"

"There's more where that came from. I can make you a rich man."

"And I can make you a dead one," Darryl said, stepping into the apartment. "All that shit you talkin' don't hold no weight. That lil' ass bit of money you just threw down; that's Brandi's money now. That will pay for all the damage you niggas just caused. As for us, don't ever come near her again. She's like family and you'll die if you fuck wit' my family."

"Understood."

Omari knew when to pick his battles. He put in his fair share of work in the streets, but he wasn't prepared to go to war. Especially, against the red flag. He didn't have the manpower to stand up to them. He had long standing agreement on territory each of the organizations would control, but they never had any gripes before this one. He didn't know Brandi was connected. He gave his men a nod and exited the apartment. Darryl kept his gun trained on them until they were out of sight.

"Give me that damn shotty," Darryl said, snatching the shotgun away from Darren. He laughed. "What the fuck was you gon' do wit' this?"

"I was going to put a hole in somebody," Darren joked.

"No the hell you weren't," Dasia chimed in.

"Right," Darryl added. "Mr. Save the World was acting like he was ready to catch a body. And the damn safety was still on."

The siblings all laughed. Although Darryl was more known for sports, he still built up his street cred once he realized he wasn't going to the NBA. He went back and forth with his aspirations to go pro but eventually, he had to let that NBA dream go. Darryl continued working and spent a few years overseas, which made him some good money. He took that money and put it back into the streets and also gave Darren some investment cash to start a non-profit organization that would benefit the people in the city that had been plagued by poverty. Darren opened up a shelter and was working towards a recreation center. He wanted to also build a rehabilitation center, but with his brother's crew being contributing factors to the city's drug issue, he thought the move would be hypocritical.

Darren was far removed from the streets, which is why his siblings laughed at the thought of him even using the shotgun. He knew his intentions were good and didn't mind protecting himself and his loved ones, but truthfully, he had no experience with guns which is why the shotgun wasn't loaded and was on safety. Out of all three siblings, he was the last one anyone expected to come in a building with guns blazing.

"Don't pay them no mind, Darren. I appreciate what you did," Brandi said.

"Thank you," Darren replied.

Dasia checked the hallway one last time and closed the door. "What the hell was that about?" she asked.

"Reign."

Hearing that name brought back so many memories for Darren. He had the biggest crush on Reign growing up, but never pursued her. When they were teens, he was timid and after years of her not being around, he just put those feelings in the back of his mind. Between him traveling with his brother and getting his organization together, he had no time to truly focus on building a relationship with any woman. However, hearing her name made those feelings work their way back.

"Wait. Reign sent those niggas over here?" Dasia asked, as she ran cold water on a rag and handed it to Brandi.

"Naw. That's her dumbass boyfriend. He came over here looking for her. I told his ass she wasn't here, but they still tore my shit up."

"Where the fuck she at?"

"I don't know. I haven't spoken to her in like a week. This ain't like her."

"You think something happened to her?"

"I doubt it. As crazy as that nigga is, ain't no way he letting anyone do anything to her," she said, picking up her phone that had been dropped on the ground. "Let me text her and warn her that he's looking for her."

"If she needs some help, let me know," Darryl muttered.

"What if I need some help?" Brandi asked softly, smiling at Darryl.

"Then I got you."

Brandi and Darryl shared history. Although they never made anything official, they often linked up with each other when he was in town. All of those nights listening through the walls of him in action made her curious and when she got the opportunity, she shot her shot. Brandi never wanted anything serious with Darryl but she did demand consistency from him. She always told him that she wasn't going to be a girl he could just hit and quit. She never wanted to ruin their friendship over the lust they had for each other. Seeing him made her forget all about the encounter with Omari. Her knight in shining armor was here to save her and he was armed with a Draco.

"So, are we still going out or do we need to give you two some time alone?" Dasia interrupted.

"Naw, yall gon' still go out. I don't want her in here, just in case those nut ass niggas come back. I gotta make some phone calls and set some shit up. I see if some of my people can slide up here to keep an eye on things."

"Oh, you don't have to do that," Brandi told him.

"Don't worry about it. I'm gon' make sure you safe."

Hearing those words sent a chill down Brandi's spine. She bit her lip and smiled at Darryl. A fire was burning inside of her that made her forget all about the nonsense she had just gone through. "Okay, I'm going to go get dressed. I'll text Reign again. I'll send her the address and maybe she'll meet us there."

"Here, take this back to the car," Darryl said as he handed the shotgun back to his brother. "Dasia, make sure he don't hurt himself with that thing."

Dasia gave Darryl a suspicious look and he gave her a sly grin back. Brandi had gone into her bedroom to change and he took that opportunity to raid her fridge. *Damn. It ain't shit in here*, he thought as he rummaged through the shelves and drawers. He grabbed a water and took it to the head. He knocked on Brandi's bedroom door. "Yo, you got some snacks in here?"

She slowly opened the door. "Yeah, right here."

Darryl rose to the occasion, as he laid his eyes on Brandi's thick, curvy body. She was wearing nothing but a bra. The clothes she was wearing were in a small pile next to her bed, along with her panties.

"You was supposed to be in here getting changed. Why you naked?"

"Cuz I saw the way you was looking at me. I knew you would come knocking eventually. So, you just gon' stand there or you gon' come get this snack?"

Darryl dropped his gun on the floor and grabbed Brandi. He lifted all 190 pounds of her in the air and began kissing on her cleavage. Darryl was like an animal and Brandi loved it. He had a thin basketball frame but his athleticism on the court showed off in the bedroom too. Brandi was very familiar with Darryl's unexpected strength. He slammed her on the soft bed and ripped off his shirt. Brandi used her index finger to signal him over to her. It only took him a second to drop his pants, exposing his long dick. He was beginning to stiffen up but wasted no time grabbing his piece and pushing it inside of Brandi's warm, juicy pussy. She moaned loudly as he entered her.

Darryl kissed her neck, while he fondled her breasts. Her hard nipples poked through the lace bra, begging for Darryl to pinch each of them. Brandi could feel Darryl growing inside of her. While he kissed her neck, she allowed her long tongue to slide up and down his ear. Darryl began stroking as she felt him getting longer and harder. Brandi dug her nails into his back and allowed her hands to slide down his back until she reached his bare ass. Brandi grabbed onto Darryl and pulled him into her. With each stroke, she continued assisting him deeper into her love box. Darryl whispered into her ear. "You missed me?"

Brandi didn't know if it was the question he asked or his warm breath on her lobe, but she could only moan a response. Goosebumps formed on her skin. Brandi kept pulling Darryl in close on his strokes, as he slowly pushed her legs back. "Oh, fuck yeah. Fuck me, Draco." He followed orders and increased the intensity of his strokes. "Harder," Brandi ordered. "Harder." Brandi filled with excitement as she panted and moaned loudly. She knew exactly what Darryl was good at and he was hitting all the right spots.

He was pounding hard. The sound of their skin smacking against each other sounded like someone was clapping their hands. Darryl squeezed on Brandi's large breasts with one hand and slid his other hand down. As he stoked, he allowed his thumb to circle her clit.

"Fuck!" Brandi yelled out as she felt a hard orgasm coming along. She tried pushing Darryl's hands away, but it was too late. He had already accomplished his goal. Brandi stared at the ceiling as she released all over his long dick. She flinched as he continued stroking her sensitive pussy. His pounding strokes began getting slower. "You 'bout to cum?"

Darryl nodded and pulled out of Brandi. He began stroking his dick, aiming the tip at her clit. Brandi took two fingers and began massaging her throbbing love button. She stared at Darryl as his eyes began to roll back. "Here it comes," he announced, as he shot his load onto her pussy. It was warm and thick. Brandi rubbed on her cum soaked pussy as Darryl admired freakiness. He was still hard and wanted another round with Brandi, but he knew it would have to wait. They had plans and if they took any longer, Darren and Dasia would be coming back up to check on them. The pinging sound from Brandi's phone caught both of their attention. She wiped her hand on her sheets then grabbed the phone.

"It's Reign."

"What she say?"

"She said she can't make lunch but she's going to meet here after where done."

"Well, that's good. At least she hit you back."

"Right. Now, let me get dressed for real this time because you know how your sister gets when she gets hungry."

"Yup. I'll go stall them," Darryl said, just before pulling up his pants and grabbing his shirt off the ground. "I'll be out here if you need me." He exited the room and closed the door behind him. That second round would have to wait until later.

CHAPTER 20

How is she doing?" Raven asked as she entered the room that Anna was recovering in. The hospital placed her in a room alongside another patient. This did not give Anna and Aliya much privacy, but they did not mind the company. The other patient was a gunshot victim that was hit by a stray bullet during a robbery. The bullet traveled in and out of her right thigh, barely missing the femoral artery. Visiting hours were over, but Raven flashed her badge to get access.

"She's okay," Aliya responded as she peeled her eyes away from the television.

"What are you watching?"

"PJ Masks."

"Oh, I've heard of that show. Do you like it?."

Aliya nodded her head.

"Can I talk to you for a second?" Raven asked, waving the young girl into the hallway. Aliya turned off the television and stepped into the hallway with Raven. "Do you want something from the vending machine?"

"Can I get candy?"

"You can get whatever you want."

"Yay!"

"We'll be right back. I'm going to take her to get a snack," Raven informed one of the nurses.

The two headed over to the visitor waiting room. Raven was shocked when she saw Aliya. The young girl looked totally different. She had showered and washed her hair. The hospital staff gave her new clothes to wear too. It was a complete transformation. "You look so pretty."

"Thank you. I like it here."

"Is everyone being nice to you?"

"Yup. They gave me food and they let me watch tv all day."

"Good. If anyone messes with you, I'll lock them up," Raven said while laughing.

Aliya laughed too. "Did you find her?"

"Did I find who?"

"The princess. You said you were going to help her."

"Oh, yes I did. She asked about you too."

"She did?"

"Yes, she did. I told her that you were fine."

"I want to go see her."

"I'll try to make that happen for you," Raven replied. "So, what kind of snack do you want?"

"Ummm. Can I have those?" Aliya asked, pointing to a pack of Skittles.

"You sure can." Raven purchased two packs and handed them to Aliya.

"I have to ask you a question."

"Okay," Aliya replied as she ripped open a pack of Skittles and tossed a handful in her mouth.

"Remember the man that took the princess? Do you remember what he looked like?" Aliya shook her head. Although she saw what happened in the alley, she was not close enough to see the shooter's face. Raven took out her phone and pulled up a picture to show Aliya. "Does this guy look familiar?"

"No."

Raven dropped her head, disappointed at the response she received. She was sure that Aliya would be able to identify Omari and she would be able to pass the information on to homicide. Instead, she was back at square one, wondering who killed Slim. *I wonder who else Reign is connected to*, she thought. "Okay, let's head back to your room."

Raven scrolled through her phone as they headed back to the room. She flipped through the biographical information sheets that were sent to her for Omari. There were almost 10 pages of known associates listed for him, along with multiple gang affiliations. *There is no way that I'm going to get through all of this tonight.*

"What the fuck are you doing?" Anna asked angrily, as she sat up in the bed. "You came back here to finish interrogating my daughter? She told me that your dumb ass was asking her a bunch of questions and shit. I told your ass that we don't know shit, so get the fuck out of here."

"It's not like that. We just went over to the vending machine to grab a couple snacks. That's all."

"Bullshit!" Anna barked. "Baby, did this lady ask you any questions?"

Aliya nodded her head. "She asked me about the man that took the princess."

"Nurse! Nurse!" Ann screamed. She was furious. "Nurse! Nurse!"

A few of the nurses ran into the room to see what the emergency was. "Is everything okay?" one of them asked as she checked Anna's vitals on the monitor.

"No, everything is not okay. This fuckin' cop keeps harassing my daughter. I want her out of here."

"What's going on?" The nurse asked Raven.

"Nothing is going on. I just took her to get a snack from the vending machine."

"And she was questioning my daughter, without my permission," Anna added.

"Is this true?" The nurse asked.

"No, it's not true, Raven replied.

"Well, it's clear that the patient does not feel comfortable with you here. So, unless, she is under arrest, I'm going to have to ask you to leave."

"That's not a problem," Raven responded.

Inside she was disappointed in Anna's decision to call her out. All Raven wanted to do was gather information to assist in the investigation. She did not appreciate being portrayed in a bad light. She waved goodbye to Aliya and made a hasty exit. The ride home for Raven was a sorrow one. She was no closer to solving Slim's murder and she just crossed the line with Anna and Aliya. Raven knew that if Anna made a formal complaint with the police department, this would surely get her suspended. Not only was she violating the department juvenile policy by speaking to Aliya without her mother present, but she was technically interfering with the Homicide Unit's investigation. That would get her at least a 30-day suspension. As much as Raven wanted to avoid any disciplinary issues at work, she truly felt that she was doing a good deed by trying to assist in this case. It was going to break her if she did not put forth some effort in finding some answers.

Raven headed over to a diner on W Lombard Street. This was her go-to spot when she needed comfort food to take her away from the stresses of work. Currently, she was stressed out enough to need four full-course meals. This was nothing that an order of chicken and waffles and a medium coffee with cream and sugar would not solve. Raven could literally taste the syrup on her lips, and she had not even pulled up to the location yet. Once she got there, she was greeted by Ms. Bev, who was an elderly black woman with silver streaks of curly hair that covered her head. She was about 5-foot-3 and only about 130 pounds soaking wet. Ms. Bev reminded Raven of her Aunt Mabel. Her Aunt Mabel was from the south and she ensured that everyone around her displayed that southern hospitality. Even her family was from Baltimore. Ms.

Bev was the same way. She gave respect and she also demanded it.

"Well hello, sugar," Ms. Bev greeted Raven with a smile. "Why are you looking so blue in the face?"

"Hello, Ms. Bev. It's been a long day at work and I'm just ready to eat and go to bed."

"Oh, sorry to hear that. Well, your favorite seat is available. Hopefully, that is some good news that can drown out all of the bad from today."

Raven smiled. "Yes, that is some good news." She followed Ms. Bev to a corner booth, that allowed Raven to have a view of the entire diner with no one sitting behind her. Just like a typical cop, she never wanted to sit with her back towards the entrances or exits. She needed to see everything that was going on inside any establishment that she frequented. The last thing she needed was to get ambushed or become a victim of a robbery if someone decided to come in and stick up the place.

"Do you want your usual?"

"Yes, please."

"Okay, perfect. I'll bring you out some tea while they start frying the chicken."

"Oh, I was thinking about ordering a coffee."

"Now, honey, you came in here and said you wanted to get something to eat and then go to bed. That coffee will keep you up all night. I'm going to bring you some new tea we just got in. Everyone loves it. It's supposed to get you relaxed and that's just what you need."

"Yes ma'am," Raven responded. *Just like Aunt Mabel*, she thought. Ms. Bev was like that family member that you hated and loved. The one that told you what you needed to hear, rather than what you wanted to hear. Raven appreciated that.

Ms. Bev headed to the back to get the tea. Raven scanned the diner, checking to see if she recognized anyone. She was never off-duty. Raven loved her job and took her responsibilities as a police officer seriously. She never wanted to get complacent, even if that meant while she was enjoying a meal at one of her favorite spots. Little did she know, this type of fire that burned inside of officers doesn't go out. The fire just gets fueled and at some point, it consumes you. She had not gotten to that point in her life yet, but the actions she was taking were leading her down that path. There was no way for her to balance life outside of her career because she never turned the switch off. She was always working, no matter where she was. Scanning faces that were around her, looking at people's expressions to make sure they looked safe, checking e-mails and text messages from colleagues no matter what time of the day or night it was. There was never a time when she was not in cop-mode.

Raven opened her phone and scrolled through a few new messages from Sharon. A new case came in about a teenage girl that was reporting she was sexually assaulted in a parking garage. One of the veteran detectives was assigned to the case, but Sharon shared the information with Raven, hoping to get her focus off

Slim's murder. Sharon's plan worked and Raven was not scouring through old emails to see if they had any similar cases in the past 90 days.

"Here's your tea, honey," Ms. Bev said, placing the steaming cup on the table.

"Thank you, so much."

"Your food will be out shortly. If you need anything else, I'll be right over there at the counter."

"Thank you, ma'am." Raven dove right back into her emails, allowing the tea to cool off a bit before she began sipping on it. *I could have sworn we had a case that occurred in a parking garage back in February,* she thought as she continued her search. Raven never gave up. She was persistent and that was the same characteristic that made her an outstanding investigator.

"Chicken and waffles," a young waiter said, as he approached the table.

"Yes, that's mine," Raven responded.

The young man slid the first plate on the table. Raven took one look at the fried chicken wings and just knew coming to the diner was a good decision. Then he slid the plate with the Belgium waffles next to the wings. Fresh strawberries and powdered sugar decorated the waffles. Food was one of the only things that could get Raven to put her phone down. This particular meal was her favorite because she grew up on it. Every Sunday morning, she put in this exact request with her mother. Raven had the best of both worlds. Her mother was African American and her father was Puerto Rican. One thing her family did was eat well. The combination of both cultures under their roof was an amazing experience growing up. Her mother and father constantly battled in the kitchen, to see who could win over the praise from Raven and her siblings. Raven's mother won her over when she introduced her to chicken and waffles.

Raven took one of the chicken wings and placed it on top of one of the waffles. She then drizzled the thick, warm maple syrup on top of the wing and waffle. Raven felt instant joy at that moment. It was like she was back home on a Sunday morning with her family. She wasted no time holding the waffle and chicken wing combo up and biting into it. The sweet and savory flavors sent her eyes rolling into the back of her head. Raven followed up with another bite before being disrupted by the ringing of her phone.

Raven looked at her phone and the unknown number that was calling. "Hello?" She answered.

"Officer Ramos," the soft voice said.

"Yes. Who is this?"

"It's Reign. Reign Bryant."

Raven was not expecting that name to be said. She dropped her food and quickly wiped her mouth. "Reign, what's going on? Is everything okay?"

"He did it."

"Who did what?"

"Omari. He killed Slim in the alley."

It was like everything was moving in slow motion. Raven took the phone away from her ear and looked at the screen. She was in disbelief. *This can't be here*, she thought. Her last interaction with Reign did not go over too well, so she was skeptical about the random phone call. "Do you understand what you're saying to me?"

"Yes."

"Listen, Reign. I appreciate you calling me but I'm going to have to get the Homicide Unit involved. You are going to have to tell them everything you know. Can I patch them into this call?"

"Yes."

CHAPTER 21

All was quiet in Ellicott City. The cool night breeze blew through the air. As the clock struck midnight, the suburb had a peaceful silence to it. Omari had just come in the house about an hour ago but was now sound asleep. He was out all night looking for Reign. After the fiasco at Brandi's apartment, Omari did not know where Reign ran off to. A part of him wanted to go back to Brandi to get more answers but he didn't know if Darryl was still around. He spent the entire day driving around trying to find Reign but had no luck. There were not many places that she frequented, so he did not know exactly where to look. Brandi was the only friend that Reign communicated with daily, and Omari already checked that spot off the list.

The ride from West Baltimore back to Ellicott City allowed Omari to clear his head. He wanted to clear the air between him and Reign, but he did not know how to do it. He still wasn't sure if she was the one that called the cops on him. It was difficult to understand the pain and betrayal she felt when Slim told her the secret. It was hard to believe after all these years, Omari could never find the courage to tell her the truth. Although he committed the act, he never intended to harm Stoney. He was only after Slim. He waited patiently for Slim that night, but Slim never walked in the front door of the apartment building. Slim crept through the back to avoid detection. Omari knew Stoney had a relationship with Slim and figured he would ask her about his whereabouts. Unfortunately, Stoney was protecting Slim and lied to Omari. When Omari forced his way into her apartment, he spotted Slim hiding inside. He confronted Slim about the drugs he stole from him and pulled out a gun when Slim denied involvement in the theft. Stoney got in between both men when Omari fired his shots. The shots that killed Stoney were meant for Slim. Once Stoney dropped, Omari chased after Slim, trying to finish what he started. He fired more shots at Slim but only wounded him. Once Slim disappeared, Omari figured he had died.

Omari struggled with the fact that he killed an innocent woman. That guilt drove him to do everything in his power to support Reign. His plan to support her turned into love. If it were not for Slim, popping up in that alley, Reign would not have known the truth and the two would not be going through their current issues. Unfortunately, Slim revealed Omari's secret, and now he was sound asleep in preparation for another day of searching for Reign.

The front door exploded open. Omari popped up. His bedroom windows shattered as metal canisters were propelled through them. CS gas seeped out of the canisters and filled the bedroom. Omari was violently coughing as he tried his best not to breathe in the chemical agent. His eyes began burning and his vision began to blur. He did not know who had launched an attack on him, but he was prepared to defend himself. Omari rolled out of the bed and blindly crawled towards the nightstand. His pistol was inside of the nightstand, and he desperately wanted to get his hands on it. It was brutal trying to crawl through the gas. Omari's eyes felt like they were on fire, and like he was coughing up a lung. Another canister was launched into the bedroom, preventing the air from clearing.

Omari couldn't stay on his mission to get to the nightstand. His knowledge of the bedroom had faded at that moment. His priority became getting some fresh air. Omari crawled over to the wall and followed alongside it until he reached the bedroom door. Another canister flew through one of the windows and hit the wall. Omari pushed the bedroom door open and crawled out to the hallway. The air was clear outside of the bedroom, but Omari was still having difficulty breathing.

"POLICE!"

"DON'T MOVE!"

"GET ON THE FUCKIN' GROUND!"

"POLICE!"

"CONTACT, CONTACT, CONTACT!"

"POLICE. DON'T FUCKIN' MOVE!"

Omari was bombarded by commands and physical force. SWAT officers bum-rushed him while he was crawling out of the bedroom. He couldn't see due to the tear gas filling his room and only felt a large amount of weight being driven into his back. "Get the fuck off me!" Omari said as he pulled his arm away from one of the officers that were grabbing it.

"STOP RESISTING!" One of the officers yelled out as he drove his knee into the middle of Omari's back.

He was sure to intentionally press all of his 230 pounds into Omari. Omari shrieked in pain. Between the officer that was on his back and the others that were pinning him down, Omari had almost 1000 pounds on his back.

"Get the fuck off me!" He repeated, doing his best to resist the officers' control holds.

Omari's efforts were ineffective. The ratcheting of the handcuffs against his wrists were uncomfortable. He yelled out as the officers were putting them on and when they were wrenching his arm behind his back. Omari was pulled off the ground and violently escorted downstairs. He still had his eye closed, hoping that the burning sensation would stop. "Omari Washington, you are under arrest for the murder of Sean Nichols." Omari could not believe what he was hearing. Although he did not recognize Slim's government name, he knew what the word murder meant. "You have the right to remain silent. Anything you say, can and will be used in a court of law. You have a right to an attorney. If you cannot afford an attorney, one will be appointed to you."

It did not take Omari long to put two and two together. He knew this arrest had to be about Slim because that was the only action he had seen in a while. As a boss, he sat back for years and let his crews handle business. The one time, he decided to take matters into his own hands and ends up getting him drug out of his home in handcuffs. Neighbors were glued to their windows, watching everything unfold.

Not only did the officers have an arrest warrant for Omari, but they also had a search warrant for his home. The warrant specifically permitted the officers to search anywhere a possible firearm could be stashed. Officers had a field day with Omari's residence. They wrecked everything they could in the home. Every door was knocked off the hinges. Cabinets and drawers were ripped open and searched. Some of the officers that were searching had knocked holes into the walls, in search of guns and drugs that may have been hidden behind the drywall. Although the arrest warrant was in relation to a murder, it didn't stop the officers from acting on their intuition from the criminal intelligence worksheets they pulled on Omari. They saw all the run-ins he had and figured there had to be some stashed in the home. Their suspicions led them in the right direction when they entered one of the guest bedrooms of the home. The officers tore that room apart too, flipping the bed in the process. When one of the officers flipped the mattress, he felt something odd. The mattress felt heavy. Cash and kilos of cocaine lined the thin mattress and the officer knew he hit the jackpot, after slicing the mattress open.

Omari's eyes still burned from the tear gas, but the sound of cheers and chatter left him defeated. He knew what was stashed in his home and now he had to mentally prepare to face the consequences.

"Take his ass to the station and get him cleaned up," the sergeant ordered.

"Yes, sir," the officers responded as they gripped Omari by his arms and guided him outside the home and into the back of one of the patrol cars. The rigid plastic seat provided no type of comfort for the prisoner. The officers did not even bother putting a seatbelt on Omari. He bounced around the back of the car, during the sketchy ride back to the district. He kept his eyes shut the entire ride, but he could hear the vehicle accelerate just before he bounced off the back of the seat. Then he crashed against the car's cage when the driver intentionally slammed on the brakes. The ride to the station was rough, to say the least. With his hands cuffed tightly behind and unable to see, Omari could not brace for the impacts. By the time the ride was done, there was pain shooting through his entire body. It had been years since Omari had a run-in with the police. Those days were done when he stopped slinging on the corners. Once he became a boss and moved out of the hood, he was out of the reach of the Baltimore Police Department. He had a few routine encounters with the Maryland State Police, but it was all related to traffic violations and it was nothing he could not handle.

Once they got to the station, the officers yanked Omari out of the back of the patrol car. "What the fuck was all of that about?" Omari asked.

"Shut up," one of the officers responded.

"Oh, you real tough with a man that's cuffed behind his back. If I wasn't in these, you wouldn't be doing this shit."

"You're lucky that Homicide wants you or we'd be taking another ride."

"Yeah, whatever pussy. Ain't nobody scared of you fuckin' pigs. You doing all this nut shit for what? You trynna make up for all of those years you got bullied in high school or something?"

"It seems like you're the one that's trying to make up for something. Are you mad because you're about to go to jail for life?" The officer replied while laughing.

"Fuck you!" Omari barked.

"Tilt your head back," a soft female voice ordered.

Omari initially hesitated, but then follow directions. He leaned his head back and immediately felt a cold liquid being poured over his face and eyes. The liquid ran off his face and down his back and chest. It provided a cooling sensation to the lingering burn from the tear gas. Omari slowly opened his eyes, allowing his blurry vision to clear up. Once it did, he was face to face with Raven. The cat had his tongue when he saw the officer that assisted him.

"Does it still burn?" She asked.

"Naw. I'm cool now. Where did those officers go that brought me here?"

"They are in the car over there," Raven said while pointing to the Ford Taurus slowly pulling away. Omari had some choice words for those officers, but he had to show great restraint because they were not even close enough to hear him yell. "Let's go," Raven instructed. She escorted him inside of the building and back to a small interview room.

"I'm going to let you know now that you're wasting your time bringing me in here. I don't got shit to say," he said as he sat in one of three chairs in the room.

Raven did not respond to his statement. She removed the handcuffs from his wrists and exited the room. Omari heard the lock being secured on the other side of the door. He smirked. *Where the fuck do she think I'm gonna go?* He slouched in the chair, getting comfortable. The hard chair he was sitting in was much more comfortable than having his hands bound behind his back, with a face full of the residue from the tear gas and rolling around on the hard plastic seat in the back of the patrol car. Omari was sturdy. Being in the interrogation room didn't faze him at all. It was not the first time he sat in one of these rooms and he knew that it would not be his last. He was more upset about the officers and the raid that was conducted at his home. Omari wanted revenge and he was going to get it.

"What do you think is going through his mind right now?" Detective Allen asked as he watched Omari through the two-way mirror, along with his partner and supervisor. A smile was plastered on his face.

"I can't tell. It looks like he's making himself at home," Raven replied.

"That's all a front. I know his type. He wants to act all though while he's in here, but deep down inside he is feeling it. When you come down here, you know you are in some deep shit. It's not like being questioned by regular detectives, you know that. I'm sure the SVU suspects feel the same way. They know they're done."

Raven nodded. Detective Allen made a point. She knew first-hand how suspects crumble under the pressure of major criminal offenses. Every time she stepped foot in an SVU interrogation room, suspects were either already in tears or confessing to the crimes before she could ask them her first question. Raven was hoping that Omari crumbled the same way.

"Okay, let's get this over with," Detective Allen stated. "Anyone want to bet on how long it takes him to confess?"

"I say less than 30 minutes," Detective Patrick Harris blurted out. The young detective did and said anything to stay get on the good side of his partner. He spent his shifts sucking up to Detective Allen. Most called him a kiss-ass, but Detective Harris did not care. He was only twenty-five years old and was very green as a detective. After graduating from the police academy at 21-years old, he didn't do much as a patrol officer. He rode the coattails of his father, Thomas

Harris, who happened to be a Sergeant in the Homicide Unit.

"Thirty minutes? You have a lot of faith in your partner," Sergeant Harris said. He stepped forward and placed his hand on Detective Allen's shoulder. "I think he's going to make you earn it. I'll say it will take you two hours to get it and I'll put a hundred dollars on that."

"Two hours? Damn Sarge, you don't have faith in me?" Detective Allen laughed. "Now, I'm going to make sure I get it in less than an hour." He turned to make it to the mirror and glared at Omari. "What about you Raven? How long do you think it's going to take me?"

Raven looked over at Detective Allen. "Sorry to say this, but I don't he's going to give it up." Her response was not a dig at the detective, but more so because of Omari's energy when she placed him in the room. He already told her that bringing him into the room was a waste of time and she believed him.

"Wow. You don't have faith in me?" Detective Allen said while laughing. He grabbed a box from the table and headed out. "Come on rook, let's get this done."

Omari watched as the detectives entered the interrogation room. He had the look of a mad man in his eyes. This was a look that Detective Allen had seen hundreds of times, but this was a new experience for Detective Harris. Omari's gaze made him nervous. Detective Allen had been in rooms with murderers often and was confident that their safety was not in jeopardy being in the room with Omari while he was uncuffed. However, this was still new to Detective Harris. He had only been in the room in a shadow role, in which he stood in the corner and watched two other detectives break down suspects. This was his first time being one of the lead interrogators. Detective Allen disapproved of it, but the sergeant gave the order so his son could gain more experience and get his name on some of the arrest cards.

Omari stared at the younger detective, noticing he appeared nervous and avoiding eye contact. Even after sitting, the young detective did not look up at his suspect. His eyes were focused on the box that his partner had placed on the table. Like a lion on a gazelle, Omari was ready to pounce on Detective Harris. However, his attack was going to be more mental than physical. "What's up?" Omari asked, while still staring at Detective Harris.

"How are you doing Mr. Washington?" Detective Allen asked. "You seem like a guy that's been around the block a few times, so let's cut straight to the chase. You know why we are, just tell me why you did it."

Omari cut his eye over at the detective. "First of all, I don't know you and I don't know why the fuck I'm in here."

"I'm Detective Allen. Now you know who I am, can we get down to business?"

"What's your name?" Omari asked the other detective.

"Umm, it' Patrick," he responded nervously.

"Detective Harris. His name is Detective Harris," his partner interrupted.

Omari cut his eyes back over to Detective Allen and then smirked. "Where's the chick at?"

"What?"

"That chick that brought me in here. She was kinda cute. Where she at?" Omari looked over at the two-way mirror. "She behind this glass?" He asked, as he stood up and walked towards the mirror. "You out there?" He shouted.

"Sit the fuck down!" Detective Allen barked. "We aren't here to play games."

"I don't give a fuck what you here to do."

"You have a choice. You can sit the fuck down or I can call some officers in here that will sit you down."

"Do what you gotta do."

Omari did not take well to threats, especially from law enforcement. He was not one to be easily intimidated and Detective Allen was finding that out the hard way. Omari readjusted his pants, preparing himself to go to war with any officer that Detective Allen called in the room.

"Hold on. Everybody, calm down," Detective Harris interjected. "Mr. Washington, we just want to ask you a few questions. That's it. There's no need for all of this animosity in the room."

"Tell that to your boy," Omari responded.

"Tell that to yourself!" Detective Allen yelled.

"Hold on," Detective Harris stated, placing his hand on his partner's chest. Detective Allen smacked his hand down. He let his aggression and ego get the best of him. A few hard knocks on the two-way mirror brought Detective Allen back to reality. He knew it was Sergeant Harris banging on the mirror in response to his actions. For a second, he forgot that his partner was the son of his supervisor. He did not mean to disrespect him, but Omari had gotten under his skin.

Omari's smirk had now turned into a smile. His focus was on the wrong detective. He was too busy trying to focus on Detective Harris and breaking him, but he realized that Detective Allen was the one he had broken. Detective Allen had stepped out of his comfort zone and now they were ticking close to the thirty-minute mark.

"Now Mr. Washington, as I said, we would like to ask you a few questions and then get you out of here."

"I'm not talking to that asshole."

"Well, will you talk to me?"

"What you want to know?"

Detective Harris opened the box and removed one of the case folders. Detective Allen removed a tape recorder from the box and hit the record button. He tried to be discrete about his actions, but Omari's eyes were on him the entire time. Detective Harris opened the case folder and removed some files. "Mr. Washington, do you know Sean Nichols?"

"Nope," Omari quickly responded.

"Are you sure?"

"Never heard that name a day in my life."

"Slim. I'm sure you heard that name," Detective Allen blurted out.

Omari just looked at him but did not say a word. He then looked back at Detective Harris. "I thought I told you I was not talking to this clown."

"I know, so just talk to me."

"I don't want to just talk to you if this dickhead is going to be sitting there recording me and saying dumb shit."

"Listen. Detective Allen is just passionate about what he does, he means no harm."

"Well, I'm not going to say another word until Mr. Passionate leaves."

"I ain't going nowhere!" Detective Allen barked.

"Well, in that case, take me home because I don't got shit else to say."

The door to the interview room opened and Sergeant Harris stood in the threshold. "Detective Allen," he said with a firm and authoritative tone.

Detective Allen stood up quickly and walked towards him. "What's up, Sarge?" He whispered.

"Step out," the Sergeant said in a quiet tone so that Omari couldn't hear. Detective Allen exited the room and Sergeant Harris closed the door behind him. "Take a walk, Jonny," he ordered, returning to a normal tone.

"What? Are you serious?"

"Of course, I'm serious. What you're doing isn't helping the interview. I'm going to let Pat take this over."

"Pat? Pat can't handle this."

"It doesn't seem like you can either. From the looks of it, he's doing a much better job than you."

"I can't believe this."

"Listen, take a walk."

Detective Allen was furious. He took the advice because staying and arguing would not have been productive and would only lead to him saying or doing something that he would regret later. He stormed into the other room, where Raven was still monitoring the interview. "This is bullshit."

"What happened?" Raven asked.

"He pulled me."

"Really?"

"Yup. Now he's going to let his son take over. This kid doesn't even have experience and he's going to sit him in a room with this guy and expect results."

"You never know. Maybe he'll get the confession."

"He's not going to get shit. That kid is an imbecile and I'm the one stuck with him because the Sergeant made him my partner. He shouldn't even be a cop, let alone in Homicide."

Raven understood why Detective Allen was pulled. Even just being in the same room as him and hearing him go on the rant about his partner, she could feel the anger steaming off his body. She continued watching the interrogation, hoping that Omari would confess to the murder.

Sergeant Harris entered the interrogation room and stood by the door. "Who are you?" Omari asked, sizing up the sergeant. He immediately noticed the heavy-set frame, the balding head, and the baggy suit. He also noticed that the Sergeant chose to stand rather than sit at the table.

"I am Sergeant Harris. I'm not here to interrupt. I'll just be over here in the corner."

"Okay, we got a Sergeant in here now. It must be important. Where did the dickhead dude go? Is he behind the mirror too?"

"He went to go cool off. Let's just focus on the questions that the detective is asking you."

Omari stared at the sergeant for about thirty seconds. "Who do you think you are? You trynna' tell me what to do and shit. I don't like that shit."

"Well, I apologize. I didn't mean to offend."

"Too late, you already did, nigga. I'm over this shit. When can I get the fuck outta here?"

"You can leave as soon as we are done asking these questions and you answer them," Sergeant Harris replied. "The longer this takes, the longer it's going to take for you to get out of here."

Omari leaned back on the mirror. "What's the next question?"

"Do you know a guy that goes by the name, Slim?"

"Nope."

Detective Harris took a deep breath. "So, you don't know this man?" he asked as a held up two pictures of Slim. One was an arrest photograph and the other was a photograph of his face taken at the crime scene.

"Nope," Omari answered, without even looking at either of the photographs."

"Were you in the Cherry Hill neighborhood on July 21st around one in the afternoon?"

"Nope."

"You weren't in the alley at all that day?"

"Nope."

"Did you drive your Ferrari that day?"

"Nope."

"Do you own a gun, Mr. Washington?"

"Nope."

"So, this doesn't belong to you?" The detective asked.

"Nope."

"Are you going to say that to every question?" Detective Harris asked. He could see the frustration on the young detective's face. Between him continually looking over his shoulder at his father and the way he thumbed through the case file, the lion had now pounced on the gazelle. Omari stared at Detective Harris. "Ok, this obviously going nowhere. Let's just get down to why we are here. Why did you kill Sean Nichols?"

"I don't know a nigga named Sean nothing. I told you that."

"Mr. Washington, we have video of you leaving the scene of the crime. We have your car on that video, and we found the murder weapon during the raid. All I want is the truth from you. Why did you do it? Why did you kill Sean Nichols?"

"I don't know who you're talking about," Omari responded. The game he was playing with the detective almost went left with the mention of the murder weapon. Omari knew they had to be bluffing because all his guns, product and cash are all professionally hidden within the home and his vehicles. He paid thousands of dollars to have those secret compartments installed and he was the only one that knew how to access them.

"Come on. You don't have to keep doing this. We have everything we need to charge you and send you away for a very long time. We are giving you the opportunity to help yourself."

"You don't have shit on me, nigga. I'm solid and when I get out of here, I'm going to sue your entire department."

"We have multiple witnesses that saw you do it."

"I find that hard to believe."

"You shot a man in cold blood in an alley full of people. We have more than enough witnesses to put you away."

"I doubt it," Omari arrogantly responded.

He knew there was a code in the streets and snitching got people killed. He knew everyone in that alley knew how powerful he was. He ran those streets and would start dropping bodies to make the case disappear.

"So, you still are going to claim that you don't know Sean Nichols?"

"Don't know who that is."

"What about Aliya Moore. Does that name ring a bell?"

"Not at all."

"What about Reign Brooks. Do you know her?"

That question almost rocked Omari. He wasn't sure why they were asking about Reign. *Do they got Reign locked up in here too?* he thought. Although they were not currently on the best of terms, the last thing Omari wanted was Reign being blamed for Slim's murder. He was not going to let that happen to her. "I don't know who that is."

Detective Harris continued flipping through the papers that were in the case file. "Well, according to Reign..."

The pounding on the mirror interrupted his statement. Omari turned around quickly after feeling the vibration of the pounding on his back. The door burst open, and Detective Allen barged in with three stocky patrol officers.

"Take him down and get him processed," Detective Allen ordered.

The officers rushed Omari and pinned him against the glass. He put a struggle with them for a while, but they were more than prepared for it. One of them smashed his face into the mirror while the other two pulled on her arms, eventually getting them locked behind his back. Those officers were handpicked by the Homicide Unit to deal with suspects like Omari. Those officers invited confrontation and then shut it down as soon as it reared its ugly head. They dragged Omari out of the room and down towards the intake area to get him processed.

"What the hell is going on?" Sergeant Harris asked.

"Junior over here just gave away the name to our eyewitnesses," Detective Allen said.

"Why would you say their names?" Raven asked as she ran into the room.

"I'm— I'm sorry. I didn't know who those names belonged to. I just saw them written down on these sticky notes. I thought they were other victims or something."

"You fuckin' idiot!" Detective Allen barked.

"What your mouth, Jonny," Sergeant Harris ordered. "He may have slipped up, but I'm not going to sit here and let you disrespect him."

"Sarge, this is bad. He just put a target on Reign and Aliya."

CHAPTER 22

It was the crack of dawn and Reign couldn't sleep, so she started making breakfast. She jumped back, reacting to the bacon grease that was popping in the pan. She used a fork to flip the thick slices of pork as they cooked. The vent was on, but the aroma still filled the condo. Reign took in a big whiff. *I just love bacon; it smells so good.* She felt at peace with her decision to report Omari to the police. However, a part of her still wanted answers. She still could not figure out why he never told her the truth after all these years. He led her to believe that her mother was killed by a junkie but instead she was killed by the man she now loved. A man she just put behind bars.

She opened the refrigerator and grabbed a bottle of orange juice. She poured herself a cup and went right back to flipping the bacon. Her meal was almost complete. She made scrambled eggs and home fries. She flipped the bacon one more time as the grease popped and landed on her arm. "Owww!" She yelled out as the grease burned her forearm. Reign turned off the stove, allowing the bacon to finish cooking on top of the existing heat. Reign grabbed the sweet Hawaiian rolls from the top of the fridge and opened them. She immediately got a whiff of the rolls as the bag opened. *These are Omari's favorite.* She closed the bag and threw the rolls back on top of the fridge.

As she piled the bacon on top of the plate, Reign's phone rang. She grabbed a slice of bacon and bit into it before answering her phone. "Hello."

"Reign."

"Yes."

"Good morning, it's Detective Ramos."

"Oh, good morning. Is everything okay?"

"Yes, everything is fine," Raven lied. "I'm just calling to inform you that we arrested Omari for Slim's murder."

"Good," Reign responded.

A part of her was relieved but a part of her felt sick to her stomach. She was still in love with Omari and now did not know what to do without his guidance and protection. They were planning an entire future together and now those plans are behind bars.

"We also got the gun he used in the murder. We did a preliminary ballistic test on the weapon based on those results, we believe the gun was used in several unsolved homicides, including your mother."

Reign's knees buckled. The weight that just dropped on her seemed unbearable. She sat down on one of the stools and tried to process the information she was just given. "So, he did it? He killed my mom," Reign muttered as she tried to fight back tears.

"It seems that way. Or at least, the weapon was used in your mother's murder. Whether or not he was the shooter, is hard to determine."

"Oh, I know he was. Slim said he was."

"I understand that. More than likely, that was probably the motive behind the murder."

"Did he say he did it? Did Omari say he killed my mom?"

"Unfortunately, he didn't. He wouldn't confess to Slim's murder either. We tried asking him several times, but he just kept playing games."

Reign crumbled inside. Her heart just could not take any more disappointment. For some reason she expected Omari to be a man and finally tell the truth. If not to her, at least to the detectives that were investigating the murders. She knew how stubborn he was though. She still didn't feel like she got justice for her mother. She wouldn't get that feeling until Omari admitted what he had done. "Are you guys going to ask him again?"

"We can try, but I doubt he'll give in. He wasn't saying a word. His preliminary hearing is next week. The homicide detectives are going to want you to be there, but I don't think it's a good idea."

"I have to testify?"

"I don't know. If he confessed, then we wouldn't need you to. But since he didn't, we have nothing else tying him to the murder. He could potentially go free."

"But you have the gun and I told you he did it."

"Yes, we have the gun, however, without your testimony, we lose everything. We lose the probable cause for the search warrant that got us the gun."

"I don't think I can do that. I don't think I can go to court and testify. He wasn't supposed to know I told you this stuff."

"I know he wasn't and he still doesn't," Raven lied. "We just need to take precautions."

"He knows a lot of people and he will probably try to send someone after me if he thinks that I'm the one that ratted him out. What am I going to do?"

"Don't worry, none of that is going to happen. We are going to do everything in our power to protect you. You have nothing to worry about."

"How are you going to protect me? You going to try to stick me in some witness protection program or something? That shit doesn't work."

Reign knew that she had taken the money from Omari's stash, she just didn't want the police to know she had it. If they did, the cash could be seized as a part of their investigation. She was more than capable of getting a place to stay with the quarter-million that she took, but she was not sure how long the money would have to last her.

"No, I'm going to contact this company I have worked with in the past. They help out all the time with these kinds of situations and they have reached in many states, so you won't have to worry about Omari getting to you."

"So, what exactly kind of situation am I in?"

"You're in a situation in which you want to stay far away from the man that killed your mother. You are the only thing that is standing in the way of Omari and his freedom. I'm sure he's going to do anything in his power to get to you and to convince you that he didn't kill your mom. The reality is he did kill her, just like he killed Slim."

"You say all of that but for some reason, it seems like he's going to get away with it."

"He's not. I promise you that. We are going to make him pay for what he did to Slim and your mom. I just want to make sure that we are being careful and protecting you as well."

"I appreciate that, detective."

"Now, like I said. I'm going to contact that company and then I'll be in touch with you, to give you their information. In the meantime, gather some important belongings to bring along."

"Okay," Reign answered as she hung up the phone. Reign placed her phone on the counter and pushed her breakfast away. The stacked plate was no longer appealing. Her stomach tightened up as she slowly lost her appetite. The news from Raven did not sit right with her. *How the hell did they not get him to confess? Cops are fuckin' useless.*

"Damn, girl. It smells good as shit in here. Why the hell you up so early?" Brandi said.

"I couldn't sleep. Why you up? This is way too early for you, night owl."

"I was sleep until I heard your loud ass on the phone," She saw as she stabbed the scrambled eggs with a fork and took a few bites off Reign's plate. "Who the hell were you talking to anyway?"

Reign hesitated to tell Brandi what was going on. She didn't want to be judged. Her current situation made her feel weak. She was finally on her own and enjoying life and now she was back in another predicament. "I was talking to a detective."

"A detective?"

"Yeah. She's helping me with this Omari situation," Reign replied, downplaying her current predicament.

"Why the hell would you be talking to cops, Rei? You trippin', girl. We don't do that."

"What else am I supposed to do? Just let him get away with killing my mom?"

"Fuck no. Ain't nobody say that but why the hell would you go to the cops? They ain't gonna do shit but make things worse than they already are."

"I don't think my life can get any worse than it already is."

"When the hood finds out you rattin' to the cops it can. You not gonna be safe out here Rei."

"Brandi, I don't have no other choice. I'm not safe out here with him anyway. Neither are you."

"There's always another choice."

"Like what?"

"You got money. Put a check on his head."

"Are you fuckin' serious? How the hell do you even do that?"

"You go find a nigga that wants to make some money and you tell him what you need done."

"Oh, it's that easy, huh?"

"And exactly where am I gonna find a nigga like this?"

"It's niggas everywhere that would do that shit. I'm sure Darryl got somebody that would do it."

"I doubt it. Omari's name rings bells out here. It's going to be hard to have somebody go after him. Especially since he's in jail."

"In jail? When the fuck did he get locked up?"

"Last night."

Brandi threw her arms in the air. "You gotta be fuckin' kidding me. You got this man arrested, Reign?"

"He got his self arrested."

"And let me guess, you just happened to be talking to a detective the day after his arrest. That ain't a fuckin' coincidence Reign. That's some bullshit," Brandi said before storming out of the kitchen.

Reign's head was about to explode. There were too many thoughts and too many emotions that were pulling at her. She was already on the fence about her decision and now Brandi made it ten times worse. *What is she's right? What if something happens to me because I cooperated with the police? Who is going to protect me?* Reign looked at her phone. Her instincts were telling her to call Raven back, but her mind was telling her to delete the number and not contact her anymore and just as she was about to hit the delete button, Raven texted her.

CHAPTER 23

Omari sat up straight in the chair. He flipped through the paperwork that the intake officers gave him. It was a criminal complaint, which charged him with 1st degree murder and a long list of related charges. *This is some fuckin' bullshit,* he thought as he read the charges that were typed up by Detective Allen. He had spent the night and entire morning in a cell and he was ready to go home. Omari thrived off making money and every second spent in the cell was a missed opportunity to make cash. Even as he flipped through the pages on the compliant, the only thing on his mind was getting the product to his blocks.

Two officers stood off in the corner of the room, behind Omari. Their mere presence made him uncomfortable. He was still on edge from the rough ride in the back of the patrol car. Those officer's faces were stuck in his head. One thing Omari could do was hold a grudge. His eyes still skimmed the complaint. He finally got through the charges and to the probable cause section of the paperwork. He read intensely as the first paragraph introduced the officer and his experience. Detective Allen spared no seconds or lines when it came to bragging about himself. The fluff introduction alone could fill an entire sheet of paper. The intensity in Omari's gaze increased as his eyes slid to the next paragraph.

The Baltimore Police Department's Homicide Unit received information from a confidential informant (hereafter referred to as CI) that OMARI WASHINGTON (hereafter referred to as the defendant) was responsible for the shooting death of Sean "Slim" Nichols. Along with several other witnesses, CI was present during the shooting. CI observed the defendant with the handgun and saw the defendant enter an orange Ferrari after the shooting. A search of the defendant's assets revealed that he is the owner of a Ferrari 488 Pista. CI informed us that the defendant "owns several properties, and that the Ferrari was stored in the garage of his primary residence located in Ellicott City, Maryland." A search warrant was obtained for this property and a search was conducted of the home. This search led to the recovery of a large amount of cash, drugs, and weapons. One of the weapons that was recovered is believed to be the weapon that the defendant used to murder Sean Nichols.

Reign, Omari immediately thought. He was ready to flip out. He suspected she had something to do with his arrest after Detective Harris mentioned her name but now the proof was right in front of him. In black and white on an official police document were Reign's words. The words incriminated Omari in several crimes and led the police directly to all of the evidence. Omari crumbled up the complaint, imagining that the paper was Reign's neck.

"Mr. Washington," a deep voice said, as an image popped up on the monitor that Omari was sitting in front of. "How are you doing today?" Omari did not initially respond, as he was still in an anger-filled daze. It was as if he was planning what he would do to Reign once he got the opportunity to confront her. "Mr. Washington," the voice said again, in a more stern tone. Omari looked up. He did not say a word. He just stared at the judge, who was on the screen and appeared to be flipping through paperwork on his end. "It seems that you've gotten yourself into quite the predicament," the judge mentioned as he skimmed through each page. "Did you get a chance to look at the criminal complaint?"

Omari still did not respond. He was looking at the monitor but he was still stuck in a daze. A daze that Reign left him in after he read the words in that complaint. There was no hiding the fact that she was the informant that the police were referring to. Everything lined up. From the dates in the complaint to the way that Reign had been acting. In Omari's mind, it seemed like she spilled more than the beans about Slim's murder. He suspected that she also told the cops about his drug organization. That means that many lives were at stake, not just his.

"Mr. Washington, did you read the criminal complaint?" The judge asked. His tone even more stern than before.

"Yeah, I read it," Omari responded, after snapping out the daze. His tone was just as stern as the judge's. One thing Omari did not care for was the justice system. He had no regard for the judge's position. The only thing he knew was that he never let anyone speak to him in that tone and he was not going to allow it to happen now.

"Okay, it looks like you've been charged with First Degree Murder, Second Degree Murder, Voluntary Manslaughter, Aggravated Assault, Simple Assault, Illegal Possession of a Firearm, Possession of Narcotics, Possession of Drug Paraphernalia and Possession of Narcotics with the Intent to Deliver. These are some very serious charges, Mr. Washington."

"I ain't do none of that shit," Omari yelled out.

"Hold on," the judge interrupted. "Today is not about whether you believe you are innocent or not. Today I am only here to arraign you, schedule a date for your preliminary hearing, and set your bail. Your bail will be set based on the severity of the crimes you are charged with and your criminal history."

"I need to call my lawyer."

"Mr. Washington, this is just a preliminary hearing. You will be able to contact your attorney once this is complete."

"Naw, this is some bullshit. Yall trynna' set me up. I ain't saying nothing else 'til I call my lawyer."

"You need to watch your mouth, Mr. Washington."

"I ain't watchin' shit, nigga."

"You know what, we are done here. Bail for the defendant has been denied. Officers, you can take him back to his cell," the judge ordered.

"Fuck outta here," Omari blurted out. "Fuck you." The intake officers grabbed Omari and pulled him from the chair. "Get the fuck off me," he yelled while putting up a little struggle. One of the officers quickly put Omari in a wrist lock, to get compliance through pain. The technique worked and a sharp pain shot up Omari's wrist and arm. He attempted to pull away from the officers, but they were locked on him. The officer maintained the wrist lock as they forcefully escorted Omari back to his cell.

The cell door slammed shut, a sound that was all too familiar to Omari. His cellmate looked at him and smiled. "You ain't gonna' win against them," the man said. Still, on the ground, Omari looked back at his cellmate. He was a thin, black man that was ripped from years of prison workouts. To Omari, the male couldn't have been older than 30 years old. Although, there was a lot of experience in the man's eyes.

"Man, fuck them niggas," Omari muttered under his breath as he stood to his feet. He eyed up the man that he had to share a cell with.

"Like I said, you ain't going to win that war. Those motherfuckas control everything in here. You piss them off and you won't ever see or speak to your family again. They'll shut down all of your visitations and won't give you no phone time."

"How you know all of this shit 'bout them?"

"Cuz, I'm vigilant. I'm the eyes and ears around this place, so I peep game. I understand how the guards move. Most of them are dirty and have people in here that will get at you. The others just go on ego trips and just shut ya shit down, whenever they feel like it. You'll see."

"Well, I ain't with none of that dumb shit. I gotta get the fuck outta here."

"We all trynna get the fuck outta here. You just gotta wait until it's your time. Did you see the judge yet?"

"My man, you're asking a whole lot of questions and I don't even know you."

"The name's Pyrex," the man stated as he approached Omari. "Like I said, I'm the eyes and ears around here. Whatever you need, I can get you. And if I can't get it, then I know somebody that can."

Omari just stared at the man. This was not his first rodeo behind bars and he knew better than to tell all of his business to a man that he did not know. In his book, rule number one was always stay to yourself. That is how he operated on the street and that was not going to change now. "All that shit is cool, but I'm good bro. If there's something I need, I'll get it myself. I'm not the type to take handouts anyway."

"It wouldn't be a handout. I'm sure there's something you can help me out with too," Pyrex said, looking Omari up and down.

Omari hit Pyrex with a left hook, that sent him stumbling back. He then rushed Pyrex and slammed him against the cell bars. "What type of shit you on, nigga?" Omari asked in a loud voice. He had Pyrex hemmed up on the bars that it was difficult for the injured man to speak. "I will fuckin' kill you."

The sound of a baton being banged against the cell bars grabbed Omari's attention. "Inmate, is there a problem here?" One of the correctional officers asked. He was a large white man, with a bald head and a beer belly that almost popped the buttons on his uniform shirt. He had a tight grip on the baton and seeing as though it was his usual weapon of choice, he was ready to enter the cell and put it to work.

"Naw, everything's good," Omari replied, after releasing his grip on Pyrex.

"I wasn't talking to you, boy," the officer said. He banged the baton on the bars again. "I asked is there a problem, inmate?"

Pyrex looked over at the officer. Blood dripped from a fresh cut on his lip. "Naw, we good."

"Make sure it stays that way," the officer said while eyeing them both up. Just as the correctional officer began walking away, Omari yelled towards him.

"Hey, guard. I need to make a phone call."

The officer walked back towards the cell. "A phone call? You in here trying to make demands, boy?"

"I ain't no fuckin' boy."

"You are whatever the fuck I say you are," the officer shot back. "Now I suggest you ask your little friend in there how things work. You ain't getting no phone call unless I say you can get one."

"It's my right to get one call."

"You ain't got no rights in here, boy. Now if I gots to say one more word to you, I'm throwing you in the hole. You got too much mouth."

"It's okay, officer. He's new here," Pyrex interjected. "I'll let him know how things work."

The officer looked at Pyrex and then at Omari. He slid the baton into the holder that was on his belt and then walked away. He had mentally placed Omari on his list. This particular correctional officer was one of the ones that Pyrex tried to warn Omari about. He was one of the ones that were in the pockets of one of the local prison gangs. He did favors for them in return for cash on the outside. They had his number and he had power beyond his wildest belief. That power allowed him to disrespect other prisoners. Those who resisted had to deal with the gang.

"Fuckin' bullshit," Pyrex mumbled as he walked over to his bunk and grabbed a t-shirt. He placed the shirt on his mouth, cleaning up the blood.

"I don't need your help, nigga," Omari barked.

"Yes, you do," Pyrex replied. "Do you know what he can do to you?"

"I'll fuck that fat nigga up."

"Shut up," Pyrex whispered, then signaled for Omari to look at the cell door.

Omari turned around and saw four inmates slowly walking by the cell while staring at him. The inmates were all white men, with tattoos covering their bodies. Some of those tattoos included Swashticas. Each of the men had shaved heads. Two of them had beards, one rocked a goatee and the other was clean shaven. Each of the men were jacked. They continued staring at Omari as they walked by the cell.

"That's his people," Pyrex whispered.

Omari looked back at Pyrex, who was still nursing his injury. "That's whose people?"

"The C.O. that you were giving all that fuckin' attitude to. He just marked you with his people."

"Fuck do that mean?"

"That means that you're a target now and they have just gave you a warning."

"Get the fuck outta here."

"I'm serious. Your mouth is going to get you in a lot of trouble in here. There aren't many niggas that survive the trouble in here."

"But somehow you made it."

"Yeah, because I know how to survive. I'm the eyes and ears, so I know everything that's going on. That's what I was trying to explain to you before you jumped all down my neck."

"Naw, nigga. You was getting weird."

"Fuck that's 'posed to mean."

"You was getting' fuckin weird, nigga. I don't play that shit."

Nigga, you serious? Ain't nobody on that type of time. I was just telling you that I need protection in here and I can get you some things for that protection."

"Protection from who?"

"A few people. Like the niggas that just walked by the cell."

"If you the eyes and ears in this place, why the fuck do you need protection?"

"Because I'm not the eyes and ears for them. The people I work with are their rivals. The white gangs don't like it. I just need to make it long enough til I get shipped out."

"That makes no sense. If you got people that you work with, they should be protecting you."

Pyrex threw the towel on the ground. "You don't get it. This is chess, not checkers. They took me and put me on a different block from everybody else. I'm all alone over here."

"Well, that seems like your problem, not mine."

"I can get you a phone call if you help me."

"How?"

"I can't tell you that right now. I need you to promise that you'll help me and I'll get you a phone call."

"I'll do it," Omari said. "Now how can I get a call?"

Pyrex lifted the thin mattress on the bunk and pulled out a bible. He opened the bible, which had a square carved into the pages, and removed a small, black flip phone. Omari's eyes lit up once he saw the phone. He knew exactly who he was going to contact with his first call.

CHAPTER 24

The ringing of the cellphone blared in Reign's ear. She ignored it and rolled over in the bed. A cool breeze was creeping through the bedroom window. It was cool enough for her to pull the blanket up over her feet, but not her entire body. Reign was in a deep sleep, thanks to a couple of Melatonin pills Brandi suggested she take. Stress had Reign up at all hours of the night. She could not help but to worry about what her next move was going to be. The Melatonin wasted no time kicking in and putting her down.

Reign's cellphone began ringing again, this time it seemed to be gradually getting louder. Along with ringing, the phone was also vibrating while on the nightstand. It had rung so many times, that it started in the middle of the nightstand and was now teetering on the edge of it. "The phone then became silent." Reign still had not awoken from the deep slumber. The phone began ringing again, this time the vibration caused it to fall off of the nightstand. The phone fell face down onto the carpet, muffling the sound a bit.

"Who the fuck keeps calling?" Brandi asked as she entered the room.

Although the loud ringing could not wake Reign up, it was annoying Brandi. She was such a light sleeper, she could have heard a phone ringing across the street and had gotten up. Brandi picked up the phone and briefly stared at the unfamiliar number that was calling. She pressed the side button on the phone twice, declining the call.

Brandi placed the phone back on the nightstand and it began ringing again. She took a deep breath and looked at the phone, noticing the same number calling again. She declined the call again and then put the phone on silent mode. Before she could put the phone back on the nightstand, the same number called back.

"Who this?" Brandi answered.

"Where the fuck is my money at?"

"Who the fuck is this?"

"Come on, rat. You don't recognize the voice?"

"Yo, you got the wrong number," Brandi said, just before ending the call. Seconds later the phone began vibrating in her hand. "I said you got the wrong number," she answered.

"Who this? Brandi?"

"Who the fuck is this?" She asked, wondering who would be calling her by name at three in the morning.

There were not many people who still called Brandi by her government name. Most people called her by her nickname, so hearing someone say her actual first name was weird."

"This O. Where your snitch ass friend at?"

"I don't know who you talkin 'bout. Ain't none of my friends no snitches."

"That's not what this paperwork in front of me says!" Omari barked.

He was still upset that Reign's words were mentioned in the criminal complaint."

"Like I said, I don't know who or what you talkin 'bout."

"I'm talkin 'bout Reign. Your friend is a rat, and she stole my money."

"Reign ain't do shit and she ain't got no money that belongs to you. She got her money."

"Get the fuck outta here. That bitch ain't earn a dollar a day in her life. That money that she took belongs to me and I want it back or it's gon' be a problem."

"Is that a threat? 'Cuz ain't nobody scared of ya nut ass, Omari!" Brandi yelled into the phone.

Reign sat up in the bed, after being awoken by Brandi's yelling. She wiped her eyes with the back of her hand and stared at her friend, who was now pacing back and forth in the room.

"Nut ass? Who the fuck you think you talkin' to, bitch?"

"Who the fuck are you callin' a bitch? Get the fuck off this line you bitch ass nigga!" She hollered, before ending the call again.

"What the hell is going on?" Reign asked. Her voice cracked on each word.

"That was Omari's dumb ass."

Reign's heart skipped a beat. "What did he say?"

"I don't fuckin' know. Something about money. All I know is that this nigga called me out my fuckin' name and I don't like that shit."

Reign could see the steam blowing out of Brandi's ears. She was still pacing back and forth. The phone began vibrating, grabbing Reign's attention. She picked it up and answered, "Hello."

"So, you a rat now?" Omari asked.

"Why are you callin' me?" Reign asked, ignoring his question.

"I'm callin' you 'cuz you got my money."

"I don't have anything of yours. I took everything that belongs to me."

"Reign, don't play with me. I need my money."

"I'm not playin' with you. This money is mine. After everything you put me through, I can't believe you have the nerve to call me on some bullshit."

"Listen, I'm not even going back and forth wit' yo rat ass. You give me my money or we gon' have a problem."

"What you gon' do kill me? Just like you killed Slim and my mom?"

"Here you go on your rat shit again. I don't know what you talkin' bout."

"You can't even be a man and tell the truth. Admit what you did."

Omari laughed. "What you around the cops? You on some real goofy shit right now."

"Fuck you. Leave me the fuck alone."

"I'm coming for my money, and you better have it."

"I don't think you're coming for anything. Last time I checked, you were behind bars."

"Stop acting like you don't know who the fuck I am! You know exactly what I can do to you without even lifting a finger. You can keep talking that shit in front of your lil' friend, but you know what the fuck is going to happen."

"Nobody is scared of you."

"I don't need you to be scared of me. Just have my fuckin' money." Omari said before hanging up the phone.

Reign looked at the number that Omari called from. She did not recognize the number. She scrolled down and clicked on the block button.

"You think Omari is really gonna try to do something to me?" Reign asked Brandi as she sat on the edge of the bed.

"Girl, no. He's just trynna scare you. That nigga ain't crazy enough to try no shit with you."

Reign looked worried. "Why you say that?"

"Cuz there is just certain shit that niggas don't do and Omari ain't gonna fuck wit' you. You did some fucked up shit by going to the cops and he just said all that shit to get you shook. You gon' be fine."

"I hope you're right." Reign exhaled. "I just don't know what I would do..."

"You gon' do what I told you to do," Brandi interrupted. "If I happen to be wrong, and that's a big if. Just make sure you got something waiting for that nigga if he acts up. We can go to the gun store if you want."

"Girl, I'm not touchin' no fuckin' gun," Reign replied as she stood up and stormed out the room.

Brandi looked at Reign like she was crazy, before thinking about what she said. "Oh, I'm sorry," Brandi said, following behind Reign. "I know how you feel about guns. I was just making a suggestion."

"It's cool. I'm gonna go take a ride."

"Where you going?" Brandi asked. "I know you not mad at me."

"No, girl. I'm not mad. I just need to clear my head. It's just too much going on."

"Okay. Just make sure you come back here. I told you that my place is your place."

Reign did not respond and just walked out the door. Brandi felt terrible. She was not even thinking about Reign's PTSD. She was only a child when her father was murdered and a teen when her mother was murdered, but the pain would stick with her for eternity. Even having a gun-toting boyfriend did not change Reign's views on guns. While they were dating, she made Omari keep all of his guns away from her. Even when he carried one on him, she never wanted to know. The only times, she had been up close and personal with his guns was the first time he pulled one out around her and the day he killed Slim.

CHAPTER 25

"**A**re you just getting off or are you heading in for the graveyard shift?" Ms. Bev asked as she poured the decaf coffee in Raven's mug.

"I just got off. I'm meeting a friend here."

"You don't have to lie to me, darling. For as long as I've known you, I've never seen you bring a friend in here. It's always work with you."

Raven chuckled. "Yeah, I guess it is always work. I just got some follow up to do on a case. It's nothing major," she admitted. Raven knew she wasn't getting anything past Ms. Bev. She was a pro when it came to psychoanalyzing cops. Her husband spent thirty years on the force before retiring, so she has seen many careers rise to the top and even more send officers over the edge. Ms. Bev saw right through Raven's nonchalant demeanor. She knew that Raven was doing something off the books, just like her husband used to do for years.

The bell on the door rang as someone entered the diner. Ms. Bev recognized the familiar face and then shot Raven a look. "Your friend is here," she said, as she poured a second cup of coffee and walked off.

"Thanks for meeting me here," Reign said as she sat down at the table.

"I figured if you were hitting me up, it had to be important."

"It is. I need somewhere to stay."

"What do you mean? I thought you were staying with a friend."

"I am, but Omari just called me and he was pretty pissed off. I don't want to put my friend at risk. I have some money, but anything I get would be in my name and he would be able to track me down."

Raven picked up her phone and her thumbs began moving a mile a minute. Without warning, Reign received a notification on her phone.

"That's a website to a facility you can go to. Go on the site and request a tour of the facility. Once you're on your tour, just tell the person giving you the tour that I sent you. All you will have to do is fill out some paperwork and you'll be good to go. If you run into any problems just give me a call."

"Thank you so much," Reign responded. She clicked on the website immediately, pulling up the organization's information. *The House of Personal Empowerment*, she read. *HOPE*. Reign scrolled through the pictures of the facility. "What is this place?"

"It's hard to describe. But it's a place for people in need."

"Like a shelter?"

"Not really. It's much more than that. I would say it was more like a gated community but only with apartments instead of homes. It's very private and secure."

"Is this a place for witness protection?"

"Not really. I know the owner of the facility, so he does me favors when I really need them. He's a good guy and wants to help this community. He started the program to help inner city youth who became victims of their environment. Kids that lose their parents to gun violence or drug addiction are allowed to stay at the facility, so they don't get caught up in the system."

Reign immediately flashed back to her time in the group home and having to be taken in by Omari. Images of her mother popped up in her head. She imagined what her life would have been like if she didn't have to be forced to make life-altering decisions at such a young age. Of course, life with Omari was incredible but now her life was on the line. No amount of money or vacations made it worth being in her current predicament. "All of this sounds amazing."

"It is. He's done such a good thing for people. Wait until you see it. He has an on-site gym, a learning facility, a huge library and an all-night cafeteria."

"All of that is in here?"

"Yup. It's astonishing when you see it in person."

"It sounds too good to be true. There has to be a downside to it."

"The only downside to the facility is the limitations."

"What do you mean?"

"There isn't much space available, which is why they are very selective about who they take. There is also no drug or alcohol counseling at the facility, so that eliminates people dealing with those issues from being able to live there. I know he was working on opening a second site and hopefully incorporating those programs into the new facility."

Reign drifted off. It was all coming back to her. The dingy smell of her mother's sofa. The odor of cigarette smoke that was embedded in the curtains. The sounds of forceful sex coming from her mother's bedroom, as Stoney worked for a couple dollars. The blaring police sirens that drowned out the television every night. *We could have been free*, Reign thought. *But mom wouldn't have been able to go.* "They have to open that second site."

"What?"

"The second site. You said they were going to open one to allow people with addictions to have access to the program."

"Yes, that's his goal."

"It needs to happen. My mom was an addict and she needed help in the worst way. I've seen her try outpatient rehab and it was a joke. She needed inpatient resources, but she couldn't leave me alone. Having a program that would allow the parents and children to stay together is crucial."

"I agree. But a place like that needs funding."

"I'm sure there is funding out there for that."

"Well, when you get signed up, make sure you talk to the owner. I'm sure he would love to hear any ideas you have."

Reign was happy to have this information. She knew that Raven wasn't obligated to provide her with this type of resource, and it definitely made her reconsider her role in the case. She wanted to see Omari behind bars for what he did, she just couldn't afford to have any blow back from testifying. She had to protect herself and the people that were close to her. Her one concern with the facility was their strict rules. Not being able to come and go as she pleased was something that Reign was not thrilled about. She didn't want to feel like a prisoner, all because she was seeking help.

Raven cut her eye over and saw Ms. Bev glaring at her from across the diner. Raven finished her cup of coffee and before she knew it, Ms. Bev was back at the table to give her a refill. "At least you're drinking decaf," she said. "I would hate to see you forcing yourself to stay up all night." Raven looked at Ms. Bev and then at Reign. "Can I get you anything honey?" Ms. Bev asked Reign, noticing that the second cup of coffee that she poured hadn't been touched.

"Just some tea, please."

"We have regular, and we also have green tea."

"Regular is fine. Thank you."

"Coming right up," the elderly woman said, before shooting a look at Raven.

"What was that about?" Reign asked, seeing an awkward look on the detective's face.

"What?"

"That waitress mentioned you staying up all night. What was she talking about?"

"Oh, nothing. I come in here all the time and I guess she's just worried about me working too late."

"I'm sorry if I'm being a burden."

"No, it's okay. I'm just doing my job."

"No, you aren't."

"What?"

"You're not doing your job. You don't work for the Homicide Unit. You don't think I didn't notice that you never have me come to the station to talk and you call me from your personal cellphone. I just want to know why. Why are you helping me?"

Raven took a deep breath and then another sip of her coffee. "I owe it to you and your mom. I was on scene at the apartment when was killed. That case stuck with me, and I just want to see it through. The homicide detectives obviously know that I'm helping out, so it's not a big deal."

"Do they know you're with me right now?" Raven looked away. Reign noticed the shift in her body language. "And let me guess, they don't know that you're sending me to this facility either."

"If it was up to them, you'd be all on your own. You see how these stories go. Witnesses get murdered all the time. I'm not going to let that happen to you."

"I appreciate it."

"It's no problem. Now, let's get on to more important matters. They make a mean strawberry French toast here. I think you should try it."

Reign smiled. "Only if it's real strawberries and not that puree crap."

"Oh, it's the real stuff."

They two women laughed, and Raven flagged Ms. Bev over to take the order. Reign was grateful to have Raven by her side. There was something special about the detective.

CHAPTER 26

Reign didn't know how to feel after leaving the diner. As she cruised the street, she occasionally glanced down at her phone as she swiped through pictures of the HOPE facility. Raven's suggestion seemed like some sort of luxury witness protection program and that's not a life that Reign envisioned herself living. She didn't want to be looking over her shoulder for the rest of her life, but she had no other choice after Omari threatened her. Reign was shocked to see red and blue lights when she pulled up to Brandi's apartment building. There were four police cars parked outside. Officers were placing yellow markers on the ground.

What the hell are the cops doing here, she thought. Reign parked and approached the building. There was a line of residents waiting to get inside the building, along with a small crowd that had gathered to see what was going on.

"Make sure you have identification out or you won't be able to access the building," an officer announced.

Reign's purse was slung over her shoulder, and she was carrying her bagged up leftovers from the diner. She reached in her purse, pulling out her license. The line was moving steadily and soon she was face to face with the officer that was guarding the front door.

"Only residents can enter the building ma'am," he said.

"I am a resident."

"That's not what your license says. You're a long way from Ellicott City."

"I don't stay there anymore. I just moved here with my friend."

"Well, I don't know what to tell you. You should have updated your license."

"So, you're not gonna let me inside my own apartment?"

"I can't."

"Why not?"

"Because your license doesn't have this address on it. You will have to come back in a few hours when we finish processing the scene. Right now, we are only letting residents in."

"Hurry up," someone yelled from the back of the line. "My kids are inside, and I need to get to them."

"You're going to have step to the side ma'am."

Reign rolled her eyes and headed back to her car. She was pissed that the officers refused to allow her entrance into the building. Officers were scattered throughout the block. It reminded her of the morning she found out about her mother's death, which had her worried. *I hope Brandi is okay.* Her heart sunk into her stomach at the thought of something terrible happening to her best friend. Reign's hands shook as she grabbed her keys out her purse. She unlocked the car door and through her bags inside. She immediately pulled out her phone and Reign returned to her vehicle and called Brandi.

Reign's heart began racing as the call went to voicemail.

Yo B! Hit me back!

Reign called again, after sending the text message. The call went to voicemail again.

The cops out here. CALL ME!!!
ARE U OK?!

Reign called again.

"Hello," Brandi answered.

"Yo, I was having a fuckin' heart attack. Where you at?"

"We at the hospital. Omari sent some niggas over there."

"What happened? The cops are out here deep as shit."

"They was out there shootin' and shit."

"You didn't get hurt did you?"

"Fuck no. Draco knew some shit was about to go down. He hired security for me and they saw Omari's niggas creepin' outside. Then all them niggas started shootin' at each other."

"Damn, that's fuckin' crazy."

"Yup, but you know I'm good. I got my nigga wit' me and he said ain't shit gon' happen to me. We just came to check on the guard that got hit."

"I can't believe this. I'm so sorry. I should have never put you in the middle of this."

"Reign, cut it out. This ain't your fault. This shit is all on Omari's nut ass and Draco gon' deal wit' that nigga."

"We need to get out of here. I have somewhere we can go."

"That's cool. We can talk about that later."

"Okay, I have to find somewhere to go cuz' the cops not letting me in the building because they said only residents can go in."

"Fuck them. Come down here and meet us."

The sound of a car door slamming snatched Reign's attention. She turned and saw someone quickly walking towards her. It was a man in a black hoodie and black jeans. He almost blended in with the night sky. A black mask covered his face, but Reign could see that his beady eyes were focused on her.

"Hey, did you hear me? I said meet us down here at the hospital."

Brandi's request fell on deaf ears, as her friend's focus was on the mystery man that was approaching her. He slowly pulled out a gun from his waistband. Panicking, Reign turned around to head back to the officers that were processing the crime scene, but there was another man walking towards her from that direction too. He was wearing a blue denim jacket with a gray hoodie underneath. She recognized him as one of the people standing in the residents' line to get back in the building.

Reign was boxed in with nowhere to go. "Brandi, they're here."

"Who? The cops?"

"No. Two guys. I think they're with Omari."

"Get the fuck outta there."

Reign hopped in the car and started it. Just as she shifted into gear, a vehicle pulled up next to her and blocked her in the parking spot. Her mouth dropped when she spotted the driver. It was Omari's cousin.

Fuck. She put her vehicle in drive and tried inching out the spot, but Ant's silver Tahoe didn't leave her any room for escape. Both men that were approaching had reached her vehicle. Reign hit the power locks, preventing them from gaining entry. *Where the fuck are the cops*, she thought, as her heart beat out of her chest. The officers that were on scene were busy collecting evidence and controlling the crowd that had gathered in front of the building. Not one officer was even looking in Reign's direction.

Reign had to think quick before Omari's henchmen carried out their mission. She blared on the car horn. The loud noise caused heads to turn, including the officers that were processing the scene. With the horn still blaring, a few officers began working their way over to Reign's vehicle. Ant noticed the unwanted attention and signaled for his guys to take off.

"What the fuck," Brandi muttered, holding the phone away from her ear.

"What happened?" Darryl asked.

"This horn is loud as shit in my ear."

"That's Reign?"

"Yeah. She said Omari's niggas were up there and then all of a sudden that fuckin' horn was going off."

"What the fuck. Did she crash or somethin'?"

"I don't fuckin' know."

"Give me the phone," Darryl demanded, taking it from Brandi.

"Yo. Reign. Yo." The horn still blared through the phone. "Fuck." He ended the call and handed the phone back to Brandi. "Where she say she was at?"

"Outside my apartment."

"Fuck. Okay, let me go talk to these security niggas and see if they can send somebody over there."

Darryl approached a small group of uniformed men that were gathered in the waiting room. One of the men stepped forward as Darryl approached. "What are you doing here?" he asked.

"I wanted to check on your guy and to see what happened to him."

"He's good. He's going to survive, but right now isn't a good time. He's still in the operating room and the doctors said he's going to need a lot of rest."

"Well, I need a couple guys to head back to the apartment to check on my girl's friend."

"That ain't happening."

"Fuck you mean that ain't happenin'?" Darryl barked. "I hired you niggas to do a job and it ain't done. Yall are private security and I need some shit secured."

"Exactly, we are security. We aren't gangbangers and you got us in the middle of some bullshit. That ain't our job. One of my guys took a bullet for you and the other three got taken in for questioning by the police. This type of stuff isn't in our job description."

"Nigga you need to make it part of yo job description."

"Listen, young man. We did this out of a favor to your brother. I'm five seconds away from pulling out of the contract we have with him, if this is the type of business your family conducts."

"Nigga, fuck you." Darryl headed back towards Brandi and hopped on the phone quick. The only reason he didn't fuck that guard up is because the man was right. They were a referral from his brother and Darryl didn't want to fuck shit up for Darren. He even hesitated to let his brother know what happened because he knew Darren was going to be pissed.

Darryl didn't expect a shootout to take place, which is why he hired the company in the first place. He figured with a bunch of legitimate armed men watching Brandi, they wouldn't have to worry about Omari's crew or the cops. Little did he know, Omari's crew was determined to carry out their mission. They tried to get into the apartment building, to find Brandi and Reign and encountered the guards. When the guards denied them access into the building, guns started blazing.

"What happened?" Brandi asked.

"Those nut ass top flight niggas are bitchin' 'bout the shootin' and said they ain't goin' to the apartment."

"So, what are we going to do about Reign?"

"I'm 'bout to send my niggas over there to get here. She'll be fine." Darryl immediately began making phone calls and making the arrangements. Although Brandi was concerned, she knew her man would take care of everything.

CHAPTER 27

Reign looked at the photograph on the pamphlet and then up at the large white building. *At least it looks just like it does in the pictures,* she thought as she walked up to the House of Personal Empowerment. The construction of the buildings were very unique. There were two massive white buildings with a walkway that led to a digital sign, with directions on where everything was located. Two breezeways connected both buildings. One of the breezeways was on the ground level and the other was on the third floor. Reign was impressed. She made an assumption about H.O.P.E., thinking it was just like the typical shelter or woman's center. She quickly realized that it was much more than that.

She had been dropped off by Darryl and Brandi after he had arranged for her to be escorted to the hospital to meet them. Brandi told Reign that she didn't have to leave the apartment, but Reign was being smothered with guilt. She had not only put her best friend's life in danger but also other innocent people at the apartment building. The only thing that would put her at peace was getting away from everyone until the case was officially over.

"Good morning, Ms. Bryant," a young woman greeted as she exited one of the buildings.

"Good morning," Reign replied.

"I am Aja and I'll be your guide for today. I'll show you around and then get you settled in your room."

"My room? I'm just here for a tour."

Aja looked at her tablet and began scrolling. "It looks like you have completed preregistration. My boss has already assigned you a room."

"That's impossible. I didn't complete any registration paperwork. All I did was call to schedule what I thought was a tour."

Aja continued scrolling. "It looks like the paperwork was completed by Raven Ramos. Does that name sound familiar?"

Detective Ramos. It all made sense now. "Yes, it does. I didn't know she was going to do the registration for me."

"Well, it's a good thing she did. All you have to do now is take this," Aja said, handing Reign a tote bag.

"What's in here?"

"Everything. Your room key, the building key card, a map of the facility, a phone directory, café menu and a list of daily activities. There is also some paperwork in there that needs to be filled out, but you can get that back to me by the end of the week."

"I don't know what to say," Reign muttered as tears began to fall from her eyes. "I wasn't expecting this today."

"It's okay. I'll tell you what, let's just head to your room first. This will give you the opportunity to unwind and drop your belongings off. Then, I'll take you over to the cafeteria to get something to eat before the tour."

"Sounds like a plan," Reign replied, doing her best to wipe her tears away. The last thing she wanted was to be an emotional wreck in front of a stranger. Reign followed Aja as she guided her through the facility. Upon entering through the large glass doors, they walked through the breezeway. It looked like something out of the future. Silver tiles covered the floor and glowed when they stepped on them. Glass windows and ceilings allowed Reign to get a view of the beautiful garden that surrounded the breezeway. There were children running around in the garden, enjoying the weather and chasing each other. Colorful flowers had blossomed throughout the garden. "This is absolutely stunning."

"This is nothing. Wait until you see your room."

The anticipation was killing Reign. The more she walked through the facility, the more excited she became about her new life. The two women reached an intersection in the breezeway.

Aja pointed to a sign that was posted on the wall. "If you go to the left, you will be headed towards the administration offices, the gym, the pool, the cafeteria and all of the other amenities. When you go right, you head over to the residential section."

The two women headed over to the residential side. Reign's mind was blown. "This place looks like a five-star resort. The pictures don't do it any justice."

"You're going to love it here. I promise you that."

"How long have you been working here?"

"I started last year as soon as I graduated college. I couldn't ask for a better job. We truly give people a chance at a good life here. Plus, I have the best boss in the world."

"So, I was curious about something. Detect...I mean the person that told me about this place said that there are certain rules that have to be followed. What happens to someone that doesn't follow those rules?"

"If someone doesn't follow the rules, they are removed from the program."

"Even the kids?"

"Yup. It's not like we just kick them out on the street or anything. We contact Child Protective Services and they come get the child."

"Then put them in foster care."

"Sometimes, yes. They also try to reach back out to relatives to see if they would help out and take the child in."

"It seems kind of harsh to be taken from such a nice place and then thrown back into that shameful system. CPS doesn't protect those children. They just dump them off at the nearest group home and that's it."

"The rules here aren't bad though and everyone follows them. The only thing you really can't do here is bring visitors inside the facility. We work very hard to keep everyone safe and secure while they are in here and having random people going in and out daily would defeat that purpose."

Omari crossed Reign's mind. She needed that security, and it was reassuring that he wouldn't be able to get to her while she was at the facility. She knew he wouldn't stop until he got his hands on her and she needed time to plan her next move.

Reign and Aja continued over to the residence section. Reign's mouth dropped to the floor when she spotted the giant sculptures that lined the hallways and the paintings that hung from the walls. Each piece was empowering. Whether it was a painting of a black woman with a bouquet of flowers for an afro or a sculpture of a fist being raised in the air, Reign couldn't help but admire the art. However, there was one painting that stopped her in her tracks. "This is remarkable," she commented as her eyes scanned the art. It was an image of a garden but instead of flowers blooming from stems, it was children.

"I love this one. It's called *GROWTH*."

Reign touched the corner of the painting and closed her eyes, envisioning her childhood before tragedy struck. Memories of her as a young girl flashed in her mind. She smiled, seeing her father and mother sitting at the dining room table eating dinner. They were truly in love. Her father was a provider and protector. At that time, her mother was a nurturer. Young Reign's world was perfect. The memory was bittersweet because although her family was together, it was the same night that her father was murdered. They ate dinner a couple of hours before the home invasion occurred.

"Can we get something to eat, mommy?"

Reign's eyes popped open. She recognized the voice. "Oh my God," she muttered as she saw the young girl turn the corner.

"Princess," the young girl shouted as she ran into Reign's arms, giving her a tight hug.

"I can't believe it. How are you?"

"I'm good."

"What are you doing here?"

"Mr. Darren said me and mommy can live here. We have a big house in here and I have my own room," Aliya said proudly.

"I wish I could give you whole house, but it's just an apartment," Darren said as he turned the corner with Aliya's mother. Aliya laughed.

"Darren?!" Reign said.

"Reign?!" he replied, spotting his old friend.

"What the heck is going on? First, I see her and now you. This is so weird."

"You say it lie it's a bad thing."

"No, it's not. I haven't seen you in so long. I was just with Brandi and your brother. What are you doing here?"

"I..."

"Mr. Darren, can we go get something to eat?" Aliya interrupted.

"Yes, you can. Ms. Aja is going to take you and your mom over to the cafeteria."

"Are you coming?"

"Yes, I am. I'm going to catch up with my friend and I'll be right over," he told Aliya. "Make sure you tell James to hook her up with some ice cream," Darren instructed Aja.

"Will do, Mr. Knight," Aja responded, before escorting Aliya and her mother to the cafeteria.

"Mr. Knight?! What was that all about?" Reign asked.

"What do you mean?"

"Why was she so formal with you? You work here?"

Darren chuckled. No, not quite. I actually own the facility."

"Are you serious?" Reign couldn't believe it. She remembered Darren as the young kid that lived next door to Brandi. After she started her life with Omari, she hadn't heard from him or seen him around.

"Yeah, I'm serious. Why is it so hard to believe?"

"I didn't mean to offend you or anything but it's just weird because you and Darryl seem to be complete opposites. You own all of this and your brother goes by the name Draco." They both laughed.

"Me and Darryl have always been different. Even since we were young and he was hoopin'. I had no basketball skills at all. I was average at best and he was a star."

"From the looks of it, you seem to be the star now."

Darren felt those words in his soul. The girl he once had a teenage crush on was now standing in front of him and she just gave him a compliment. He was feeling himself. Reign was just a beautiful as he remembered her. Although she hadn't seen him in years, Darren couldn't say the same. He spotted her out a few times, while she was with Omari. He didn't dare approach her because he didn't want to cause any problems and knew he couldn't compete with the drug dealer lifestyle.

Darren worked hard to get where he was in life. He created the H.O.P.E. program and funded it through donations, grants, and other silent investing. Despite their differences, Darren and Darryl had good hearts and his big brother didn't hesitate to put some cash behind his dream.

"I'm no star. I'm just trying to help our community."

"Sounds like a star to me."

"Not at all. So, how do you know Aliya and Anna?"

Reign paused. She was embarrassed to tell Darren the truth. She didn't want him judging her for the way her life turned out. Especially, with Darren being so successful. She didn't need him looking at her sideways because she decided to cooperate with the investigation against Omari. "Let's just say, we have a mutual friend," she lied. "Speaking of them, I thought you didn't take addicts here. How did they get in."

"We usually don't but I made an exception as a favor to Raven."

"Are you two a thing?"

"Who?"

"You and the detective. She got them in here and then she got me in here. It just feels like there's a little bit more there than just a friendship."

Darren smiled. "Naw, it ain't like that at all. Me and Raven go way back. We're just really good friends and plus, she ain't into men."

"Oh, I'm so stupid," Reign joked. "Sorry."

"It's all good. For the record, I'm single."

Reign perked up. "I find that hard to believe."

"Why is that?"

"You're handsome and successful. I'm sure there are plenty of women lined up to get a chance with you."

"I appreciate the compliment but that ain't happening. I stay to myself mostly because I'm always busy with work. There is so much to do here, and I have to make sure this place is in order. So, I guess you can say that I really don't have time for a relationship."

"What do you have time for?"

"Ice cream. I know a guy that makes a mean chocolate sundae. If you want, we can discuss my boring dating life over in the cafeteria."

Reign smiled. "Let's go."

CHAPTER 28

"Damn, it smells good as shit in here," Ant said as he entered the home.

"I just made breakfast," India replied.

"How you up here trynna' make my cousin trap house into a home? You cookin' and shit, being all domestic."

"Nigga, I ain't none of those lil' scruffy hoes yall used to fuckin wit'. My momma raised me right."

"Well, tell yo mom that I appreciate it. But that ain't just food I'm smellin'. I smell some green too."

"Yeah, I rolled up before I cooked. That shit on the counter."

Ant walked over to the kitchen counter and grabbed one of the blunts that India rolled up. He lit it and inhaled the potent herb. He needed to smoke to calm his nerves. He was expecting a call from Omari, and he knew his cousin was going to want some answers. "O gon' be hittin' me up in a few. What that bread lookin' like?"

"We got a little over fifty."

"Fifty racks? I thought it was gon' be more than that, but that ain't bad."

"It ain't good either. Some of that shit is borrowed money from yall crew. Those niggas gonna want they bread back, sooner than later, especially because the work is dryin' up. How yall gon' get it back to them? Omari locked the fuck up and there ain't no access to the connect. You can't even get product to yo niggas."

"Don't worry your pretty lil' head over that shit. We'll get it taken care of."

Ant knew that India was right about the connect. They hadn't made any moves since Omari got locked up and things needed to change. Ant took another hit of the blunt, as he watched India walk into the kitchen. Her fat ass mesmerized him. He wanted her, but she was forbidden fruit. India belonged to Omari and Ant wasn't the snake type to try and lay up with one of his cousin's chicks. It didn't matter that India was just a side chick that Omari fucked with when he came to the hood, Ant knew he couldn't make any moves on her.

Ant couldn't keep his eyes off her. India was wearing a tank top and shorts that allowed her ass to peek through. Ant couldn't help but stare. *I would fuck the shit out of her sexy chocolate ass*, he thought as he took another hit. It wasn't just India's curvy body that made Ant curious, it was the work she put in on the streets too. India's brother introduced her to the stick-up game. He had a small crew that did robberies all around the city. He never wanted his sister to get in the game, but she watched his every move. Before he knew it, India was laying up with niggas and then stealing from them. She had a group of girls that she partied with and they were all on the same mission. They targeted thirsty men that looked like they had money. They would get the men drunk and even slip them something that would knock them out. Once the men were out cold, India and her crew would take them for everything they had.

As soon as her brother found out what she was doing, he upgraded her little hustle to planned robberies. His crew and her friends joined forces and began setting up people they were guaranteed to come up from. The jobs got riskier, but the rewards were worth it. It wasn't long before the *Pretty Pistols* name began ringing bells on in the streets and even in different cities. India and her friends welcomed the new street name that they earned from being fine ass bitches that wouldn't hesitate to put a hole in your head and steal your shit. Once India got around Omari, she sunk her claws into him. He tried his best to stay loyal to Reign, but India would not take no for an answer. She was persistent with her advances on Omari, until she got what she wanted.

Ant's phone rang. He didn't even look to see who was calling before answering on speaker, "Yo."

"Did you take care of that bitch?" Omari asked in a stern voice. He spoke low because he snuck to make the call on a burner phone.

"Not exactly."

"The fuck you mean, not exactly?"

"We ran into some problems. There were security guards outside the spot and our niggas got into it with them."

"I don't even know what the fuck you talkin' bout right now. All I know is that bitch better be dead or we gon' have a problem."

"Listen cuz, we was choppin' out there and now it's hot as shit. The motherfuckin' cops is out there heavy."

"I don't give a fuck. I got this nut ass case to deal with and I need that rat ass bitch dead. Without her, they don't got no case."

"I got you. I'm gon' take care of her. You ain't got nothin' to worry about."

"You better take care of that shit quick. What's up with that money? I need India to bring that shit down here today for the lawyers."

"Say no more. She right here, she said we got fifty to give to you?"

"Fifty? What the fuck I'mma do wit' that? These lawyers are hittin' me up for ten racks just for them to take care of this bail hearing for me. I still need money for trial and money to pay bail if I get it. I can't do shit wit' fifty."

"That's all we got."

"Nigga go find that bitch and get my money. I know she got that shit on her."

"I will, but in the meantime we gotta get some work back on the streets. Shit dry out here," Ant suggested. He inhaled the weed and blew out the thick smoke.

"I'm going to send you the connect's info. Just give me a couple days to see what's happening with the case. If I'm still in here, I'm just gon' let you pick up the next shipment. We gon' need some money to pay for it tho."

"We ain't got nothin' extra right now."

"We gotta do what we can. We prolly gon' have to dip in that fifty. Where India at?"

"She just walked in the kitchen."

"Okay, this what we gon' do, take ten more racks out of that and pay those niggas to go after Reign. Tell India to take the other forty to my lawyer, so I can get shit taken care of here."

"Yo, I don't think ten is gon' be enough for them niggas," Ant said. "Hello?"

Omari quickly shut the phone off and tucked it under an opening that was next to the toilet. His celly had dug out the opening to hide drugs and the phone. He allowed Omari to use the phone, with the agreement that Omari would take care of his folks on the outside. Little did the celly know that Omari's operation was running on fumes and there wasn't much to go around.

"Washington," a correctional officer announced. "You got a visitor."

"Who is it?" Omari asked, because he wasn't expecting anyone. The guard didn't respond and just opened the cell. "Yall nut ass niggas don't never got answers," he muttered.

"Get on the wall," the correctional officer ordered. He was a tall, lanky man. He had a thick mustache salt and pepper mustache. His dark brown skin was rough, and bags sat under his eyes. It was apparent the career was aging the man twice as fast as he should be. "Assume the position." Omari placed his hands on the wall and spread his feet, allowing the officer to pat him down. "Turn around." The officer handcuffed Omari in the front with a transport belt and then escorted him to the secure visiting room, where two men awaited his arrival.

"What you doing here?" Omari asked when he spotted his attorney in the room.

"How are you doing, Mr. Washington?"

"I'm good. What's up? What's going on?"

The attorney nodded his head to the correctional officer, who then left the room. "I got some good news and some bad news for you."

Omari sat down across from the two men. "What's the good news?"

"The good news is you may be going home."

"What?" Omari sat up in the chair. "Don't bullshit me. How the fuck can I go home.?"

"I just had an emergency bail hearing and requested that your bail be set to a reasonable amount. The judge agreed with my argument and set your bail at ten percent of two hundred and fifty thousand dollars."

"So how much do I need to get out?"

"Twenty-five thousand."

"Shit. That's great news. I can post that today," Omari said, thinking about the money that India was supposed to take to the lawyer.

"Glad to hear that."

Omari was ecstatic at the news. He was ready to hit the streets and get back to work. He wasn't going let this minor setback stand in the way of his expansion plan. A wide, sinister smile spread across his face. Omari noticed the energy in the room didn't match his excitement. His attorney and the odd man sitting next to him had on their poker faces. "Who is this dude?"

The attorney cleared his throat. "Mr. Washington, unfortunately he is a part of the bad news. This is Albert Weiner. He is an attorney with the Public Defenders Office."

"Why the fuck is a public defender here, when I got you?"

"Your preliminary hearing is next week, and you are going to need proper representation. You are facing some serious charges and I would hate to see you go in there and get blindsided."

"I do have proper representation. I got you. That's why I paid that high ass retainer. You trynna play me, nigga?" Omari was ready to jump across the table and catch wreck.

"Mr. Washington, unfortunately your retainer fee had to go towards the bail hearing that took place. You would need to pay another retainer fee for the preliminary hearing."

"And where the fuck am I supposed to get that type of money from?"

"I have no idea, sir. That's why I brought Mr. Weiner here today. I'd rather you speak to him and prepare for the case now, instead of waiting until the day of the hearing."

"Man, I ain't talkin' to this fat, sloppy ass nigga. You my fuckin' lawyer."

"I will need payment prior to the hearing."

"I'mma get your fuckin' payment. Listen, I'mma have someone come down to your office today with some cash. You can use that to bail me out and take a deposit for court."

"Okay. As soon as I get that money, I'll get you bailed out."

CHAPTER 29

"You know Reign wants me to go to one of your brother's spots with her?"

Darryl took a swig of the rum and coke that Brandi made him. "His spots aren't that bad. They're not like regular shelters. They are like housing developments. Like the shit, we grew up in."

Brandi rolled her eyes. She poured herself another glass of wine. "I just don't know how I feel about this whole situation."

"What you mean?"

"As much as I don't fuck with that nigga Omari, I don't think it's cool Reign went to the cops on him."

"Why not?" Darryl asked, taking another swig of his drink. "She ain't in these streets, so she is basically a civilian."

"What? That girl used to move his product, help him sell that shit, and laid up in one of his stash houses for years. She was definitely in this street shit."

"Damn, I ain't know all that."

"Exactly. That's why I don't fuck with this cop shit. I don't care if he killed her mom or not. That shit needs to be handled in the streets."

"You know she ain't built like you."

"I don't give a fuck how she built. Once you step foot in this game, you have to oblige by the rules. No matter what happens."

"Facts."

"She should have killed that nigga herself if she felt some type of way about what he did to her momma. I know I would of."

"You a fuckin' rider, that's why. You built for all this shit," he said leaning in for a kiss.

"That's because I fucked wit' one of the realest niggas in the game."

"Is that right?"

"Yup. You came to my rescue like you always do."

"That ain't never gon' change. You my lil' baby and I got you."

"You got me, huh?"

"Of course, I do."

"Well, then I need a favor."

"I need you to hook my girl up with someone."

"Like a date?"

"No, nigga," Brandi laughed. "I know you can find someone that would put this work in. Reign has money to pay whatever price needs to be paid. I just need you to make the connection."

Darryl put his drink down on the coffee table. He took a deep breath, thinking about Brandi's request.

"You know what would happen if I asked one of my people to do something like that?"

"Yeah. I wouldn't have to move and my friend could stop looking over her shoulder."

"Fuck all that. This would fuck up business. That nigga is a bitch, but he got the streets flooded right now. Everybody is making money off the product that he's providing. If I put a hit out on him, there's going to be a lot of motherfuckas' out here starving. We don't need those type of problems."

"That nigga in jail right now. He ain't moving product right now. Not with this type of heat on him."

"The last time I checked, his operation was still delivering on time. So, he got somebody holdin' it down for him out here."

Brandi chugged the contents in her glass, then slammed it on the table. "So, what about when he threatened me? You came up in this bitch, ready to air his ass out. What would be the difference if you would have killed him right there?"

"He made the first move, not me. That's the difference."

"I don't get it."

"You're asking me to draw first blood. If that happens, I'm gon' have a lot of questions to answer."

"Well, is there anything else we could do to get rid of that nigga?"

"I'll have to get an outside contract if we do this. Some niggas that can't be traced back to us."

"Could you do it?"

"It depends."

"Depends on what?"

"On how bad you want this favor?" He said softly as he ran his hand up her leg.

His touch sent a bolt of electricity thrumming through her body. Darryl was filled with anticipation. He was curious to see what her response was going to be. Brandi poured herself another glass of wine, emptying the bottle. She sat back on the couch and took a sip. Staring into Darryl's deep brown eyes, she slowly spread her legs, exposing him to everything that was under her short skirt.

As if he were reading her thoughts, he slid his hand up her thigh until his fingers brushed across her lower lips. They were warm and wet. Brandi let out a deep sigh when she felt his touch. Darryl took another swig of his drink, finishing it, and scooted closer to Brandi. "No panties, huh."

"Nope." She smiled.

"Perfect." Darryl climbed on top of Brandi, plunging his tongue into her mouth.

He unbuttoned her blouse, exposing her large chocolate breasts. He kept his lips pressed against hers as he continued exploring her body. His hands roamed from her hips to her ass, as he squeezed her plump cheeks. Brandi sighed again. She lifted her hips allowing him to get a better grip of her goods. As their tongues continued dancing, Brandi allowed her hands to explore his body. She unbuckled his belt, then his pants. Darryl anticipated her reaching for his hard dick, as it tried to bust out his jeans but instead, she headed north. Brandi ran her hands up his solid abs and up to his chest. She brushed past his nipple and rubbed his chest and shoulders. The more she explored, the more turned on she became.

Her pussy was pulsing, waiting to be entered. Brandi wasn't one to wait and hope that a man made the right moves. She made sure she got what she wanted. She kept her hand on Darryl's shoulders and pushed down on them, forcing him to slide down on the couch. Looking into her eyes, he could see exactly what she wanted. Brandi pulled her hands out from under his shirt and placed them on her head. She continued guiding him down until he disappeared beneath her thick torso.

Darryl took in Brandi's sweet aroma, before pushing his lips against her wet pussy. He enjoyed the taste of her. He cupped her breasts, thumbing on her nipples until they stiffened. He licked viscously like he was cleaning up the last bit of ice cream from the bowl. Brandi gasped as he liberated his long tongue inside of her. She wasted no time rubbing on her clit as Darryl fucked her with his tongue. "Oh shit, Draco. I'm bout to cum." Brandi used her fingers to spread her lips apart, as Darryl continued working his tongue in and out her pussy. "I'm cummin'," Brandi moaned as she reached an explosive orgasm and squirted all over her lover.

Darryl had just introduced her to a new experience. One that sent her over the edge of pleasure. Brandi's body quivered as the orgasm continued. Darryl didn't stop his feast, as Brandi tried her best to push him away. He grabbed her wrists and pinned them to her side. His tongue slid out her pussy and up towards her clit. "I'm cummin' again!" Brandi screamed as she felt his warm mouth engulfing her clit. Brandi felt helpless. She was intoxicated by the level of pleasure she just experienced.

"Let me taste you," she said as she tried catching her breath.

Darryl wasted no time, following her order as he stood up in front of her. Brandi sat up on the couch and looked up at him. Once again, she found herself hypnotized in his deep brown eyes. She was craving him. Brandi couldn't wait to get her hands on his hard dick. His print was prominent through the denim, exciting her even more. She didn't even want to pull it through the zipper, she wanted to admire it. "This my dick?" She asked as he pulled the jeans down.

"If you want it to be," he responded.

Just as she freed his dick from its bondage, the hard piece stood at attention for her. Brandi kissed the tip, teasing Darryl. She felt it throbbing as her full lips pressed against it. She squeezed his shaft, causing his dick to throb again. Darryl bit his lip. Brandi noticed the precum that was oozing out. She licked the tip, tasting it. Darryl looked down watching as his long dick slowly disappeared in her mouth. Brandi knew she could only go so far. With other lovers, she could easily deep throat them but not with Darryl. He was too big.

She only made it three quarters down the shaft before she started to gag.

"Damn," he growled.

Brandi sucked on his dick, rocking her head back and forth. Darryl placed his hand on the back of her head, assisting with her motion. Brandi left his dick wet and sloppy. She beat it while she slowly sucked on the tip. She looked up at Darryl, trying to lock eyes but his were rolling to the back of his head. Brandi cupped his balls, while she licked the shaft and jerked him off at the tip. This was a combination that she knew put Darryl right where he wanted to be.

"Spit on it," Darryl whispered.

Brandi gathered the saliva in her mouth and spit on the tip of his dick. She continued jerking him off and massaging his balls.

"Spit on it again."

She fulfilled his wish, spitting on the tip once more. She then slipped her tongue across his shaft and down to his balls.

"Fuck, I'm 'bout to cum."

Brandi slid his dick back into her warm mouth. She continued jerking his shaft, as she circled the tip with her tongue. Without warning, she felt him release into her mouth. His dick was pulsated as he came. Brandi continued jerking him, ensuring every drop landed in her mouth.

"Chill," he joked as he pulled away from her. "You know that shit gets sensitive."

Brandi spit the cum into the empty wine bottle.

"Why you ain't swallow that shit?"

"Boy, ain't nobody doing all that. That shit too thick and I don't want it caught in the back of my throat all night."

Darryl laughed. "Let me go wipe my shit off," he said as he wobbled to her bedroom, with his pants down by his knees. She laughed at him and pulled her skirt down. *I love that nigga*, she thought as she began cleaning up. *Let me make him another drink.*

Brandi picked up the glasses and grabbed the wine bottle. As she was walking towards the kitchen, the apartment door got kicked in. Brandi jumped back as the door almost fell off the hinges. "Bitch!" Someone yelled out before firing multiple shots at her. The wine bottle and glasses fell and shattered on the floor. Brandi dove behind the couch as two gunmen continued firing into the apartment. It sounded like a warzone as they riddled the apartment with bullets. Each of them was loaded with 30-round extended clips that they emptied during the assault. Ant was one of the men. Omari gave him strict orders to find Reign and get his money back and that was exactly what he was there to do. After the last time, his men came to the apartment, he didn't plan on taking any chances or leaving any witnesses.

Ant dropped his clip and reloaded. "Reign, where the fuck you at?!" He yelled out. "O, wants his motherfuckin' money." He slowly approached the couch. "Get your ass out here and give me the fuckin' money!" He chambered a round. "Yo girlfriend dead, but we gon' let you live if you just give us the money." Ant pointed his gun at the couch. The closer he got, he saw Brandi lying face down on the ground. Blood began staining the carpet. "Rot in hell bitch," he muttered as he pulled the trigger.

Shots ripped through the flesh. Ant fell to the ground, dropping his weapon. Darryl had tore through him with a quick burst from the Draco, as he emerged from the bedroom. His accomplice attempted to reload but Darryl put him down quick. He walked up on him and put two more shots through his head for good measure. He then stood over Ant, who was gasping for air. "Tell the devil, I said what up," he muttered, just before sending two shots through Ant's forehead.

"Brandi, you okay?" Darryl asked, pulling the couch away.

"Yeah," she answered, rolling over. Brandi was shaking and tears were flowing down her face. "What the fuck is going on?" She asked, panicking at the thought of almost losing her life.

"Nothin' I can't handle." Darryl assisted her up and gave her a tight hug. Brandi was in shock. Everything happened so fast, and she didn't have time to process what took place. "You bleedin' on your arm. You got hit?"

"No. I think that happened when I hit that table after I jumped on the ground."

"Well, let's get this shit wrapped up, and let's get out of here. It won't be long until the cops come, or these niggas send reinforcements."

BULLET HOLES & BROKEN HEARTS

"Where the hell am I gonna go?"

"You gon' stay wit' me."

CHAPTER 30

Darren sat in his office, thumbing through paperwork. A knock at the door caused him to shift his attention. "Come in."

The door slowly opened, causing him to jump when he saw Reign enter. "Hey, what's going on?"

"Hey. Sorry to bother you, but I just wanted to know if you had a minute to talk?"

"Of course, I do. Come have a seat." Darren sat back down and slid his paperwork back into the folder. "What's on your mind?"

"So, I just want to start by saying that you have an amazing thing going on."

"Thank you," Darren responded with a bit of confusion in his tone. "Is there a but coming?"

"What?" Reign laughed.

Darren chuckled. "Usually when someone gives you a compliment, it's followed up by a 'but' most of the time. So, they'll say hey I like your car but it's kinda small. So, I figured there's a but coming, so what is it?"

"There is no but," Reign replied. "You truly have great things going on. I just want to know if you could help me do something similar."

"You want to invest or something?"

"Umm…I guess. I don't know. I just want to be able to help people the way you are. I went through a lot when my mom died and there weren't many resources out there for me at that age. So, I figured maybe you could help me create a program or something. I have a little bit of money stashed away and would love to put it into something like this."

"To be honest with you, it isn't easy. There are a lot of politics behind the scenes and not a lot of funding for startups. I got lucky my brother believed in me and invested in the company. As I built, I began getting funding and government contracts. But if I didn't have Darryl's help, I wouldn't have made it this far."

"So, what should I do?"

"We could partner if you want. I was looking to expand outside of Baltimore. So, if you're serious about this, I could bring you in as a partner. One of my friends is a business guru. She could get you all set up on the business side of things and then we could make some great things happen. Plus, if you do it this way, you won't have to worry about any of the startup bullshit. M company has all the required documentation to get contracts from the city."

"Is it good to have contracts?"

"Absolutely. They payout to retain rooms even if they aren't filled yet. It's kind of like a retainer fee that you would pay an attorney. The city needs to have availability in safe locations for victims and witnesses. I'm able to provide that safety and security to the people that they recommend for our programs."

"Like Aliya and her mom."

"Yup."

"So, if a witness gets put in the program here, how long do they get to stay?"

"I believe it's up until their case is over. The thing is, we don't get the specifics about their situations. We just come and talk to them to see if they're a good fit for our facility. Then it's all about getting the paperwork together. They don't tell us anything about the cases they were involved in. That would be too much of a security risk for them."

"That's true. This is so much information to take in."

"It's okay. You've got me, so you don't have to do it alone. All my resources are now your resources."

"That's so sweet of you," Reign said as she adjusted herself in the chair and looked around the officer. "I still can't believe you did all this."

Darren smirked, "What did you think I'd be doing?"

"Truthfully, I pictured you following in your brother's footsteps."

"Nope. That life was never for me. I was lucky enough to find out what my purpose in life was and I haven't looked back since."

"Your purpose?"

"Yeah. The reason why you are on this earth. Some people are here to entertain others, some are here to lead people others are here to create change in our world. I believe that everyone has a purpose but it's up to us to live within that purpose."

Reign was hit hard by those words. She knew she struggled in that area of life. She didn't know what her purpose was. Thinking about it, she definitely knew it couldn't be following orders from Omari, her whole life. She then wondered what his purpose was. He profited off drugs and didn't hesitate to kill. *What the hell could he be here for?* "Is purpose always good?"

"What do you mean?"

"What is the purpose of people who aren't good? Like rapists and murderers. There's no way that their purpose was to be doing those things."

"What if I told you they are doing those things because they have no purpose."

Darren just blew her mind. He completely flipped her view of the example she gave. She smiled. The conversation she had with Darren was intriguing and inspiring. They continued chatting about the organization and reminiscing on old times at the Gilmor Homes. Reign hadn't laughed so hard in a long time. It felt good. "How did you get so smart?" Reign asked.

"I wouldn't say I'm that smart. I just follow my heart and usually doesn't let me down."

"Is that so?"

"Yup."

A notification pinged on Darren's phone. He grabbed it and checked the reminder.

"Do you need to take that?" Reign asked.

"Naw. That's just a reminder of a dinner reservation I made. I think I'm going to be a few minutes late to it."

"Oh, I'm so sorry. I didn't mean to hold you up. I didn't know you had plans."

"It's nothing to be sorry about. It's just dinner. I can be late."

"Won't your date be upset if you come late?"

Darren chuckled. "Oh no. It's not a date. It's a solo dinner."

"A solo dinner? Like you're eating by yourself."

"Yeah. I do it all the time."

"I didn't know that was a thing," she clowned.

"It is for me. Unless you care to join me."

Reign looked at Darren and thought long and hard about his offer. She already ate but she wouldn't mind keeping their conversation going. "It depends."

"On what?"

"On where we are going. I don't know what type of food you like. This could be a setup."

"Never. It's an Italian joint and their food is to die for. They also have a spectacular selection of wine."

"Spectacular, huh?"

"Spec...fuckin'...tacular."

They both laughed. "Yeah, I'll go with you."

"Perfect, I'll bring this with me," he said as he scooped up two folders off his desk. "I'll show you some properties that are available and see if there are any you like."

The ride to the restaurant wasn't long. Reign spent that time imagining what her life was going to look like in a few years. Darren inspired her to find out what her purpose was in life. She thought long and hard about her journey through life so far. Even thinking about her maturity surprised her. She was able to navigate through life even though her back was always against the wall. Even though Reign was just finding out who she really was, she was still proud of herself for never giving up.

"What you over there thinking about?" Darren asked, noticing that Reign was in deep thought.

"I'm thinking about what I'm going to order if we ever get to the restaurant," she teased. "Don't get me wrong, I appreciate you offering to drive, but I feel like I'm in the car with my grandma."

Darren laughed. "Oh really. Since when did it become a crime to drive cautiously?"

"If it was a crime, you would be locked up."

"I ain't that bad."

"For life." Darren shot Reign a sinister look. "Death row," she kidded.

"How about now?" Darren questioned as pushed down on the gas pedal, taking his Acura TL twenty miles over the speed limit. Reign scrunched her face up, then shook her head. Needless to say, she wasn't impressed by his poor attempt to live on the wild side.

"Come on, I'm going sixty. That don't count for nothin'?"

"Nope."

"At least it got us here faster," he said, pulling up to the restaurant. Darren exited the car and worked his way to the passenger side. He opened the passenger door for Reign and held his hand out, assisting her out of the vehicle.

"Thank you," she said, shocked by the chivalry.

"Why are you acting surprised?"

"I'm not. That was just a little different for me." Reign tried to think back to a time when Omari assisted her out of the car, and she couldn't. She watched as Darren opened the door to the restaurant for her as well. "Thank you, again. I must say, you suck as a driver, but you are one hell of a gentleman."

"Ha! The last time I checked you made it here safe and sound. I would say that makes me an excellent driver," he countered. The two approached the hostess. "Hello. I made a reservation online, but I'm a little late."

"That's no problem. What name is the reservation under?" The hostess asked.

"Knight. Darren Knight."

She scrolled on a tablet. "Here you are."

"Excuse me. My reservation was for just me. Would it be possible to change it to add my guest?"

"That won't be a problem at all, Mr. Knight. Follow me."

Darren headed to the table and Reign made her way to the bathroom. She was in a brief state of panic once she entered. *Why the hell didn't he tell me that this place was so nice? I'm definitely underdressed*, she thought as she checked herself out in the mirror. Reign stared at the way her silk blouse fell off her shoulders. She wished she at least had on a skirt instead of the denim jeans. *Even black jeans would have made this look a little dressier.* She tilted her head, allowing her curly ponytail to fall to the side. She did her best to pull out her curls, attempting to make them look fuller.

"This look is not going to work," she muttered, pulling her blouse up over one shoulder. "This is no way to look on a date. Hold up, this ain't no date. This is just dinner." She thought about Darren's attire. The fitted gray suit and white turtleneck, that he wore. "Wait. This is a date. He's out there looking amazing and I'm in here looking like this. I'm so stupid. I should have changed."

A toilet flushed and Reign did her best to act like she wasn't just talking to herself. A middle-aged woman exited a stall and approached the mirror. She glanced at Reign in the mirror before running the water to wash her hands. Reign put on a fake smile, hoping the woman wouldn't she was crazy. She couldn't help but notice that black, cape-neck pencil dress that the woman was wearing. "I just want to say that you look amazing."

"Thank you," the woman replied. "You do too."

"Oh, please stop lying. I look like I'm dressed for the movies or something."

"You still look good. I'm sure your date thinks the same thing."

Date. There goes that word again. Reign didn't even know what it meant to be on a date with someone other than Omari. She started sweating as her nerves began sending her anxiety through the roof. *I need some advice.* Reign tried calling Brandi but there was no answer. "Fuck. I just gotta wing it." Reign exited the bathroom and headed towards Darren, who was tucked away in a corner booth. Reign felt like all eyes were on her and not in a good way. She spotted everyone's attire, and no one was dressed as casually as she was. "Before you say anything. I just want you to know that I'm mad at you."

"Mad at me?" Darren asked, scooting over in the booth. "What you mad at me for?"

"You failed to inform me about one very important detail about this date. I needed to be dressed up. You got me out here looking a mess."

"First of all, I didn't even know this was a date. I just thought we were going to be discussing your new business plan and check out these properties that I told you about."

Reign was so embarrassed. The only thing she heard was that it wasn't a date. She felt like storming out of the restaurant and crawling under a rock. She couldn't believe she just put her foot in her mouth like that. "Did I say date? I didn't mean like a real date. I just meant like coming out to eat." Reign grabbed one of the two glasses of water on the table and took a sip.

Darren gave her a doubtful look. "Sure, you did."

"Sooo... what are you getting to eat?" She asked, changing the subject.

"The steak and penne pasta entree is amazing. You can swap out the steak with chicken or vegetables if you want to, but I definitely recommend it."

"I'll try it."

"Cool. I'll put our order in." Darren tapped on the tabletop tablet to order their food. "What kind of wine do you like? Red or white?"

"White is fine."

"Alright. The order is in."

It wasn't long before the server showed up with their wine. Reign was still trying to avoid addressing her embarrassment. She looked around the dimly lit room that was full of couples. All of them were dressed like they had come from a red-carpet film premiere. Then there was her. The undressed woman swore she was on a date. Reign couldn't help but laugh at herself. The ambiance in the restaurant was very romantic. *There's no way that he was coming here by himself. Whatever, maybe he was. Stop dwelling on it, girl. You already embarrassed yourself.*

"I think I got it," Reign blurted out.

"You think you got what?"

"I think I know what my purpose is."

"What is it?"

"I think my purpose here is to help out young women who don't have parental figures in their lives."

Darren's gears began turning. "Tell me more."

"Umm... I just think about my situation. I got lucky. Both times. When my dad dies, my mom and I had to reinvent our lives with no assistance. Not from family or the community. We had to just figure it out and that didn't work out for us. Then when my mom died, I had to figure it all out on my own. That led me to Omari and now look at me. I figured that my purpose can be to help other young women not go through what I went through...what I'm going through."

Darren smiled. "You're going to be an inspiration to so many women and girls."

"You think so?"

"I know so," he replied. "Now, check these out." Darren put his folder on the table and opened it.

Reign flipped through the documents in the folder. "These places look nice," she said as she looked at the pictures of each property. The ones in Virginia have a lot of land.

"I know. Can you imagine having a property on all of those acres? You could do farming, camping and all types of stuff. That would be a dream come true."

"It definitely would be nice. Have you been to Virginia?"

"Yeah. A few times."

"How is it?"

"Well for what I do, everywhere is the same. There are ghettos in every state, no matter where you turn.

That's why I could pick up and go to any city and still make a difference. There will always be people in need."

"So how do you choose where you want to go?"

"B-More was easy. This is our city and I had to start helping in the place we grew up, but honestly, I'm choosing them now based on location. I want them to be close enough that I could visit them weekly if I wanted to. Check out that spot on Georgia Ave in D.C."

"Damn. I love this one."

"It's nice, right? That's brand new construction."

"I would love to have a place like this."

"How 'bout we go check it out?"

"Are you serious?"

"Absolutely. I can reach out to the contractor and schedule a visit. Just let me know when you're free to take the trip."

"Could I bring Brandi with me? I might want to check out the city afterwards."

"What kind of question is that? You definitely can bring your best friend. Plus, you're an adult which means you don't have to ask for permission to do anything."

Reign wanted to jump for joy, but she maintained her composure in the elegant restaurant. The server approached with their food. It looked and smelled delicious. Reign had just picked up her fork when her phone rang. She removed it from her purse. *It's Brandi.* She declined the call, wanting to focus on dinner. Darren's phone began ringing. It was on the table, and he immediately silence it, without checking to see who was calling. Her phone began ringing again. *Brandi.*

"Hello," she answered.

"This nigga tried to kill me!" Brandi yelled.

"What? Who?"

"Omari, he sent some niggas to my apartment, and they shot my place up! They tried to kill me!"

"Are you fuckin' serious?"

"Yeah, bitch. If it wasn't for Darryl, I'd be dead right now. He came out bustin' at them niggas and you won't guess who one of the niggas was."

"Who?"

"Bitch ass Ant."

"Omari's cousin?"

"Yup. I watched his bitch ass that his last breath. Darryl slumped his ass."

"Where you at now?"

"I'm at Darryl's crib. Where you at?"

"I'm out with Darren."

"Tell that nigga to answer his phone. His brother just tried callin' him."

Reign put her hand over her phone and looked at Darren. "Answer your phone."

"What?" He asked, confused as to why she told him to do that. Before he could ponder another thought, his phone rang. He watched her storm out of the restaurant to continue her call.

"Yo, Darryl. What's up?"

"Where you at?"

"I'm out with Reign. Why?"

"Her boyfriend just sent some niggas to hit up Brandi."

"What? When did this happen?"

"Just now. They shot her shit all up."

"Is Brandi okay?"

"Yeah. I got her out of there. There's a problem though?"

"What's the problem?"

"The problem is that I had to put them niggas down. The cops are going to have questions for her and I think it would be better if she had an alibi for tonight."

Darren took a minute to think. "Just bring her here. She can say that we were at this restaurant all night."

"Are there cameras?"

Darren looked up and spotted cameras in every corner of the restaurant. "Yeah. It's a bunch of them in here."

"That ain't gon' work."

"Why don't you just take her to your spot?"

"I thought about it, but I don't really want to be involved. The cop's gon' be all in my shit if they found out that she was wit' me."

"Take her to the housing building. The cops won't suspect anything if she's in there."

"You sure?"

"Yeah. Just make sure she has a solid story because the cops are going to come knocking if yall left bodies behind."

"I know. We'll get that shit together."

"Ok. We're going to wrap things up here and I'll meet you over there," Darren said before hanging up. He then had the waitress pack up their entrees. They then headed back to the facility, so Darren could get things together for Brandi.

CHAPTER 31

Reign looked around at the restaurant. The elegant atmosphere of Ambar put Reign at ease. With so much craziness going on in the past month, she enjoyed the peacefulness that Washington D.C. provided her. The incidents involving Omari had her paranoid and she wanted to get out of the city. Darren gave her the information for a property to look at while she was in the area and there was only one person that she wanted by her side when she went to go check out the property.

"Oh, this place is nice," Brandi announced as she entered the restaurant. Dasia agreed as she spotted the pants that were displayed throughout the dining area.

"Hey, ladies," Reign greeted, as she hugged both of them. "Thanks for coming out here."

"How'd you find out about this spot?" Dasia asked.

"Your brother recommended it to me."

"I bet he did," she countered.

"Girl, listen," Brandi chimed in. "This was a long ride, I need a drink."

"I already ordered us some mimosas to start with."

"Mimosas? What the heck am I gon' do with that? I need to order something strong. I almost got killed the other night."

"I still can't believe that shit happened."

"Thank God that my brother was there with you," Dasia said.

"Girl, who you tellin'. He is like my guardian angel. You should have saw him in action."

"First of all, let's rewind. Tell me exactly what happened from the beginning."

"It was a regular ass night at first. Me and Darryl were just chillin' and drinking. Next thing I know, he goes into the bedroom and my door was kicked in. These niggas shot my whole place up. Luckily, I dived out the way and they missed me. Your girl was out there like G.I. Jane, low crawling and shit. Next thing I know, one of those niggas was calling out your name and asking for money. Then my boo came out bustin' on them niggas. We was in there like India and Dirk," Brandi joked.

"Not India and Durk though," Dasia laughed. "Wasn't India shooting back?"

"Bye girl. Don't be fuckin' up my story. If I had a gun, I would have been bussin' in that bitch too."

"How the hell are you joking about this?" Reign asked. "Someone tried to kill you," she whispered as the waiter approached with the mimosas.

"Here you go, ladies," he said, placing the pitcher on the table with three wine glasses.

"Thank you," they all said in unison.

"Are you ready to order yet?"

"Can you give us one minute? We haven't looked at the menu yet," Reign responded.

"No problem. I'll be back in a few minutes."

"Thank you." Reign poured three glasses of mimosas and took hers to the head. The cool beverage was refreshing. "Now back to you," she said to Brandi. "How the hell could you be sittin' in here and laughing about all of that? That's crazy shit."

"It's nothin'. It's not even that big of a deal and I feel like you are going to overreact to it," Dasia butted in.

"It's nothin'? How could you sit here and say something like that in front of me? You know damn well how I feel about this shit." Reign stormed off to the bathroom. To her, it felt like Dasia wasn't taking the situation seriously. Reign splashed water on her face to wash off the tears. She second-guessed herself and purpose in the world. *Why am I here? Everything I touch turns to shit and everyone I love ends up dying.* Reign splashed water on her face again. When she opened her eyes, Brandi was standing behind her in the bathroom. "I'm so sorry," Reign said, hugging her friend.

"Sorry for what?"

"Sorry for putting you through this nightmare."

"This ain't on you. Well, maybe it is because you decided to talk to the cops and shit," Brandi joked.

Reign chuckled, as tears continued running down her face. "I feel so guilty for getting you involved in all of this," she admitted sorrowfully.

"You didn't put me through anything. You're my friend and I got involved because I wanted to. Yeah, the past couple weeks have been scary, but it is what it is. I keep tellin' you that this shit comes with the lifestyle. Besides, if it wasn't for all this drama, me and Darryl would have never hooked back up."

Reign rolled her eyes. "That's like the fifth time you done mentioned his name. Let me find out you sprung or something."

"Girl, hell yeah. I'm head over heels for that nigga. Not only is the sex good, but this nigga also saved my life two times. I ain't never had a man do that for me and he got me feeling some type of way." Brandi grabbed a paper towel and began patting the sweat on her forehead. "Just thinking about him got me all hot and shit."

Reign laughed. She had never seen Brandi act like this over a man. Usually, she was doing her best to get rid of them once they start catching feelings for her. This was a good look. Reign wasn't too happy about the new connection. It reminded her a lot of the current relationship she was in. Darryl was in the streets just as much as Omari and Reign didn't want Brandi going through the same pain she had to endure. It was something about being with a street nigga that wasn't appealing anymore to her. Reign knew if she ever got back into the dating scene, the man she chose to be with would have to be the complete opposite of Omari. Of course, the trips and lifestyle were unbelievable, but they came at a price that she couldn't afford. Reign freshened up and the two-headed back to their table.

"Damn, I thought I was going to have to send a search party after you," Dasia muttered. "What the hell were you two off doing?"

"Talkin' bout your brother," Reign responded, smirking as she sat down.

"It's about time. Now Darren can shut up about that childish crush he has on you."

Reign and Brandi both looked at each other before Reign turned back towards Dasia. She watched as Dasia poured herself another mimosa. *What the hell is she talking about? Darren has a crush on me? She's lying.*

"Don't look so surprised," Dasia added. "You just said you were talkin' bout him, so I'm guessing you two are a thing now."

"We were talkin' bout Darryl," Brandi said, smiling and refilling her glass too. "My boo. Big Draco."

Dasia laughed. "You too amaze me. Yall known each other yall entire lives and yall wait all this time to become an item. I don't get it."

Brandi smiled and sipped her drink, rather than respond to Dasia. The history between Brandi and Darryl had been discreet. When the two first hooked up, Brandi was a senior in high school. She knew that he was a playa, so it was nothing serious. He would lie and say he was going out, just to go next door and chill with Brandi. With her mother always being at work, this gave her all the opportunity in the world to invite Darryl over. When Brandi spent time at their apartment, she was there to see Dasia. Brandi and Darryl put on a front like they weren't messing around when they were in front of her.

The waitress returned to the table with another pitcher of mimosa and an array of appetizers. Dasia reached over and grabbed a piece of the grilled vegetable flatbread. "I ordered a bunch of stuff while you two were playing in the bathroom."

"Hold on. You're not going to brush past the Darren comment. What do you mean he has a crush on me?"

"You've gotta be kiddin' me, Reign. This must be a joke. That boy is head over heels for you. He always has been."

Reign looked over at Brandi. "Definitely head over heels for you," she said.

"That can't be true. Darren and I are just old friends. He's never even made a move on me or said anything to me that would even suggest that he was interested in me."

"That's because he's a nice guy," Dasia commented. "The problem is you two are so used to these hood ass niggas that are all aggressive and up in your face. Believe it or not, there are other types of men in this world." They all laughed. "Darren doesn't have that aggressive demeanor. I knew he liked you because he always asked about you. Always wondered what Lil' Reign was up to. Even after you got with ol' boy, Darren still asked about you. That's why I'm not surprised that he's meeting you out here to show you a property. He'd do anything for you. I know he would."

Reign was flattered but was still in disbelief. Despite Dasia's take on men, Reign wasn't that naïve not to notice a sign if Darren was interested. The notification on her phone startled her a bit. She had been so used to Omari harassing her, that she got nervous every time her phone went off. Reluctantly she picked it up and checked the notification. *It's Darren.* "It seems like we spoke your brother up. He just texted me the address of the building."

The three women finished up their meals. They had about two hours until they had to meet Darren and the realtor at the property. They shared nothing but laughs as the mimosas continued flowing. They all needed this time together, especially Reign. This was the first time in a while she was able to let her hair down and be relaxed. There was always a reminder of her pain, no matter what she did, but Dasia and Brandi took her mind off everything for a few hours.

Once they left Ambar, they headed over to the property. Upon arriving, Reign looked at the address that Darren sent her and then the matching numbers on the five-story building. "It looks like this is it," she said as they all exited the car that Darren sent for them. He stood outside the building, waiting for their arrival.

"Damn this place looks nice," Brandi commented, as she admired the modern construction build.

"It is," Dasia agreed.

Reign had her eyes on something else and paid no attention to the building. Her eyes were glued to Darren. He stood in front of the building, wearing a fitted navy-blue suit and navy-blue dress shirt. A gold chain hung from his neck, and he was rocking gold Cartier frames. *Damn, he looks good.* She shot him a smile and a wave as they approached.

"Okay, D. I see you. All fly and shit," Brandi blurted.

"You know I try," he responded. "But yall the ones looking all good." Although he complimented all three ladies, he was looking at Reign. He liked her style, with the leopard print blouse, knee-length leather skirt and black YSL heels. "Come inside. I want to introduce you to the realtor."

Darren held the door as the women entered and were greeted by a handsome bearded man. He had a low fade that tapered perfectly into his groomed mane. Just like Darren, he was fly from head to toe. He rocked a tailored three-piece suit, which hugged his thin frame. The ladies could smell his invigorating cologne as he approached to shake their hands.

"Well, hello Mr. GQ," Dasia said.

"Good afternoon, ladies. I'm Rashawn and have the pleasure of providing you with a tour of this incredible thirty-unit building. So, if you follow me, we can start with the common areas. Dasia scurried up to Rashawn's side with a million questions like she was the buyer. Brandi was not too far behind him, hovering like a bee on a flower.

Reign hung back with Darren as they walked through the property at their own pace. "The pictures don't do this place any justice. This is gorgeous" she said, admiring the elegant light fixtures, dark hardwood floors, and unique artwork that hung on the walls.

"Each of these paintings were designed by local black artists. I figured it was a nice touch one a place like this."

"That's amazing." Reign stood in front of a painting of a dozen roses. All of them were wilted and dying, except one. It was in the middle and it was full of color and fully bloomed.

"This one reminds me of you."

Reign glanced over at Darren. "How so?"

"The one in the middle is beautiful and stands out. You're light at the end of a dark tunnel. The sunshine after a storm."

Reign was speechless. Her heart skipped a beat, hearing Darren say that about her. Her whole life, she looked at herself as someone that brought pain and suffering to others, and he looked at her as the complete opposite. Reign didn't see what Darren saw. Even as she made plans to step into the world of helping others, in a way she felt like it would somehow balance out years of pain and suffering. Yes, she would be helping plenty of people but on the other hand, it would give her a sense of purpose that she didn't currently have. Up until this point, her happiness relied on the choices others made for her. Whether it was her mother, Omari, or even the police that was pestering her to testify. She finally would be able to control her own life and destiny.

"Look at this office."

Reign peeked her head in the room that had already been furnished. A white marble table sat in the middle of the room with a white padded chair behind it. Gold accents decorated the entire office. "This is beautiful. I wouldn't ever leave this room."

"I know. I would have to put a bed in here and just make this my bedroom." He laughed.

"This office looks ten times better than it did online."

"Come on. Let me show you something else." Darren headed towards the common areas with the others. They passed Dasia and Brandi, as Rashawn took them upstairs. Dasia gave Reign the thumbs up as they passed, and she smiled. She still didn't see what Dasia saw. Darren was very nice to her, but he wasn't giving out any signals that would suggest that he was romantically interested in her. "Check this out," he said opening two double doors.

Reign's mouth dropped when she saw the recreation area. There was a fireplace in the center of the room surrounded by couches and other seating along the walls. Six other doors were already labeled. *GYM, SPA, POOL, ARCADE, COMPUTER LAB, STUDIO.*

"What is all of this. I didn't see this in the pictures."

"Exactly. It's amazing right?"

"Hell yeah. How do you have all of this in one building?"

"I don't know, but the builders did one hell of a job."

"Look at this." Darren walked over to the wrap-around fireplace and grabbed a ribbon that was hanging from the top of it. He pulled the ribbon down, revealing a large sign.

Reign's mouth dropped and tears fell from her eyes, as she read the sign. *STONEY WAY.* The gold letter shined bright, matching the other décor in the room. It felt like her heart stopped and she was frozen in place. Memories of her mother popped in her head as more tears began falling. All the emotions she felt were overwhelming. "What's going on? Why is my mom's name up there?"

"Well, I figured that this would be the place where all the families come to spend time and to make their own memories. So, I thought it would be a good idea to honor your mother by naming this place after her. So now you can help build great memories in her honor."

Reign ran over to Darren and jumped in his arms. "You didn't have to do this." Having her in his arms felt good. He didn't want to let her go. He took in her sweet scent, and they continued embracing each other. "How were they able to put a sign up on a property we don't own?"

"Because we do own it. I put in an offer as soon as you told me you liked it. I figured we could be partners, and this would help jump start you into this industry." Reign hugged Darren again. "The only thing you gotta do now is, sign on the dotted line," he said as the two worked their way back to the office.

Reign looked back at the sign as the left the recreation area. They entered the office and Darren closed the door behind them. Reign never noticed the bottles of champagne and paperwork on the desk when she was standing in the hallway.

"I don't know about all of this," Reign said hesitantly as she looked around the luxurious office once more. It was like a dream come true, being in the building and knowing that her vision was coming together. She was so used to being under Omari, she couldn't even describe the feeling of having something that belonged to her.

"Take your time," Darren muttered, as he sat on the desk. "There's no rush for any of this. We can go check out other spots too. I still have the information for the Virginia properties and the realtor there is good folk. I can put this property solely under my organization if you don't want it."

"It's not that," she muttered, pacing back and forth.

"Then what is it?"

"Can I be honest with you?"

"Of course, you can."

Reign walked over to him. "I'm not like you. I'm not all educated and knowledgeable about this stuff and it's scary. I don't want to be a disappointment. Not to you or anyone else."

"You would never be a disappointment to me," Darren said, placing his hand gently on Reign's hand.

She could feel the electricity in the air as his hand caressed hers. "Whatever we need to do to get you comfortable in this field, we'll do. If you have to go back to college to get the education you want, then so be it."

"GED."

"What?"

"A GED. That's what I need to get first. I dropped out of high school."

"After your mom died?"

Reign nodded her head. She was embarrassed after telling Darren her business, but she wanted to be honest with him. She knew this was something she had to put behind her because it wasn't likely to happen.

"We can still make that happen. There are a ton of GED programs available out here. We can just get you enrolled in one and I can recommend a few webinars you could check out about managing a property."

Reign wasn't expecting that response. The last time she mentioned getting her GED, the idea was shut down immediately. Darren encouraged and inspired her to follow her dreams. She envisioned showing Aliya this building and ensuring the little girl that she and her mother had a safe place to stay without the worries of Slim's case hovering over them. Having Darren's support meant the world to her. "Why are you doing this?" Reign asked as she got closer to Darren. She looked him in his, demanding an honest answer.

"Why am I doing what?"

"Why are helping? Why are you being so nice to me?"

"This is what I do, Reign. I built a life dedicated to helping others. The lives we lived growing up were filled with so much pain and heartbreak. I kept telling myself that over the years things would change. The world would get better. But it didn't. Our neighborhoods are still afflicted by violent crime and poverty. I had to do something."

"So, I'm just a charity case to you," she muttered, pulling her hand away from his. She knew everything Dasia was saying was bullshit. Darren admitted that he would have done these things for anyone in her predicament. Reign was embarrassed. She didn't know what to expect but she couldn't fight what she felt for Darren. She was grateful to have him in her life, but she also didn't want to be a burden to him or his family any longer.

"I didn't say that," he scoffed, grabbing her hand and pulling her back into his space. Reign was so close she could smell the mint on his breath. "You aren't a charity case at all. You're special. You've always been special."

The electricity that was in the air was now moving through their bodies. It just seemed like Darren knew exactly what to say at the right time. Reign moved forward and the mint she once smelled, she was now tasting. As the two passionately kissed, Reign felt a fire burning inside her that she hadn't felt in a long time. Inside, Darren was a nervous wreck. Butterflies fluttered in his stomach. This was a moment he waited for since he was a teenager and now it was happening.

Darren pulled away, allowing their eyes to me. The sun rays peeking through the blinds landed perfectly on Reign's face. It bounced off her smooth caramel skin and her light brown eyes. She is the epitome of beauty, he thought as he stared at her and smiled nervously. In any other room, Darren was a statue of confidence. However, Reign made him feel like he was sixteen again. She stared back at him and could tell his nerves her getting the best of him. "What's wrong?"

"Nothin'. This just all seems unreal."

"Ouch!" Reign yelled out feeling a sudden pain in her hand. "Did you just pinch me?"

"I'm so sorry," Darren pleaded. He felt horrible. "I was trying to pinch myself." The two shared in laughter. "This is definitely the worst romance movie." Reign laughed in agreement.

"I still can get over the fact that you just pinched me for no reason," she joked.

"There was a reason. I just wanted to make sure I wasn't dreaming."

The two gazed at each other. Although the line was cliché, Reign felt the sincerity behind every word. Once again, he knew exactly what to say to make her feel like the only woman in the world. She stole another kiss. *His lips are so soft*, she thought as she went in for another. "So, if this was a dream, why would you pinch yourself and wake up from it?"

"Because dreams don't last. I want this to be real."

Reign melted in his arms as the two locked lips again. Darren gripped the back of her shoulders, locking her in place as his tongue intertwined with hers. Then he allowed his hands to fall, gently brushing against her back. She had no clue how to respond to his hands rubbing down her back. His touch was so light and subtle, but it fueled the fire inside of her. Before she knew what was happening, she had straddled Darren. He sat back on the desk, allowing Reign to get a more comfortable position. He could feel her warmth on top of him. Darren slightly leaned back, allowing Reign's lips to hover over his.

She leaned in for more passion, but he leaned back again. Reign wasn't used to being teased and it left her wanting him even more. She had only been with Omari and now longed for the touch of another man. She felt a bit selfish, knowing that she had personal reason as to why she was giving herself to Darren. Now his hands were resting lightly on her hips. Reign bit her lip, knowing he wanted to touch her in other places but was still being the perfect gentleman. She did the honors of unzipping his dress pants, releasing his hard dick that seemed eager to be free. Reign rubbed her hand up and down his hard dick. It had only been the second one she had ever touched. She immediately noticed that Darren wasn't as thick as Omari but was a few inches longer.

She was nervous to feel it inside of her. Her mind was a jumbled mess as different thoughts spun around and reasons for not proceeding began to pop up. The main one is loyalty. As much as Reign hated Omari, she never officially broke up with him. *Would this be considered cheating? Should I wait to do this? Does*

Darren have a girlfriend? Her mind was getting the best of her.

Darren was done teasing. He slowly lifted his hips, pushing the tip of his hard dick against Reign's wet pussy. If she weren't wearing panties, he would have slipped right in her. Reign gasped as the thoughts escaped her mind and pleasure took over. She locked eyes with Darren again, before reaching down and pulling her panties to the side. There were no more excuses. She wanted it.

A moan slipped from her mouth as she sat on the tip. Her wetness guided him deeper into her, as he tried to control himself. It was so tight and so wet, that Darren was about to cum just after a few pumps. He looked over at the window, focusing on the blinds. Reign continued riding him as his dick went deeper than Omari ever could. Darren was hitting a spot that Reign didn't even know existed.

A long moan escaped her lips as he blew a flow of cool air against her warm skin. *What the fuck is he doing to me*, she thought before letting out another moan. Darren then ran the back of his hands down her smooth thighs, sending chills through her body. "Oh shit, do that again," Reign ordered. Repeating his actions but switching it up, he softly ran his fingertips down her thighs. "Fuck," she nearly screamed as he drove her to a newfound high of lovemaking.

Unexpectedly, Reign's knees began trembling. Darren could feel it too and began thrusting his hips upward and his hands locked on to her ass. His touch was so gentle and intentional. It drove Reign insane. "Cum on it," Darren whispered in her ear, allowing his breath to brush across her lobe.

Suddenly, Reign exploded. There was a loud moan and then she could only hear the loud beating of her heart. She arched her back and curled her toes during her release. She grabbed onto the desk with one hand and gripped Darren's suit jacket with the other. Darren didn't even realize his focus had shifted from the blinds back to Reign as he reached his peak and filled her warm pussy with cum.

Reign collapsed on his chest, with a smile that spread from ear to ear. Darren wrapped his arms around her, holding her tight against his body. He could feel her heartbreaking and she could feel his. He was a little disappointed in himself because he usually lasts longer than he did, but anticipation got the best of him. Reign didn't even notice. He hit new spots inside of her that left her soul floating above her body. She couldn't move. The two stayed down there as Dasia and Brandi continued checking out the rest of the building.

CHAPTER 32

"This is the sixth time we've called her and she hasn't answered," Detective Allen's voice roared in the small conference room. "This is why I don't use witness protection. It has no guarantees that these people will show up."

"This isn't like Reign," Raven said. "She wants to see her mother get justice."

"I'm not worried about what she wants for her mother. I'm worried about the Omari Washington case that we are pointing on tomorrow. If we don't have her, we'll need to get the little girl over here to get prepped.

"That's not how this works. We agreed that Reign would testify, so that Aliya wouldn't have to. She is too young for this."

"I don't care how young she is. We need to have a witness prepared to testify tomorrow. If that doesn't happen, you're going to have a big problem on your hands."

"How so?" Raven asked, not taking kindly to the empty threat.

"You interfered with a homicide investigation. This was never a special victims case, but yet there you were every step of the way. I don't know why my boss allowed this to happen, but I promise that if things go left tomorrow, I'm going to rip that badge out of your hands for messing with my case."

"Messing with your case? You wouldn't even have a case if it weren't for me," Raven barked, getting in Detective Allen's face. "These are my witnesses. I found them and if weren't because of me, you would still be in that alley way with no leads. I solved this case, not you. Remember that."

"You can say what you want, but my name is on the paperwork. All you did was get in my way."

Raven couldn't believe what she was hearing. It's sad to say, but it wasn't surprising. Minorities always got the short end of the stick when it came to police department. Not only was she a woman, but she was a lesbian and also Black and Puerto Rican. It was as if all the chips were stacked against her from day one. No matter how hard she worked, she had to work harder than everyone else in the department. When they put in eight hours, she had to put in ten to twelve hours. When they gave a hundred percent, she had to give a hundred and fifty percent. When they went home to their families at night, she had to meet witnesses in a diner to ensure them that she was going to do everything in her power to support them.

Raven didn't understand the weight of the burdens she carried around each day, but she would soon find out. She made a promise to Anna and Aliya that she would do her best to keep the young girl from taking the stand, but without Reign, she had no other choice. Raven began panicking as the walls seemed to be closing in around her. "What if something happened to her?"

"I doubt it."

"What's that supposed to mean?"

"Her little boyfriend made bail and we haven't heard a peep out of him. Then last week his cousin pops up dead in an apartment. That same apartment is leased to an associate of the witness. There were shell casings everywhere. I would say there's a connection between all of it."

"What? Why didn't anyone tell me about this."

"Like I said, you aren't in this unit."

"So, you think Reign had something to do with the shooting?"

"Maybe. You want me to believe that it's just a coincidence that our witness goes missing right after this dude gets killed and then she doesn't show up to case prep. My guess is that she's taking matters into her own hands."

"No, she wouldn't. She's not that type of person."

"And how would you know?"

"I...uh...I don't really know. She just doesn't seem like the type that wanted revenge. She just wanted justice."

"You don't know these people."

"What people? Because that's not the first time you used that term when referring to Reign."

"You know what I mean."

"No, I don't. Feel free to enlighten me."

"I say these people because they operate under a different set of rules than we do. We don't grow up how they do, we don't act how they do and we don't think like they do. They're animals and they eat their young. Kids in the ghetto don't stand a chance in our world. You know it and I know it."

"I don't know shit. All I know is that you sound like an asshole because I'm one of those kids that you're talking 'bout. I didn't grow up with no silver spoon in my mouth or generations of officers in my family that paved the way for my career. I worked my ass off to get everything I've gotten and all those kids you talking 'bout can do the same thing."

Detective Allen laughed. "Yeah, okay. If you ever get the opportunity to come on this side of the fence, you'll see this city in a very different light. They're killing each other left and right and no one is doing a thing about it. No one has the courage to step forward and do the right thing. They call it snitching but the reality is that the streets have their minds so corrupted that they don't know how to differentiate right and wrong."

"You're not different from them. We are all human beings on this fucked up planet. We all have an expiration date and we've all done our part to contributing to the good or the bad that this world has to offer. The only difference between you and the people you're talking 'bout is that you have a fucked up mindset and think you're better than them. Did you even grow up in the city?"

"I grew up just outside of it. I didn't need to live in the city to see how fucked up it was. You can see it from a mile away. Just watch the news and you see everything that goes on."

"The news? That gotta be a joke. The news doesn't tell you shit. Being in the streets tells you everything you need to know. Maybe if you got your lazy ass up and out of the office sometimes you could see what's really going on in the streets.

"You sound like you've got so much love for the streets. What happens when those same streets break your little heart? You won't be left with nothing. That's the difference between me and you. This gun and badge are all I need. You're right. It's tradition in my family and at the end of the day, I don't have to worry about it turning on me because I never turned on it. I hope you can say the same."

"What's that supposed to mean?"

"It means you need to pick a side. Either you want to be a cop or be in the streets. You can't do both. Clearly it hasn't worked out because we're sitting here in the District Attorney's Office and we need to prep for case but we don't have any witnesses. The streets don't love you. The sooner you realize that, the better off you'll be. You put too much faith in those animals."

Raven's phone rang before Detective Allen could finish his offensive rant. She picked up the phone and the weight of the world lifted off her shoulders. Raven exited the conference room and answered the call.

"Where the hell are you?"

"I'm in D.C. and I have some great news," Reign said.

"Did you forget that we had to prepare for the case. We are all down here waiting for you."

"Oh my God. Was that today?"

"Yes and Detective Allen is pissed. He thinks you flaked on the case."

"Why would I do that?"

"I don't know. Maybe because Omari's cousin got killed and you need to lay low."

"What? You think I had something to do with that?"

"Honestly, I don't know what to think. The only thing that I know is that you were supposed to be here and you're not. Then I get hit with the news about Omari's cousin."

"That shit ain't got nothin' to do wit' me."

"What happened?"

"Omari sent them to my friend's spot. They were lookin' for me, but I was at H.O.P.E. with Darren."

"So how did Omari's cousin end up dead?"

"I have no idea," Reign lied.

"Who says at the apartment?"

"My friend."

"What friend?"

"Why are you asking me so many questions? You're makin' me feel like I did something wrong."

"I'm just need to make sure that you aren't playing me. I put career on the line to help you and I don't want to find out that you are being a vigilante and taking the law into your own hands."

"I would never do that."

Raven needed that reassurance. She allowed Detective Allen to put those doubts in her head about Reign. "I knew you wouldn't. I just needed to be sure."

"You don't have to worry about me ever doing anything crazy like that. I am staying as far away from Omari as I can. I really didn't remember that we had to prep today. I'm sorry."

"It's okay. They are going to prep Aliya for the case."

"What? They can't do that. You said if I testified, then she wouldn't have to."

"I know what I said, but you didn't show up to today and they need a backup plan in case you don't show up tomorrow. They are threatening to kick her out of the H.O.P.E. program if she doesn't cooperate with the case."

"How can they do that?"

"They are the ones paying for her to be there. The city isn't just going to cut a check for a housing allowance for a witness that won't cooperate with the case."

"You said we had time. You said it would be months before they bothered Aliya. I could make something happen for her then but if they kick her out now, there is nothin' I can do."

"Everything was good until you didn't show up today. Detective Allen is pretty pissed and I'm sure he's going to be calling Darren's company soon to arrange for Aliya and her mom to be picked up.

"Well, Darren is here with me. I'll talk to him to see if there is something we could do about Aliya."

"There's something else. It looks like the District Attorney is going to offer Omari a plea deal."

"A plea deal? Is that common for a murder?"

"Sometimes it is, especially when they don't believe that they have a solid case."

"How don't they have a solid case? Yall have the weapon and I told yall that he did it. That seems pretty solid to me."

"But you'll need to testify in order for that case to be solid."

Reign thought about Brandi and the crazy ordeal she had to go through. "I don't know if I can do that. Omari has his people coming after me because I'm cooperating with you. What if we just let him take that deal and we all move on."

"That's an option. They are going to offer him ten years, so we'll just see if he takes it or not."

"Ten years? How the fuck can we get ten years for killin' two people?"

Raven let out a deep sigh. It became difficult for her to form the sentence, but she knew that it was vital for her to be transparent with Reign. "They are only focusing on Slim's murder for the deal."

"So, Omari gets away with killin' my mom?"

Raven could hear the pain in her voice. She hated to be the one to break the bad news to Reign, but the situation was out of her hands. "If it were up to me, he wouldn't even get a deal."

"But it's not up to you, right? You made me believe that doing all of this was going to finally get my mom some justice. You lied. You had to know about this deal all along."

"I didn't know. I promise you that I didn't know they were going to do this. If you come tomorrow to testify, maybe we can change their mind and just go through with the full hearing."

"I'm not doin' shit. For what?"

"Because it's the right thing to do."

"The right thing to do would be not to lie to people. Don't feed people with a bunch of bullshit and make promises that you can't keep."

"Reign, please..." Raven begged, before the call ended. She leaned against the wall and sunk down into she was sitting on the floor. She knew Reign was right about the promise that Raven made her. She guaranteed her justice that she knew was out of her hands. Raven wasn't even in the homicide unit and shouldn't have been involved in the case. A part of her wished she hadn't injected herself into the investigation.

The conference room door opened. Detective Allen exited and spotted Raven sitting on the ground. "I guess that conversation didn't go as planned." Raven ignored

C.L. LOWRY

"Don't start with me."

"Like I said, choose a side."

CHAPTER 33

"All rise," the bailiff announced.

Raven stood to her feet, along with everyone else that was present in the courtroom. It was the day of Omari's preliminary hearing, and she didn't feel confident about the case. In the back of her mind was the guilt of feeling like she betrayed Reign. Raven had good intentions when she stepped foot into that alleyway, but somewhere down the line everything fell apart.

She sat in the back of the courtroom and watched the prosecutor pull out multiple folders from a file box and carefully align them on the table. She then looked over at the defense attorney, who appeared to be nervous and had his head on a swivel. *Why is the public defender up there?* Raven knew that Omari had deep pockets and couldn't imagine anyone using a public defender to fight a murder case. She had seen the white chubby man before and knew he wasn't built to take on a case like this. Besides the thick bifocals that sat on the bridge of his nose, his balding hair and baggy suit, he was hard to miss because he carried around a dingy green briefcase that looked like it should have been thrown in the trash years ago. The shoulder strap to the briefcase was being held together by safety pins.

The courtroom was packed, but there was no sign of Omari or any of the witnesses. Raven checked her cellphone. *No calls or messages.* She couldn't help but worry. She scrolled down her contacts until she got to Reign's name. She thought about making the call but had a feeling that it would be denied. She looked up and spotted a set of beady eyes staring at her. Detective Allen was in the front row but was focused on her. Raven knew precisely what he was thinking, He had already threatened her career because of her involvement in his case and now with no witnesses present in the courtroom, he was ready to follow up on that threat.

"You may be seated," the judge announced. "Counsel, are we ready to proceed?"

"We are, your honor," the prosecutor responded. "I would just like to point out that the defendant doesn't appear to be present."

"Is this true?" the judge asked the public defender.

"Umm...I guess so, your honor. Forgive me, but I don't know what client looks like," he responded, turning his fat head around and scanning the crowd. "If I could respectfully ask the court for a few minutes. I would like the chance to give him a call." He opened a folder and flipped through the paperwork. "I believe I have his number written down somewhere."

"Make it quick," the judge responded.

The doors to the courtroom opened and everyone turned to see who was entering. Raven sat up in her seat. The clicking of shoes on the tile left everyone in anticipation. The public defender stood up, hoping his client had just been running a little late and was now coming in to face his accusers.

Reign entered the courtroom with Darren by her side. Her nerves got the best of her because she wasn't ready to face Omari or any of his folks that may be in attendance. Darren held her hand and they found two seats in the back row. Raven looked over and gave a little smile to Darren. He acknowledged her with a slight head nod. Reign spotted Raven but remained emotionless. She still wasn't happy about the conversation that took place between them.

"I don't see him in here," Reign whispered.

Darren scanned the courtroom. "Where do you think he's at?"

"I don't know."

"There's no way he wouldn't show up to this. Something ain't right."

Reign felt a knot in her stomach. She had never been in a courtroom before and never imagined she would be involved with a criminal case. This was entirely out of her comfort zone. She hadn't spoken to any of the detectives that were involved in the case or the prosecutor. "I got a bad feeling about this."

"Don't worry 'bout it. We went over this already. You're not going to testify. We are just here so they don't try to kick Aliya and Anna out of the program. Once this case is over, we can transfer them over to your spot and we won't even have to deal with the city anymore. They'll have a new start."

"I can't wait."

"Let's just wait and see what happens here." Darren held Reign's hand. He could feel the sweat on her palms. After everything that was going on and the attack on Brandi, Reign wanted no parts of the case. Even if it meant Omari would walk on the murder charges for what he did to Slim. Once Reign found out that her mother's death was not added to the charges, she was no longer invested in the case. Reign couldn't help to think that she let her mother down. She now had two parents that were murdered in cold blood and neither of them received justice.

Once the couple entered the courtroom and Detective Allen saw Reign sitting in the back of the courtroom, he scurried over to the prosecutor to make him aware of her presence. The prosecutor looked back at Reign and then addressed the judge. "Your honor, I would just like to inform you that our eyewitness is present in the courtroom, and we are ready to proceed with the hearing."

The public defender dropped his paperwork on the table. "Your honor, I request that the witness and all officers involved in the investigation be sequestered."

"Counsel, you are in no position to make a request to the court when your client hasn't showed up yet. Did you make the call yet?"

"Umm...I apologize sir. I can't find his phone number. I know it was on one of these papers, but I just don't know which one. If I could just have a few more minutes to look."

"Your honor, he has had more than enough time to look for that number. Something tells me that even if he finds it, his client still won't be showing up. I'm sure his client was aware that we were going to make a bail argument seeing as though a string of violent events took place, which we linked to this case. My guess is that the defendant is in the wind," the prosecutor said.

The judge rubbed his chin and glanced at the public defender. "I am inclined to agree with the prosecution." He lifted his gavel and announced "the defendant has failed to appear for this preliminary hearing and all charges will be held and his bail revoked. A warrant for will be issued for the defendant. Court adjourned."

Darren turned to Reign. "He really didn't show up."

"This can't be good. That means he's still out there."

"Maybe it is good and something happened to him."

"Here come the detectives, let's ask them."

"Ms. Bryant?" Sergeant Harris asked.

"Yes."

"I am Detective Sergeant Harris of the Homicide Unit. You have already met Detective Allen. I would just like to extend my gratitude to you for showing up today. I know things like this aren't easy, so I just want to thank you for being here."

"What happened to Omari?" Reign asked.

"We don't know. We were going to ask you the same thing. Have you heard from him at all?"

"Hell no."

"We will keep an eye out for him and let you know if anything comes up."

"Why wasn't he charged for my mom's murder? It's not fair that he gets away with that."

Sergeant Harris looked over at Detective Allen and then back at Reign. "We are still putting the pieces together in that case, to ensure that it's solid. We don't want any surprises coming up. That's why we were getting this case out of the way first."

"Are you sure you will charge him for my mom's murder? That's the only reason I agreed to cooperate with yall in the first place. I want justice for my mom."

"You have my word."

"And I want her to work the case," Reign replied, nodding her head in the direction of Raven.

"Unfortunately, Detective Ramos isn't a part of our unit," Sergeant Harris responded, after seeing who Reign was referring to.

"Why not?"

"She works for the Special Victims Unit. We allowed her to help out with this case, but it was never going to be a permanent thing."

"Well, it needs to be. I want her working my mom's case."

"Okay, I'll see what I can do. In the meantime, here's my card. Call me if you ever need anything."

"Thank you."

Reign and Darren exited the courtroom with the everyone else. There was relief that she wasn't called to testify, but there was still concern because they didn't know if something happened to Omari. With Darren's help, she was moving forward with her life and didn't plan on looking back. Sergeant Harris' word meant nothing to her. Reign wasn't optimistic about the case they would build for Stoney's murder. They already had the murder weapon and, in her mind, there was plenty of evidence seized on the night of the raid.

"I can't wait to get to D.C."

"I know you can't. I just shocked that you got Brandi to agree to move with you," Darren teased.

"Shit, me too. She said she's gon' be back and forth tho' because of your brother."

"Those two are something else." Darren laughed.

"I like it tho'. I've never seen Brandi like this before. You know how she used to be. She used to have a new nigga every other week. I like what your brother has done for her."

"I just hope he stays consistent with her. Especially with everything that's going on."

"I think he will."

Darren smiled and reached his hand out. Reign held it, sliding her fingers in between his. The couple headed down the courthouse steps and towards the garage.

I should kill this bitch. Omari was heated, watching Reign leave the courthouse with another man. He gripped the sawed-off shotgun that rested on his lap and turned the corner in the rental car. He slowly drove down the street approaching the couple. *This bitch really came here to snitch on me. I knew this was a set up.* He adjusted his grip on the shotgun as he pulled up right behind them. Just as he was pulling up next to the couple, Omari spotted a familiar face. Raven ran to catch up to Darren and Reign. *That fuckin' cop bitch.*

Omari slid the shotgun over to the passenger seat. He was ready to air Reign out but wasn't prepared for a shootout with the cops. Seeing Raven, caused him to change his plans. The couple never noticed he had driven by them in the silver Toyota Camry. *I'm gon' to get you bitch*, he thought as he headed away from the courthouse.

CHAPTER 34

I NDIA!" Omari yelled as he entered one of his stash houses.

"Hey, what's up?" she replied, exiting the kitchen.

"You know who this nigga is?" he asked, showing her a picture that he took on his phone.

India grabbed the phone and examined the couple in the picture. She then swiped over to a few more pictures. "That look like Draco's brother. He fuckin' wit' dat bitch?"

"That's what it look like. The nigga was all hugged up on that rat ass bitch when they came outta' court." Omari put the shotgun on the couch. "I gotta find this nigga. I'mma kill all of these motherfuckas."

"I thought you went up there to do that."

"I was 'bout to but one of those fuckin' cops popped up."

"I told you it was a bad idea. It's a fuckin' courthouse. Of course, it's gon' be cops up there."

"I ain't have no choice. That bitch hidin' out somewhere and that's the only place I knew I was gon' find her. What the fuck you want me to do, let this shit ride and rot in a cell cuz of this bitch? Without her they ain't got no case."

"You gotta chill out. It's way too much heat on you right now. What if one of those cops saw you in that car? You gon' bring all that fuckin' heat down on me."

"Ain't nobody see me in it. Plus, you can take it back to the rental spot if you want and get another one. It ain't a big deal."

"It is a big deal. I don't want no bullshit comin' my way."

"And what if it do?" Omari asked, walking up on India. "What you gon' do?"

He was so close that their lips almost touched as he spoke. India bit her lip. "I'm hold it down," she muttered sensually.

"That's what I like to here," Omari said as his lips brushed against hers. "Now go and get my money."

Omari slapped India on the ass, once she turned to get the cash she was holding for him. Her low-cut shorts allowed his palm to slap against the bottom of her ass that was hanging out. Omari's eyes followed India, every step of the way. It was like her ass had him in a hypnosis. For a second, he forgot about his failed mission. Her curves always grabbed his attention but seeing Reign with another man made Omari want to give India some special treatment.

"Here you go," India said, handing Omari a thick wad of cash.

"How much more I need?"

"Like thirty."

"Fuck," Omari blurted out, knowing that he would have to retain a private attorney in order to take care of his case. He no idea that his former attorney never put in the continuance request and that the public defender dropped the ball at the hearing. "I'm 'bout to text these niggas and get the rest of my money."

"You sure you wanna' do that?"

"Hell yeah. I paid these niggas to handle this shit and it still ain't been handled. If I gotta do this shit myself then I'm getting' my fuckin' money back."

"Why don't you give them time to do what they gotta do? You act like they just sittin' around doing nothin'. You told them that Reign was at that bitch apartment and they went over there three times to handle business, but she was only there once and Ant and 'em almost got caught by the cops when they tried to run up on her. Give it a lil' more time."

"I ain't got no more time to give. The sooner that bitch die, the sooner I can get rid of this case and get back to my old life. Ain't that what you want?"

"I ain't picky. I'm gon' hold you down regardless of if you make this shit happen or not."

"Ain't gon' be no regardless. I'm gon' make all this shit happen and give you the world," he muttered, pulling her in close.

India let out a soft moan, as the bulge in Omari's pants pressed against her. "You better stop," she whispered, knowing she really wanted to say *give me that big ass dick.*

Omari cupped her ass and pressed against her again. "I ain't stoppin' shit."

India couldn't take it anymore and dropped down to her knees. She was ready to get a mouthful of Omari. He had been so wrapped up in his mission to kill Reign, he didn't really have time to give India what she longed for. It meant the world to her to have his attention and to finally be his main bitch. India knew she complemented Omari well. She was getting to know the ins and outs of his business, preparing herself to one day call shots of her own.

India unzipped Omari's pants. She looked up at him and smiled, knowing she was about to suck his soul out of his body. Omari stopped India. "Chill," he said as he picked her up.

"Why you stop me?" she asked. Omari smiled and pushed India against the wall. "What the fuck." She was ready to swing on him but saw the look in his eyes. His aggression wasn't rage; it was seduction.

Omari grabbed India by her braids and turned her around, pushing her face against the wall. She was like puddy in his hands, allowing him to man-handle her. India felt his thumbs slide inside her shorts as he slowly pulled them down. She didn't know what was coming next.

"Fuck," she moaned as Omari gently sunk his teeth into her earlobe, following up with his warm tongue sliding into her ear. India's eyes rolled to the back of her head. "You know I need you, right?"

Hearing those words made India weak. She nodded her head then looked back at Omari. He dropped to his knees and was now staring at her round ass. He smacked it, and the strike from his hand forced both cheeks to jiggle. Omari loved India's body and he was ready for a taste. Kissing one cheek at a time, he teased her and allowed the anticipation to drive her insane. India tried to stay focused on him, but each soft kiss forced her eyes into the back of her head.

"You gon' keep playing with me, daddy?"

Omari stared at India, as she looked back at him and smirked. Their eyes were locked. Omari stuck out his tongue and shoved it deep between her ass cheeks as the tip of his tongue reached its destination. "Oh fuck," India yelled out in pleasure. Omari placed his left hand on the small of her back, keeping her pinned against the wall. Then he slid his other hand against her soaked pussy, allowing two fingers to enter. India moaned louder. She tried pushing off the wall because she was losing control of her body, but Omari left her weak.

Her body began trembling as she Omari continued consuming her. He continued working his fingers in and out of her, occasionally massaging her clit. India's moans turned to pleasurable screams. She clawed at the wall, trying to find something to grab. "Arch that shit back," Omari ordered. India obeyed the command, poking her ass out and allowing Omari to continue feasting. "You like this shit?"

"Naw, nigga." India moaned. "I love this shit."

"Tell me you love it."

"I love it," she moaned.

"Tell me you love this shit."

"I love this shit."

"Tell me you love me."

India was in state of euphoria. "I love you, nigga," she screamed as she climaxed. Omari continued fingering her as she released all over his hand. "Damn, nigga," she moaned as her body continued shuddering. Omari kept her pinned against the wall. India couldn't escape. Everything was sensitive. She couldn't handle his touch anymore and just collapsed to the floor.

Omari laughed. "Why the fuck you just fall down like that?"

"Cuz, you driving me fuckin' crazy. You knew what the fuck you was doing."

"I was just givin' you what you want."

"Naw, nigga. That was more than that. You trynna have a bitch on one of those Lifetime movies and shit because you did this to me and I snap and kill any bitch that think about lookin' at you."

Omari picked up India's shorts and handed them to her. "I wasn't even done with yo ass yet. He pulled out his phone and looked at the time. "You lucky I got shit to do or I'd be right back on that ass."

"What you gotta do?"

Omari ignored the question and headed to the bathroom. He grabbed a washcloth and ran warm water on it, along with soap. He began wiping his face and beard, cleaning himself up after his meal.

India came in the bathroom and stared at Omari. "You just gon' ignore me? What you gotta do?"

"I gotta meet up wit' this crazy nigga, so we can get this job done. But first I gotta get that money back from those niggas that Ant hired. They are a waste of time. I'mma do this shit myself. All I need is someone crazy enough to ride wit' me."

"Why don't you bring me wit' you?"

"I need you to do something else. You gotta get close to that nigga Draco. I need to know where he at and who he wit' at all times. If I can catch any of these motherfuckas' slippin', I'm takin' that shot."

"I already tried that and it ain't work. I couldn't even get close to that nigga. He movin' different. He don't be at the clubs no more or on his blocks. He's like a ghost out here."

"I'mma make that nigga a ghost for real," Omari said, putting the washcloth on the sink and turnin' to India. "I don't need you to do nothin' crazy, baby. Just find out how he be moving and where he be at. I'll handle the rest."

"What if somethin' happen to me?"

"Ain't nothin' gon' happen to you. These niggas are all on alert cuz of me. They gon' be lookin' for some niggas to run up on 'em. They ain't checkin' for no females. You'll blend right in if you're down their hood and they won't even know. "

"Okay. I'll do it. I need one of your guns tho."

"What you need a gun for?"

"I need to be strapped at all times. I'm not going out there naked."

"Cool, get one of the pistols out the closet. Just make sure you don't do nothin' stupid. I'm gon' be the one to kill Reign and her lil' boyfriend. That shit on me."

"Gotchu," India said as she headed upstairs to get ready. Omari could say what he wanted about being the one who pulls the trigger on Reign, but India didn't plan on letting an opening slip through her fingers. She knew that if the opportunity presented itself, she wouldn't hesitate to put Reign down. India needed Reign out of the way, so Omari could be focused. India needed him to be the hustler that flooded the streets again, not a has-been that was obsessed over his ex-girlfriend and a court case. There was only one way to solidify her spot and she was going to get it by blood.

CHAPTER 35

"I can't believe Brandi agreed to move to D.C. with me," Reign said.

"I can't believe it either, but I'm happy that she did," Darren responded as he pulled up to the apartment building. "I think those are the movers. Do you have the key?"

"Yup." Reign handed Darren a set of keys and he exited the car and approached the men. Reign's head was on a swivel. Darren agreed to drive one of his tinted-out company vehicles, but she was still on high alert. Brandi's apartment was a complete mess as a result of the shooting, but they both had belongings that they needed to get out of there.

Darren knew it was too risky for Brandi and Reign to be packing themselves, so he hired a moving company to do the packing and shipping for them. The ladies wouldn't even have to step foot back into the apartment. The moving crew was going to pack all of their valuables up, while Darren and Reign made their way over to The Elk Room to meet up with their friends.

"We are good to go," Darren said as he entered the tinted-out Dodge Charger. "They said they will text me when they are finished."

"This is really it. It's like a dream come true."

Darren slowly pulled off. "Why do you say that?"

"I spent my entire life under someone. Whether it was my mom, the people at the group home, or Omari, someone always made my decisions for me. This is my first big decision that I made solely for myself without being concerned about how anyone else felt about it."

"How does it feel?"

"It feels amazing." Reign wanted to say more to Darren, but she kept it to herself. She was grateful to have him by her side. She knew that she wouldn't have been able to maneuver through the past few weeks without him. Darren was different in so many ways. Reign felt secure with him and never questioned his intentions. He never asked her for anything, which made her want to give him everything. "So, you never told me your plans."

"What plans?"

"Your plans for H.O.P.E. and your plans with me."

Darren smirked. "Let's just see how things go. I'm a hundred and ten percent dedicated to you. I'll do what it takes to be with you, but I refuse to pressure you into making any decisions right now. I'll be out D.C. as much as you want me to be."

"What if I wanted you to be there all the time?"

"Then, I'll be there," he responded, leaning in for a kiss. Their lips locked, igniting the fire inside them both.

Reign didn't quite know what she was feeling. So many emotions took over in that moment. She cracked the window, allowing for the breeze to cool her down. She took in the beauty of her city one last time. For Reign, this wasn't a permanent goodbye to Baltimore but it was definitely a lot of pain and trauma she wanted to leave behind. "Hey, make a left turn and go around the block," Reign requested as she leaned forward and stared at the side mirror.

"Why, what was it?"

"I don't know yet. There's a silver car back there and I could of sworn that I saw it over at the apartment. It's just weird that it's behind us now. I want to make sure they aren't following us."

Darren made a left turn and checked the rearview mirror. The silver Toyota Camry that was a few car lengths behind them also made the left turn. Darren and Reign looked at each other. Her heart began racing. "Hold on," Darren said as he made another left. The Toyota made the same turn. "They're still behind us. Open the glove compartment."

"What?"

"Open it. It's a gun in there." Reign opened the glove compartment and froze when she saw the pistol. Sounds of gun shots went off in her head and images of her mother and father flashed in her mind. Her hand shook as she went to grab the gun. Darren's eyes danced around from straight ahead to the reaver view mirror. He looked over and noticed Reign's hand. He grabbed Reign's hand. "It's okay."

Darren made a right turn and pulled over. The Toyota made the right turn too. Darren released Reign's hand and grabbed the gun. "Get down," he instructed Reign, as he clenched the weapon. He checked the side mirror to see if the Toyota pulled over too. He raised the gun once he saw the vehicle pulling up next to him. Darren's finger slid over the trigger, as he prepared to air out the Toyota. Reign pulled her seat back and closed her eyes. The Toyota pulled up and passed them. "Oh shit," he muttered, letting out a deep sigh as he watched the Toyota continue down the road. His heart was racing. "False alarm."

"Sorry." Reign pulled her seat up. "I feel paranoid. You prolly think I'm crazy or something."

"You're not crazy at all. That car definitely looked like it was following us. I know exactly what you need. "Darren put the gun back into the glove compartment. "You need to go have a couple drinks with your Brandi and my sister and then tonight we are going out for dinner. Just the two of us."

Reign smiled. It never failed. Darren always knew the right things to say and it was always at the right time. He headed to the lounge and even though everything turned out to be some bullshit, her intuition didn't allow her to put her guard down.

"Yall better slow down wit' all those drinks. Yall gon' be drunk as shit by the time they get here," Darryl said.

"Nigga, these are mimosas. Ain't nobody getting' drunk off this shit," Dasia responded. "Where they at anyway?"

"They should be pullin' up," Brandi stated, as she poured herself another drink.

"Well, I'll be right back. I'm going to the bathroom," Dasia announced. "Make sure nobody touch my drink." Reign and Darren entered the lounge, just as Dasia headed to the back. They were on their second pitcher of mimosas, and it was running right through her.

"Hey yall," Brandi greeted as she hugged Reign and Darren. "What those movers say?"

"They said they'll take care of everything for us. We ain't have to do nothin' at all."

"They better be careful with my shit and none of my bags better be missing."

"These dudes are legit. They aren't going to fuck with your stuff. I use this company all the time and I've never had an issue with them."

"Good but if something is missing, you're going to have to replace."

"I'll leave that up to my brother," Darren kidded.

Damn, I gotta weak ass bladder. Dasia flushed the toilet and exited the stall. As she washed her hands, the bathroom door opened. Dasia looked up and spotted a familiar face. "Oh my God. India, is that you?"

"Yes, girl. What a coincidence. What you doing here?"

"I'm just here with my brothers. What about you? You here for business or pleasure?"

"Definitely not business. I just stopped in for a quick drink."

"The streets are talkin' about you and your girls."

India scrunched up her face. "What they sayin'?"

"They sayin' that yall are gettin' at the bag." Dasia said, as dried her hands with paper towel. "I heard yall be runnin' shit over in Philly and Jersey too."

"Somethin' like that. You gotta come get down with us."

"You know damn well, I ain't fuckin' wit' that shit around here. My brother would kill me if I got caught up in some bullshit."

"Who said you gotta be around here?"

"What you mean?"

"You remember Londyn? She went to school with us too."

"I think so."

"Light skinned, green-eyes, big forehead," India joked.

Dasia laughed. "I prolly gotta see her to recognize her."

"Anyway, she just hit me up about some work in Atlanta that she's 'bout to get into. I'mma head down there with her next month. Let me know if you trynna get on this money train."

"I'll think about it. Give me your number and I'll definitely hit you up about it." Dasia took her phone out her purse and handed it to India. India put her number in the phone. "You might as well come out here and chill with us. We 'bout to order another round of drinks."

"I appreciate the offer, but I'm just gon' grab a drink and them I'm heading out. I've got some business to take care of and a few errands to run."

"Okay, girl. I'll hit you up tomorrow and maybe we can do lunch to discuss a few things."

"No problem," India said as she opened the door to exit. "Wait, are you gon' be here for a while? Maybe I'll come back after I handle everything."

"I doubt it. My brother is taking his girl out to dinner later, so we'll prolly only be here for a couple hours."

"Alright, that's good to know. Don't forget to hit me up tomorrow, so we can link up."

"Definitely."

India headed back to the lounge area. She didn't hesitate to pull out her phone and give Omari an update. She sat at the bar and watched from across the room. India wanted to pull the strap out and blasting at that entire section. She hated letting opportunities pass her by, but she had no choice in this situation. Omari told her to stand down and that's what she planned to do. Besides, the bulge on Darryl's hip, reassured India that he wouldn't go out without a fight. She couldn't afford to get into a shootout in a packed lounge. She played it smart and continued watching them, waiting for Omari to tell her what to do.

CHAPTER 36

Omari sat in his Ferrari, contemplating his next move. India had given him the intel he needed to complete the task at hand. He was impressed by her cunningness, to not only tail Reign and Darren but to also get info from Darren's sister. Everyone walking by admired Omari's luxury vehicle. Some people even snapped pictures of it while passing. No matter where he went in the vehicle, the Ferrari grabbed everyone's attention. For the first time, it seemed like he had finally come to grips with his issues. He called it loving a woman, but one could argue that he was just infatuated and obsessed with Reign. He was used to being on top of the world and the fact that when it came to true love, he was not able to keep the woman that held him down through his most challenging times was a hard pill to swallow. Just thinking about her made him want to snap. Omari reached into the glove compartment and pulled out a Crown Royal bag. The small sack was being used to hold a bunch of small glass vials filled with cocaine. He grabbed one of the vials and carefully emptied the white powder onto the dashboard of the foreign car, next to a rolled up hundred-dollar bill. Omari leaned forward and use the rolled-up bill to snort the powder into his nostrils. He rocked back in the seat, patiently waiting for the high to hit him. Minutes ticked away as Omari's mouth began to water and his eyes rolled to the back of his head. He had been sitting in the car for over two hours and watched as the clock finally hit midnight.

The picture he received on his phone of the couple kissing had to be a misunderstanding in his mind. *This bitch got me locked up and has the nerve to be running around kissing on this nigga and shit.* Omari tried his best to understand what was going on in his life right now. *It had to be a friend of hers she was just out to dinner with,* he thought, but he was informed that it seemed much more between Reign and her date. Still in disbelief, he came to the Topside restaurant to see for himself. Omari planned on going to the restaurant to confront the two and out their situation. He also wanted to express his love for the woman whose heart he had broken into a million pieces. He never planned on Reign finding out what he did to Stoney, and he could not believe that his secret was finally out. To Omari, an apology from him would be sincere but he doubted if Reign was going to accept the apology. An apology attached to her mother's death would never be accepted. That is an everlasting pain that she would always feel.

However, Omari did not think he deserved the karma that Reign bestowed upon him. It was rule number one of the street code; *no snitching*. He felt that Reign violated the street code once she had their home raided and him arrested. He felt deceived by a woman he truly loved. The last thing he expected her to do was go to the cops. Especially after seeing the lavish lifestyle that he was providing her. But since she did cooperate, he needed to get rid of Reign or else he would risk spending the rest of his life in jail for murder. His chances were not going to be good with a bench or jury trial, and her as the eyewitness.

He was still in disbelief. He knew in his heart that killing Stoney was an accident, but that did not matter to Reign. His intended target had always been Slim. Stoney was an unexpected casualty. He figured that taking care of Reign would be the ultimate repayment for his despicable actions. He was willing to take that secret to the grave with him. Even in jail, he was constantly thinking about everything he accomplished with Reign. To have his whole life taken away from him while sitting behind bars was a harsh reality. He assumed that once he got out of jail, that Reign would somehow forgive him, and they would be able move on from this situation. However, that was not the case at all.

An AK-47 automatic rifle was propped up on the front passenger seat. Omari cocked the rifle, sending a round into the chamber. He was prepared to paint the city red. He was parked across the street from the restaurant, with a perfect view of the entrance and exit. He patiently waited for the perfect time to strike. The drugs were currently flowing throw his system and he felt invincible. Omari was ready for war. Another message came through his phone.

They are leaving now.

Omari stared at the front of the restaurant. He was focused. The rage began to suffocate him, as he watched the couple exit the restaurant. Reign was being carried by her date. *This can't be right.* In Omari's head there had to be an explanation and he wanted to hear what it was. He was rotting in that cell before he was granted a bail hearing and to see Reign hugged up with another man was infuriating. His heart raced intensely as his hands began to shake. It was time to strike.

Omari exited the Ferrari and started walking towards the couple, hoping to run into them as they made their way down the sidewalk. The plan was simple and it replayed over and over in his head. He was going to rip them both in half with the assault rifle. His plan was interrupted when the couple stopped at a white Dodge Charger and entered the vehicle. Omari picked up his pace, before the vehicle had a chance to take off. He did not plan on letting Reign go that easily.

As he approached the Charger, he could see the couple making out through the rear windshield. It felt like his racing heart had shattered into a million pieces. But for most, a moment that would have brought out sadness seemed to bring out more rage in Omari. "If I can't have you, nobody can," he muttered just before walking up to the driver's door and raising the rifle. Omari pointed the high-powered weapon at the occupants of the vehicle and squeezed on the trigger, without hesitation. His index finger kept slapping on the trigger until there was nothing more than a clicking noise with each trigger pull. All he saw was red as he advanced on the Charger and grabbed the door handle. The job was not done. He wanted to ensure they both were dead. A line was crossed and there would have to be a price to pay.

Omari opened the door, but the driver gathered enough strength to pull back on it and hit the gas. The Charger scraped the vehicle it was parked behind, which made it jerk. During that minor collision, Omari was knocked to the ground. "Ahhhh," he screamed. A sharp pain exploded in his body as the left rear tire of the Charger ran over his legs. Through the pain, Omari managed to throw another clip in his rifle and bust of more shots at the Charger as it sped off down the street. The first few shots shattered the back windshield of the Charger, but the remaining shots just whizzed by the vehicle. After making a sharp turn, the Charger was out of view.

Omari was in a lot of pain, but his prior drug use made it manageable. He only had a few minutes before police officers would swarm the area, collecting evidence and looking for witnesses. He used all the strength he had to crawl towards his vehicle. Once he made it to the Ferrari, he muscled his way inside. The pain was killing him, but he still had the ability to move his legs. Even if he didn't, there was still unfinished business he had to handle before it was too late. Omari was determined to find Reign.

Omari bumped another line of coke before heading out to find his prized possession and intended target. The Ferrari sped down the street, hitting the same turns the Charger made earlier. There was no sign of the Charger anywhere. Omari was sure it would be pulled to the side of the road somewhere, after the assault he unleashed on the occupants. *There is no way they got far.* Omari was all up and down the Mount Vernon area. All hope was lost, until he heard police sirens and spotted their emergency lights in the distance. They were going in the opposite direction of the restaurant. "That has to be for them," he mumbled as he headed in the direction of the emergency vehicles. Omari ended up at the intersection of W Lexington Street and N Greene Street. Beyond the flashing red and blue lights, he spotted the Charger which was currently flipped on the side. He pulled over and watched as fire fighters and paramedics extricated the occupants of the vehicle and loaded them onto stretchers. The police had the intersection surrounded, so there was no way that Omari would be able to get close to the scene.

It was like a wild animal was let out of a cage; the way Omari was preying on Reign. A part of him wanted to start letting off shots at the ambulances as they loaded the victims in the rear of the vehicle. However, he did not want the large number of officers to react to him. He knew he could not win a gun battle against an army of cops. The thought did cross his mind a couple more times, but the move just was not practical. Omari felt like a failure. He only had one thing to do, and he did not know if he correctly executed his plan. Omari had no other option but to get out of the area before the cops spotted his vehicle.

Omari's legs felt like they were on fire. He sent out a few text messages and headed over to Cherry Hill. Once he pulled up, he was assisted by a few of the remaining members of his once lucrative drug organization. Once he got locked up, the territory was open for the taking and someone took it. With the MS-13 gang controlling most of the territory, the remaining blocks belonged to the Bookert Bloods. They ran a small pocket of Cherry Hill that spanned from Round Road to Carver Road. Most of the crew was still cool with Omari but their leader, Staxx, did not care for him. Staxx did not like Omari's in and out presence in their hood. He knew Omari used to get a lot of money, but he also knew that money had run dry. The only thing that Omari had left was the home in Ellicott City, a couple row homes in Cherry Hill, and a few cars. Omari would always pop in and out of the hood, whenever he needed something. Whether it was getting guns or fuckin' with a few of the chicks in the hood, he made sure he kept a presence.

Staxx inhaled the thick smoke from the blunt and blew it out through his nose. He was a prominent figure in the hood, literally and figuratively. He stood around

6'5" and weighed about 240 pounds. As with every hood story, his skills growing up were in sports. He played football and basketball all around the city. However, between a lack of focus in school and his run-ins with the law, Staxx never had the opportunity to excel at anything besides gangbanging. Tattoos covered his light brown skin, each of them colored or accented with red ink. His trademark piece was inked directly over his left eyebrow. Completed in calligraphy font and red ink, he represented his crew by getting Bookert tattooed on his face. Wherever Staxx went, you knew exactly where he was from.

He stood on the front step of one of the homes and watched members of his crew help the injured Omari into a home across the street. He took another hit from the blunt and headed across the street. Omari owned the home that he was carried into. It was initially one of his trap houses, but now it was just abandoned. The gang posted up at the home, but no one claimed rights to operate out of it, nor were they given permission. The tiny two-bedroom and two-bathroom home looked like it was going to crumble. There were rotten wood planks that covered the floors, broken tiles in the kitchen and bathrooms, and mold spreading from the walls to the ceiling.

"What the fuck is going on, blood?" Staxx asked as he barged into the home.

"He's hurt," one of his men said.

"What the fuck happened to you?" Staxx asked Omari.

"Got hit by a car," Omari mumbled as he grimaced. The pain in his legs began shooting up into his back. He pulled up his pant legs to examine his injuries.

"I don't see shit."

"I think my knee is dislocated."

"Yo, it ain't nothing wrong with this nigga. Yall up here treating this nigga like a baby and he ain't even bleeding."

"Chill out," Omari shouted. "I'm really fucked up."

"How you get hit, blood?"

"I was crossing the street, and somebody must have not been looking or something. I don't fuckin' know." Omari scooted himself up onto the wall. He was still scowling in pain. "Somebody go get India for me. I need her help."

One of the men, was about to head out the door and Staxx pulled his gun on him. "Who you work for, blood?" Staxx barked. "This is the shit I'm talking 'bout. Yall be jumping for this bitch ass nigga and he ain't even gang."

"Yo, watch your fuckin' mouth," Omari yelled. "I was puttin' food in these niggas mouths before you even hit the scene."

"Who the fuck you talkin' to. We will get it brackin' if you want, blood. I'd smoke yo ass right here."

Everybody turned when the door burst open. Brizz came running in the house. He was wearing a fitted suit, but had his red bandana tied around his head. "Yo that shit was crazy," he said to Omari. "You lit their asses up."

"Fuck you talkin' 'bout?" Staxx asked. "And why the fuck do you got a suit on, nigga?"

"O, just lit this fuckin' car up over in the Art District," Brizz said excitingly. "He had the K out and shit and blasted those motherfuckas."

"Oh, you just happened to leave that fuckin' part out of the story, huh?" Staxx asked Omari. "Aye, Brizz. Who did this bitch ass nigga light up?"

"I don't know. It was a couple. They were at this fancy ass restaurant."

"So, what the fuck were you doing there?"

"He asked me to go and watch them. That's why I got this fly as suit on. I was in the restaurant and shit. Once they left, he lit they asses up."

"So, these motherfuckas are dead, huh?"

"Yeah, they're dead. Well, they pulled off, but they prolly banged out somewhere. Ain't nobody surviving all those shots from the K."

"Oh, so yall don't even know if they survived that bullshit?" Staxx turned to Omari and raised his gun into the injured man's face. "And your dumbass thought it was a good idea to bring this shit over here? Are you fuckin' stupid nigga?"

"I didn't have anywhere else to go," Omari hollered.

"Go to that fancy fuckin' home you got. Don't bring the bullshit to me. These motherfuckas might have followed you down here. The fuckin' pigs might have followed your dumbass too and you thought it was a good idea to bring all of that heat down here?"

"It ain't no heat," Omari responded. We're good."

"It ain't no *we* nigga. It's you and your bullshit. You tried to drag Brizz into it, but you better leave him the fuck out of it. Matter of fact, get the fuck out of here."

"Where the fuck am I gonna go?" Omari asked.

"I don't give a fuck where you go," Staxx barked as he hovered over the injured. "I just know you've got five minutes to get the fuck out of here."

"This is my house nigga, I don't gotta go nowhere."

"I ain't gonna repeat myself," Staxx said before turning to his men. "Drag his ass right back out there to that foreign and let's get back to work."

Staxx's men immediately followed orders and gripped Omari up, dragging him out of the house. Omari did his best to fight them off, but his injury left him at a disadvantage. The men dropped Omari off at his Ferrari and then went back to their corners. They knew Staxx was still watching and the last thing they wanted was to be on his bad side. Omari was a dangerous man, but Staxx was a maniac. Omari continuously operated off emotion. Staxx just didn't care and operated off pure evil. It was surprising to the others that Staxx let Omari off with a warning instead of just airing him out. However, although he was evil, Staxx wasn 't dumb. He knew that whatever heat Omari had on him would lead back to his hood and he did not want any association with that. With Omari gone, Staxx could have his people just focus on getting money.

CHAPTER 37

"**I think he's waking up. Go and get the doctor.**" The sound of the door slamming could be heard over the repeated beeping that was coming from the monitor. Darren struggled to open his eyes.

When he did, he was staring at the ceiling. The lights were turned off, but the window was open, and the sun was shining through. He lifted his hand to scratch his face, noticing the tubes and cords that were attached it. He followed the tubes and cords with his eyes. One led to an IV that was putting fluids in his body and the others were hooked up to an electronic monitor. This was the same machine that was letting off the annoying noise. A hand brushed across Darren's leg. He looked over and saw Dasia by his side.

"I can't believe you're up," she said. Tears had pooled in her eyes but had not fallen yet.

"What happened to me?"

"You need to rest, Darren. I sent Darryl to get the doctor."

"Where is Reign?"

The tears were slowly running down Dasia's eyes. "M—Mom is in the waiting room too. She wants to see you but wanted to wait until you got up." She was clearly choked up.

"Reign. Is Reign here?"

"...and dad is on his way here from Virginia."

"Dasia, what the fuck is going on? Where is Reign?" Darren muttered, as he tried to sit up. Despite a valiant effort, the pain that attacked every part of his body prevented that movement from happening. The grimacing expression on Darren's face made Dasia get squeamish. She stood up and walked to the window.

The door opened and in walked an older white man, wearing a white lab coat and holding a clipboard. "Mr. Knight, I'm glad to see you're awake. I'm Dr. Gooden and I was with you since you came into the emergency room. How are you feeling?"

"Everything hurts and I can barely move."

"Yes, we have you on medication for the pain and you should be up for another dosage within the next hour," the doctor said as he looked down at his watch. "Other than that, I need you to get some rest and start letting your body heal."

"What happened to me?"

The doctor looked over at Dasia. He figured one of the family members would have informed Darren about the incident he was involved in. Seeing the sister in tears and the desperation on Darren's face let the doctor know that his patient was unaware of what took place. "Well, you were involved in a horrible shooting and a car accident. It is a miracle that you survived. You were shot multiple times and when you crashed your car, you didn't have a seatbelt on which caused you and your passenger to get tossed around the inside of the car. I believe you sustained a concussion from the accident. We were able to patch your wounds up, but you have a long road to recovery and need to rest."

Everything was all coming back to Darren. He thought the events that took place were from a bad dream, but they were indeed a reality. The muzzle flashing during the first initial shots was fresh in his mind. His heart began racing and sweat beads formed on his head. The beeping on the machine began speeding up.

"Mr. Knight, calm down. You are safe now. There's no need to worry."

Darren could barely move his body. He tried scooting up in the bed but only moved about an inch before scowling in pain. He felt defeated.

"Doctor."

"Yes, Mr. Knight."

"Reign. Where is Reign? She was in the car with me."

He was hesitant to answer. "Can you give us a minute?" the doctor asked Dasia. She walked over and kissed Darren's hand, then left the room. His eyes followed her and then refocused on the doctor.

"Mr. Knight, the passenger was severely injured during the shooting incident and the crash. She lost a lot of blood after the shooting, and she is still in surgery."

"She's not just a passenger; she's my fiancé. Why is she in surgery?"

"Yes. You had surgery too, so we could remove the bullets and repair your arm. Your arm broke after one of the bullets hit the bone," The doctor said as he scanned the notes on his clipboard. "Your fiancé on the other hand, has organ damage and we are still in the process of trying to repair the organs and stop some internal bleeding around her lungs."

"NOOOOO," Darren yelled out. "No. This can't be true." He tried sitting up again.

"Mr. Knight, please calm down. We are doing our best to help her. There's something else. Two of the bullets entered her stomach and there was nothing we could do to save the baby."

"Baby? What baby?" Darren asked in confusion.

"Your fiancé was pregnant."

"What?" Darren yelled. The information he was given was not processing correctly in his head. "Get out and go help Reign. I don't need you here."

"Mr. Knig—"

"Get the fuck out," Darren barked. If he had any amount of energy, he would have lunged at the doctor or thrown something at him. He only had enough energy to cry. Darren never knew that Reign was pregnant. She never told him. He wondered if she even knew she was pregnant. There were so many questions that needed to be answered. Darren could not stop the tears that were falling from his eyes. His whole life had been turned around in one night. Not only was his future wife badly injured, but they just unexpectedly lost a child. He did not even know why this happened to him or who targeted them. He felt an intense headache coming over him and just sat back in the bed.

"Yo bro," Darryl said as he entered the room. "What was all that yelling about?"

"I gotta' get the fuck out of here. Reign needs me." Darren began pulling at the cords, trying to disconnect them. Darryl grabbed his wrist.

"Bro, you have to chill. She's in surgery. It ain't nothing you can do for her right now." Noticing his brother's painful gaze, Darryl released his wrist and sat in the chair next to the hospital bed. "Who did this to yall?" Darryl asked.

Darren recognized the fire in his brother's eyes. He wished he had an answer for him. "I don't know. The came out of nowhere when we got in the car. I couldn't react fast enough." More tears fell from his eyes.

"This ain't your fault, don't you dare put this on yaself. I'm going to make some calls and find out who did this. You gotta' promise me that you're going to chill while I'm gone," Darryl said. "Let these doctors do their job and let me do mine. The only thing you need to do is chill out." Darren cut his eyes away. "You gotta' make that promise or I ain't leaving your side."

Darren looked back at this brother. "I promise," he reluctantly replied. He could not bear to feel this vulnerable. Darren was a strong-willed man and he didn't want anyone handling this situation but him. *Reign, you're going to pull through this. We're going to pull through this.*

"I'm bout to go make a couple of phone calls. Can mom, come in and see you? I know she's worried sick out there."

Darren nodded. He knew his mother had to be devastated when she got the news. She felt like she had been sitting in the waiting room for days, patiently expecting to be told that Darren had awakened. She was ecstatic when Dasia came out and told her the good news. She wasted no time running back to see her baby. Darryl held the door open, as his mom rushed in to see Darren.

Darryl began texting, to see if anyone heard about the shooting. It was only a matter of time before he got some information because the streets are always talking. Darryl just wanted to find out who was responsible before the police did. He was not a fan of the justice system and figured that real justice was street justice.

"Darryl," Brandi yelled from down the hallway.

"Brandi."

"Dasia called me," she said, giving him a hug. "Where are they?"

"Darren is in a room recovering and Reign is still in surgery."

"Oh my God. Did they say when she'll be out of surgery?"

He shook his head. "The only thing they said is that she was hurt badly," Darryl replied. Brandi could not believe what she was hearing. She knew Darren and Reign were legitimate people. They were not in the streets in any way, so it was only one person to blame for the attack. Reign had been through so much in life, from the death of her parents to the craziness with Omari and now this. Brandi's heart went out to her best friend. *If anyone can survive something like this, it's Reign,* she thought.

Brandi stepped forward and looked through the window of Darren's room. She saw his mom by his side and immediately thought about her best friend being all alone. "Do you know what floor she's on? I have to be there for her."

"They didn't tell us that. But I'm sure you can just go ask the nurse at the desk and she'll let you know. They've been cool with us."

"Okay, I'll head up there now. Are yall good?"

"Naw, we ain't good," Darryl responded. He was filled with rage. "I need to know who did this to them."

Brandi did not even hesitate to answer him. Once she got the call from Dasia, she immediately had a suspect. "I think I know exactly who did this."

CHAPTER 38

Omari grimaced as his new swollen legs began to throb. He started the Ferrari, allowing the growl of the vehicle to echo in the air. He eyed up Staxx, who was standing across the street, watching him like a hawk. Omari slid his hand over to the assault rifle that was still in the passenger seat. A part of him wanted to end Staxx's reign of terror and get his streets back, and now with Reign and Darren possibly out of the way, he could now focus on that goal.

Omar needed to get his money back. He had not been this concerned about money since he was a teenager. That brief jail sentence threw his business all out of whack. His connect only wanted to meet with him and then after the arrest, he did not want to meet at all. No one wants drama with law enforcement, no matter if it's on the local level or the Feds knocking at your door. Anyone who comes out of jail is a liability for at least their first free year. They are constantly going to have to check-in with their probation or parole officer or they are being stalked because the cops have other charges, they want to pin on you and they like to get them in at the preliminary hearing. So, as of now he was out of luck. There was no way that his plug would touch him this year, so he needed to find a new one. This would mean a war for territory. A war that neither side is prepared to fight, let alone win.

Omari's hands began to itch as his instincts told him to raise that gun and light Staxx up. Omari's hand rubbed along the barrel and then onto the handle. He was ready to put in some work. He drove by Staxx, and it seemed like their eyes were locked on each other the entire time. He navigated his way through the hood and ended up on the corner of Bridgeview and Round Roads. This was India's old block. She still resided in this neighborhood, although she spent most of her time at the stash house. He pulled out his phone and dialed a number.

"9-1-1, what's your emergency?"

"Hello, I would like to provide you with information regarding a shooting," Omari said, trying his best to mask his voice.

"A shooting where, sir?"

"There was a shooting at the Topside restaurant, and I know who the shooter is."

"Who is the shooter, sir?"

"His name is Staxx. He just dropped off an AK-47 on the corner of Bridgeview Road."

"Okay, sir. We have units on the way. I need you to stay on the line with me, so I can gather more infor – "

Omari hung up the phone. He tossed the rifle and his cellphone outside into a thick bush at the corner. Despite the excruciating pain in his legs, a smile spread across his face. He had a plan in place and this was the most crucial part of it. By the time he got over to his home in Ellicott City, the police would have swarmed Cherry Hill and snatched up Staxx for the shooting. With Staxx out of the way, he would be able to reclaim the blocks he once owned. Unfortunately, most of his old territory was taken over by MS-13. To get those back, he would need more than an anonymous phone call to the police. He would need an army and if Staxx was gone, The Bookert Bloods would become his troops. They had the numbers and the firepower, and Omari had the desire to win. He always did.

Next, Omari pulled up in front of India's home. Unable to walk up to the front door on his own, he honked the horn multiple times, until he spotted someone standing in the window. He was praying that it was not her dad, because that man hated Omari. He felt that his daughter was too good to date a drug dealer. After his son became adopted by the streets, India's parents fought hard to prevent her from following in those same footsteps. Her father also didn't like the fact that Omari was older than his daughter. India's dad constantly hounded her about Omari's age, but she never gave him a straight answer about how old he actually was. It was ironic because their home was one of the few that Omari owned. That also caused a bit of tension between the two men.

India's family was renting the home for years, but she and her family ran into some financial trouble. Once she started hanging around Omari, he began handling those issues for her, including dropping a pile of cash to avoid the home going in foreclosure. This gave her father another reason to dislike Omari. His pride would not let him accept the help and the acquisition was completed without his knowledge. India's brother tried multiple times to pay off the home, but their father refused the help because he knew the money wasn't clean. He did not want to feel like he owed Omari, but it was too late.

India looked out the living room window, to see who was making all the noise. Once she saw it was Omari's Ferrari, she immediately ran outside and hopped in the car. Omari wasted no time taking off, knowing that the neighborhood would soon be swarmed by red and blue lights.

"What are you doing here?" India asked.

"I need your help."

"What's wrong?" she followed up, seeing that he was in pain.

"I was in an accident earlier and my legs are hurting. I need you to see if you can help me out."

"How the fuck you get in an accident?"

"Reign and her boyfriend ran me over."

"So, this bitch got away again?"

"I don't know. I lit their shit up but he drove off on some scary shit."

India shook her head and then hopped on her phone. Her thumbs were tapping away at the screen and her eyes were focused on it. "There are a couple pharmacies up near you, we can stop there and pick up some stuff" she suggested.

By the time the couple made it to Omari's Ellicott City home, they were stocked up on first-aid supplies. India had purchased ice packs, pain relievers, leg wraps and a cane. Omari pulled into the garage. "Here, let me help you inside so you can get settled. I'll come back out and lock everything up." The interior of the luxury home was a mess. Without a feminine presence in the home, Omari did not bother with the upkeep. The damage caused by the Swat team, during the raid, was still present. Gaping holes decorated the walls, doors to the kitchen cabinets had been ripped off, and deep rips covered the leather couches from the claws of the K-9 drug dogs.

If Reign was still in his life, she would have had hired someone to fix the damage and to clean the home, but instead there was India. India did not mind that the house was in shambles because it was still lovely to her standard. She admired how large the home was and not the condition of it. Just being in the suburban neighborhood was a come up to her.

She assisted Omari to the couch in the den, before running back out to the garage to get the supplies from the pharmacy. "Lay back and let me put these on your legs," she said. India opened the icepacks and put them on Omari's legs. The bruising from the tires was beginning to show. She walked to the kitchen and grabbed a glass from the sink. She filled it with tap water and brought it over to Omari. "Here drink some of this and take these," she said, placing three pills in his hand. He immediately took the pills, hoping that the pain relievers would allow him to finally get comfortable. India had also given Omari a sleep aid. She figured he had been through so much that the only way he would actually get some rest is with assistance.

Hours had passed since Omari and India got to his home. India's idea worked. Omari was knocked out. She was able to replace the icepacks and even wrap his legs while he was sleeping. Without warning, Omari felt a blunt object crashing down against the side of his face. The force from the strike knocked him off the couch. His body crashed onto the floor, causing a sharp pain to shoot up his right shoulder. "What the fuck," he mumbled, turning to see what just struck him. As his blurred vision began to focus, all Omari could see is the color red. Red bandanas, red t-shirts, red hats, and there was India standing in the front rocking the red shorts that Omari complimented earlier in the night. "What the fuck is this?"

"You know what this is," Staxx said.

Omari's eyes widened when he saw Staxx standing in his home. He was not alone. There were four other members of his gang standing behind him. Omari's heart was racing and felt like it was going to jump out of his chest. He still did not process what was actually happening. "Fuck are you doing in my crib?"

"You left something in my hood, and I had to return it to you," Staxx said, tossing the large object at Omari. Omari looked down at the AK-47 that he discarded in Cherry Hill. "You thought you were slick, you fuckin rat," Staxx barked as he slammed a cellphone next to Omari, shattering it.

"This ain't what it look like."

"Then what is it, nigga?" Staxx asked. Omari could not think quick enough to provide him with a valid response. "Look at you. You're a fuckin' nut. Stand on your shit nigga," Staxx yelled. His roaring voice echoed throughout the large home.

"You did this? You let them in here?" Omari looked over and asked India.

"Shut the fuck up," Staxx interrupted. "You don't get to talk to her, you fuckin' rat." Staxx walked over to India was put his arm around her shoulder. "She's my bitch and she's gang. You were just a job."

Omari's heart shattered into fragments of disappointment. He was betrayed by another woman. He had feelings for India and felt like he did right by her. To see her standing with Staxx was a complete disappointment. Everything started playing back his head and the pieces of the puzzle were finally coming together. Omari remembered India tapping away on her phone while they were driving up to his home and the amount of time she spent in the garage after she said she was going to lock everything up. *It was her.* She was setting him up the entire time and did it right under his nose. "Why did you have to bring her into this?"

"You brought her into this, nigga. I told you to leave. I told you to not come the fuck back. And what's the first thing you do? You go and get her and bring her here, after you try to set us up."

"I ain't try to do nothin'."

"My phone has been blowing up since we got up here. You made the hood hot. It's pigs everywhere and my people told me that they are askin' for me by name. But you're a slick ass, dumb ass nigga." Staxx laughed. "You thought you were gon' set me up for the bull shit that you pulled off tonight, but that ain't happenin' nigga. The streets talk and that shit travels. Imagine my surprise when my homeboy from back in my ballin' days just hit my line. He told me his brother just got shot and that he needed a favor from me. He wanted to know if I could find out who shot his brother and now look at this. It all makes sense now. Brizz ran around braggin' that you shot somebody, and I find out my nigga Draco's brother got hit. That's real fuckin' ironic, nigga."

Omari grabbed the AK-47 from next to him. He aimed it at Staxx, leaned back, and pulled the trigger. Omari wanted to end it all right now and get back to his original plan. If the set up with the cops did not work, a bullet to the head would definitely put Staxx out of commission. The loud click in the firearm sent a sea of frustration through Omari. His last desperate act just failed.

"Is this nigga serious?" Staxx asked. "He thought we would be dumb enough to hand him a loaded gun." India and the other men began laughing. "Pick his ass up." The other gang members immediately followed orders and gripped up Omari. One of them delivered a gut-wrenching body shot in response to Omari's failed attempt to take out Staxx. "You really thought it was going to be that easy?" Staxx asked.

"You're so lucky. I should have killed you a long time ago," Omari exclaimed.

"You should have killed me? Nigga I'm a god. You can't kill me."

"You ain't no god. You're a man just like the rest of us. You bleed just like us."

"And you're a fuckin' rat," Staxx yelled as he shoved an ice pick into Omari's torso. Omari screamed out in pain. "You feel that? That feels good, doesn't it?" Staxx delivered another strike, puncturing the skin right next to the original wound. Omari screamed again. However, his screamed was muffled when India shoved a rolled-up ball of gauze into his mouth. Watching her assist in his torture hurt more than the stab wounds. There wasn't a bit of remorse on her face. He was truly just a job in her eyes. From the moment they met, India's goal was just to get close to Omari. To learn how he moved and where he was getting all of his money from. Once he got locked up, he trusted India to move a few things around for him. He was so focused on Reign, he never noticed that India was skimming off the top. She lined her pockets with extra cash until it all began to run out. She also had the paperwork to the Ferrari and all the rest of Omari's properties.

All of this was reported to her brother and Staxx. The only thing Staxx wanted was Omari's connect, which he got. It was not hard manipulating Omari when India was constantly pulling at his heartstrings. They say that behind every good man, there's a great woman. In this case, behind every broken man, there's a woman that can easily control him. India was Omari's puppeteer. She played innocent but she knew the game well. Every week The Pretty Pistols had a new victim, who thought he was going to get lucky with a pretty girl and the next thing they knew there were five red shirts in their house taking everything they could.

"I want this whole place cleaned out," Staxx ordered. "Anything valuable is coming with us."

Omari had been thrown back to the ground. He lifted his tank top, revealing the deep stab wounds. Blood dripped from each of the wounds, staining his pants. Omari had no fight left in him. He still couldn't get his legs under him and now the fresh wounds made it hard for him to do anything other than crawl around the floor.

"How does it feel? Does it burn or does it sting?" Staxx laughed sinisterly.

Omari didn't bother responding. He couldn't. He held his hand over the wound, slightly applying pressure. He let out another scream. The pressure he applied to slow down the bleeding hurt just as bad as the stabbing. Deep breaths escaped his mouth as he tried his best to control his breathing. The AK-47 was still on the floor. He wished it was loaded because this would all be over. He would have let it rip on everyone in the house, including India. But unfortunately, his fate had been sealed and he was not in control of it. "Just do it. Just kill me," Omari begged.

"Not yet. You need to suffer first." Staxx replied. Omari let out another groan. He looked up at his belongings being taken away by Staxx's crew. He was filled with anger. "Karma is a bitch ain't it?" Staxx lifted his leg and delivered a devastating kick to the side of Omari's face. "That's for trying to set me up." He delivered another kick. "And that's for being a fuckin' snake." Omari was broken. He could barely scream through all of the pain. Blood dripped from his swollen lips and open wounds. The beating he was currently taking was put on hold as Staxx's phone began ringing. "Yo," he answered, still hovering over Omari. "How's your brother doing?" he asked. His eyes stared a hole through Omari as he listened to the response. "That's good. Well like I said. We got this snake ass nigga right here. Let me know what you want to do."

Omari listened intently. His fate was currently being decided and he had no control of the outcome. It was not much he could do physically, and he knew there was no reasoning with someone as ruthless as Staxx. He was left with no other choice but to pray that it ended quickly.

"Okay, I got you," Staxx said before ending the call. He then stepped forward and continued hovering over

Omari. "Do you have any last wishes?" Staxx asked, pulling out a chrome Desert Eagle handgun from his waistband.

Omari groaned. "In – India." He could barely say her name.

"India?" Staxx asked. He looked over at her. "Oh, you want her to do it? You want her to pull the trigger?"

Omari nodded. "Yes," he muttered. "Please."

"Let me guess, you're still hooked on her. Even after all of this, you still worried about her. So, with your dying breath, you request that she be the one to pull the trigger. Why? Is it because it will give you closure or some shit?"

Omari nodded again.

"Fuck your closure, nigga," Staxx shouted before unloading his gun. Omari was riddled with bullets and slumped over on the floor. Blood poured from each bullet wound. Staxx watched Omari take his left breath, ensuring that there was not a chance of survival. He spit on Omari's lifeless body, before exiting the home and heading back to the hood.

CHAPTER 39

arryl slid his phone into his pocket and entered the hospital room. Everyone huddled around Darren's bed. Their mother was holding his hand firmly, refusing to let go. Their father was still on his way from Virginia. Dasia and Brandi were conversing and shot Darryl a look when he entered. He gave them a nod, confirming that their problem was solved. Brandi was relieved. She couldn't wait until Reign got out of surgery so that she could deliver the good news. They no longer had to look over their shoulders. The days of Omari hunting them down were finally over.

"Are they still out there?" Their mother asked.

"Who ma'?" Darryl wondered.

"Those two officers. They came in here asking Darren all of these questions like he was a suspect. I told them that he was in a lot of pain and wasn't in the right mind to answer those types of questions."

"Fuck them niggas. We ain't got shit to say to them."

"It's okay. They're just doing their job," Darren muttered.

His mother clenched his hand. "It's not okay. They have no right to question you like that. They asked you if you were shooting back at the person who shot you. If you were a white man, they wouldn't be asking you that. They would prolly have the case solved by now."

"Well, I hope they do solve it." Darren grimaced as he attempted to sit up.

"How bad is the pain, honey?"

"It's bad. I can feel everything. My arm is killing me."

His mother stared at the left arm, which was wrapped in a cast. She couldn't even imagine the type of pain Darren was currently experiencing. "Darryl, go get the nurse. Tell her that your brother needs something stronger for the pain."

"Okay," Darryl responded as he turned to head to the nurses' station. "It looks like they 'bout to come in here now."

Two doctors and three nurses entered the room. Their mother stood up. "He needs some more pain medication. Whatever you gave him before must have worn off."

"No problem," Dr. Gooden responded. "I'll make sure that we up his dosage."

"Good. Can we also get one of the nurses to help him to the bathroom? He hasn't gone in a while."

"Absolutely. Is there anything else you need?"

"No. That should be it."

"Where is Reign?" Darren asked.

"Yeah, is she out of surgery yet?" Brandi followed.

Dr. Gooden looked at Darren and took a deep breath. "There is something I need to tell you."

"No," Darren muttered. It didn't take a rocket scientist to figure out what was about to happen. The doctors didn't have to speak a word. Their body language displayed the bad news before they ever opened their mouths. "No. Don't say it. You better not say it."

"There was nothing that we could do."

"No," Darren yelled. "Where is Reign? Where is she at?" Tears poured from his eyes and once again, he tried scooting up. His entire world just crumbled. He waited his entire life to be with Reign and she was taken away from him in a split second. "I have to see her."

"It's okay, baby," his mother said, grabbing his hand. "Try to relax."

"I can't relax," Darren hollered. "I want Reign. I need her. I need my baby." Tears poured from his eyes. He had lost his fiancé and unborn child in a matter of hours. "Why, Lord? Why would you take her? You could have just taken me."

Darren's mother did her best to comfort him, but he was inconsolable. Nothing she could say or do would make his pain go away.

"This can't be true," Brandi said, as her voice cracked. Mascara ran down her cheeks. "Reign is a fighter. She has to be alive. You don't understand what she's been through. She can survive this.

Dr. Gooden sighed. "She did fight. However, the injuries were just too severe. One of the bullets entered her chest and caused penetrating cardiac trauma."

"What the fuck does that mean?"

"It means that the bullet struck her in the heart."

Brandi stumbled forward and fainted. She would have hit the floor if Darryl didn't run over and catch her. This was too much. Reign and Brandi had been best friends since middle school. The news broke her heart. Brandi knew that Reign deserved the life she planned on living. After all that she had been through, Darren seemed like the perfect guy to help make her dreams come true. Brandi saw the difference in her friend immediately after Reign met Darren. He made Reign so happy in ways that she never imagined. Reign told Brandi about the pregnancy, but it was their little secret. No one else had any idea that Reign was carrying Darren's child.

"Get her to a room," Dr. Gooden ordered. The nurses ran over and assisted Darryl with Brandi. They escorted her out of Darren's room and into her own. She slowly regained consciousness but was still distraught.

Darren was ready to jump out of bed. "Take me to my fiancé right now," he barked. I need to see my baby. She needs me right now." Darren didn't care about the words that came out of the doctor's mouth. He was only concerned about seeing Reign.

"Mr. Knight, I will get someone to bring a wheelchair up for you. You're in no condition to see anyone, but we will make an exception. Once the wheelchair comes up and the nurse gets your meds, we will take you up to the room."

The words went in one ear and out the other. Darren was breathing heavily. It felt like an elephant was sitting on his chest. The sounds of gunshots and glass shattering were repeatedly playing in his ears. Darren had to find a way to focus between the sad news that he had just received and the shooting replaying in his mind. He flinched at the thought of the attack. At the time, Darren was defenseless and so was Reign. He wondered if there was anything he could have done to save her. *We should have just left once we got in the car. We shouldn't have been making out. I should have had a gun with me.* "Please tell me this isn't real."

"I wish I could," Dr. Gooden replied.

"Everyone, can we get the room to ourselves," Darren's mother requested. Dasia and the medical staff obeyed the request and exited the room. "Listen, I know this hurts. I don't want you to feel like you can't let your emotions out."

"It's my fault."

"How so?"

"It was my idea to go to that restaurant. It was my idea to head back to the facility and get my Charger instead of staying in the company vehicle. I could have been strapped."

"And what were you going to do if you were strapped? Whoever did this to you had it planned out.

With all those shots they fired into your car, it wouldn't have mattered if you had a gun on you."

"I know, but I should have done something. Ma, you always told me that a real man stands behind his decisions. I can't stand behind these because they ended up getting Reign killed."

Darren's mother broke down and was in tears, right along with him. She has never seen this side of her son before. He was one of the strongest young men she had ever met, and she couldn't believe he was so hard on himself. "What can I do to make this better for you?"

"Better? You can't do nothin'. She was the love of my life and now she's gone."

"Look at me, son. She wouldn't want you acting like this. It's okay to grieve, but I also want you to think about what Reign would have wanted you to do."

Darren turned his head and stared at the ceiling. "She would want me to keep her name alive, especially at H.O.P.E."

"Don't just keep her name alive. She stood for something greater than herself. Make sure you keep her legacy alive too."

There was a firm knock at the door before two nurses entered. One of the nurses was carrying a small cup that contained two pills and a cup of ice water. The other brought in the wheelchair. The nurses assisted Darren with the pills and water. The pain was excruciating, and he wanted the pills to make it all go away. The nurses lifted him and guided him to the chair.

"Do you need me to go with you?" his mom asked.

Darren shook his head before being wheeled out of the room. Darryl and Dasia were in the room with Brandi, as a doctor attended to her needs. As Darren was wheeled through the hallway, it seemed like all eyes were on him. As they reached the elevator, Darren caught a glimpse of himself in the reflection of the metal door. He was banged up. There were bandages on his head and legs and a cast on his arm. He was unrecognizable, even to himself.

It was painfully ironic that he was one of the few people growing up in the hood that wasn't directly impacted by the violence in his environment. Darryl had always been his safety blanket. It wasn't until he was grown that he found himself in such a volatile situation. *I know it isn't true*, he thought as the elevator door opened and the nurse rolled him inside. *I'm gon' get up there and Reign is gon' be just fine. We will help each other heal and then we are getting out of here. Everything is going to be okay.*

Flashes of the shooting and the crash flooded his mind. Occasionally a positive memory of Reign also popped up. He remembered her reaction to the building he helped her acquire. *She is going to make such a difference when we open that place.* The elevator door opened, and the nurse rolled him into the restricted area.

"Here we are, Mr. Knight." The nurse parked him in front of a room.

Darren looked through a window and there she was. *Reign.* He tried placing his hand on the glass, but the pain prevented him from doing so. *Get up!* "Get up, baby!" he whispered. "Reign, get up!" Darren yelled. "Get up!" None of his other pain compared to the one he felt in his chest. Reign hadn't moved. She couldn't move. Her lifeless body sat on the table with a bloody sheet covering everything below her neck. "Get up, Reign. I can't do this without you." Tears poured down Darren's face as he faced the reality of the situation. "I can't do this without you," he sobbed. "I don't want to do this without you. You are the only person I imagined being with. I'm sorry I couldn't protect you. I'm sorry I didn't come up here sooner. I'm sorry you had to suffer. I should have done more."

Darren leaned forward, trying to wheel himself in the room. "Fuck," he yelled out, after falling out of the wheelchair and crashing onto the ground.

"Mr. Knight, are you okay?" the nurse ran over to assist him.

"Leave me alone. I don't want your help," he shouted. "I deserve to be down here." Darren began hysterically crying. He looked up at Reign's body. "I didn't deserve her."

Some would say Darren saved Reign and put her on a new path but in fact, it was the opposite. Reign opened Darren's eyes and heart up for love to find its way in again. This meant more to Darren than anything he had ever done for Reign. Although things ended tragically, it is still better to have loved and lost than to never have loved at all.

THE END

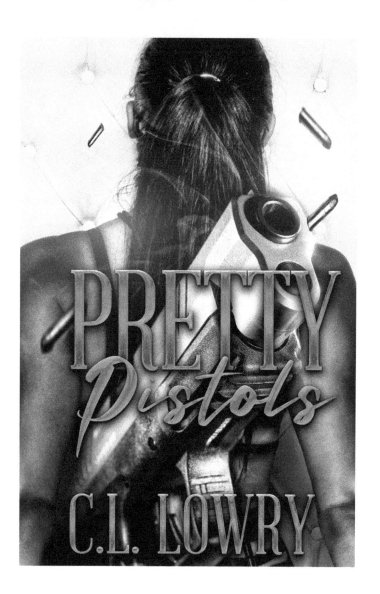

COMING SOON...

COMING SOON...

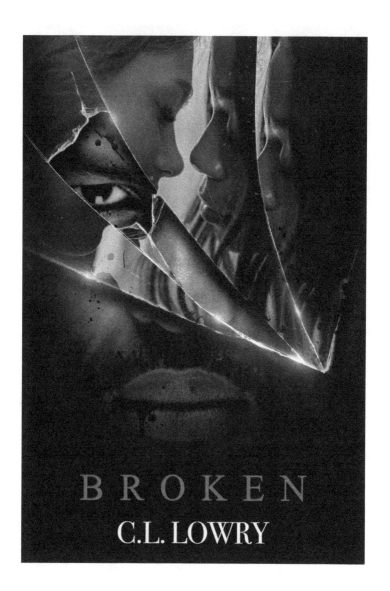

BROKEN
C.L. LOWRY

COMING SOON...

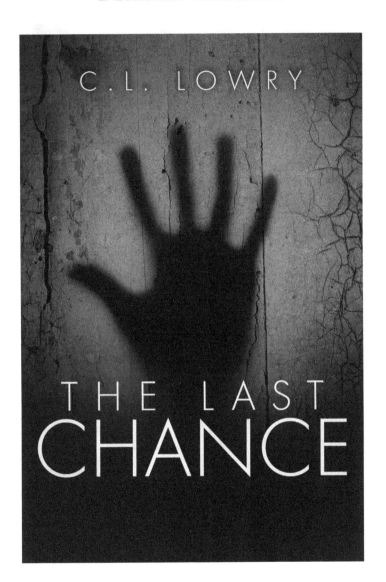

COMING SOON...

COMING SOON...

ABOUT THE AUTHOR

C.L. Lowry is an award-winning author and filmmaker. Although he prides himself as being a prolific crime novelist, his pen game is versatile and allows him to navigate through multiple genres. Lowry was born and raised in Philadelphia, Pennsylvania but his family roots trace back to the beautiful island of Barbados, West Indies. Lowry uses his life experiences and creativity to demand his readers' attention with realistic scenarios throughout his stories.

When he isn't penning a page-turning novel, Lowry is behind the camera creating high-quality films under his production company, Black Lens Cinema. Lowry is also the host of the Fiction Addiction Podcast, where he interviews authors, filmmakers, and other creatives. Sign up for Lowry's spam-free newsletter to learn more about future releases, sneak peeks, special offers, and bonus content. Subscribers will also receive access to exclusive giveaways. To sign up, visit his website at **www.authorcllowry.com**.

CREEDOM PUBLISHING COMPANY

Creedom Publishing is a fully incorporated publishing company. Much like our slogan "The Home of Creative Freedom," we are committed to providing new and upcoming authors with the resources and opportunity to share their creativity with the world.

Creedom Book Services is the parent company to Creedom Publishing Company. Under our publishing company, we provide quality books for readers of all ages. Whether it's the eye-catching childrens book series for young readers or the page-turning crime thrillers by award-winning author C.L. Lowry, every book under Creedom Publishing Company is worthy of being added to your library.

Our books are available for purchase on our site and eBooks are available through Amazon Kindle.

CONTACT THE CREEDOM PUBLISHING COMPANY AT:

CREEDOMPUBLISHING@OUTLOOK.COM

CPSIA information can be obtained
at www.ICGtesting.com
Printed in the USA
LVHW111740060622
720550LV00007B/23

9 781946 897077